Typewriter Pub, an imprint of Blvnp Incorporated
A Nevada Corporation
1887 Whitney Mesa DR #2002
Henderson, NV 89014
www.typewriterpub.com/info@typewriterpub.com

ISBN: 978-1-64434-017-2

DISCLAIMER
This book is a work of fiction. The characters, incidents, and dialogue are drawn from the author's imagination and are not to be construed as real. While references might be made to actual historical events or existing locations, the names, characters, places, and incidents are either products of the author's imagination or are used fictitiously, and any resemblance to actual persons living or dead, business establishments, events or locales is entirely coincidental.

AMOR ETERNO

MARA LYNNE

type writer pub

To my Mom and Dad,
whom I love the most in this world.

FREE DOWNLOAD

Get these freebies and more when you sign up for the author's mailing list!

maralynne.awesomeauthors.org

PROLOGUE

The wind raged against the *nipa* leaves that made the roof of the house. It was after the sun had kissed the floor of the earth that the air got lonely and chilly. Soft music came out from the flute of an almost emaciated old man, who was sitting on the footsteps of the stairs. It accompanied the mellow gush of wind. Meanwhile mothers in the village busied themselves preparing a hearty dinner for their families.

By the window stood an elderly woman wearing an ankle-length skirt and a thick rough elbow-length sleeve blouse. She watched the solitary moon shine in the sky.

"When will it happen?" asked another woman who just entered the room that was walled by thick timber. She was slightly thinner, but her hair was as gray as the old woman's near the window.

"Very soon."

"Is it going to be different this time? Can we claim victory this soon?"

"I believe so," answered the old woman as she trekked toward the middle of the room where a small wooden table was resting. She sat just beside the table in a squatting position on a woven mat that was lying on the cold wooden floor. "We can't let the curse change the course of time. We have all been waiting for this for centuries. Today is the best time to fulfill the prophecy."

"What did the old priestess say about this? Have they found the warrior?"

"She has Cahaya, while I have my eyes on one man. I just need to be sure that he is the one."

"And the stone? Have you found the stone, *Manang*?" asked the thinner woman while pouring green concoction with an obnoxious smell into her cup.

"No," she answered with a shake of her head. "I don't know where it is, but my instincts are telling me that it is being guarded. I just don't know where to look for it."

"We will need it to break the curse. Everything is useless without it even if we find the warrior."

"I have to travel back there once in a while to gather news from the old priestess. We have to keep our hopes high that she finds the stone."

"Then you have to hurry. The warrior's blood must be shed before the stars align. We can't miss the day, or we'll have to wait for centuries for another rebirth," said the woman whose eyes narrowed and darkened. "This will become your endless pursuit, *Manang*. This won't end unless we become victorious this time. I know you are tired and you'd love to see your sister again."

"We have a second option though." *Manang* said with a smile. "We still have the present."

But in her mind, she knew she couldn't go forward with the present, and it disappointed her. Two chances; neither of which she did not want to waste.

The thinner woman sipped her concoction and gulped a large volume of air after she saw a remarkable sign of hope on *Manang's* face.

"I commend you for using your powers to protect the world and to fulfill the prophecy. But I'm afraid using two rebirths is quite a danger for you, *Manang*."

"I do not worry over losing my powers. It was bestowed upon me by Bulan to correct the mistakes of the past. By the time I

2

lose them, the warrior will be gone. The prophecy will have been fulfilled, and the curse broken."

Flash!

The other woman held onto the edge of the table as her face grew pale. The Sight had just warned her of an impending event.

"Do you see anything?" *Manang* asked her anxiously as she leaned forward, knocking the cups and the teapot off the table.

"A boy." Her voice was dead and dull. Coldness stroked her limbs and spine. This happens whenever the Sight came like a flash. She wavered. "I can hear him laughing. He sounds so happy. Poor little one."

"You see the warrior?" *Manang* moved to the other side of the table and put her arm around her trembling friend.

"Is he the warrior, *Manang*?"

"Is he?"

"But he's… just a child."

"What else do you see?"

The visions kept on coming and it became more difficult to control.

Cars rushed to avoid traffic. Two adults listened to this funny small box in front of them that talked about a storm coming into the city undetected by any weather station in the country. A little boy around five was tucked in the back of the car, looking outside the window and watching other cars pass by. He looked forward to getting on the rides that he kept asking the lady at the front seat how long it would take to get there. But they did not pay attention to him. They were both glued to this strange box.

The little boy shrugged his shoulders and went on watching the cars speeding. He did not even bother to wonder how the dark skies got angrier each time lightning lashed. The man who had the steering wheel pressed on the gas accelerator, overtaking others behind. It was smooth and fast at first, but something went wrong after a couple of minutes.

The car started to move in jerky motions. almost crashing into nearby vehicles. The steering wheel was out of control. A truck carter appeared a few distances away, and the man had to stop the car to prevent an imminent collision. His foot pressed down on the brake pedal, but the car did not slow down. The lady screamed at the top of her lungs. The boy did not know what exactly was happening, but he knew that the woman was afraid.

"Son!" the woman reached for his hand. She pulled the seatbelt and made sure that he was snugly tucked in.

"What's happening, Mommy?" he asked as he marveled at his mother's eyes.

The woman did not say a word. Her grasp tightened as they came close to the slowing truck carter. Rain torrentially poured and hit the windshield like it was about to shatter.

"*Manang!*" She grabbed the old woman's arm and said, "You must save the child! He shouldn't die this way…"

"Die?"

"Yes."

The old woman moved her head sideways. Her voice was absent of panic or even remorse. "He will be unharmed. The curse will save him."

PART I

CHAPTER I
The Inheritance

"Why do they call me bad luck, Grandpa?" he cried one afternoon after returning home.

His kind grandfather sat on the stone stairs beside him and hung his arm around the boy's shoulders, and answered with a warm smile, *"You are not bad luck, Xander. People just don't know you. You are a very sweet and loving kid. If they know that, they will love you."*

"But they avoid me…"

"Then you must not stop being good to them until they realize who you really are."

"The kids are afraid of me. They said I bring disaster to the village. They said I am a monster because I survived the car crash…"

Grandpa embraced him.

"It was a miracle. It was God's doing that you were saved, and the disasters are also from God," he said. *"He made them for us to be better occupants of his kingdom."*

He looked straight into his grandpa's eyes. His nose bridge was high, and his lips were thin. He was losing hair at the top of his head, but his mustache still grew.

"But they say that our family is a useless guardian of the shrine. We let the shintai be stolen from the temple. So, the gods are angry!" he said curiously.

"That was a long, long time ago! And a lot of shintais had been stolen, too. It did not just happen in our place," Grandpa explained. "Natural calamities don't necessarily come from the loss of a shintai."

"But without the shintai, Kami will never protect the village!" A look of worry descended on Xander's face. "People think Kami sent me here to bring misfortune!"

His grandpa chuckled, his face turning red with suppressed laughter.

"You have too much of your grandmother's stories!" He laughed. "You will make a fine guardian of the shrine!"

"You're joking. Right, Grandpa?" Xander's eyebrow raised.

He winked at him. "You are still a guardian of the shrine even without the shintai. That has been our family's task for centuries. Our ancestors were great warriors of the Sun God. Did your grandma tell you that?"

He shook his head. "Only how we got the shrine from the imperial family."

"Well, our ancestors, centuries and centuries and centuries ago, were imperial warriors whose duty was to protect the emperor who was a descendant of the Sun God. When the thirteenth emperor died, he gave his imperial sword, the Kusanagi, to his favorite warrior, Kazuma. The Kusanagi was a gift from the Sun God to the thirteenth emperor for successfully winning wars against the neighboring tribes and for acquiring vast lands.

"When emperors die, they become kamis or gods, and their spirits dwell in an object of their choosing. The sword became a shintai that houses the spirit of the God of Conquest, Hamichan, who was the thirteenth emperor in person.

"You see, the emperor was a valiant, cunning, and ambitious man. He liked to go to places, which he could dominate by force. And as for Kazuma's duty to protect the sword and to fulfill Hamichan's wish, he traveled all over the world to find lands, which he could conquer in the kami's name. He brought with him the sword.

"For quite a time, Kazuma's family heard that he had been in the south and had subjugated kingdoms. But years after years, they stopped hearing from him. He never returned, and that is how our shrine lost the sword and the protection of the kami."

Xander's eyes marveled with awe.

"Had Kazuma returned, we would still have the sword, and this village would have been bigger and mightier than any territories," added his Grandpa.

"Is it Kazuma's fault why people hate us?"

"I honestly think it's the reason."

"Why didn't he return, Grandpa?"

"Nobody knows. Even our ancestors could not answer that question."

"Did that really happen, Grandpa?" He tugged his grandpa's sleeve to take his eyes away from the setting sun on the horizon.

"It is a myth, Xander, but it will not hurt if we believe." The old man faced him. "After all, Kazuma was our ancestor, and we came from him." He directed his grandson's gaze back to the setting sun.

*   *   *

His eyes opened, and his pupils dilated. A chaotic blizzard seemed to have almost blinded him. After blinking his lids a couple of times, he realized that the unknown white spots were just artifice created by the luminous light from the ceiling.

Big drops of sweat plummeted from his forehead and wetted his collar.

That same dream again.

His heart pounded like the thunders outside his window in that dark field of raging sky.

It was just a dream. He made himself believe.

Rough air came out from nowhere and lasted for several minutes. The aircraft's body started shaking. Children clung to their mothers and cried their hearts out. Some adults held their breath and tightly gripped their prayer books and rosaries.

It was just turbulence. It would not cause the wings to fall off or break the plane into half or crash the aircraft into the open sea. Nevertheless, he still held onto his own chair and put on his safety belt per the flight attendant's instruction.

Once the aircraft was stable again, coffees were distributed through trolleys and handed out by petite stewardesses in skimpy blue uniforms.

"No, thanks," he calmly said to the flight attendant who kept her poise despite the turbulence that still rocked them from time to time.

He just had no appetite for anything at the moment, not even for a cup of hot coffee. He was still barely recovering from the same dream that had been hunting him for several days now.

He hurriedly reached for his backpack and pulled out his sketchbook. His fingers trembled as he searched for his drawing pencil before it fell off his bag's pocket. The pencil rolled horizontally on the floor for a couple of seconds then stayed under his chair for the rest of the time. He tried locating it with one hand, tapping the carpeted floor for a thin elongated object with a sharp end.

Then, a huge and loud thunder rattled him. His heart jumped off its place spontaneously. The thunder momentarily shushed, and his heart recovered from that shock, but the squeaky tingling sensation on both his ears deafened him for a while.

The aircraft quaked again, stronger and longer than the first one. Children screamed. The flight attendants scampered to their chambers with anxiety written all over their faces and anxiously fastened themselves into their chairs.

He turned to his window and saw dark, heavy nimbus clouds moving quickly and bumping each other. Lightning appeared every after one strong roar from the angry heavens. There was no news of storms when he left for his flight.

He clearly remembered what the weatherman said, "Bright and sunny!"

When everything seemed back to normal—the children a bit calmer, the aircraft more stable, and thunder and lightning less intense—he resumed searching for his drawing pencil. He got it in a matter of seconds. Then, he immediately opened his sketchpad and started sketching against the thick paper. Only by drawing could he calm his nerves. He must draw what he dreamed about, or it would continue to irk him.

After a while, the sky cleared.

The lightning and the scary thunder were completely gone. Anxious cries of children waned down, and the passengers calmed down. The flight attendants unfastened their seatbelts and started to roam around to check on everyone's safety.

Yet his focus was solely on his drawing. No amount of teasing cupcakes or cookies could divert his attention away. His hands were smudged and sullied with charcoal and his own sweat, but he wasn't stopping.

Three circles aligned each other. The one in the front was larger and had more shadowy parts. It was exactly what he saw in his dream. Things in his dream changed a lot, though sometimes they repeated. He had seen these circles quite a few times already, and it filled the pages of his drawing book. These circles always came after a nice dream, disrupting beautiful memories of his childhood or even anything that was just beautiful, and turned them into a nightmare.

After he finished his drawing, he was calmer. He instantly kept his drawing stuff in his bag and started checking a few documents from a white envelope. He began reading the document with a title head "Last Will and Testament." Several pictures of an old house were revealed as he scanned the pages.

He was going back to his grandpa's home. It took him sixteen years to return. But this occasion was not something he would have done if he had a choice. He was not that seven-year-old kid anymore.

When he was more relaxed, he turned to the tranquil scenery outside his window. He saw what he didn't expect to see. Three vague rings in formation shocked him. They were as big as the bright moon but indistinct as mist.

"Please turn to your windows," a flight attendant started speaking over the microphone. "You will see a rare phenomenon that happens only once in a hundred years. Outside, you will see the planets Jupiter, Mercury, and Venus. Normally, they just appear as tiny dots like stars. Today is quite an exception. It is believed that this spectacle will last for a week or two. Please enjoy this exciting celestial display!"

*   *   *

"Is this it?" inquired Xander with an eyebrow raised as he came out of the car.

A big stone house with grubby white walls and red roof stood alone in a wide land. Some wide green plants and tall trees could be seen a few distances away from the house. Large checkered windows surrounded the upper floor. The window sashes were decorated with *capiz* shell panes and could be opened wide on broad daylight and peaceful nights for the cool breeze, and closed down if storms came. There were also vents that were protected by roof eaves above the large windows that let in fresh air during rainy days. *Ventanillas*, small windows below the larger ones, were also noticeable. A huge portico with stone columns greeted the entrance. The door, wide as the length of two horses combined, slid from one side to the other.

"It looks different from the photos," he added.

"The pictures are personal belongings of your grandfather. They were taken in the 1920s. He wanted you to see the house how he had seen it before," replied the lawyer, Atty. Tan.

"That old man!" he snapped. He marched toward the wide entrance. It appeared so creepy that he already made up his mind about his very brief stay. "I can't wait to sell this property, then I could go back to Japan to do my own thing!" he exclaimed as he set foot at the tiled floor of the portico.

"But you cannot sell this place until you meet all the conditions in his will. You must know that. For you will not inherit a single cent," countered the lawyer.

"Then make this thing easier for me, Atty. Tan," Xander said confidently. "I have no time for this bullshit!"

"I wonder if you have read all the provisions in his will," marveled Atty. Tan.

"It's your job! Just tell me what is in there and what is advantageous for me!" His face flared with annoyance and he stormed inside.

The inside of the house was astonishingly large compared to what his limited imagination had offered. The foyer had polished mahogany walls that were carved with miniscule patterns of tree branches and veins. There were columns with arches attached to the high ceiling. The furniture was well polished and seemed to have been well taken care of for years. There was a grand staircase made of wood that led to the upper level. Rows of candlesticks lined the stairs.

He began to wonder if the place still didn't have electricity because of the presence of fresh candles. The first thing he did before he continued examining the entire hallway was to look for electrical wirings.

"Did this place even recover from ancient civilization?" he kidded.

"There is electricity here, sir although power shortage does happen in unlikely circumstances."

He did not fully grasp the meaning behind the spine-chilling sensation that bothered him. He felt it first when he passed through the doorway. It was like eyes were following his every move like the walls had ears, and the staircase had some magnet that compelled him to go upstairs. It was not just the dullness or the lack of life that made it look sinister. Unexplainable strangeness was the best way to describe it.

"I'm not living alone here, am I?" He sounded funny as he directed his gaze to one majestic portrait that hung on top of the staircase.

It was a picture of a man in a blue officer uniform. His austere look and the badges on his uniform made Xander believe that the man could have been a very important person during his lifetime.

"No, you will not. The cook, *Manang* Leticia, will be with you in the morning till late afternoon. And the caretaker, Ayang, will be here 24/7. She lives at the small space at the back of the house, which used to be the *zaguan* in the old times," answered the lawyer as he silently followed Xander's pace.

In his mind, the lawyer was celebrating Xander's discreet fear, which was way beyond everyone's knowledge. People close to Xander knew him to be daring and most certainly unafraid of old houses, yet Atty. Tan did not dare assert his observation.

Xander chuckled upon hearing the strange word *zaguan*. He remembered how he used to play there with his grandpa's old carriage and carts. Now, it had turned into a simple space for the caretaker. He recalled his indifferent encounters with Ayang.

She was never a friendly woman. He thought.

He never really had the chance to talk to her though. She always gave him the creeps, and she looked so stern and ugly. But his grandpa seemed to like this woman so much. He was the only person whom he knew who fostered a pleasant relationship with the eerie Ayang.

Now, that he was a lot older, he was certain that Ayang grew colder and stricter. It is a fact that older adults get crankier and more sensitive as they age. Moreover, it would be nice if Ayang just worked around the house discreetly. After all, she would have the house back in two weeks or so and would have a new master by then.

"Do you want me to summon them, sir?"

"No!" he answered quickly. He did not want to see Ayang at the moment. He thought of just going to his room and have the rest of the day for sleeping.

"Well, then! Do you want me to give you a tour?"

"No, I can do it alone. I still remember my way around here," he sharply said after surveying the upper floor.

The receiving room was surrounded by several bedrooms. The kitchen and dining room were a few distances apart. The living room had wooden settees and a rectangular table in the middle. The floor was carpeted, and the walls had portraits and tapestries. Fresh plants in gigantic pots guarded the doors that surround the *sala* or the living room. But the thing that captured his attention was the old piano set covered with a mantelpiece. Tall bronze candlesticks were laid on top of it with new black candles. The *sala* didn't change a bit since his last visit. Everything was where they should be.

Atty. Tan nodded. He was pleased with Xander's decision. "Just give me a call when you have queries. I'll inform you as soon as I have found potential buyers."

"Alright!" He snobbishly left the lawyer at the end of the stairs.

Atty. Tan unhesitatingly marched his way out of the house. Spending time with Xander was comparable to lifetime imprisonment. They both shared the same sentiments. Neither of the two liked each other. If Xander was just too excited to sell the house and head back to Japan in no time, then he was no different. He would gladly do the job for his advantage.

Xander headed to the room, which used to be his the last time he was here. He could have easily acquired the master's bedroom, but he preferred a haven, not a place where he would be constantly reminded of his unfeeling grandfather.

The room was made. Ayang very well knew that Xander would always choose dime over gold. The bed sheets were fresh and clean. The curtains were neat and fragrant. He laid his bag on the side table and hurried to the bed for a good sleep. He thought of waking up by the time dinner was served. He was pretty confident that *Manang* Leticia would not forget that he was here.

He slowly closed his eyes, and enjoyed the cool breeze of the wind. Things that he loved about the province were the fresh air, the clean water, and the bright sun in the country compared to what the bustling Manila had.

The stillness was inviting him to deep sleep. The soft mattress seemed to be pulling him down to the abyss of calmness, and the blankets wrapped his entire body like a cocoon to a caterpillar.

He was just so exhausted, but a lot of things were going on in his mind, yet they were not troubling him at all. Instead, excitement surged through him. He just could not wait for tomorrow. He thought of painting nature or anything extraordinary that amazes his sight. He also wished to take pictures of the old houses in the area and include them in his portfolio.

Art had been his constant passion in the twenty-three years of his life. He attained an art degree at a university in Japan and then worked as a professional photographer and painter. He had built his little museum when he was twenty-one, with the help of his family's fortune. He was quite popular in his field.

His parents died in a car accident when he was five. Since then, he was taken in by his Japanese grandparents.

His paternal grandpa, the one who owned this ancient house in *Barrio* Makinlang in the province of Quezon, did not even try to reach out. It was one of the few reasons he didn't like him. Even though the lifestyle in Japan was more convenient for him, he still wished to live in the Philippines because of the several good things he heard from his dad. He could have forgiven his grandpa if he only showed interest in taking him in.

He only heard from him once, and that was when he was sick and afraid of dying. The old man called and invited him for a few weeks' stay. When he got well, he was automatically sent back to Japan. Just like that.

Xander did not just hate his grandpa's lack of care but his unusual and unhealthy habits as well. He was an avid fan of gambling. He played cards and cockfights with his neighbors. He'd also drink palm wine or *tuba* almost every day while smoking a stick of tobacco.

However, he heard great accounts from Atty. Tan about his grandpa's kindness toward the people whom he had helped. They were his poor neighbors and farmer tenants. He would let his neighbors borrow money without even making a list. Xander always wondered how his grandpa recovered his money, or perhaps he never asked them back. Perhaps, it was one of the good traits people admired about him.

Despite his indifference with his grandpa, he never questioned his good relations with the people around him. How he wished he had experienced it firsthand!

Sleep did not come to him, despite the temptations the ambiance gave him. He tried to, but his excitement and thoughts were just too hard to ignore. Then the strange incident during his flight to Manila came to mind. He recalled the three rings that his eyes had clearly seen outside his window. They looked just like the three circles in his dream.

It was not just a coincidence, was it?

Jupiter.

Mercury.

Venus.

What did these planets have to do with his dream and to him?

His head ached as he forced his mind to clear. These dreams were not helping him at all. They were just so many of them, and they seemed to get more bothersome each day.

He rose from his bed, reached for his bag, and took his photobook. He thought that the pictures could help him calm his nerves. They were, after all, his comfort blanket next to his sketch pad. As he browsed the pages, he began to miss the little village in the countryside of Japan where he grew up. He imagined himself walking at the cold streets of the village, taking pictures of old temples and old houses.

Oh, how he missed the tenderness and charm of the little colorful leaves, *koyo*, as they dropped to the ground to create a canopy. The soft sound of the flowing river along the bank always enticed him to stop for a while and watch the reflection of the setting sun.

Autumn is finally there, he thought.

The old temples and shrines in the photos were his favorite spots to sneak a photo of. They were just enigmatic and beautiful. Every time he went there, he felt that a part of him was made complete. There were no specific reasons he could point out to explain this odd fondness over temples. He just liked them. He always thought that it could be because of the calmness and peace it brought him.

He reached for his pencil and started drawing his home—the shrine where he lived all his life. He was taken in by his grandparents to live with them in the countryside of Honshu, a peace-loving town up the mountain. His grandparents had been living in the old temple for the longest time and owned a Shinto shrine, which they inherited from their ancestors.

The shrine was erected near a mountain peak that supplied water to the plains and valleys of the low lands. His grandfather, Hiroko, kept the shrine attended for decades, although it no longer housed a sacred object or a *shintai*. Despite its absence, the shrine kept its reputed sacredness through the ruins that remained after centuries of natural and man-made disasters.

He drew the *torii* or the Shinto gate first. The gate was made of two wooden pillars united by a tie beam and a lintel that spanned the space between two pillars. There were stone stairs that led to the *sando* or the approach or pathway to the shrine. The *sando* was bordered with *toros* or stone lanterns that are lit with flames at night.

The *toro's* structure represented the elements of the universe. The bottom part was the *chi* or the earth. Above it was the *sui* or water. The section that encased the lantern's fire was the *ka*, and the topmost parts that point toward the sky represented the *fu* or air and *ku* or spirit.

There was a small roofed area where people cleansed themselves before entering the shrine, though rarely used at present as the number of worshippers and visitors declined. Small auxiliary shrines spread all over the area. Statues of lion-dogs called *komainu* were erected at the doorway of the *haiden* or the hall of worship and were believed to be the guardians of the shrine.

Behind the *haiden* was the *honden* or the main hall that kept the *shintai* which enshrined the *kami* or a god. But Hiroki's shrine no longer had the *shintai*. It was lost a long, long time ago after his early ancestors inherited the shrine from the imperial family. It had become a shrine by architecture and not by essence anymore.

There was nothing that could beat the peace of mind that he got whenever he was in the shrine. He loved the shrine because of its mystery. He loved it for the serenity it gave him. He loved it for everything, except for the people who made his life miserable when he was growing up—the village people.

While looking for his sharpener in his bag, his grasp loosened and the bag fell off the floor, and let slip its contents: a few gadgets, some books, the envelope that contained his grandpa's last will and testament, and a few personal things. He picked them up one by one when a box sloppily covered with brown paper caught his eye.

He had almost forgotten about it.

He carefully laid it in front of him and opened it, starting with the sides. He was surprised to know that his grandfather was a quixotic man who loved to keep uncanny treasures. Sure, he was old and cranky, but Xander never thought he would be melodramatic.

The box revealed a medium-sized leather book that looked like fire almost engulfed it. Its cover looked fragile and old, and its carvings almost deteriorated. Time had aged it, and fire almost destroyed it. In the middle of the jacket was a small stone, the size of a cherry tomato and black as charcoal.

He tried to pull it out once after curiosity won him over, but he failed. It seemed that the stone was strongly glued to the book. However, the key lock just below the stone made him think of the possibility of having it removed with the use of the right key. He just had to find it.

Along with the book was a Victorian pen. It looked worn out with its blackened surface. The fire must have destroyed it too, and Xander started marveling why his grandpa left such useless and odd objects to him.

Did he ever think of how they were going to benefit him? An old book with a useless pen? Did he want him to be a writer? Did he want him to be a secret overdramatic man like him? He just had no idea what to do with them.

CHAPTER 2
The Caretaker

Heartbreaking music filled his ears. It took him several seconds to recognize what it was and where it came from. It sounded so sad and piercing, yet it was as good as a lullaby. Its misery went on for over a minute until it knocked him to sleep completely, and then it began to fade slowly. He wanted more of it, strangely, but it was dying out inevitably.

As soon as he opened his eyes, Ayang's large ones flabbergasted him. He almost had a heart attack. He covered his mouth to prevent himself from screaming. He did not imagine seeing her this way. He opened his eyes to look for the source of the strange music, but what he got was Ayang's piercing glare.

They stared at each other for quite a while. She stood just a few feet away from him. He wondered whether he should greet her good morning or ask her about her sleep. His voice would not come out, so he chose to wait for her to say something first. But, as aloof as he knew her to be, Ayang did not even bother to utter a word, or even sigh at the very least. She, in her old plain *baro't saya,* which he had always seen her wear since time immemorial, looked away and started putting out the yellow candles inside his room.

He could not understand why he felt so scared seeing her. She was a very weird woman, to begin with. There was just something about her that Xander just could not like. And she looked like she never aged.

Had she discovered the fountain of youth?

She would have been around sixty when he first met her sixteen years ago, yet now, she did not look any different at all. Her clothes and her low bun were the same. Her hair had not turned gray either. She was giving him the creeps. Ayang was not a pretty woman, but neither was she repulsive. Her features were just so strikingly strong and bizarre that Xander found them far from being visually appealing.

Ayang had a fairly round head with a protruding forehead crammed with wrinkles. She was short, only about five feet tall. She had a single strand of whisker right on top of her mole on her right cheek that made her face look so bloodcurdling. She also walked so slowly, with her back always bent forward. Her shoulders were not symmetrical as well. Doing the household chores might be so taxing for her, given her physical condition.

As soon as all the candles were lit off, Ayang opened the windows. Bright sunlight entered the room and woke him up fully. He, then, realized that he had fallen asleep last night without even having dinner. He heard his stomach grumble.

"Good morning, *señorito*!" greeted a plump brown-skinned woman who just came into his room.

She must be Manang Leticia, the cook.

"You must be starving now," she said. "We did not wake you up last night because you were so sound asleep. But I have made you a wonderful breakfast you will love!"

He turned to *Manang* Leticia, and answered, "Thanks. I'll just come down in a moment."

"Well, you better hurry up, *señorito*."

"And don't call me *señorito*. I don't like how it sounds," he said shyly.

"Oh!" *Manang* Leticia uttered with surprise. "How shall I call you then, Mr. Montejo?"

"Just Xander."

22

Then, both their eyes instantly turned to the sluggishly walking Ayang.

"Oh, right!" exclaimed *Manang* Leticia. "Ayang needs your used clothes. She's going to do the laundry this morning."

"Can she even use the washing machine?" he straightforwardly asked with a laugh.

Ayang was a very traditional woman, and she seemed to be someone who had never used a washing machine in her life.

"We don't use them here."

Aha!

"Ayang does the laundry with her hands," answered the cook.

Then, he saw Ayang waiting at the doorstep. He felt a little sorry for her. Her old age was one factor to empathize with. Really, he thought it was time for Ayang to retire.

"I'll do my laundry on my own!" he asserted.

Manang Leticia frowned.

"I meant…" he stuttered as soon as he realized that *Manang* Leticia could have misinterpreted him and thought that he did not like Ayang doing stuff for him because of her odd appearance. "I do my own laundry. She doesn't have to work so hard."

"But Ayang will not like that. She wants to make good use of her time always," said *Manang* Leticia. "You must let her do it, Xander."

The old woman was not even moving at all. She probably heard what they were talking about. He just hoped that she would not take any of what he said against him. He still had a little sense of care for her despite the fright she always gave him.

"Okay. I'll bring out my laundry after I hit the shower."

"But this house doesn't have a shower either. We use buckets and dippers here," said *Manang* Leticia.

"That's not a problem," he replied. He was used to using them at the shrine.

"So, I'll see you at the dining table in a few minutes." Then, *Manang* Leticia and Ayang left the room.

What a daunting way to welcome his first morning in this house!

It was still six in the morning, and people were already up.

He hurried to the bathroom where windows were not part of its structural design. There was even no electrical connection. He wondered how his grandpa used the lavatory with just candles. He just could not imagine himself carrying a candlestick in pajamas and walking through the hallway and the staircase at night, alone.

He was astonished to see no pipes in the bathroom, only a big sized bucket filled with water and a wooden dipper made out of coconut shell. There was no way *Manang* Leticia or Ayang could have brought this heavy bucket inside.

Where did they even get the water? There was no water connection in this tiny room.

This place was absolute primeval!

It was a good thing he brought his own soap and shampoo, or else he would be forced to use some of his grandpa's old fragrance or oil. Well, that would be far from awesome. It would definitely be horrendous! Xander was not prehistoric.

He had just been here for less than twenty-four hours, yet he was already raging. It was not a paradise after all! Where were the good things and happy experiences his dad talked about in this place? Surely, he must not have misheard him.

After one cold bath, he gathered his used clothes and dumped them all together in a rattan basket, which Ayang would surely take with her. A silly idea passed through his mind. He felt bad for making fun of Ayang's misfortune, but he couldn't just help it. The house had no washing machine, had no television most probably, no internet connection, or good water source. Then it probably would not have space in the backyard for washing clothes.

It must be lacking a sewerage system. Then, Ayang would surely do the laundry in a flowing body of water just like what he

24

has seen in historical films. There must be a stream or a river nearby, and Ayang would walk to get there, carrying the rattan basket with her wrinkled hands.

*　　*　　*

"Does the piano in the *sala* still work?" he asked *Manang* Leticia over breakfast.

The menu was a little revolting to his taste. A simple salted egg was a better choice. He did not remember eating something like it sixteen years ago. The cook then was *Manang* Marcela, and she made excellent pudding and rice cakes. Her sautéed vegetables too were scrumptious. But, it seemed that *Manang* Leticia had her own cooking style and had an exotic taste.

The obvious shape of the frogs on the plate did not make the dish pleasant to the eyes. He even thought of skipping breakfast and search for some cafeteria in town. But that would probably hurt the woman's feelings, and he didn't want to instill bad impressions on her. She was the only normal person in the house and the only one whom he could have a decent conversation with.

"The one in the *sala?*" she said as she pointed the living room that was just a few meters away from the *comedor* or the dining room with her lips. "I don't know why your grandpa kept that there. He never used it."

"I heard someone playing it this morning."

"It might be Ayang. Though I have not personally seen her play it, she's the only person in the house who gets up before six. She could have been doing it for years, and *Don* Santiago seemed to have no objections about it."

"When will the electricity come back?"

"We don't know. It comes and goes," replied *Manang* Leticia while scooping another spoonful of brown rice on his plate.

"Is it the same in your house?"

"Oh, no! We have a good electrical connection in the rest of the *barrio*. It's just this house that has some problem," said she. "*Don* Santiago had it fixed years ago, but it never changed. It might be because we're a bit far from the *barrio* and the electricity is too weak to reach here. There are a lot of new establishments down in the town, so I guess their consumption is a lot bigger than ours."

Xander immediately thought of Atty. Tan. Perhaps he could help with this matter. He had connections with the local engineers.

"There's a *fiesta* in two weeks, Xander," added *Manang* Leticia. "I thought you would want to go. It's going to be fun. There will be lots of food like *lechon, paella,* and *pancit.* And a carnival will also open. There is going to be a lot of games too! And most of all, we must not forget about our Lady Patron, the *Immaculada Concepcion.* Masses will be held before the fiesta."

Xander remembered the last time he entered a Catholic church. He was with his parents on a sunny Sunday. It was his birthday, and they were planning to go to the amusement park to celebrate it after attending mass. It was not a good memory, and he had no time to rekindle certain emotions.

"But we're hoping that the weather will turn out good. Lately, thunderstorms and extreme weather conditions hit the *barrio.* If this continues, the *fiesta* will definitely be canceled for everyone's safety," started *Manang* Leticia whose cheerful aura amazingly turned into apprehension. "I wonder why storms only strike our place and not others."

"There was a storm in the Manila sky yesterday," he replied after remembering the heavy turbulence in the plane.

It seemed that catastrophe always followed him. Back in the days, their little village in Honshu got hit by a series of calamities when he came there, and people made that as an excuse to hate him for being the bad omen.

"But it never hit the land. It's a different story with ours." She sounded so perplexed. "It's not like this before, you know."

"Climate change, *Manang*. I heard it first from Al Gore."

"And there's this strange thing in the sky," she went on. "We heard from the elders that the lining of the three planets is a bad omen. They were saying something about an angry goddess and a curse. We just cannot celebrate the *fiesta* with that thing in the sky! Who knows what will happen? They say it'll last for weeks."

The three planets again…

"What did the elders say about it?" Curiosity got the better of him. He had the feeling that she must know the story behind it.

"I don't really know. I am not a native of this *barrio*. My husband is though."

"Seems like your people also believe in myths. Way back home, I've got a library filled with books about mythology."

"It's an old folktale. I don't really believe in it, though some do." She smirked with delight. "I didn't think you'd be interested in folktales."

"It's the atypical phenomenon I was curious about and not that silly old tale!" he barked.

He remembered how his old grandpa, Hiroko, and his grandma, Reina, filled his mind with tales of nonsense when he was young, and he was so stupid to have believed them.

"There's no way I'd believe such baby stories!" He laughed after.

Manang Leticia shrugged her shoulders and left the *comedor* to take away the empty dishes for cleaning.

In the meantime, Xander chose to stretch some muscles. He went out of the old house and toured around the large garden. He was quite surprised how Ayang had done a good job in preserving the beauty of the vicinity. It was something that an old woman with skeletal defect could not have done alone. He wondered if hired gardeners came to help.

The garden was filled with trimmed white cedars, coral woods, and garden dills. Flowers like cape jasmine and hibiscus lined the stone pathway to the marbled gazebo near a swamp

27

planted with mangroves and water lilies. What a breathtaking sight it was!

This creepy old ancestral home has its own secret of beauty—he thought—*that was worth the attention.*

He was more amazed to see the window of his bedroom overlooking this fine beauty. What a sight it would be in the early morning and early dusk!

Another thing in the backyard caught his attention. A vintage dome-like structure that looked like a mausoleum stood near a willow tree just a few meters away from the swamp and the gazebo. A cryptic message was carved at its wooden door. He could not even decipher if it was Latin or Spanish.

It said, *A sojo ed leuqa euq son oma.*

He thought of destroying the door so that he could see what was inside. His grandfather was buried somewhere else and not in this expensive looking chamber. Therefore, something really, really important must be inside. He was just about to use the crowbar, which he saw behind the bushes, to open the door when he heard *Manang* Leticia's voice roar from behind.

"That mustn't be opened!"

Xander felt all the blood in his body rush to his face.

Manang Leticia's face went ashen pale. She ran all the way from the kitchen to the backyard when she saw him trying to break entry.

"It's the resting place of a witch," her voice toned down as she enunciated the last word. She looked so cautious, with her eyes scanning the surroundings.

"What?" he said in one breath.

Manang Leticia pulled him back to the house unhesitatingly.

"*Por pabor, señorito!* Don't ever try to break the chain again!" she exclaimed anxiously.

The poor woman had never looked so worried since the first moment he saw her. She appeared so different with her round eyes so big like a tarsier's.

"The town priest had to sprinkle holy water all over the entrance because it is cursed. You don't want to disturb the spirit of the witch, do you?"

"A witch?" He laughed at the idea.

Manang Leticia hurriedly secured herself on a chair and started swishing her *abaniko* fan to her face. "You nearly gave me a heart attack!"

"Right. What else have you got for me, *Manang*? Entertain me!"

"That place always gives me the creeps! Even *Don* Santiago doesn't go there, nor did he order to have it eradicated. I heard from the town people that before your family took over this property, this was owned by a strange family from Europe. They called them bloodsuckers or vampires. Others call them witches."

"That's not true. There are no witches or vampires!" he insisted.

"I'm not saying they're true. But they could be! And almost everyone in the *barrio* believes so."

"It's just a tomb from centuries ago," he said confidently. "And those stories about vampires and witches are all fictitious. So, why don't you relax and just finish your cooking?"

He observed that the dirty kitchen did not even have a gas range or a stove. It would perhaps take hours to finish one dish. There were earthenwares, mostly jars and pots; wooden and tin boxes in cabinets near the high ceiling where silver utensils were stored; and a wood burning stove, which used a chimney made up the kitchen. Fresh vegetables and fruits were stored in a basket. Clean water for drinking was kept in big jars. And the meat was not stored in a refrigerator.

Poultry animals were killed an hour before they were going to be cooked. Nevertheless, there were occasions when *Manang* Leticia would stow meat in vinegar or sugar cane, salt, powdered pepper, and other herbs and spices to prolong its shelf life.

"Even so, don't go near that place! It is better that way!" said *Manang* Leticia.

Then, Ayang came. She was carrying the rattan basket, which was now empty.

"Where are my clothes?" he asked.

"Ayang left them to dry outside," answered *Manang* Leticia.

Then, Xander turned his attention to the old Ayang who was scooping water from a jar with a mug. He spoke to her for the first time, "What do you know about the mausoleum in the backyard, Ayang?"

Ayang paused. She instantly closed the lid of the water jar and returned the mug to its storage.

A long silence bored Xander. What was he expecting? A decent conversation with a woman who never liked him? *Manang* Leticia was about to say something when they heard a guttural sound come from Ayang's throat.

"There are no witches." Her voice sounded so serious but a little shaky.

Xander was surprised of this sudden improvement, and so was *Manang* Leticia.

"It's just a tomb where the dead peacefully lay," added Ayang as she turned to face the stunned Xander.

"Of course you will say that!" countered *Manang* Leticia.

She had always thought that Ayang was deprived of creativity or imagination. She was sometimes the subject of gossip among the *barrio* people, accusing her of witchcraft because of her hermit-like way of life. However, there were no records of this woman's tomfoolery. She lived harmoniously with everyone, though she preferred to be always alone.

"I think Ayang is right!" seconded the amused Xander.

He finally realized that Ayang is not that strange. At least, she got a bit of sense as compared to normal people. He smiled at her, hoping to receive a smile back from her. But Ayang immediately left the kitchen without leaving a word.

"Oh, yes! She's a little bit strange," commented *Manang* Leticia as she started washing the rice grain. "You will get used to her."

CHAPTER 3
Mysteries of the House

Rain poured in torrents. His attempts to contact Atty. Tan always failed. His mobile phone started to run out of battery, and he had no way of charging it. What a sad life he had in the old house! It was totally worse than the Bronze Age!

His windows were open, letting the air and the moonlight in. He was still not used to the meager light the candles gave off. And the moon was not shining brightly.

"What a clever man!" he uttered after a deep sigh.

He was reading the terms of his grandpa's will. He was generous to give him everything he had, but the conditions were just too over the top. He would have the house and the forty-five-hectare farm. And to add to that, he'd also become the tenant's employer. But all these he would have, only if he abided to his terms.

The terms sounded quite simple. First, he had to stay in the house and learn to love the ways of life in the *barrio*. Well, it was a no-brainer. He could always lie to Atty. Tan and make a sworn statement that he had fallen in love with the place.

Second, he must sacrifice something for the tenants. This one was kind of hard. What would he sacrifice them? Apparently not his life! He was not Jesus Christ or some national hero. Perhaps he would need more days to think about how to handle this.

Third, he had to find a missing painting, which the document called "The Window through Time" and a rare white pearl. He was a bit confused why his grandpa would want these things. He was rich enough not to covet them.

An antique painting not even at par with a Michelangelo, a Rafael, or a Picasso, was worth nothing, he thought.

But the rare white pearl maybe. He could sell it once he had it in his hands. Nevertheless, he was quite unsure how to find them. There were no other details about these items' whereabouts except for what they were.

He was getting tired, and retiring for the night crossed his mind. So he reached for his bag to return the will to its safe place when a strange leather book caught his eye. He had not opened it since the first day Atty. Tan handed it over to him. He wondered what could be inside. *Could be his grandpa's diary or a book about witches maybe.* His mind was pushing him to peek inside over the idea of finding a map that would lead him to find the items in term number three.

The book was old and fragile, but it was so easy to open.

The insides of the flap cover had letters handsomely engraved in the English language.

It read, "*A Personal Property of…*" then the rest was burned.

He remembered that his grandfather was fond of putting his name on his belongings. It must be his name that was erased. The book was from him in the first place. As he browsed the dated yellow parchment, he saw nothing but empty pages with just splotches of old age. It did not seem like a book but a notebook or a journal to be specific.

He examined the thing again, checked the front cover, ran through the pages, and double checked the back, yet he found no traces of content. What did his grandpa want to say by giving him an empty diary? Did he want him to put into writing all the accounts of his life to be read by the next generation? Xander just

33

could not understand him. Too bad his grandfather was not around anymore to clarify the confusion.

Xander even thought that his grandpa was just playing games with him and actually had no plans of giving over his inheritance. It might sound so judgmental, but Xander never trusted the man. Frustration over the useless empty diary pissed him off. If he could contact Atty. Tan tonight, he would definitely demand the earliest flight out of the country. He hated to be played, and his good-for-nothing grandfather was doing it to him in the most exciting way he could have imagined.

Losing his temper, he hurled the diary outside his window.

Enough of this game! He thought.

The diary must be soaked wet by now or must be caught by the thick bushes. But he did not care. It was just a piece of junk that got into his nerves.

The downpour got so strong and the wind angrier that it blew his curtains into turmoil.

He walked straight to the side table where an oval shaped mirror was attached, and he laid his backpack to rest before retiring for the night. Unusually, he felt the spine-chilling coldness of the wind. It was colder and creepier than he thought. He felt the hair on his nape rise, and his knees shake. Then, the black candles' flare brightened more. His room turned peculiarly lighter and brighter like the sun had shoved its luminosity to it.

His heart pounded like a gong. He could hear and count each beat with his fingers.

Then, the rain calmed, and the wind stopped blowing.

He turned to the murky sky outside his window and saw the three rings slowly appearing. Now, they had colors. Each glowed scarlet red. Though faint and little, he could clearly see the red color. It was mind-blowing.

The spectacle must not be left unnoticed or unrecorded. It ohappens rarely for centuries, he thought. So, he quickly searched for his camera in his backpack. There was no way he'd miss this chance.

34

His hands quickly installed the parts of his camera when he noticed something in his mirror.

He froze.

It wasn't something.

He rubbed his eyes and blinked a couple of times. For a moment, his heart stopped. Time slowed down. He couldn't believe what he was seeing.

There's a woman in his mirror.

He stared at her for quite a time. He was waiting for himself to scream—scared but he had no clue where he got the audacity to stay composed—but his voice was trapped somewhere that it might perhaps take more than eternity to find.

The woman gracefully brushed her hair with a beige comb. She looked beautiful with her light brown hair.

As surprise caught him, he unintentionally dropped his camera. The loud sound it made as it touched the floor was besieged by the growl of the mighty thunder. Lightning stroke and the wind angrily blustered, clattering his windows and curtains. His quick eyes noticed how the candles were put off.

As darkness enveloped his room, the radiant sky where the moon lies brightened even more. He was relatively worried about the recent changes in the weather. Rain, lightning, and thunder oddly appearing, and intervals of tranquility were quite short. It did not give him the impression that global warming was causing it. There must be something strange behind the change of weather.

He turned back to the mirror and was quite astounded to lose sight of the beautiful woman. She was gone, strangely.

He waited for seconds and had his eyes on the mirror. He had no idea why he was doing it, but he wanted to see her again to make sure she was real and not a hallucination. Oddly, he did not feel frightened. Surprised, yes, but not frightened, and he wondered why.

Then, the rain instantly stopped. No more lightning and thunder. Only the bright moon and the three vague planets illuminating his dark room.

She did not reappear. He could see only his reflection.

"Ayang?" He almost jumped off his feet as Ayang's face appeared in the mirror.

She was standing behind him carrying a piece of white lit candle.

"You scared me!" He felt his heart fluttered.

"The storm was strong," she plainly said as she walked towards the candlesticks and changed the black ones with white ones, which she brought as spare and started lighting them. "You must close your window."

"Yes, I will." He finally found his calm back.

Ayang gave him the chills. *Why did she have to appear like that?*

Soon, the room was well-lighted.

"You look startled," commented Ayang as she studied his face. She observed how tedious and robotic the young man had turned after she came into his room.

Xander did not opt to tell the old woman about what he saw in the mirror.

It happened quickly. He started doubting whether it actually happened. It could be his brain playing with him because of the oddity of the weather or whatever solid and sensible reason he could think of. It was just so impossible to see a reflection of a woman who was not even there in real life.

It was just his mind. He forced himself to believe.

"Why did you change the candles?" he curiously asked while watching Ayang kept the black candles inside her pocket.

"The white candles emanate calmness. It will help you sleep well tonight," answered she.

"Oh!" he uttered. Then, he went on asking before Ayang could step out of the room, "How old is this mirror?"

36

"Two centuries old." Her voice was dreary like there was no life in it. "Why do you ask?"

Her piercing stare bothered him again.

"Nothing in particular," he lied.

"Are the lights good enough?" she questioned.

"Yes, they are. Thanks!" He smiled at her. He felt weird smiling at a very cold woman, but he must, however, show that he appreciated all the work she had done for him.

Ayang slowly marched her short legs out of the room. Her footsteps were discrete despite the weight of her wooden slippers. He thought he heard her hum a song before she totally vanished from his sight.

As soon as he was alone again, he turned back to the mirror. There was nothing in it but his curious and anxious reflection. He was certain of what he saw, but his rationality was saying otherwise. Which should he believe? His sight or his logic?

He began pacing around his room, trying to erase the astonishing image of the woman from his mind.

Have I gone mad? He thought. As he walked anxiously, his foot stepped on something hollow. Its sound differed from the rest of the floor area. It sounded like an empty space where trapped air was hidden. He kneeled down and knocked off the piece of wood around the hollow part. And a compartment, just like he thought, bewildered him.

There was a tidy polished wooden chest inside the compartment. He quickly pulled it out and laid it on the smooth surface next to the now empty compartment. There were strange flower carvings on the lid of the box, which he delicately touched with his fingers.

There were just so many strange things in this house, and his brain couldn't keep up.

As he opened the box, he saw a collection of papers folded into squares. They were old papers like the ones in his grandpa's diary, but he did not quickly assume that the box was his grandpa's.

One reason was the box was unearthed in his room. There was no way his grandpa owned it. Perhaps the previous occupant could have hidden it to avoid questioning.

He looked both ways to check if someone was watching him. When he realized there's no one, he opened a few and read them. They were poems written in a language he could not understand. But there were a few poems in English that talked about romance and dreams.

One caught his attention. It was a very short but lovely poem.

It is not forever when you doubt.
It is not real when you fear.
It is not happening when you give up.
Genuine love is worth all the sacrifices.
To be with each other, I will give all that I have
Even if I have to die.

A smile was painted on his face. He wondered if such love still existed, or just a fantasy which these words were trying to blind him with. However, he felt good after reading it.

The poet must be so inspired when he wrote this, he thought. *He must have been so in love to be inspired to make poems.*

*   *   *

He walked down the stairs to the kitchen with a candlestick in his hand. It was dangerous to trek a dark hallway especially when senses were so high up as though one sees, hears, feels, or even smells minute things along the way.

There he saw the two women helping each other clean the kitchen.

"What can we do for you, Xander?" asked the jovial *Manang* Leticia.

Ayang seemed not to care about his surprising presence. Instead of paying attention to him, she went on drying the glasses with a piece of cloth.

"Is everything okay here? There was like a storm earlier," he said.

"We're okay. We're used to the darkness," answered the cook. "And the storm passed so quickly. It did not touch us. We're big girls."

"Listen. I can't live without electricity. We need it," said he.

"Electricity comes and goes in this house." There was a hidden laugh in Leticia's answer, and Xander could identify it.

"Are the candles not enough for you?" Ayang spoke.

"They barely produce light. I can't do all my paintings using candles only. I need proper light."

Ayang turned her back to him and walked out of the kitchen.

"Where is she going? It's dark."

"She can find her way. Ayang has many eyes," kidded Leticia.

"But where is she going?"

"Probably to town to get some supplies. She has been telling me about storing food while the weather is okay."

Indeed, Ayang behaved rather suspiciously creepy.

"*Manang,* I want to ask you about my room." He pulled one chair from under the table and sat down. He placed the candlestick in the middle of the table, which made the entire room looked so much brighter and warmer. "Who occupied the room before me?"

"Nobody."

"Nobody?"

"All I know is that room is uninhabited for years. Why do you ask?"

He shook his head as the image of the uncanny woman flashed in his mind again.

"When was the last time that room was inhabited?"

"I don't really know. If you have questions about the house, ask Ayang. She knows everything from the rooftop to the floor."

"Don't you think this house is a little bit eerie?"

"Oh, it is. But it's normal for old houses. Are you by any chance scared?"

"No way!" He gathered his legs and rose from his seat, looking as though he was proving the woman wrong. He was not scared. He was curious about the mystery that wrapped the house. It didn't look different than how it looked sixteen years ago, but there was something off about it.

"Well, good night, *Manang!*"

CHAPTER 4
Message in Fresh Ink

It happened again—the dream.

He woke up soaked in sweat.

It was not the three rings this time but a silhouette of a woman with long hair adorned with a headdress of golden coins and thick long patterned clothes. His dream was vague, but just like the three rings, it bothered him tremendously. It was the first time he dreamt of it after he came to this house.

He heard the crowing of the roosters, long and constant.

They crowed in chorus, hurting his ears. Nevertheless, he was annoyed not because of the roosters but because of the odd dreams. He just had enough of them, and he couldn't bear living his life forever having strange dreams that had no connection to him at all. Thinking about them made his heart explode. He always felt like he was on the run, or some hungry and terrifying predator was after him.

Then, there was Ayang's eerie music again, penetrating his ears. The dream, the crowing of the roosters, and Ayang's music were pestering him all at once.

He stormed out of his room to the *sala*.

"Stop it, will you?" he yelled.

But when he laid his eyes on the piano, he saw no one. The lid of the piano was even closed. A white knitted mantle covered the entire piano.

He was positive that he heard the piano play, but where was Ayang?

"I'm sorry it bothered you."

He heard a voice coming out of the *comedor.* Ayang appeared carrying a broomstick and a dustpan.

"How did you get there?" His eyebrow raised in curiosity.

"I was downstairs to get these." She showed him the broom and the dustpan.

Xander turned to the piano again, which looked untouched.

"But I heard the piano play," he insisted. "How did you manage to go downstairs in a flick of a second?"

"I did not touch the piano. I do not know how to use it," she responded calmly.

Xander just smirked with skepticism. Ayang was just scared to admit it. She might be thinking that if she admitted, Xander would get mad and punish her. It was not a new thing among employers and employees. It happens all the time. Employees protect themselves by fibbing, and Xander could only think of this as Ayang's excuse.

"Alright, I get it," he said. "I'm amused by your denial, Ayang, but please, stop playing the piano early in the morning. It's not because it sounds repugnant. It sounds great actually. It's just that it annoys me. I've got a lot of things in my mind right now, and I need silence to think!"

Ayang nodded. Finally, she admitted.

"Anyway, I'll be going to town today," he said.

"To the *barrio?*"

"Yes." He badly needed some distraction. "Tell *Manang* I'm getting food on my way there." He hurried back to his room.

*   *   *

He brought his camera and his sketch pad along with him. He had to find activities that could clear his mind for a bit.

His first stop was the morning mass. The church was old, and it looked like an architectural structure from the sixteenth century or earlier. It was a small church, but its buttresses were majestic and towering. The door was large; it could let in at least seven people at the same time.

It was not about his fear of remembering his parents that pushed him to go there. He wanted to do something new— something that would pull him out of his comfort zone. He was thinking about the cause of the dreams, and one major reason he considered was the unsolved issues he had with himself.

He had been a product of his own foolishness all this while. Pretensions was his sole companion for sixteen years: pretending to be strong, unyielding, and happy. The dreams might be telling him to stop and for once be vulnerable. Sometimes, admitting one's imperfections was a part of healing. But it was easier said than done. It had always been like that.

After the mass, he hurried to get out of the church to avoid the traffic of people when he noticed a group of elderly women in navy blue blouses, knee-length skirts, and laced veils on top of their heads, gazing at him.

One woman approached him in a friendly way, and said, "You are *Don* Santiago's grandson, aren't you?"

He nodded curiously.

Then, the rest of the group came running toward him. He had never seen a troop of middle-aged women so exuberant and loud.

"We are just wondering if you're interested in participating in our *fiesta* two weeks from now. We will be so honored to have you as a judge for a flower arrangement competition," said one of the them.

With the way she spoke, one could identify how loquacious she was.

43

"Me?" he sounded flabbergasted.

The group of cherubic women bobbed their heads altogether.

"But I have no experience in flower arrangements," he reasoned out.

"Oh, it does not matter! As long as you can choose the most beautiful flowers and designs, you're good to go!"

How could these women think he was apt for this challenge?

"Just think of selecting from a bunch of beautiful ladies," said the one with a pair of round thick-brimmed glasses. "You pick whom you think is the loveliest in the group, the one who catches your attention the most. I think you are quite an expert at that," she kidded the last part.

Xander blushed. He was not sure if it was a compliment or a tactic to get him aboard. He never had any serious relationships before. Perhaps he had good taste in women for he had been attached to quite attractive ladies in the past six years. But he did not think picking flowers was similar to that. With flowers, one would just see the exterior. The flowers' beauty wilted soon after, and none of its splendor would remain but the memory of how it looked before. Women, on the other hand, were deeper subjects than flowers. To find the right one, men had to consider what goes beyond the surface. They lasted longer than anything in the world.

As they said, women love and care the longest compared to men. Women might sometime appear changeable, but their greatest quality is that they remain true despite tribulations. They might appear weak, yet they draw strength out of their weakness. Their magic is keeping men incessantly in love with them, and this Xander failed to ponder. He had always fallen out of love with all the girls he was with. He never sought a resolution to any of them.

"I will think about it," he said.

"That's great! Then you will be able to meet some of your farmer tenants. They always join the contest for the cash prize!"

The women seemed to be so caught up with the conversation that he began to think of it as an unending punishment. Thus, he was forced to accept the invitation just to cut the conversation short.

He had this feeling that he would become the subject of tattletales across the *barrio* before the day ended. To have a foreign person get involved in their beloved *fiesta* was quite an accomplishment. And those tattletales would surely boast of how they convinced him.

He dashed off the church to avoid queries from the townspeople as soon as he found the opportunity to escape the clutches of the eager women. Apparently, his presence and his identity had been leaked to almost half of the population of churchgoers. They were so friendly and would talk about any kind of things, and seemed not to run out of what to say. It was weird, really, to be treated like a superstar, but he found no reason to be treated as such. He started to think if his grandfather was treated similarly.

What would grandpa do if he were in my shoes? Would he allow these people to incessantly talk about flowers, or women, or even their neighbors' cows or livestock? He thought. He found it so different because he had never been mobbed in his entire life.

His neighbors in Honshu never showed this kind of interest in him, not even when they learned of his success in Tokyo. They never cared. But everyone here was different. They were all so nice, but they were also starting to get into his nerves. He was even chased as he trekked his way out of the church's vicinity until he reached the empty pavements.

When he was finally clear of the rampaging townspeople, he finally slowed down and breathed freely. He stayed for a while in one street corner to cool himself when he noticed a stranger glaring at him. She was sitting on a spot where a big rainbow-colored umbrella stood.

She called for him, "*Pssst!*"

45

Xander immediately went to see her.

What a strange way to get his attention, he thought.

"You got a fifty there?" she asked.

He looked inside his wallet and saw bills in hundreds and thousands. He took the one hundred bill and said, "I've got this."

Then, the woman hurriedly grabbed the money bill and hid it inside her belt bag. She began, "Give me your hand. I'll read your future."

Xander smirked with incredulity. The people in this *barrio* were very novel and queer. They were not like the ones he met before. They were extremely and annoyingly nice, yet strangely confounding. He had not yet fully recovered from the townspeople's extreme hospitality.

And here comes another strange character with a strange agendum, he thought.

He replied coldly, "Give me back my hundred!"

Fortune telling was a travesty for him. No man could predict one's future. Everything depended on the choices made in the present.

"It's just a meager amount, young lad, when you can have your future read!" commented the uncanny woman whose gray hair was in a single braid.

"Okay!" he expressed boldly. He thought of giving it a shot. His opinion about it would never change anyway.

The woman held his hand and stretched out his palm. Her eyes surprisingly widened after a few seconds of dead air.

Xander found it funny seeing the woman's expression.

"What? Did you see anything?" he challenged. It was like she saw animation in his palm. "Am I going to hear something new? Perhaps save the world from doomsday?"

She replied in a low voice, "Your quest for answers will be abridged. At twilight, when the sun has kissed the peak and when the moon has risen above the pillars of heaven, time and space will be breached. Yet, it will just be short-lived. Until blood is not shed, more of your ties will suffer. The stars have been warning you."

He snickered. "That's funny! I wonder if you have been telling the same lies to others."

The woman just stared at him.

"You can keep my money though, but I don't believe in fortune telling!" he managed to calm his voice. He was not angry about getting lied to. He was actually amazed by the woman's creativity.

"It's not going to be easy for you, young lad," she went on, not minding Xander's indifference. "But time will come, and you will have to believe me."

He shrugged and hurriedly left the street corner.

It was total nonsense to believe what she said. The strange things happening to him were mainly caused by his confused state of mind. He forced himself to believe. All he had experienced in his childhood led him to this condition. With a few psychological therapies, he would soon be back on track.

"Sorry!" he immediately said as he collided with someone in a corner.

"It's okay… Not your fault."

He paused after seeing whom he bumped into. A young lady in plain clothes started picking up objects that fell out of her grip after the collision.

Xander unleashed the gentleman in him and immediately helped.

"Are you selling these by any chance?" he asked. "Are you a businesswoman?"

"Bananas! They are bananas made into chips. Sweetened!" A faint smile formed on her face. "I am delivering these to the church," she answered as she hastily picked the packs and put them back in her basket. She seemed to be in a hurry that she did not even bother to face him while talking.

"Is this yours, too?" he asked as he showed her a necklace with a crucifix that was under his foot.

The young lady's eyes brightened. They were almond shaped and almost light brown in color. For once, Xander stopped to study someone else's face.

She took the necklace and put it back around her neck.

"Thanks!" She smiled shyly.

Xander just watched her lips curved.

There is something so distinctively engaging about her, he thought.

"Are your eyes really brown? I mean that brown?" he asked as he thought he saw them glistened as sunlight reflected on them. It was like he had seen the sun in them.

She blushed coyly as she quickly looked away. She thought it was appallingly shocking for strangers to look directly into a woman's eyes in the first meeting.

Xander hurriedly picked up his camera and asked, "Is it okay if I take a picture of you? I am a professional photographer and a painter too. I love to collect beautiful things."

The young lady flinched.

"What I meant is, I would love to have a souvenir of you and keep it as one of my collections," he clarified as he found himself flushing with embarrassment. He should have been more careful with what he said. "Obviously you are beautiful. That's why I would love to take a picture of you. I am not in any way objectifying you."

"I'm sorry but…"

She looked so doubtful. He wasn't just too bold for asking about her eyes but taking a picture of her was quite wild for strangers to do.

"I can pay you!" slipped from his mouth. "How much do you want?" He sounded really desperate.

There was an awkward silence.

Xander, then, realized what a fool he had been. He should not have bribed her! He saw how her facial expression transformed into complete disgust.

"I did not mean it that way!" he countered quickly.

The young lady decided on ignoring him. She walked away without saying a word. In her head, what just transpired was a perfect example of boys' luring tactics to get girls. She thought that she was mature enough to know what was real and what was not. Avoiding men like him was the best way out of trouble.

He was obviously perturbed by how he got rejected. He completely understood why she refused and he knew he was wrong. Girls in this country were bought up conservatively, and hitting on them the way he did earlier was just way beyond proper. Truth be told, girls in this country could get a little hard to please at times, and he couldn't blame them.

That girl had all the goods to decline a man like him. True, she was attractive, and she had the attitude that most women didn't. No girl had ever rejected his request, except her, and it was the reason he found her appealing.

Anyhow, if there were another thing that made her stand out in his book, it would be her pair of astounding eyes. They were mesmerizing. He thought it was the first time he had seen such color. And it was true that he wanted to take a picture of her for his collection. It was a rare chance to see that kind of color. They were almost golden with the sun's reflection. He started wondering how they would look without the sun.

He went back home after dinner. That was after six in the evening.

Manang Leticia was so worried that she repeatedly asked him how he managed to walk the dark roads to the house. But Xander did not have to walk the five-mile dark roads when he gained good friends in the *barrio* who genuinely offered to drive their carts for him.

49

Riding on wooden carts heaved by farm animals was thrilling, though not as exciting as a drag racing ride or a shuttle ride. It was the first time he was transported home by a fierce and strong *carabao* that had long arched horns on top of its head. But traveling with his friends along the dark silent roads was quite fun. It made the slow ride more fun than a shuttle ride.

These people were extremely fun to be with. There were music and singing, and a lot of talking. They shared their stories of survival, and Xander realized how simple these people were. They only wanted what was enough for them. They were very contented people and happy with what they had. A simple dream was already big for them, and it was what pushed them to strive hard—family, friends, and love.

Before he retired for the night, he sketched the face of the girl who refused to have her picture taken. At least, he got a vivid memory of her, and he could draw her anytime. But it would have been better if he got those eyes in full color or in the picture so that he could see them anytime he wished to.

While sketching, he noticed how silent the house was. Perhaps *Manang* Leticia had gone home, and Ayang… he had no idea where that eccentric woman was. She could have retired to bed already. But he did not care where she could be. He had no need of her at this time. She could be, perhaps, resting in her room, the old *zaguan*.

When he was almost finished with his sketch, he noticed that something was missing in his drawing. He got the eyes perfectly, except for the lack of colors. The nose and the lips looked the same as far as his memory served him right. However, her hair that curled down to her shoulders was a little bit exaggerated in his drawing.

He was about to reach for his sharpener from the desk when he took notice of his grandpa's diary carefully laid on top of the side table. He recalled that he got rid of it last night. He held it with his hands with full wonder. It still looked the same: fragile and worn out. However, the papers had become dirtier as water marks were left.

What was it doing on his nightstand? He was sure he threw it outside his window while the storm was ravaging his backyard. It was just too impossible for the diary to find its way back to his room. It was not like the diary had legs to crawl back to his room or had some extraordinary powers to magically appear.

How to eliminate it?

He decided to burn the diary for good. He detached one candle from the metal holder and took one antique porcelain dish that was hanging on the wall, opened the diary, and was just about to dismantle the pages when he saw something peculiar on the third page. His eyes widened with shock. The last time he saw the diary it was empty. Only the proprietorship writing was present at the cover. He was absolute that the pages were free of anything.

But it wasn't the case now. There was a strange message written in beautiful longhand.

PART 2

CHAPTER 5
The del Fierros

She carefully wrote.

The weather is insane. It's sunny during the day and rainy at night.

"Dinner will be served in a few minutes, *señorita*." A young maid in a plain thin *baro't saya* stepped into her room.

"Yes, thank you, Maying," said she.

And the maid, Maying, courteously closed the door behind her.

It was raining that night. Her windows were closed, but the angry wind was able to knock one *capiz* shell piece out of her window frame. She climbed out of her bed and hurriedly picked the shell up and stuck it back with hot glue made from animal collagen. Putting back the square piece shell was difficult as the wind was mightily strong. The loud clamor of the thunder even caused the entire window to shake.

Lightning hit a coconut tree outside. She saw through the hole in her window how the long thin leaves of the tree burned, fell off, and got doused as it touched the pool of rainwater. The heavens were angry. The moon had even showcased its great cowardice as it moved behind the chunky nimbus dark clouds. Storms appeared in seconds and disappeared after minutes.

After safely putting back the shell piece, she excitedly jumped back to her bed and opened the notebook her deceased grandmother gave her. The notebook looked beautiful. Its black leather cover made it look so expensive, and the dull dark gemstone in the middle added to its mystery. The papers were thick and finely coarse, and they were the finest parchment in town.

She freely lay prone on her bed as her mother was not around to reprimand her for behaving outlandishly improper. She took her quill pen from a metal case with her initials engraved on it. Her favorite quill was from a swan in Spain, and she preferred to use it than the new steel pen points. Hers had been boiled in a few minutes with a little alum and salt to harden and then dried in the oven for about two hours in very low heat. She got her ink placed in a little crystal jar where it was preserved for centuries as what her grandmother told her in her stories.

She continued writing.

A shell from my window fell off, and I had to stick it with glue, which my maid had been hiding in my dresser. I'm quite scared of the lightning. My abuelita, Lola Priya, is not here to console me. So, I have to stop fearing the lightning or the thunder. She went to heaven, and the thing she told me before passing away was to start practicing my English and Filipino. I'm quite good with both because my maid, Maying, speaks to me in Filipino, and I have books in English in Papa's library.

She gave me a piece of her jewelry. I have always wanted it, and she gave it to me on her deathbed.

This diary came along with the jewelry. I was a bit surprised to see this empty because I was expecting to be reading abuelita's life story and to know her more. Maybe she was saving this for some important occasion, which didn't happen. Had it happened otherwise, I would probably not have this.

Anyway, this is my first entry to this journal, and I am genuinely excited to be writing my everyday story. Before I go down for dinner and before my parents return from Doña Stella's house, I'll leave this short quote from an English writer. She said in one of her novels, "To be fond of dancing was a certain step towards falling in love."

Oh, how I wish I fall in love in the sweetest and most romantic way! I don't mind dancing. And I don't mind being serenaded with music and poetry.

She ended it with her initials.

C. d. F.

She waited for the ink to dry.

The rain had stopped, and she opened the windows to let air through. The soft wind would dry the ink quicker.

Her face was painted with bewilderment when she set her eyes on the sky. Three bright scarlet rings appeared. It was like heaven was in the war for shedding blood. It was the most peculiar thing that night.

The sound of horses and their shoes clanking against the stone pathway reached her bedroom, and she quickly closed her diary. A *kalesa* or carriage entered the gates. Oh, what an unfortunate time to welcome her *madre's* ire. Her mother hated to travel when the downpour was strong, more so detested the circumstances when mud got into her apparels.

She scurried to the dresser, looked into the mirror, brushed her long curly hair, and fixed it in a neat low bun adorned with a tiny flower hairclip.

"Señorita?" Maying came in. "Your parents have come back!"

"Maying, have you seen the sky?" she asked excitedly.

"Oh, yes, *señorita!* It looked magical!" replied Maying as she helped her mistress put on her clothes. "The same rings also appeared last night."

"Really?"

With pressure under her sleeves, she hurriedly hid her diary under the bed and returned her quill and ink back to her dresser.

Her mother's rowdy voice got louder and louder as she ambled up the stairs. Nothing about her mother's protests surprised her. The bad weather was at fault for the woman's exasperation.

Don Jaime, a considerably tall man with wide and broad shoulders, just beamed with common amusement. They came in with their clothes roughly drenched.

Dinner was delayed for an hour to accommodate *Doña* Guada's prejudiced inclination towards self-care. The woman directly headed to her room for a change of outfit, while *Don* Jaime sat across the *sala* and warmed himself near the lamp.

The kerosene lamp on the table made the food more appetizing as it emanated light throughout the whole *comedor.*

Doña Guada came out of her room in a new set of clean clothes. Her *camisa* had a collarless and translucent chemise made from pineapple fabric, with sleeves shaped like bells. The *pañuelo* covered the low-necked *camisa.* Her *saya* was an ankle-length skirt that shaped like a bubble and was hugged by a *tapis,* a muslin knee-length over-skirt. She sashayed her way to the dining table with her hand swishing her feathered fan. The maids secretly made fun of her by sneaking glances at each other.

Tamales, a dish made of corn-based starchy dough filled with pork meat, cheese, vegetables, herbs, and spices; and *Paella Valenciana,* cooked with white rice, vegetables, chicken meat, beans, and seasoning, were the main attractions of the night. They also had a bottle of Mexican wine and watermelon and mango for dessert.

Don Jaime discussed raising the farmers' pay by 10% by the end of the year, and by inviting a doctor to conduct free medical check-ups for the farmers and their families. But his wife declined to listen. She started talking about the new fashion trend in Spain and expressed her excitement over the arrival of her older sister.

"I couldn't wait to have my dresses recreated!" she stated theatrically. "Consuelo will certainly bring new fabrics from across Europe. Oh, I just can't wait to show them to my *amigas!* For sure, Jaime, they will envy me!"

"Hold your horses, Guada!" Jaime warned leniently. "You have to tone down your expenses. Wealth is not eternal."

"Who cares about money, Jaime, when we're financially secured?" She laughed confidently. "I can have whatever I want. You cannot make me stoop down below my level! And I will not conform to your unnecessary generosity towards the *indios*. They are as good as savages and infidels! In my body runs the blood of Spain, and through my actions shall reflect that I am above anyone else!"

Jaime ordered the maids to leave the *comedor* for a while. His wife condemning the *indios* in front of these humble servants was too much for his conscience to handle.

"You must not forget that you married a man with savage roots! If not for my paternal grandparents' Spanish blood, I could have been the *indio* you hate the most!" Though he knew he was still an *indio* in the eyes of some aristocrats despite his wealth.

"But my love!" Her voice rose. "Your grandparents are *insulares!* They might have been born and raised in this place, but they are still *Español!* That's why you're wealthy. It's because you have their money and legacy! And we are rich because I have got money too, which these poor *indios* don't. That's the difference between them and us. Don't you agree, Clarissa?" She turned to her daughter who was mum while watching them argue.

Guada continuously boasted her full Spanish ancestry to the people whom she thought to be beneath her. Her kind considered themselves as *blanco*, or people with full Spanish blood who were either born in Spain (*Peninsulares*) or in the Philippines (*Insulares*). Guada's family was from the rich region of Catalan. They had a tinge of nobility as their ancestors were dukes and duchesses, marquises and marchionesses, and barons and baronets, a long, long time ago. Guadalope Diaz Vargas had been proud of this her entire life.

Her family moved to the east via the Manila-Acapulco Trade. Since then, they kept the sanctity of their blood by marrying to fellow *Espanyol.* The Vargases started their own businesses, owning hectares of lands all over the country, but fate altered the story of the Vargases. Guada had to marry the half Spanish, half Filipino, Jaime del Fierro.

The reason for the intermarriage was unknown to many. Only Guada and her mother knew why she had to marry a man who could have been an *indio* because of his pure Filipina mother, a savage in their dictionary. However, Jaime's inheritance from his Spanish father tamed the superior and arrogant Vargases and made the former more than marriageable.

Jaime was a grandson to a *gobernadorcillo*, and this connection gave him a reputable name. He had always adored the love story of his parents. His father was a good and intelligent man, had studied in Madrid for years, and traveled to the Philippines to spend a vacation with his grandfather, who was then a high ranking official. In one of his trips to the *barrio*, he met this beautiful and simple girl whose hair was as black as a raven and whose skin was sun-kissed, almost golden. They fell in love with each other and got married. There was a little rebellion from the family over this marriage, but love overpowered everything. Jaime's father settled in the country and died in old age after his beloved wife left him two years earlier.

He had always dreamed of this kind of romance, but Guada was a different woman. She had changed over time. The sweetness and kindness she bore when they first met gradually vanished. Despite this transformation, Jaime remained faithful to her.

More importantly, *Don* Jaime believed that he was fortunate to have a daughter like Clarissa—a young, sweet, and charming girl of eighteen. This gift made up for not being able to have the perfect wife. He was grateful that Clarissa did not get her mother's pomposity. She was neither rude nor insensitive to the people around her. As a matter of fact, she was friends with the servants of the house, and she barely mingled with aristocrat children.

Clarissa was homeschooled. Her mother taught her to read and write. Women didn't have the privilege of receiving a university education like men did. Neither did they have the right to get involved in civic matters. They were taught to be excellent housewives and mothers. But her mind was as deep as the ocean like an empty jar ready to be filled with just anything. She read everything that interested her. Her father's library was the best place in the house for her, her favorite as a matter of fact. *Doña* Guada would sometimes tell her off for reading too much. She preferred to have Clarissa study needlework and music than waste her time with reading and writing poetry.

Dinner ended with *Doña* Guada emerging as the victor. Her husband chose to seal his mouth and not to aggravate the conversation any further.

CHAPTER 6
A Daughter's Run

In the morning, when the sky was free from dark angry clouds and eccentric rings, Clarissa and her mother went to the *barrio* to attend mass. Guada, like the townspeople, was so keen to hear about the priest's opinion about the peculiar astronomical phenomenon. They flocked the church in time for *Padre* Cito's sermon.

The stout and short priest in brown robes assured everyone that last night's phenomenon was just one of the universe's wonder. He was so confident about it that he kept laughing throughout the mass. Assurance from the Dominican priest was what the townspeople needed. They regarded him as the prophet of the sacrilegious doctrines, and whatever that came out from his mouth was the truth and would always be the truth.

They peacefully marched out of the church in high spirits. The ambiance of the vicinity instantly filled with good energy. Fear was erased from everyone's faces.

Clarissa waited for her mother inside the *kalesa*, watching the latter laughing with her *amigas*. They were probably talking about dresses or gossiping.

"I don't think I can wait for mother!" she complained as she took the white laced veil off her face.

"Where are you off to, *señorita?*" asked Maying who was sitting at the driver's seat as she saw her lady mounting off the carriage.

"I think I'll go for a short walk." She scuttled away from the *kalesa* before Maying could stop her.

She lifted her long, heavy skirt and train to avoid the quagmires on the muddy road. Last night's heavy rain left craters on the ground jammed with rainwater. Her *bakya* or wooden clogs adorned with floral carvings were quickly sullied with dirt. Nonetheless, Clarissa went on to achieve her transient freedom. She just felt like a free bird.

Getting away meant not being in her mother's circle of rich friends. It meant not behaving according to norms. She just wanted to be her real self. Her high spirits screamed for freedom every time she curbed herself with propriety. Exploring the woods and the *barrio*, and driving the *kalesa* were just a few of the things she wanted to do, which she could hardly do if Guada's iron claws were clutched around her neck. She grew tired of acting docile and prim.

She did not care about the dirt that gathered around the hem of her skirt or the sweat that was dripping down her forehead and neck. She continued running away anyway. She reached the streets of the busy market where the natives and the *sangleys,* or Filipinos with Chinese ancestry, ruled trade and business. People used copper coins or *barillas* for purchasing products. Obviously, the rich people had their purses and pockets filled with it and could just buy anything they wanted.

The houses in the *barrio* were so close to each other that neighbors often talk through their large windows, but none surpassed the regality of the del Fierro's stone house. Some were built in wood and stones with large windows on the upper level while stores opened at the ground floor.

At one store, *abaniko* fans were sold. The fans were of great help especially to mothers who needed to tend to their crying infants because of the warm weather. The *abaniko* fans were made by skilled craftsmen working in *Aling* Lucing's shop. She thought of buying one for her mother, but then she realized that the latter would prefer silken embroidered fans from New Spain.

Clarissa enjoyed watching maidens hold their *abanikos* close to their chest whenever they were praised by the elders for their beauty and wit, while she enjoyed more seeing them whiff their fans in rapid movements when they encountered cocky young men teasing them for their looks.

There were headgears made from pearls too, but she was not interested in them at all.

It was the first time she toured the *barrio* market alone, and she massively enjoyed it. Her short walk did not turn out to be short as she lost track of time. There were just so many things around that fed her hungry eyes, and time seemed so short to see everything.

She was hurrying back to the church when she met a female native from the uplands. If her mother were here, she would probably make a scene and embarrass the native woman by calling her a savage. She knew by the time the native blocked her way that she was in trouble.

The native glared intently at her.

Clarissa smiled at her in return instead.

Fear is not an option at the moment, she thought.

The native seemed tame. She stood petitely, and her skin was like the color of the mahogany tree. Her eyes were large and dark, and her curly hair was made into a small bun at the back of her head.

"What a beautiful necklace you have!" exclaimed the native with her eyes ogling the piece of jewelry on her neck.

"Oh, thank you!" Clarissa replied as she touched the necklace with her fingers. "My grandmother gave it to me."

"You should guard it with your life."

She fell into silence and wondered. She knew she must take care of it. It was her beloved grandma's heirloom.

64

"It does not look like an ordinary piece of jewel." Her voice was monotonous, yet something uncanny in it bothered Clarissa.

The native could not be referring about the cross pendant and Christianity because the former had no recognized religion. Their kind flew to the uplands to avoid Spanish friars from converting them. Clarissa did not just believe it was about religion.

"It might help you with the answers you're desperate about."

"What do you mean?" she asked as nicely as possible.

"Eternal sufferings shall you bequeath to your children until the heavens cease from turning red. One mistake from the past shall hound you, and you cannot get out of it unless you sacrifice the one thing you desire the most!" she uttered gravely after pushing Clarissa to the wall.

Her fingers slid to the cross on Clarissa's necklace. Clarissa's face turned ashen white, and her lips trembled with fear. The native's sudden act bewildered her. The native's stare looked ferocious and scary, dark and piercing like a vulture's.

The native persisted with her breath almost suffocating the trembling young lady, "You must spare no room for mistakes! You must not repeat history! You must end this eternal misery! It's desire against destiny all over again."

Clarissa gripped the woman's hands and thrust them away. As soon as she got her breath back, she immediately ran off, securing the necklace with her fingers. Her heart was skimming with every breath she puffed out. The woman petrified her. What she blurted out seemed to be complete nonsense. Clarissa did not believe any of it.

Natives were against Christianity, and they always attacked people who followed the Christian laws when they happened to meet one. What she experienced was plain savage brutality. Now, she understood why *Padre* Cito was so adamant on converting the upland natives. He wanted them to learn discipline, to be taught manners and the divine power of one God, and to recognize the church as the instrument to salvation.

As she reached the pavements leading to the church gates, she paused for a while to calm her nerves down at a corner. She had been walking and running for most of the morning, and her legs started to feel exhaustion. She felt her right ankle get swollen from twisting it while running.

"*Señorita?*" A voice emerged from the other side of the corner.

"Alejandro?" A tinge of hope in her voice surfaced.

A man in *camisa de chino*—a thin fabric shirt with long sleeves—and loose trousers appeared.

"Oh, Alejandro!" Clarissa heaved a sigh. Dread immediately dispersed as the man's familiar face greeted her.

Alejandro noticed Clarissa touching her ankle.

"Did you hurt yourself?" He sounded anxious.

Clarissa brought down her skirt right away to hide her reddened ankle.

"Where's Mama?" she asked.

"I drove her and Maying back to the mansion," replied Alejandro whose eyes were still on her feet. "What happened to you, *señorita?* You look appalled when you saw me."

She cleared her throat, and said, "I was attacked by a native in the market."

"Attacked?"

"Don't fret, Alejandro! She didn't hurt me. I twisted my ankle while running away."

"You must have it checked by a doctor," he suggested.

"No! I will be fine. Mama must not know about this," she told him. "You must not tell anyone, Alejandro."

He nodded.

"Now, if you will be so kind as to take me home. I can't let people see me in this state."

"Can you walk?" He offered his hand.

66

"Yes, I can. Just watch me from behind," she answered as she declined his hand. Young women must always be wary of men and Alejandro was not an exception. "People might see us, and you would not want to be the center of gossip."

"Okay." He silently followed her from behind.

*   *   *

She told Alejandro to get the *kalesa* through the gates as quietly as possible. She did not want to catch her parents' attention. Her mother must be in her room crying over the idea of losing her only daughter. Her father might be in the *barrio* seeking help from the officials to find her.

"*Señorita!*" Maying came running to her as she went down the *kalesa*.

Her ankle was hurting so bad.

"Where have you been? *Doña* Guada flew into hysterics when you disappeared. I just could not say you ran away. Now, they all thought you were abducted by the savages!"

She eyed Alejandro who was listening to the conversation. She expected him to keep quiet.

"I was in the market," she told Maying. "And I, unfortunately, hurt myself."

"Oh, *señorita!*" Maying's face sparked with worry.

"But I'll be fine!" she assured the worry-stricken Maying. "Now, if you would just please help me walk up the stairs?"

Maying brought a bowl of herbal decoction to Clarissa's bedside. It would take more than a day to rest her foot, but the herbs would help in easing the pain.

"Did Ayang help you with the decoction?" asked Clarissa as she lay down on her bed.

"Yes, *señorita,*" replied Maying. "She went to the woods to get the herbs."

"I should be studying more about plants," commented Clarissa as she read the book of prayers. "And Mama?"

"She's in bed. She said she'd talk to you over dinner." Maying laid warm leaves above Clarissa's ankle and wrapped it with a clean piece of cloth. "Alejandro went to the *barrio* to inform your father."

"Oh, Maying! Mama's voice will surely deafen me tonight!"

Maying chuckled.

"You cannot blame her, *senorita*. You're her only child."

"Oh, how I wish I were a boy!" the words unconsciously came out her mouth. "Then, I will not have to follow what Mama says. I can travel to Europe on my own and go to universities, and she will not have to say that I always have my nose buried in a book!"

"I'll bring your lunch over, *señorita.*"

"Not here, Maying. Bring it over to Papa's study."

"You are well aware that people know that that's a known secret?"

She bobbed her head enthusiastically and jumped off her bed. Her ankle ached after her feet landed on the floor, but it went away quickly. Her papa's library was the best place to be herself.

"I still have four books in my list before this month ends." She hurried out of her room.

Maying warned her not to run to prevent straining her foot, but Clarissa was as hardheaded as a toddler as she can be. She entered her papa's study rather silently to avoid waking her temperamental mother up.

The study was not big, just enough for three big shelves attached to the walls, and three smaller cabinets with plenty of books in fragile binding.

She hurried to the chair near the window and started reading a pocket-sized book, which she hid inside a secret chamber in her father's desk. It was a book about legends and myths that was banned by the Catholic faith as it contained stories of the pre-Spanish Philippines, which could cause a revival of pagan beliefs.

Doña Guada would completely admonish her if she found out about this. Clarissa received the book from a savage native who worked for their family without even getting caught of being unconverted. It was only Clarissa and Maying who knew about Ayang owning a savage's life.

Creak!

She heard a sound from the *narra* cabinet. It sounded like the flipping of pages and friction created by papers rubbing each other. Vigilantly walking towards the cabinet with her book clasped in her hands, her eyes widened as anticipation heightened.

"Alejandro?" Her voice quavered as she set her eyes on the man sitting on the floor with his back against the cabinet wall.

His eyes were directed to the book he was holding but lost his focus when he saw her.

"*Señorita?*" He instantly stood up and hid the book behind him. He looked surprised as his face turned so pallid like the cotton woven material on top of the tea table.

A smile formed on her face. She was amazed to discover Alejandro's secrets. He had been hanging around her papa's study for quite a time and borrowing books too.

"I'm sorry I interrupted you," she said.

"No, *senorita.* I'm about to leave anyway…"

"No, Alejandro! You can stay here as long as you want!" She smiled again. "What are you reading?"

"World History," he replied shyly. "*Don* Jaime is too kind to let me borrow his books for my schoolwork."

"That sounds interesting!" Her eyes lit up. "How long have you been hiding here?" She sounded so amused. "I mean, you can grab a chair and sit near the window. The view outside is exhilarating!"

Alejandro unexplainably went red.

"I think I know why you're hiding!" she teased, seeing how uncomfortable the poor man became. "You are afraid of Ayang!"

"No, I am not!" he countered.

"I heard from Maying and from the other maids that Ayang gives you the creeps, and she has been watching you all the time!" she added.

"That's a different story!" He laughed.

The barrier of awkwardness was broken.

"How's your foot, *señorita?*"

"It's still hurting, but I think I can still run off anytime," she joked.

Her cheeks glowed like a primrose. She felt so good with laughing; something she couldn't freely do with her mother around. It felt so wonderful to say anything you wanted without thinking what would be the consequence for saying it.

"I think I should go back to the stable, *señorita,*" said he.

"Are you done with the book?"

"I will continue reading it in my room tonight."

She nodded with a trace of doubt. She believed that Alejandro was just shy to stay in the library because she was there.

"You must come back here," she quickly said before the man could step out from the room. "This room needs to be livened up a bit. The books prefer to be read by scholars, and I just cannot read them all!"

"I will, *señorita.*"

"Alejandro! It's so nice talking to you again like how we used to when we were children."

CHAPTER 7
The Hole in Time

"Who could be visiting at this hour?" *Doña* Guada asked herself as she heard horses neighing.

She dashed towards her window without expectation of her husband's return. She would know if it was Jaime's horse.

"Consuelo?" Her eyes widened as she saw an expensively dressed lady exiting the *kalesa*.

Her arrival was premature. The letter the del Fierros received from Consuelo indicated her visit to be a week later. Guada was just so surprised and thrilled at the same time that she rushed down to the main door to greet her darling sister.

"Guada!" Consuelo entered the main door and called out.

Her petticoat was big enough and was jammed in the doorway. Her servants needed to pull her through. Her cherubic face looked like it was going to explode of embarrassment from getting stuck.

"You should widen your door, Guada!" she reprimanded her sister. "Our doors in Spain are as big as an elephant's trunk!"

Guada kissed her sister on the cheek and asked, "Why did you arrive so prematurely?"

Consuelo replied once she freed herself from the door's hold, "My husband traveled back to Mexico earlier than expected. I did not want to stay alone in our house, so I boarded the ship that travels to *Filipinas* a week earlier."

"I am just so thrilled you're here!" uttered the elated Guada. "Did you bring the fabrics?"

"Oh, yes! Mind you, they are the best in Europe!"

"Oh, I love your dress, Concha!" Guada exclaimed as she touched the delicate beadwork on Consuelo's chest and waist.

The petticoat too was colorful and filled with floral designs and gems. Her sister just looked like a perfect European noble.

"Oh, how I wish I could wear this kind of dress again! I look so dull and plain when I stand beside you!"

"Yours is the most stylish wardrobe I have ever seen in this island!" commented Consuelo.

"Not as stylish as the ones I had before!" she replied sharply. "If I could only get this *pañuelo* out of this design and make the waist fit better, then I'd be happier."

"That's the consequence of marrying a conservative man, Guada!" laughed Consuelo.

Then, they walked straight to the *sala*.

"Does my niece still play the piano?" she asked.

"Yes, she does but only in the early morning. I prohibit music throughout the day as it gets into my nerves," informed Guada after ordering a maid to prepare some hot chocolate.

"Where is she by the way?" Consuelo searched the entire living room for her favorite girl.

Guada's face wrinkled. She told her sister about her daughter's *barrio* adventure that nearly caused her a heart attack.

"You really have to impose strict rules now, my dear. Clarissa is not getting any younger. She is eighteen and marriageable. I married at sixteen and you at her age! I only think that it's time for her to realize her duty as the daughter of a wealthy and noble clan," said Consuelo.

"I'm afraid it will take us light years to straighten her up!"

"You sound like you failed your parental duties!" ribbed Consuelo.

"She has not acquired the class of the Vargases!" murmured Guada in desperation. "Neither did she try to learn it! She has Jaime's *indio* mother's character! She might have earned a Christian name, but she is still a savage by blood!"

"That formidable woman!"

"Clarissa might have our beauty, but her morals are so alike with the *indios,* and that includes her simple-mindedness and the lack of motivation! She does not even wear her best clothes. She even chooses to mingle with servants than my *amigas'* children!"

Then, their gazes turned to Jaime's study, which was just across the *sala.* At the doorstep was a stunned Alejandro.

"What is this bastard still doing here?" inquired Consuelo to Guada. "I always thought you had gotten rid of him."

Alejandro immediately greeted them a good afternoon, calling Consuelo as *Doña.*

"Oh, please, Concha! Don't start with me on this!" she slothfully said after sipping the cup of hot chocolate. Guada spoke to Alejandro, "Don't you have some tasks in the stable?"

"Yes, *Doña*," he answered directly. "I am just borrowing *Don* Jaime's book."

Consuelo chuckled with mockery. "What a generous husband you have, dear sister!"

"Now, off you go, boy!" she stridently commanded Alejandro with her finger pointing to the staircase.

Alejandro rushed down the stairs and did not even bother to look back.

"What will Jaime get for taking that boy as his ward?"

"I have no idea!"

"Are you certain that he's not Jaime's bastard?" Consuelo's eyebrow arched. Her forehead creased.

Guada laughed at the idea. "Jaime would never betray me!" she said boldly. "The boy does not even look a bit like Jaime! It's Jaime's *indio* mother who brought that bastard here."

"Oh, God! You never told me about that!" Consuelo's eyes widened.

"Jaime doesn't want to talk about it. He said that his parents wanted to keep the child's origin a secret," whispered Guada.

"Oh, heavens, dear sister! That boy could still be a del Fierro bastard! He could be Jaime's little brother. Not really sure if he is the *indio* woman's son or his father's boy."

"Exactly the reason why I cannot easily get him out of this household. Jaime is giving him too much attention!"

Then, the study's door opened, and the two ladies in the *sala* almost dropped their cups upon seeing Clarissa walk out of the room.

"Dear child, what are you doing in that room with the bastard kid?" Consuelo rose from her seat and stomped her foot.

Utter astonishment was painted all over their faces.

Guada held unto the armchair. She could only pray that her eyeballs were deceiving her. She felt her legs wobbling as shock penetrated her soul.

Clarissa felt the urgent need to respond. Drawn on the women's faces were horror and disbelief. She told them, "I was just reading a book, *Tiya*, and Alejandro was there to study his lessons in World History."

Guada let out a sigh of relief. She dramatically fell down the long settee and started demanding for a glass of water.

"You must know, dear child, that being seen with a man, more so alone in a single room, is a humungous disgrace to your integrity as a woman!" lectured Consuelo. Her face slowly recovered from shock and fury. "Worse case is, if this man has no expectations, just like that bastard! Can you imagine yourself forced to marry a man with no title and fortune?"

"Alejandro is a friend, *Tiya*. He's like a brother to me!" she reasoned out. "We've known each other all our lives."

Consuelo calmed herself. She approached her niece, and told her, "I know that you consider him a friend, but he is not like us. You should not be socializing with his kind. Now, let us stop this squabble. I just arrived from sea, and I need to get the water out of my head!" Consuelo gave a fascinating smile and opened her arms to receive a hug from Clarissa.

"Welcome back, *Tiya*." Her voice sounded dreary.

"Take what I said as a lesson, but do not be mad at me."

"Oh, please, enough of that! Don't you see how I need to be nursed?" conveyed Guada exaggeratedly.

Two maids tended to her "needs." One whiffed the *abaniko* to her face, and the other massaged her forehead.

*   *   *

The conversation around dinner was mainly about *Tiya* Consuelo's developing wealth in South America. Unfortunately, she had no children to inherit her husband's money. Thus, she considered Clarissa as her own and was as concerned as a real mother should be.

Don Jaime barely had the chance to open his mouth. The night was dominated by the women.

As dinner ended, Clarissa hurried to her bedroom to start reading the books her aunt brought from Europe.

Maying feasted on the boxes of dark chocolates.

"Ayang changed the candles again," said Clarissa as she observed the black candles in her room.

"She said that the black candles make you sleep soundly."

"I better give one to *Tiya*," she said. "And Mama too!"

"I doubt the black candle could still remedy *Doña's* sleeplessness," Maying said humorously.

Clarissa chortled.

"It's getting late, *señorita*. Time for bed. Good night!"

"Maying, take the chocolates with you. Share it with the others."

"Thank you, *señorita!*" Maying carried the boxes of chocolates in her short arms without difficulty.

Clarissa took out her quill and ink from the drawer and the diary from under the mattress. She lit the lamp on her study table and positioned herself near the window. The sky was clear and bright. The moon shone vibrantly together with the three rings. The scarlet color had even lightened up a bit.

She just had so many things to write; from the native encounter to Alejandro to *Tiya* Consuelo's premature arrival. Excitedly, she opened the diary and searched for her first entry.

"Can this be happening?" she read at the bottom of her written paragraph.

PART 3

CHAPTER 8
Behind the Pen

Xander impatiently waited for the words to appear like magic. His fingers continuously tapped the table, which he had dragged near the window. It took him more than an hour to decide on what to do with the remarkable entry on his diary. Curiosity, confusion, and great anticipation overwhelmed him.

He waited for a few more minutes. He started pacing around his room while throwing a few glances on the odd diary from time to time. He was nervous and excited at the same time. He felt butterflies in his stomach. Only by pacing would he be able to let go of this uncontrollable anxiety.

He walked back to the table and picked the Victorian pen with his left hand, and wrote.

I need to get an answer! So, please, if you're a ghost from another dimension, just show yourself and tell me what you need. I demand you to stop this baloney!

Then, he held back his breath as he waited for the response to magically come out. His heart was clamoring for it. He could hear it pumping violently.

I am not a ghost!

Appeared gradually right before his eyes.

His heart almost jumped out of his chest.

He was out of words.

He saw it! He saw the words came out from nowhere!

Then, he unconsciously started laughing out loud.

"Huh! You think you can fool me!" he shouted with all his might. His voice echoed in his room. "What is this? Some joke?"

Xander did not know who he was talking to. He had no idea how the words appeared. Yes, he was expecting a response, but he did not know it was really possible. It was. It appeared just like how he wished for it to happen.

Crap! What tomfoolery had he gotten into now?

He suddenly fell into seriousness as he glared back at the beautifully written words with utmost attention.

This isn't a trick, is it?

It was really happening. His eyes were not deceiving him.

Xander finally decided to write again.

This is not a joke. This is actually happening.

How is this possible?

He scribbled fast.

I don't know. Why don't you tell me?

I think this diary let us communicate.

Xander studied the diary again. This time more intently.

Do you mean there are two diaries, and you have the other one?

Yes, I think so.

The response was quick.

Mine is a leather-bound notebook with a black stone in the middle.

His eyes enlarged with astonishment.

Mine too.

He answered. Then, he lacked the words to write. For a few seconds, he just stared at the open diary, reading the words printed over and over again.

Are you still there?

He did not know how it happened, but it was like his hand had its own mind.

I am.

Where are you now?

It took him a lot of courage to ask it.

In my bedroom.

He glanced around and felt the hair on his arms and neck rising.

Are you sure you're really not a ghost?

I told you. I am not!

He smirked with disbelief. If he was dreaming, he wanted this dream to quickly end. Everything that was happening seemed too unreal to believe. Appearing texts in an ancient diary and communicating with a ghost through it was just totally surreal.

Why do you keep on asking me if I am a ghost?
How will I know that you're not one?

He noticed a tinge of irritation from the latest message.

You want proof? Well, right now, I am sitting by my window and seeing a spectacular display in the sky. Does that sound human to you?

What spectacular display?
Do you mean the strange scarlet rings in the sky?

His eyes immediately turned to the bright sky outside his window.

How did you know about the rings?

I see them too, outside my window!

Xander shut the diary in a snap. It was a crazy thing to be communicating with someone you didn't even know through a notebook. He extended his arm to the trash bin near the corner wall and next to the table to where he was writing and was just about to let go of the diary when the lightened black candle surprisingly fell off the wall and burned the contents of the bin. The flare was strong enough to burn everything that was inside the bin.

It was not just pure accident, he thought, the candle falling off the wall.

The holder seemed strongly attached to the wall, and in no way, could it easily have detached itself without a force acting upon it.

The fire doused off little by little.

An idea crossed his mind.

The diary could have not been just a simple notebook. It could be bearing some mystical powers that only the owner knew about. It could protect itself from destruction. There was no way it could have survived the storm, but it did, as it was back on his table the day after, partially unscathed.

Have you tried destroying this thing?

He asked directly.

No! There's no way I'd destroy this precious thing.
My grandmother gave it to me.

I got mine from my grandfather. Do you think they know
each other?

I don't know. Maybe they do.
But my grandmother passed away a long time ago.

Grandpa too.

He paused.

Had this always been your grandmother's?

With nothing but pure skepticism, he asked anyway. His grandfather having an affair with this person's grandmother could be a great back story for the mystery this journal carried. He did not know much of him. He could have spent his life loving another woman.

This diary could be the symbol of their sworn love, he thought.

What if his grandfather knew about the mystery of the diary and used it to communicate with this woman?

I think so…

This is just so strange.

I think the same.

Shaking his head, Xander wrote on the paper.

What kind of a woman is your grandma?

She is very pretty and sweet. Why are you asking about her?

Nothing. I just want to know.

Maybe he should not be raising the topic about infidelity when he rarely knew the person he was talking to, and the scale of havoc it could create.

Look, we both do not know why and how this is happening. But this is something that just does not normally happen.

I am aware of that.

What do you think should we do?

You tell me what you've got in mind.

Maybe we should just pretend this did not happen.

Do you mean that we should just forget about this?

Yes, exactly! It's just like you're reading my mind. Let's not open this diary anymore, and, on no account, should we write on it. Do you understand?

He was very certain of what he was proposing. For the first time, his hands stopped trembling.

But I promised her to write in it every day!

Don't be silly!
What is happening in this notebook is absolutely absurd. We don't know if this thing is possessed.
So forget about that silly promise! We don't even know what kind of black magic this diary hides!

Why do I have a feeling that you are a very conceited man?!

The hilarity from the message popped out from nowhere and caused the muscles of his lips to twitch and form a smirk.

Why do I get the feeling that you are a reckless little girl who just reached puberty?

He meant it as a joke. Though at the very last minute, he realized it had been too much to say.

You are so rude! Fine!
I will stop writing on this diary

84

just so I won't hear anything from you.

That's a deal!

He wrote confidently. He was also absolute that he had no intentions of keeping a connection with a child.

By the way, you will always fail to try to dispose of this thing. It will never be destroyed. So you better keep this in a place where you'll forget about it.

Then, he found himself counting every second that passed. He was actually waiting for a response. It surprised him that he felt a little disappointed when he did not receive an answer. He supposed that the person behind the strange messages unquestionably followed what he said.

He grinned with respite. All he had to do now was find a place to keep the diary away from his reach.

While looking for a safe place to hide it, he could not stop thinking whether the other person was female or male. The handwriting looked like it belonged to a woman, and the responses sounded like a pissed woman yelling at him.

Did she really keep the diary? Or did she just ignore what he said?

He thought this bizarre exhibition would leave him sleepless tonight.

"Ayang?"

His door opened wide with Ayang carrying a tray of candles.

He carefully hid the diary inside the drawer to avoid Ayang's critical eyes.

She directly went to the four walls of the room to change the black candles with fresh white ones. She noticed the empty candle holder and the burnt contents of the trash bin.

"Where's the candle?" she inquired.

He stuttered. What should he say?

"Did you burn something?" Her eyes were on the charcoaled contents of the bin.

"I burned some documents."

Her eyes spun around the room. Xander pushed the drawer silently, crossing his fingers that Ayang would not notice his uneasiness.

Then, Ayang's eyes stopped roaming and tiptoed to put the white candle on the holder.

"Let me help you with that!" He hurried to her.

"No!" She quickly avoided his hand, and their eyes met.

Xander thought he saw Ayang's pupils constrict.

"I was just thinking of helping you…" His low voice did not mean fear.

The sudden transformation in Ayang's eyes stunned him. He thought he had seen it before.

"You don't have to," Ayang said coldly.

Xander stepped backward as he forced himself to remember where and when he witnessed what Ayang did with her eyes. He felt so sure that he had seen such display before. Maybe when he was a little kid.

"Sleep well." Her guttural voice sounded terrifying, as she closed the door behind her.

Xander fell unto his chair. His head felt severe pain like large bore needles were striking it one after the other. He closed his eyes and felt the pain radiate from his forehead to the back of his head.

Where had he seen those eyes before?

*   *   *

A strong flash of light emerged right before his stunned eyes. He felt as though his entire body was being pulled by a force down below like he was being summoned by hell. His breathing became more labored, going after the amount of air he lost for breathing so hard.

Then everything around him went unexplainably dark.

He felt nothing… saw nothing… heard nothing.

It was just total darkness. The dark slowly eclipsing the little light that was left, the muffled noise he could barely hear, and even the slightest touch of warmth on his skin.

The stillness lasted not longer than a minute and he felt the hair on his arm stand. His skin tightened as he strangely felt cold.

From nothingness surfaced a tiny light, growing little by little. Its glow was not hurting his eyes at all. It was radiant enough to brighten the surrounding. As the tiny light grew, more lights appeared, competing with the glimmer the first one made.

For a time, the lights were a picture of beauty and calmness, until they all merged at once, hurting his eyes to the point that he thought he'd lost his vision. One specific picture bewildered him after the lights went off. Three eccentric rings shone beautifully. Their color was yellow like the moon and the sun.

Then, he heard soft whispers. One sound was more of a groan.

The soft sounds were too hushed that he could not make out any clear words from it. Although to him, it sounded as though it was a prayer. Gradually, the whispers waned as the rings brightened more. Then, a figure emerged from the tall trees.

A man!

A man was running with his bare feet as though being chased by a wild animal. There were so many tall trees that it was not too hard to veil the scared figure from whoever or whatever was trailing him.

Then, he felt an imprecise pain around his chest. It was a striking pain, and he knew he felt it on himself. While he felt the pain on his own body, the scared figure slowly revealed itself to him.

It was him, his very own face but in a different body. He was hurt right around the chest where he felt the pain start. Blood stained his clothes. He did not know where he got the wound, but it was hurting him and slowing him down. He kept on running and running until he felt so exhausted and frightened. He paused to breathe air when he saw the wound on his chest widen. Blood trickled endlessly. The pain was there yet death was far from taking him. He waited and waited for himself to lose consciousness, but he did not and probably would not.

The coldness on his skin built up. He started losing sight of his poor self when darkness crept its way back to his dream.

Ring! Ring!

His heart skipped a beat at the sound of his ringtone.

When he opened his eyes, he felt his sweat, cooled by the strong wind, fall down his face. The window was left open. The moon was up in the sky glowing brightly as the rings.

He rose from the chair and reached for his phone.

"Sir," Atty. Tan's voice fully wakened him up. "What took you so long to answer my call?"

"It none of your business, Attorney," he replied as he massaged his forehead.

"I was just worried…" came Atty. Tan's shaking voice.

"I appreciate your concern, Atty. Tan, but I am not a child. I am capable of looking after myself."

"Oh… anyway, sir, how was your first few days?"

"Apparently this house is primeval. There's no electricity. I don't know how long my mobile phone can stay like this," he said as he stood up from the chair and went pacing around the room. "Now, if you don't have anything important to say, please hang up."

"I have found four potential buyers for you. One of which is Mr…"

"Save it, Atty. Just come over here this weekend," he said in annoyance.

"Alright, sir," Atty. Tan's voice quavered. "I will see you Saturday."

"Hold on, Atty.!" he called.

"Yes, sir?"

Xander opened his drawer and carefully took the diary out.

"What do you know about grandpa's diary?" His eyes were directed on the messages written in longhand.

"The diary?" Atty. Tan paused. "He did not mention anything about it."

"Not even how he got it?"

"No, sir."

"Did he mention anything about a woman?"

"A few times."

A few times?

"How did he talk about her?"

"As far as I remember, there was this one woman he always wanted to find."

What, he conjectured, might be true after all: his grandpa having an affair.

"Did he find her?"

"I do not know, sir. He stopped confiding non-financial things to me after a series of failed investigations."

CHAPTER 9
Delving in Tiago's Secret

Xander sat on the settee in the *sala*. He waited for the clock to chime at six. Waking up so early was not that difficult. His weeklong stay in the province had already reset his body clock.

He was nearly losing his patience waiting for the long hand of the clock to reach the twelve-mark. In his watch, it was already four minutes past six. His purpose for waking up early was to find out who was creating the music from the piano.

His eyes were focused only on the piano set capped with a mantelpiece.

A few more seconds and he would find out if Ayang was lying or not.

Three... Two... One...

He heard nothing.

He waited for another minute, but the piano was not playing as what was expected.

His left eye caught a woman putting out the black candles near the tapestries. Ayang had shown a minute shortly after six.

"You woke up late!" he exclaimed.

"I am never late. I always wake up at four. I managed to sweep the backyard and do a little weeding out too," she replied as she collected the candles. "Just before six, I started stifling the candles downstairs."

"You saw me guarding the piano that's why you didn't touch it!" He smirked as if he was a victor.

"No. I did not expect you to be awake this early," Ayang fired away calm responses, which amused Xander. She went on, "I just came up a little later than six and a little later than the expected time the piano must play."

"Cut the crap, Ayang!"

"I told you. I don't know how to use it," she uttered every word calmly.

Xander stood up and approached the old woman curiously.

"So, you're saying that the piano plays on its own?"

She shrugged and started to walk away from him.

"There's something you're hiding about this house, Ayang!"

She halted, turned her head, looked over her shoulder, and gave him a very reserved but sneaky smile.

She spoke, "If there are secrets, then why should I reveal them to you?"

He felt his blood boiling. He had never met such a stubborn woman in his life.

If there was someone who had been in this house for so long, it would be Ayang. If there was someone who breathed the dust and air of this house all her life, it would be Ayang. And if there was someone who knew his grandfather more than anyone else, it would be none other than Ayang!

"What do you know about Grandpa's diary?" his voice rose.

"Diary?" Ayang's face looked pasty with shock. Her eyes widened as she heard the word. Xander thought Ayang's aura grew dark. "What diary?"

From Ayang's surprise, Xander did not think that she knew about the diary. Why would she look as concerned as this? It was like a balloon was blown up right in front of her.

"You do not know anything about it then?"

She shook her head. But obviously, her mood shifted. From a mysterious and confident woman, Ayang turned vulnerable just because of something she did not know existed.

What was with the diary? What was so important about it that even Ayang looked shaken as she heard about it? Why did his grandpa keep it? Was it to secretly communicate with his lover?

*   *   *

After their conversation, Ayang was not seen all throughout the morning. *Manang* Leticia said that sometimes Ayang would just disappear but would return before the day ends. Nonetheless, it was not Ayang's whereabouts that fascinated him. It was her strange reaction to hearing about the diary and the mystery that surrounded it.

He even asked *Manang* Leticia over lunch, "Is grandpa the kind of man who keeps dark secrets, *Manang?*"

"Dark secrets?" echoed *Manang* Leticia as she poured purple yam on Xander's dessert. "I don't think *Don* Santiago is a man capable of having dark secrets. He could have secrets but not dark ones."

"Do you think he had shared these secrets to anyone?"

"When he was younger, perhaps to his wife. But when your father moved abroad, he had no one else to talk to except for some friends and maybe Ayang!"

But Ayang would not say anything about what she knew. She has secrets of her own.

"Do you know any of his friends?"

"He's got a few friends who I remember," answered she. "Tomas, the owner of an old bookshop in the *barrio*, and Macaryo, one of his tenants. But Tomas had been his friend the longest."

"How did they become his friends?" He was making sure that these men could help him.

"I only know that Tomas had helped him with something. *Don* Santiago was always seen in Tomas's shop. Macaryo just became close to him when he started bringing him fresh tobaccos," replied *Manang* Leticia.

"Is there a way I could see them both?"

"Tomas is just in his bookshop. But Macaryo isn't always in the field. He's sometimes seen in town selling crops with his daughter."

*   *   *

The *barrio* was busy with everyone preparing for the *fiesta*. Middle-aged women in blue uniforms formed a booth near the *barrio* leader's house and started accepting applications for several competitions like the flower arrangement contest, a cooking contest, and even a beauty pageant. *Banderitas* or small flag shaped banners in festive colors were attached to lamp posts and traversed the streets. Children played in groups along the roads, but none of the games played were familiar to Xander.

Tomas's bookshop was a few walks away from the *barrio* proper. It was surrounded by wooden houses and is nearly covered by a big mango tree. On his way to the shop, he saw Ayang getting out of a small house with a tailor's signage outside. She was carrying heaps of thick fabrics on her back. Xander began to wonder what need did Ayang have for these materials. The house seemed to be not in need of new curtains and mantelpieces nor was it in need of blankets.

Should he follow her? His curiosity was telling him so. However, his priority as of the moment was to meet the old Tomas. It was difficult to evade curiosity, but Xander did it by walking straight to the bookshop.

Tomas's shop was small. The walls were yellowed by time, and windows grew veins. The door had a glass on it, which would allow customers to see what was inside. The "Welcome" sign signaled him to enter.

The bells chimed as he pushed the door in.

Tall shelves surrounded the shop. It was indeed a small place. There was a couch, which seemed to be Tomas's bed too. The table near the couch served to be his dining table as well. His kitchen was located behind the tall shelf, but Xander could still see the sink and burnt pots and a burner. However, the shop was fortunate to have an electrical connection. Bulbs filled the place with brightness.

"*Manong*, you have a customer!" A girl's voice from nowhere welcomed him.

Xander's eyes roamed to find her.

"*Manong?*" called the girl again.

Apparently, Tomas was not answering.

"Hello?" started Xander with eyes so wide. "I'm here to see Tomas."

A girl in neat long pleated skirt came out from the corner hidden by piles of books.

"I'm sorry for..." She halted as soon as she saw him. The smile on her face wilted.

"You?" said Xander with a smirk.

"*Manong* Tomas might be at the back of the house," she said while avoiding his smirk. "I will let him know you're here, so you just wait here." She hurried to the backyard.

Xander wondered what the girl who refused to have her picture taken was doing in Tomas's bookshop. She could be a helper or a customer.

After a few minutes, she came back with an old man walking behind her. He wore a pair of thick eyeglasses. His cotton shirt was plain but stained with yellowish marks. His pair of jeans were ragged and discolored.

"Are you Mr. Tomas, sir?" he asked courteously.

94

"The one and only! What can I do for you?" he questioned as he led Xander to the counter.

He turned his gaze to the young lady at the edge of the counter who was counting books inside her bag. *How could she act like he was not there?*

Xander felt annoyed for being ignored. Without removing his gaze from her, he told *Manong* Tomas, "I'm here to ask you a few things about my grandfather."

"Grandfather?"

"*Don* Santiago."

Tomas's eyes brightened.

"You are Tiago's grandson?" He sounded surprised.

"I am, sir."

The young lady suddenly tapped Tomas's shoulder. "Excuse me, *Manong*?"

"Yes, dear child." The old man turned to her.

"Will you mind if I leave now? I still have to bring these books to the upland students," she responded.

"Of course, you can go, dear child!" exclaimed Tomas.

"Then, I'll see you in a week, *Manong*!" She gave the man a sweet smile, which Xander wished to see more often.

"Send Macaryo my greatest gratitude for the logs."

"I will let father know."

"Good luck at the festival. Win the top prize."

"Thanks, *Manong*!"

Out of good elementary breeding, she finally faced Xander and recognized him with one courteous nod.

"*Manong*," she added after quickly shifting her glare from Xander back to the bookshop owner. "Please wear thicker and warmer clothes. The weather will be more awful in the coming days."

"Alright, sweet child! Now, off you go!" Tomas said amiably.

As soon as she had left, Xander found his place again.

"Does she work for you?" he asked curiously.

"No, she does not. She borrows books from here," responded the old man as he offered Xander a chair near the counter. He continued, "She brings them to the unfortunate students up to the mountain."

"She makes banana chips too, doesn't she?"

"Yes. She's a hard working girl!" praised Tomas. "But why are we talking about Rina when we should be talking about Tiago?" Tomas observed Xander's obvious interest over the girl.

He might admire her, thought Tomas.

Xavier coldly shrugged his shoulders to appear unconcerned. He noted that the old man had discovered his fascination toward her. But he knew that it was just plain fascination over her brown eyes.

"So, you're here to ask about Tiago! What can I help you with?"

"I heard that you became friends when you started helping him with something. I wonder what you helped you with," he began.

The chair was a bit rickety, so he set his foot to the ground to stop himself from rocking sideways.

"Just some stuff about books and legends. You see, I have a wide range of collection, which I inherited from my ancestors. Some of these books belonged to the late family who first owned your grandfather's house," he said.

"Why did he need to know about legends?" he wondered.

Xander knew his grandfather to be a well-educated man, but why need books from this tacky old shop when he could purchase quality books abroad?

"There was this one book that he wanted, which can only be found in my shop," he boasted. "The book was proclaimed seditious by the church for it contains our ancestors' animism and pagan worship, which would destroy the purpose of spreading Christianity. Originally, the legend was only known by the natives or even some of the converts. But one Mexican scholar in the 1630s came to town, and he heard about the legend. He wrote a book about it and published only fifty copies in Guadalajara. When it reached the Philippine soil, the Spaniards burned them publicly. Without their knowledge, three copies survived, and went missing for years. Until now, only one is known to be existing."

"It is with you, isn't it?"

"Yes. It's the book Tiago requested to see."

"Do you know why he wanted to see this book?"

"I had not asked him, but I heard from rumors that he needed it to find a woman."

The word rang in his ears. Just like what he theorized. Just like what Atty. Tan said about a woman his grandpa was searching for.

Who could she be?

"Did he have an affair with this woman?" The question was as direct as an arrow.

"That I cannot answer, young lad. Not because I am protecting Tiago, but I have so little knowledge about it. I just cannot say things that I am not sure of," Tomas reasoned out.

His face looked so serious. Indeed, he was a good friend. Other people would have feasted over this subject once it reached their ears.

Xander looked down. His hands clenched his pants. He searched for another way of finding the truth. Tomas just had no idea about who this woman was and if an affair really existed.

"One more thing, *Manong*," he continued. "What do you know about his diary? He might have told you something about it."

"A diary?" He sounded confused. "Oh, yes! He showed me an empty notebook once." Thrill could be heard in his voice.

Xander heard what he just desired for. He leaned a little bit more and listened.

"Is it that notebook with a tiny black stone at the center?" Tomas searched his memory.

"Yes!" Xander replied excitedly.

"He asked me to fashion a Victorian pen using the ink he gave me. I still have the crystal jar that originally contained the ink and the quill that used to be together with the diary," he said as he carefully searched the cabinets inside his counter.

Xander intently watched the old man go through his stuff. Weird objects came out of his drawers and cabinets. But one common thing that he observed about them was they were all ancient-looking.

"At last!"

Tomas held high a metallic box with his right hand. Half of his body was still inside his large cabinet. "Now, where did I put that jar?" he murmured to himself. "There it is!" he shouted gleefully. Tomas went back to the counter and cautiously laid the objects in front of him. "Here, take them with you."

"Did he say something about what the diary does?" His fingers traced the carvings of the metal box.

"No," he answered straightly. "Is there something he should have told me?"

Tomas did not seem aware of the diary's magic. Thus, Xander found no reason to disclose it to him.

"Can I see the book my grandpa borrowed from you?"

Tomas scratched his head. He replied in a slowed rate, "I don't have it at the moment. I lent it to Rina. She has the book."

CHAPTER 10
Surprise from the Heavens

Manang Leticia stormed her way up the stairs. Her face was bloated with shock, and her face was as pale as her lips. Her knees trembled as she approached Xander who was drinking a cup of coffee on the tea table.

She exclaimed, "It's snowing in the *barrio!*"

Xander almost spilled the coffee in his mouth.

What nonsense was she talking about?

She caught her breath, and spoke, "I saw it! It started last night, and the snowfall was torrential!"

"We are in a tropical country, *Manang*," he stated matter-of-factly.

"I swear in my father and mother's name. It is snowing!" she asserted. Her nose flared.

"Weird things do happen," commented Ayang who just appeared from nowhere.

She picked up an umbrella from the cabinet and covered herself with a thick jacket. She was wearing boots. She looked prepared. Xander began to wonder how Ayang could have prepared herself when no one in this village could have predicted the snowfall.

Furthermore, he remembered that he saw her leaving a tailor's shop yesterday carrying heaps of thick fabrics. He stood from his chair and glared at Ayang's jacket.

"You seem to be so prepared, Ayang," he said to try Ayang. He went on, "You seem like you know that this was going to happen."

Ayang chose not to counter his tirade. Instead, she marched downstairs with the yellow umbrella with her.

"Did Ayang tell you anything, *Manang*?" His voice sounded doubtful.

Right, she was strange in the beginning. But as days passed by, her true colors were slowly showing. Nevertheless, Xander still could not make up his mind on whose side Ayang was inclined to: his or something else. What was really in her mind? What did she want to happen?

"It is really strange! It is snowing there while it does not here!" *Manang* Leticia fell down the settee and started covering herself with the cushion.

"We have to go there, *Manang*!" he said as he rose from his seat.

"Where?"

"To the *barrio*. I want to see it with my own eyes!"

"But it is very cold out there. Even my children have to sit next to a burner!" Her eyes started to fill with tears.

Inside the woman's mind was the probable, yet unusual, cause of the phenomenon: God's punishment for the sinful world.

Xander hurried to his room and looked for some thick jackets in his dresser. There were only a few, but he took them all.

Manang Leticia wondered what the young man was doing with the pile of clothes on his bed.

"Hurry, *Manang*! Give me a hand!" he said as he placed the selected clothes in a box. "We're bringing these to the village. We can take some of Grandpa's clothes too!" Xander knew that his grandpa had traveled to cold places before, so, he was sure that he had heaps of winter clothes. "And take enough for your family." He handed the box that was half-filled with his own clothes.

100

Manang Leticia's face glowed with grateful joy. She was wordless at the young man's kindness. She thought how alike he was with his grandfather: generous and caring.

Xander darted to his grandpa's room. He had only gone there once, and that was when he first visited when he was just seven. The room hadn't changed. It was big with expensive tapestries on the walls and antique cabinets filled with old books and porcelains. The bed had a gigantic white mattress with cushioned pillows. It was well-taken care off.

He hurried to his grandpa's dresser and found fur and woolen coats. He called *Manang* Leticia to take them and separate them by sizes. The clothes they gathered were too big for children.

"These will not be enough," said *Manang* Leticia. "The children need them more than the adults."

"Didn't Grandpa use to say before that there are stocks of old clothes in the guest room? Clothes of his family?"

It was kind of awkward for him to claim these people as his family when he had not even really felt that he was part of this family.

The clothes, he remembered, looked sewn delicately and they were kept securely inside a wooden trunk, and Grandpa would always sneak into the guest room and looked at them when everyone was out in the morning. He stalked his old man, only because he was curious about what kind of a person he was.

"There's a trunk of old clothes, I remember. But they were moved to the *zaguan* for safekeeping," answered *Manang*.

"Grandpa wanted them transferred to the *zaguan*?" he clarified with his eyebrow raised.

"No. It was Ayang who transferred them there after *Don* Tiago died. She said that the guest room must be emptied because you are coming."

Why would the trunk of old clothes interest the weird old caretaker Ayang? He wondered.

101

Why did she transfer them after his grandfather died? Xander did not plainly believe that he and the mandatory emptying of the guest room was the reason for the trunk's transfer. Ayang was hiding something, and more so, she knew about the snowfall.

He asked *Manang* to ask her husband to drive them to the *barrio* and to take some chopped logs from the storage for the townspeople, while he went to the *zaguan* to find out Ayang's secret.

He scurried to the back of the house and found himself striding the whitewashed walls of the *zaguan* that connected the back gate to the back door. It was just an empty space with no sign of Ayang's personal things. There was even no bed or a bedside table or a dresser.

How did Ayang sleep then?

Though there were wooden boxes and trunks, and old carts and wheels, the place did not appear livable. The floor was made out of stones, and insects and rats crawled on it. It was weird to have the *zaguan* at the back of the house when it should be found at the entrance.

There! He found the old trunk nearly covered by rice sacks and pieces of woods from a smashed wheel.

As he pulled the lid of the trunk up, his eyes caught a glance of the smaller containers hiding behind the large trunk, jars, and knapsacks. People in the old times might have enjoyed traveling so much as evidenced by these large and heavy traveling cases. Obviously, they never traveled light.

He first opened the large trunk. There were clothes made from fine fabrics and embroidered with gems and stones, and laces. They did not look like the traditional *baro't saya* that Ayang wore. If Xander had his memory right in his History class, he assumed that the clothes were of European origin. Colorful low-necked gowns over petticoats with tight elbow-length sleeves decorated with frills and ruffles filled the first trunk. There were also caps festooned with large feathers and gigantic ribbons and furs.

102

He took out the fur muffs, cashmere shawls, neck scarves, and woolen coats, and set them aside. He, then, turned to the smaller trunks near the wall. Clothes for little girls were inside, and some *baro't saya* and small version of the frivolous gowns in the large trunk. He took all the coats from the trunks, which he thought were going to fit the barrio kids. He never thought that these old clothes would come in handy. He began to wonder how his great, great grandparents were able to have such expensive taste when his grandpa Tiago was the complete personification of humility.

"Are these all we have found?" Xander asked *Manang* Leticia who was already sitting beside her husband on the driver's seat.

She wore a thick black fur coat and her hands were covered with silk gloves. Her husband draped himself with a leather jacket, which Xander recognized to be his. *Manang* Leticia appeared to be raring to go. She knew how bad the situation was in the *barrio*. Hence, she wanted the clothes to be distributed to her needy neighbors right away.

"Yes, *señorito*," she answered.

There were a total of seven boxes in the cart. They were not going to be enough for everybody, but at least, they would be of help to some.

Juan, *Manang* Leticia's husband, hit the *carabao's* back and the cart began to move. Xander snugly positioned himself at the cart with his arms enveloped around his legs. It became colder as they got closer to the *barrio*. He did not take any coat or jacket from the boxes to make sure that the people who needed it most got it. He was used to cold seasons anyway. The heater in the shrine sometimes did not function so winter days in Japan were long and cold.

The road was bumpy, and the boxes kept on moving and jumping off the cart as they passed over potholes after potholes.

The sky turned chillier, and the winter sun seemed to be dying out.

103

"How bad was last night?" he asked.

Juan answered, "It was terrible, *señorito*. Some of the families had to evacuate their wooden houses and relocate temporarily in the church grounds. Men went to the forests while snowfall was heavy just to secure woods to burn. Father Alfredo can no longer calm the women. They were talking about the looming apocalypse!" Fright was written all over Juan's face. He reached for his wife's hand while his other one manipulated the rope that was attached to the animal.

Apocalypse?

Xander remembered when people called him a bad omen for bringing calamities to their countryside. Series of hurricanes, strong snowstorms, extreme summer heat, and mild tsunamis hit the place, which he called home, for years. He began to wonder if he really carried bad luck.

The cart stopped.

They reached the *barrio's* entrance.

Caps of ice covered the stone houses from the roofs to the eaves, and to the window lattices and ridges. The roads were emptied, no open stores or vendors selling their products with their loud, friendly voices and no happy little children playing games. The plants froze like icicles. The leaves glittered like the dewdrops were immortal. The *banderitas* fell off the ground and whiteness engulfed its festive colors.

The place was a disaster, but the snowfall had stopped.

Apparently, people who were not used to cold weather would really panic if such a thing happened. The country was a tropical place in which snowfall would always remain a mysterious disaster that would leave the residents wondering and eager for survival.

Gradually, they unloaded the cart of the boxes.

The windows lit as *Manang* Leticia called for people from their houses to get out and line up for clothes and wood.

People in light clothes came out. Some were even in slippers, and their feet numbed as they moved a step forward. Their nails slowly turned blue, and their lips trembled. They wrapped themselves with layers of fabrics, which appeared to be blankets and curtains.

It was indeed cold.

Xander in his woolen sweater felt cold too, but he had to tolerate it until everyone got enough warm clothes.

Juan distributed wood in bundles while *Manang* Leticia chose clothes for the kids and women.

"I think this phenomenon has to do with the three rings," said *Manang* Leticia with her eyes directed to the winter sun and the three intertwined rings in the sky. "Perhaps we'll have more of this in the coming days."

"I hope help from the outside comes immediately. It will be hard if we run out of food," said the woman who was in the queue.

"The farm was hit by snow, and my husband said that the crops are vulnerable to extreme weathers," said another woman. "Sooner, we will all starve to death." Their panic-stricken faces alarmed Xander.

His grandfather's farm was the source of livelihood for most people in the *barrio*. Most of the residents were his tenant farmers. If the source of food and money died, the *barrio* would perish too.

"Father Alfredo and the volunteer women are opening the church for a soup kitchen. We're lucky that Macaryo had brought enough supply of crops to the church before this catastrophe happened."

Manang Leticia commented, "Then food is no longer a problem!"

"For now…" the other women agreed.

The boxes were slowly disappearing. Everyone seemed to have warm clothing around their bodies. Xander took one coat and wrapped himself around it. He felt a lot warmer. He was lucky that there were excess, or he could have died of frostbite.

A large bonfire was lit in the middle of the road where families could warm themselves and make barbecue poultry meat for lunch. He saw how mothers wrapped their children with their arms and warmed them with kisses. Fathers, too, were busy securing their houses with more wood and food supplies. Some of them even climbed up the roofs and walls to cover holes with metal scrapes or flat timbers.

It was a sight he never had experienced but would pay anything just to have. He saw the people still smiling and being optimistic despite the ordeal they were facing. Children still had time to pick on others and play around the bonfire. Some young adults were even helping the older adults carry logs to the road when they could just stay inside and sleep on their beds as the weather was very inviting.

Xander sat near the fire with his hands level with his chest. His face flushed as warmth slowly spread.

"*Señorito!*" called Juan who was running toward his direction. He was followed by a flabby old man who Xander recognized to be the local parish priest. He gasped for air for a few seconds and continued, "*Señorito,* Father Alfredo would like to thank you for donating clothes to the townspeople."

The cherubic face of *Padre* Alfredo ballooned as he smiled to Xander. He offered the young lad a handshake, which the latter gladly accepted.

The priest sat on the large stone, which Juan and a few kids hauled from the snowless area under the tree. Xander wondered how the priest could remain so cheerful despite the calamity. His smiles never wore off.

Xander started, "How does the Bible explain this phenomenon, Father?" He had no idea how to answer his own question because he had never read the Bible. "Almost everyone is saying that the apocalypse is coming."

Father Alfredo looked him in the eye and answered, "I, too, cannot answer that. With what's happening in the world, I think all we can do is to pray for everyone's safety."

Prayers? He had forgotten how to pray, and he neither believed in it. He always ended up disappointing himself when his prayers never came true. Hence, he chose not to do it anymore. He'd be spared from frustration at the very least.

A grin of disbelief marked his face.

He continued asking, "Do you believe that certain people carry bad luck?"

"No!" the priest answered confidently. "We are all created as gifts to one another. It's not the person that is the problem but what he does that create havoc."

What Father Alfredo said slowly sank into his consciousness. He would love to believe what he said, but after all he experienced in the past, it seemed so difficult to believe the old priest.

"It looks like the *fiesta* will have to wait," he diverted the topic.

"A fortnight maybe," answered the priest. "It is everyone's safety we must prioritize over anything else. I am sure the Virgin Mary and the Lord will not hate us for calling off the festivity."

His eyes followed the woman in a white fur coat who just dismounted the cart that stopped in front of an empty fruit stand. She helped a middle-aged man unload the cart of bundles of chopped wood, sacks of corn and sweet potatoes, and baskets of various vegetables. She carried two smaller baskets filled with the same products in the cart and started walking away.

"Oh, thank God! Macaryo is here!" The priest rose from his feet. "He's a very generous man for sharing his last month's harvest to us. He could have earned bigger income by selling those outside the *barrio,* but he chose to feed it to us!"

Some men helped Macaryo carried the loads inside a house. They all looked happy when Macaryo arrived.

Father Alfredo dashed to meet the thin, short Macaryo whose head was covered with a wide-brimmed hat made from reeds. He wore a pair of black plastic boots and makeshift coat made from some old blanket.

Macaryo kissed the hand of the priest when they met, and his face brightened as he saw Xander walking towards his direction.

"It is an honor to finally meet you, *señorito!*" he cheerfully greeted as he took off his *salakot* and revealed a balding head, placed the *salakot* near his chest, and bowed.

Xander thought he had gotten used to being called *señorito*. Despite his request to be called by his name, people in the *barrio* never stopped using the label.

His eyes still followed Macaryo's daughter, Rina, who stopped in front of a wooden house to bring two bottles of warm cow's milk to a mother who cannot produce milk for her baby. She took her fur coat off her shoulders and put it around the mother who was still cold. The baby started crying, so Rina wrapped her shawl around the baby just to pacify her. Once the baby had stopped crying, Rina left for the empty boxes that were just a few steps away. As the biting wind touched her skin, Rina rubbed her hands together and felt the warmth of her breath against her skin.

Xander watched her stand there getting through the cold with only her light clothes.

"I am very sorry to tell you, s*eñorito,* that the farm field is currently not in the best state," said Macaryo with his forehead creased. "We cannot work if there is still ice, and it would take months or years to grow them again."

Xander had no idea about farming, neither had he any clue on managing a rice field or a crop farm. So he just nodded and nodded until Macaryo stopped talking. The poor man did not even notice that Xander's attention was on his daughter who was slowly fading in the young lad's eyes.

He cut Macaryo, "*Manong*, can we talk about the farm and the estimated damage next time? You can go to the mansion anytime this week."

"Oh!" Macaryo uttered in surprise.

Xander strutted to Rina's direction where she was piling the empty wooden boxes in her father's cart. He brought along with him a thick fleece throw, which *Manang* Leticia saved for him. When he got near her, he wrapped the fleece throw around her shoulders, which took Rina by surprise. When she turned around, she saw Xander's intent eyes and the cold smoke coming from his breath.

People stared at them. Even Macaryo's jaw dropped. As she looked around, she saw people wondering what just happened, which made the embarrassment a bit less tolerable.

Rina felt her throat dried up and face glowed. To her, Xander seemed to be expecting something from her. She stood there not knowing how to respond to a young man's valiant act if that was what Xander was trying to show the people.

A simple thank you might appease the strangeness that Xander was showing off, she thought.

"Thanks," she said quickly with a brief, curious look in his eyes.

Xander put his hands on his hips and looked like he was about to say something when a middle-aged woman came to him and spoke to him, "I am sorry to interrupt you, *señorito*, but my family and I are very grateful for your kindness. I remember the days when *Don* Tiago used to help my family by lending us money to pay our debts. You surely have his kind heart…"

"You're most welcome, ma'am," he answered as he took her hands with his own.

By the time the woman left, Rina was gone by his side. He looked around and saw her leaving the town center and to the narrow thoroughfare to his left.

"About the meeting…" he heard Macaryo stating while he and Father Alfredo walked towards him.

"What about Monday next week, *Manong*? Right now, I have a really important business to attend to!" He smiled at Macaryo and to Father Alfredo and tapped both shoulders before he scampered to the narrow thoroughfare where Rina went.

The way seemed familiar. Tall walls that bordered the constricted thoroughfare, wooden houses that were so close to one another, and a big fruitless tree that was swathed with snowflakes suggested that Rina was heading towards *Manong* Tomas's bookshop.

There was mist all over the place. He could not even clearly see if Rina had already entered the shop. Cautiously, Xander moved closer to the shop and hid behind the thick bushes near the entryway. He tried to peep through the glass window, but all he could see were blur silhouettes and hand gestures. The moisture on the window hindered him from seeing what Rina and Tomas might be doing. With his sleeve, he carefully wiped the window.

He saw Rina burning woods in a clay chamber in the kitchen while Tomas transferred all the goods from the basket to the cupboard. Then, Rina waved her goodbye and took one basket with her on her way out.

Xander dashed behind the mango tree to avoid being seen.

"You have to go home now, Rina." Tomas' voice sounded muffled. "It's very cold out there!"

"I will. After I deliver these sweet potatoes," she said with a smile.

Where could she be going at this hour? Xander wondered.

Rina closed the door gently and started sauntering the narrow thoroughfare again.

CHAPTER 11
Maiden of the Mountain

The hem of Rina's skirt swayed as she trekked the uneven road of the mountain. She carried the basket of crops and vegetables with both hands. She had no idea that she was being trailed by Xander.

The mountain was covered with huge and undisturbed forests rich in flora. The roads or clear pathways were narrow as plants, weeds, and trees reside in the forest. It seemed that the snowfall in the place was mild as the ice was slowly melting, nearly divulging its original state.

Xander kept his eyes on her. He transferred and hid from tree to tree every time Rina walked five meters away from him. He had no clue as to where she was going. Nonetheless, it did not cross his mind that Rina lived in the mountain.

After a while, Xander started to perceive a small community of *nipa* huts gathered in circles in the heart of the forest. The remarkable huts were small native houses made of tied bamboo walls and a roof made from *anahaw* or *nipa* leaves. They were erected on the gigantic tree roots that sprang out of the soil. Big sturdy trees surrounded them.

The wide strong tree branches formed a canopy or a shield that protected the small community. It had protected the nipa huts and the people from the snowfall. Like in the barrio, a dying bonfire was in the middle of the area, creating a thin line of smoke that connected the earth and the sky. The *nipa* huts were almost free from ice caps, and people were starting to get out of their houses to get back to their normal daily routines.

Rina was welcomed by bouncing children in makeshift coats. Their skin color was darker than the color of the coconut shell but lighter than coal. Their eyes were big and happy, and their smiles were genuine that anyone could see the trueness of their souls. They played around her and started pulling down her sleeves.

"Now is not the time to play," Rina spoke sweetly. "I need to get these potatoes to Doring's house."

Some children clung to her and kissed her cheeks.

"Will you make us some of these clothes in the future?" asked one child who was shaking her hand.

"I will see, Tado," she answered.

"They're very warm, Rina!" The girl with short curly hair exclaimed jubilantly. "I was able to sleep well last night despite of the cold wind."

"Did you burn wood in your house, Tata?" asked Rina as she walked towards the fourth *nipa* hut to the coconut tree.

"Yes! We used the wood you brought yesterday. *Tatay* made fire while *Nanay* cooked warm sautéed water spinach," Tata answered.

Xander surreptitiously followed her. The *nipa* huts were excellent cover-ups. He was able to reach the fourth hut without being noticed by the animated children or the industrious adults.

He saw Rina enter the fourth *nipa* hut, and the children were left outside the doorstep, playing stick dolls and wooden toy cars. There was no way he could get past these children, but an open window on the right side of the hut was free of them. Hence, he sneaked his way there to listen to Rina's conversation with a middle-aged woman.

"It is a good thing that we had prepared before the snowfall occurred." The voice of the woman surprised him. The window was higher than he expected, thus making it impossible for

Xander to catch a view of the voice's owner. "The makeshift coats helped a lot."

"It was kind of a little sad that we could not tell everyone about it ahead of time. It would create a ruckus," Rina talked. "I had to lie to father about the food supplies. He would not believe me if I told him about an imminent weather disturbance. I had to sneak some of the farm's crops to the church for storage. Father Alfredo had not grown suspicious, fortunately. He thinks that *Tatay* is donating everything."

"Does the farm owner know about you stealing his crops?" The woman's voice grew dark.

"You mean *Don* Tiago? But he's dead, Doring."

"No, the new master of the mansion, Rina. I am sure you have met him."

There was silence, and it was killing Xander. He was so eager to hear what Rina would say about him.

She finally spoke, "I have met him... a few times. I don't think he cares about the farm."

It struck him. How did Rina know about it?

"I also think that he does not really care about the farmers. I heard from Ayang that he is raring to sell the farm and his property as soon as possible."

"But he does not seem to be an insensitive and uncaring man, Rina."

A tinge of joy masked the disappointment he felt after hearing what Rina had to say. He had to credit the strange woman for championing him.

The unknown voice continued, "He came to the *barrio* with warm clothes and wood for the townspeople. I don't think that is the definition of uncaring."

"I suppose so." Her fingers touched the fabric of the fleece throw on her lap, and she was reminded of Xander's odd act earlier that brought a flush on her cheeks.

"Yes."

"But Ayang said that I should be wary of him and that he should not be trusted," Rina reasoned out.

She was so full of displeasure and doubt. Xander noted, and it did not please him.

Rina continued looking down to the wooden floor. She had never been so confused about judging a person's character by merely listening to others' judgments. "I don't really know him. He is a very mysterious man, so different from the men in the *barrio*. Ayang said—"

The voice cut, "What does Ayang have to do with your judgment, Rina? Does she always have a say on every decision you make?"

"No, but what she says is always true. You know it, Doring!"

"She says it because she knows that it is what you want to hear."

Rina froze in astonishment.

Xander's ears were glued to the wall. He heard everything so clearly.

"What do you mean?" she inquired curiously.

"Ayang has been with you since you were a little girl, and she has helped you and your family several times. With that, she has learned to know you more than anyone else in the *barrio*, so she knows what your mind wants to know and what your heart wants to hear. You basically breathe everything that Ayang says because you have become predictable to her."

"Is that a bad thing? I don't think it is, Doring. Ayang has not and will not hurt me," she asserted.

"Hear them out, Rina, but it is still up to you to make the decision," said Doring. "Ayang may have hold of your mind, but not your heart for it always wants what makes you happy, and that is the truth. You will never be satisfied unless your heart feels that she is heard and followed."

"But I don't know what my heart wants…"

114

"Not now but time will come," Doring said.

"It's unlikely to hear you say that, Doring."

"Your heart knows what it wants—what you want. You should listen to it more."

Rina fell into silence.

The sounds of the children's laughter filled her ears. Choosing between the mind and the heart was not an easy thing to do. What Rina just wanted was to avoid regrets at the end of every decision. It was the pain and disappointment that she feared that kept her inside her shell.

"Now what we have to do is to prepare for what lies ahead. Right now, I do not see trouble," the woman said after noticing Rina's stillness.

Rina rose from her seat and answered, "Then, let me know what I can do to help."

"Yes, thank you, Rina, for doing us this favor."

"You're welcome. I do this because this is my home, and I have to protect everyone I care for." She sighed at the end. "I will come back before this week ends."

Rina walked down the bamboo ladder with her empty basket.

Children started to surround her again and followed her until she reached the narrow road out of the small town.

Xander was just about to move out of the tree when he heard the woman, Doring, talking to someone with a strangely familiar voice.

"You just missed her," Doring said.

"There were a few things I had to settle." The voice sounded husky and old.

"Did you get to talk to Doray? Has she met her?"

"No. Not yet. Probably in the coming days when problems in her father's farm worsen," answered the voice. "Do you see anything new?"

"No. Nothing we should be alarmed of. We just have to wait," Doring said. "Rina is starting to doubt."

"Doubt what?"

"About what she must do."

Laughter erupted from the beholder of the old husky voice.

Doring ignored the laugh and went on, "Do you really think Rina can do it or maybe we should wait for another *Muling Buhay.*"

"You must be feeding her with your nonsense, Doring."

"You always know that I am on her side and not yours. I live to protect Rina," Doring's voice turned serious.

Xander felt his legs tremble. He had no clue as to what those women were talking about. *Why did Doring have to protect Rina? Was she in some kind of trouble?*

"You pledged to protect the *Muling Buhay.* Thus you must do what must be done!"

Doring fell silent. Her tongue seemed stuck with her teeth.

"If this fails, we can always reverse time." The mysterious voice sounded like she was making a threat. "We always have alternatives, don't we, Doring?"

The hair on Xander's arm rose. He felt the spine-chilling sensation travel through his skin. The canopy of tree branches and leaves swung violently as the ice cold wind raged the small town. Plants danced to the rhythm of the wind and, the children hopped around the lumber piled in the middle for the fire.

The voices faded.

He saw a middle-aged woman whose hair was tied in a low bun walking toward the children. Her loose patterned short-sleeve blouse and ankle-length skirt gave him the impression that she was the woman, Doring, whom Rina had talked with earlier. *But where was the other woman?* There were two of them: the strange husky voice he heard and Doring.

*   *   *

Everything was just so strange—the snowfall, the unexplainable weather changes, the three rings in the sky, his grandpa's diary, Doring, and now Rina. People in this *barrio* were just remarkably bizarre.

He walked down the mountain with all the questions crowding his head. *Manang* Leticia and her husband were waiting for him in the *barrio*. The bonfire was burning steadily, and more people surrounded it with their families. Father Alfredo gave him a plate filled with rice and some *pancit* when he found out from *Manang* Leticia that Xander had not eaten any lunch yet.

Xander was not able to consume everything that was on the plate. He was raring to go home. He needed time to be alone. There were just so many freaking things happening, and Xander did not know which mystery he must first deal with. He got this strong feeling that was pushing him to know the answer to those questions, but there were just so many of them. He felt that he was being constrained by time like he was being pushed to work against the clock.

His head started to ache. It was another terrible migraine attack.

When they reached the mansion, Juan took care of the cart and the *carabao* while *Manang* Leticia went straight to the dirty kitchen to prepare dinner. Xander rushed to his room to take his medication when he heard the piano play.

It was Ayang who appeared first in his mind when he heard the music. He hurried upstairs while his head felt like it was being squeezed and smashed against a brick wall.

The music continued.

He stood at the mouth of the staircase with his eyes wide in shock.

Music was coming out of it but there was no sign of a living or breathing creature. The mantelpiece remained intact on top of the lid and the wooden stool kept under the piano.

117

His eyes went straight to the single black candle that was lit on top of the piano. The sky was lonely, and the windows were open to let in the cool breeze of wind from the frozen *barrio*, yet the flame on the candle was undying.

PART 4

CHAPTER 12
Into a Lady

Her fingers halted.

Clarissa thought she heard a note go astray.

"Why did you stop, *señorita*?" Maying asked as she turned to the window to check for *Doña* Guada's carriage.

It was the best time to play the piano while the mistress of the house and her sister were out to the *barrio*, boasting off their latest fabrics.

Clarissa shook her head and continued pressing on the keys. Her long fingers gently arched downwards and rested on the black and white keys and danced together with her sweet melody that enveloped the entire *sala*.

She stopped again.

There was something so unusual about her music, like some notes were diverting from her melody, none of which she was certain she produced. This time her fingers were a few inches away from the keys, yet a strange disorderly sound continuously came out of the piano. Her eyes froze on the black and white keys with astonishment.

"Is there something wrong, *señorita*?" Maying wondered. She had never heard Clarissa play so disorderly.

Clarissa slammed her fingers against the keys to make the odd and mysterious sound stop. A piercing sound jammed their ears. The piano wobbled, and the candlestick nearby fell off the floor. The candle's flare petered out.

Silence.

Maying glanced at Clarissa with surprise.

The mysterious sound was finally gone.

"Did you hear something, Maying?" Her voice seemed to be trapped within the walls of her throat. Her fingers swelled and trembled after she slammed the piano keys. "Almost like a whisper?"

"A whisper, *señorita*?"

"Yes, a whisper."

Maying hesitantly shook her head.

She could not be mistaken. Clarissa was absolute of what she heard: the strange piano sounds and the whisper. The whisper was loud and clear in her ears.

"Can you hear me?"

She rose from her feet and scurried to her room. Her door closed behind her before Maying could even enter. She immediately took the diary from beneath the mattress and her quill and ink from her dressing table.

With her heart racing, she wrote.

I think I heard your voice.

She waited for words to appear.

She swore to never open the diary. They had a deal. But the whisper happened, and she could not stop herself from thinking about it. For days, she had been so curious and troubled by the mystery of her grandmother's diary.

Waiting for a reply felt like forever.

She dragged her study table near the window and sat snugly with her back on the chair. Her heart fluttered. She had no words to say. Everything was blank. Her eyes searched the landscape that was outside her window, hoping that she would find the right answer to such a puzzling event.

Outside was a clear swamp with blossoming water lilies and huge sturdy mangroves along the bank. Her eyes were caught by a newly built marbled gazebo, which her mother had always wanted. Alejandro and other men workers were painting the gazebo's roof white. The sun was high up in the sky, and the weather was humid and warm. It must be exhausting for the workers to work at such time of the day. Not even the thinnest *camisa de chino* could cool their sweating skin.

Her eyes were fixed on the man with the fairest skin. Alejandro was tall and well-built, and nobody would ever think he was a bastard son with the features he possessed. He got his mother's tan skin color, though lighter than the others, and his father's strong western looks.

Clarissa remembered when they were little. Rich children of her mother's *amigas* often laughed at Alejandro for being dark-skinned and for his questionable birthright. When he was surrounded by *mestizos* or people with Hispanic roots, Alejandro stood out because of his slightly darker color. When he was surrounded by regular *indios,* he stood out as well because his color was lighter than the rest.

She noticed that she was already staring at him for so long that she blushed when Alejandro turned to her direction. Their eyes met for a single second.

So you heard me?

The new message got her attention. She wondered how long she had been absent-minded.

I did.

She tried not to look back outside for the fear that Alejandro might catch her staring at him again, but waiting for the response again seemed an eternity.

The workers' voices reached her ears. She did not attempt to look back at them though, although her curiosity was killing her. Her eyes were fixed on the scribbles on the open page of the diary as she listened to them.

One man said, "I heard that a few of our men are leaving the field for a life in the *barrio*."

"There had been no rains, and the crops are wilting. It's odd that it always rains in the town but not in the field."

Alejandro spoke, "Have they told *Don* Jaime about their plan? I am sure that *Don* Jaime is doing something to solve this. He is not the type of man to abandon us."

"The man is just human. He cannot make rain!" said one man.

The others started to laugh at the comment.

What would happen to the field if farmers left? What would happen to everything her father had worked hard for? It would definitely break his heart.

The workers' voices faded. They were starting to leave the gazebo for lunch.

Clarissa left her study table and scampered her way down the staircase to the front door. The workers walked down the gravel pathway near the portico. They put down the metal buckets they were carrying as soon as they saw Clarissa walking toward them.

While bowing their heads, they greeted the lady.

She gracefully curtsied to the men and quickly looked around to find where Alejandro had gone too. Earlier on he was just with the others, and now he was nowhere to be found.

"*Señorita?*"

"Do you know where Alejandro has gone to?"

One of the men pointed his finger to the big tree that was just a couple of walks away. "He's going to get some water. There's a well behind that tree."

Clarissa quickly went there, her feet following the footprints that she assumed to be Alejandro's.

How big Alejandro's feet are, she thought.

He was wearing a pair of boots. Still, they were huge for her little ones.

"Alejandro?"

"*Señorita!*" Alejandro's face went all red as he turned his head around and saw a flustered Clarissa beside the tree.

The water bucket fell off the ground as he lost grip of it. Water was dripping from the tips of his hair to his upper body quenching the heat of the hot afternoon.

Clarissa quickly turned around her back on the man, depriving him the sight of her horrified face. She felt her cheeks burned as the image of Alejandro's nakedness constantly played in her mind. It reminded her of the books Maying lent her secretly. Maying had recently started to learn how to read, and she had easily acquired restricted books from a peddler who journeyed from New America.

She shook her head of the unwanted thoughts while saying, "I apologize for surprising you, Alejandro, but can you spare me a minute?"

Alejandro hastily put on his shirt as he felt it was improper to face a lady in such appearance.

"I'm sorry to startle you, *señorita*..." he said apologetically, his voice quavering of uncertainty.

"It is I to blame, not you... I have a few things to ask you." She felt her palms sweating. "Privately," she added as she saw three servant girls coming their way to fetch water.

Alejandro nodded and picked the bucket up from the ground.

Clarissa led him to the gazebo, not even turning around to see if Alejandro was following her. Her steps were controlled, and Alejandro noticed the apprehension in her movement.

The wind strongly blew the curls on her face and created ripples in the swamp. The three rings appeared vaguely on the sky with the vivid sun. The gazebo's shadow towered across the gravel pathway and shaded the tiny flowers that were planted along it.

"What is it that you wish to tell me, señorita? Is there anything you want me to do?"

"The truth is, Alejandro, it is about my father..." She bit her lip, traces of mortification still evident on her face.

His forehead creased.

"I know it is unladylike, but I cannot help myself from being nosy." Clarissa exhaled as she ran her fingers against her palm. "I heard your conversation with the workers. How bad is it?"

Their eyes met. Clarissa wanted answers so desperately.

"How is it going to affect Papa?"

"Weeks of no rain dried the soil and the stream," Alejandro answered. "One strong downpour can help. Otherwise, the field will be useless for the rest of the year. Growing the crops again may take months and harvest does not come in days. I am afraid it will drain our food supply and affect *Don* Jaime's business. Famine is inevitable."

"And Papa has been keeping this from us for how long?" Her voice broke. She remembered how her father leniently lectured her mother about scaling down her expenses to maintain the household economy. He was talking about raising the farmers' pay by 10% by the end of the year. This probably marked his decision for raising the farmers' pay to keep them motivated.

"Three weeks, *señorita*. And..."

"And?"

"And the bank can no longer loan money as they remain cynical of *Don* Jaime's capacity to pay," he told her in the most careful way he could.

125

"And Papa. How is he dealing with this problem?" She knew that Alejandro was not the best person to ask, but she just could not directly talk to her father. If he knew that she knew about the crisis in the field, there was no doubt he'd be more worried.

Jaime was the kind of man who hated pressing anxiety to people whom he cared about.

"He is trying his luck with the banks outside the *barrio*. I learned from him that one is willing to lend." A smile on Alejandro's face eased the worry she was carrying. "*Don* Jaime's an intelligent man. He knows how to handle this, and I think the farmers will not just abandon him after all the kindness they received from him."

Right! People in town were always grateful, and they could prove this by showing their loyalty to *Don* Jaime.

"Thank you, Alejandro," she told him with a faint smile. "I hope Mama won't go into hysteria when she finds out about this."

But both Alejandro and Clarissa knew that *Doña* Guada was only concerned about the money the field brought to her wallet and how she spent them to please her vanity to became the envy of her *amigas*.

"*Señorita!*" Maying came running breathlessly. She held her skirt high to prevent her feet from stepping onto the hem of her skirt. Disquiet was written all over her face.

"Your mother demands to see you! Oh, *señorita*. She's in a fury!" cried Maying.

Clarissa could not think of any reason for her mother to be furious. What did she do? Would she reprimand her for always running down the stairs or for reading too many books?

However, these offenses did not seem to summon an infuriating scolding, she thought.

Without wasting time, Clarissa and Maying hurried back to the mansion. She did not see her mother in the *sala*, but she saw a couple of maids outside her room.

"They are in your bedroom, *señorita*," said Maying who was behind her.

Her mother and *Tiya* Consuelo stood near the window. Her mother's arms were linked together around her chest while *Tiya* Consuelo had her hands on her hips. Their eyebrows were arched, and Clarissa could feel the livid sentiments the women were probably holding back.

The door closed behind her. Now, it was only her, her mother, and *Tiya* Consuelo's ire.

Aside from the women's piercing glares, her attention was directed to the diary on her study table that was left open in half with the quill in between the pages. She caught her breath.

Perhaps they discovered the mystifying messages and turned frantic as they thought of her practicing sorcery. Clarissa froze for a moment, her eyes only focused on the diary. Her mother's long fingers were rested on the table, and with just a little motion, they would probably reach the fragile papers.

Had they read what was inside?

"We saw you talking to the bastard again!" *Tiya* Consuelo seethed.

She heaved a sigh after finding out that it was not the diary that caused her the trouble.

"You were talking in the gazebo. For heaven's sake, Clarissa. What went through your mind to even bring him to the gazebo?" Her mother walked towards her. It was plain concern that pushed the women to reprimand her for showing the lack of decorum. Guada continued, "Had people seen you in that place, they would probably think you are flirting with a bastard!"

"Oh, please, Mama!" She walked past her to the study table and shut the diary. She carefully laid it back to the drawer. "It's not like this is something new to you... He's an old friend."

"You're not supposed to be friends with him!" countered *Tiya* Consuelo. "We heard the workers talking about you and your

127

little flirtation! Did you not think about the tattletale wives they have?"

"You could be the talk of the town by the end of the day! Have you thought of what kind of scandal this would bring to our family?" her mother cried.

"You cannot make me choose who to be friends with!" Her voice rose. She thought that any sensible explanation she would give would never be reason enough for them.

Doña Guada reached for her hand and said, "Alright. I'll allow you to make friends with the servants, but please, not with Alejandro. People are starting to talk about you two. He's going to ruin your future."

"Is there something going on with you two?" asked *Tiya* Consuelo as she approached Clarissa.

"No! Not at all!" *He doesn't even seem to like talking to me anymore,* she thought to herself. "What on earth made you think of that?"

Guada and Consuelo looked each other in the eyes as though telling the other a message that Clarissa must not know about.

Doña Guada took Clarissa in her arms and said to her softly, "We only want the best for you. A man like Alejandro does not deserve you."

"Nothing is going on between us," she said. "I know my duties, Mama. All my life, I heard nothing from you but—"

Guada cut in, "For you to start acting like a lady. A real Spanish lady, *edukada, inteligente, elegante!* And to marry rightfully."

"Mama, I will do everything you say." She loosened her mother's grasp. "But you won't be able to tell me who to marry…"

"I beg your pardon!" *Tiya* Consuelo exclaimed.

The conversation was heading nowhere but to war, she thought.

Clarissa did not want to aggravate the situation, so she stormed out of her room, leaving the two women out of words behind.

What was so wrong about talking to a friend, running on the stairs barefooted, and choosing Maying over rich kids as friends? Meekness and submissiveness were just not Clarissa's thing. She wanted to speak her mind, to be free and not manipulated, and to be different from other girls in the *barrio*. Simple things made her happy.

She ran back to the gazebo and there, she cried her heart out. She embraced her balloon-shaped skirt with her arms and dumped her face in between her thighs. Alejandro was not there to bring her more trouble, and she would not want him to appear either.

"*Señorita?*"

She looked up. Her face was entirely puffy and damp with tears. Ayang handed her a clean handkerchief with a rose knitted on it from her pocket.

"Oh, Ayang!"

The old woman's face cheered her up. Ayang had always been an angel to her.

"Did you fight with *Doña* Guada again?"

Clarissa meekly nodded.

Ayang cowered beside her.

"Have you finished reading the book I gave you?"

"No. Mama's eyes are always on me."

"Do you know what happened to the heroine at the end of the story?"

"Undoubtedly, yes. Heroines in legends die or disappear. That's why they are called legends. The heroines are not always proven to exist."

Ayang agreed with a simple bob of her head, but she added, "She died because she was stubborn and disobedient, so she was punished."

"Are you saying I'll meet the same fate just because I've been naughty?"

"Cahaya simply ignored the rules and followed her heart, which was not the right thing to do at that moment," Ayang started. "Sometimes, following your heart leads to trouble, and doing what must be done keeps us away from trouble."

A gentle smile formed on the young woman's swollen face.

"Thank you, Ayang, for that wonderful advice."

She kept in mind what Ayang said. Perhaps it was time to grow up. She had learned to be a proper lady for years—etiquette, demureness, and manners—but she was just too observant and too opinionated to get by the norms. She thought they were not important as long as you were happy. But society called for it. She couldn't escape the fact that she would have to be a mother, just like her mama, and a wife with duties and responsibilities.

Maybe it was time to put those learning into practice.

CHAPTER 13
Holocaust in the Field

Don Jaime kneaded his fingers on his forehead as a beating pain radiated from the center of his skull. The past few weeks had been severely stressful for him.

The supposed to be flooded parcel of arable land had dried out turning the *palay* or the rice grain golden yellow to brown just like the color of the parched soil. Gone were the green and the sodden fields. The *carabaos* or water buffaloes were kept inside the barn just waiting for the farmers to take them to carry products that were deemed to be the last of the harvest. Farmers took what was left consumable and sellable. It was better to have some than nothing.

A group of farmers surrounded *Don* Jaime in a *nipa* hut. They talked about a plan that would solve the selective drought—an irrigation system that would channel water from rainfall in the *barrio* to the rice field and the farm.

A thin fair-skinned old man with slanted eyes started, "But will it not take months for the water system to be made? By then, the land will surely not be arable, and the plants would have been dead."

The others nodded in agreement.

"And will it not take so much money to build, *Don* Jaime?" asked another.

"With due respect, *Don* Jaime, how are you going to raise our pay by 10% and have this water system built together?" Their voices were filled with doubt and suppressed revolt.

Poor *Don* Jaime scratched his head. He sat on the chair with his hand on his face supporting his entire head on the table.

"I have secured a loan from an outside bank. They will lend me the money for the water system, and I still have funds for your wage increase. I don't think it will be a problem unless I do not have your assurance that you will all work to make this project successful." His face suddenly brightened up. He forced himself to sound cheerful. "And our food supply is enough for the entire *barrio* for the rest of the year if we learn to economize."

"We all know that your farm is the biggest in the area, *Don* Jaime, but it is not the scarcity of food that bothers us!" A man sitting at the back rose from his feet. He was young but heavily bearded. "It's losing our job that worries us! How long can you pay us in this kind of situation wherein you release more than what you get back? If we can't be paid on a long-term basis, we cannot pay the lease to your land. Nearby farms don't have this problem. They are already harvesting the crops they had planted for months."

"If this continues, we better work in other farms even though the pay is lesser, lands are smaller, and the lease is higher."

An old man wearing a *salakot* stood. He cleared his throat, and then spoke, "Friends, we have been working for *Don* Jaime for several years, and not once has he disappointed us. He had been generous to all of us, even giving us the food he shares with his family on special occasions. He throws parties in his house when one of us gets married. Why do we question him now?"

Everyone fell into silence, even *Don* Jaime.

"We won't lose anything for a few months, and we still get our salaries 10% higher," the old man in *salakot* continued. "I am confident that by the end of the year this problem will just go away and everything will be back to normal."

Don Jaime held back from bursting into tears, but his face was starting to turn red.

Those who complained were silenced with embarrassment while others remained meek. The complaints stopped and praises rained for the old man in *salakot*.

Slowly, the *nipa* hut was emptied. The farmers left to continue working on what was workable. *Don* Jaime approached the old man in *salakot* and thanked him for courageously supporting him.

"It will always be my pleasure, *Don* Jaime," replied *Manong* Bong.

"I will try my best not to disappoint you, Bong," said *Don* Jaime as he tapped the old man's shoulders. "And remind me to get you a new *salakot*. That one has been with you for fifty years!"

Manong Bong chuckled. "It's your dear father's *salakot* that he used to wear when he attends meetings in the municipality. He gave me this when he saw me planting *palay* in the field with an old one that had a large hole on it. He was very kind to give it to me despite our difference in rank. Who would think that a rich *mestizo* would share his thing with a native? It has been my treasure ever since."

The *salakot* had silver pleating at the brim and capiz shells as design.

"*Don* Jaime?" A young man in red *camisa de chino* came in. "*Señorita* Clarissa is here, and she came by foot!"

The men turned their gaze to the open door and saw Clarissa in her plain *baro't saya* trekking the long dry but narrow dike of the paddy field. Maying and two more maids followed her with heavy baskets in their hands. The farmers greeted the maidens as they came across them, removing their hats or *salakots* and placing them near their chests as they bowed their heads.

"It seems that your daughter, *Don* Jaime, got the kindheartedness you and your father both have," commented

133

Manong Bong while marveling at the cheeriness and civility the young lady was demonstrating to the farmers.

"That is the one thing my wife has always prayed to eradicate from her," answered *Don* Jaime as he tried to stop himself from smiling too much. "Clarissa may not be as refined as what society calls her to be, but she will always be a perfect daughter to me."

"Papa!" Clarissa called as she waved her hands to Don Jaime.

"Does your mother know about this?" he asked as he went out of the *nipa* hut.

Clarissa shyly shook her head.

"I brought lunch for you and your men!" she said gaily.

Maying and the maids laid out a clean blanket over a wooden table on top of a hill where a huge mango tree stood for shade. Then, they prepared the food that they brought: freshly cooked rice, grilled *bangus,* chicken *tinola,* and *pinakbet* or steamed vegetables. The farmers left their scythes on the field and darted towards the hill after Maying called for them.

Some scurried to the *batalan* or to the area at the rear of the *nipa* hut where water is stored for washing. They washed their hands with the use of water stored in a clay jar or *tapayan.* Young farmers cut banana leaves and divided them into equal sizes to be used as plates. They used their bare hands as they ate while the females took care of serving the food with their ladles.

Manong Bong and *Don* Jaime sat beside each other on a bench near the tree. They talked about *Manong* Bong's family in the mountains and how the drought had affected their agricultural living.

"It is hard times we're living now. We get our food from the forest, and from the animals that we domesticated," said *Manong* Bong.

His face seemed sad. Life in the mountains had been difficult as most of the fertile and arable lands were procured by the church to be leased to the working class in very high amounts. Aside from the lease, they were also required to pay taxes. As for the natives who flew to the mountains to escape the Spaniards, their livelihood had drastically turned limited to hunting and growing indigenous crops in the forest.

"We only get our rice grain from your field, *Don* Jaime, and you are the only employer who allows natives to work in his land."

"As I said, Bong, we have plenty of produce stored in the warehouses. I will let you bring sufficient supply to your tribe later," he assured *Manong* Bong.

"But will not the others complain about this?"

"The others can freely purchase goods in the *barrio* while your tribe's people cannot," answered *Don* Jaime. "If you go down the mountain just to go to the *barrio* to buy food, the civil guards might see you and turn you over to the friars. It is too risky for you."

"What risk, Papa?" Clarissa came carrying an empty clay jar.

Don Jaime almost fell off his chair because of surprise. He uttered, "Dear child, your mother will not approve of you listening to other people's conversation!"

"I apologize," Clarissa responded forlornly.

The man noted how the radiance and smile faded from her face. He was expecting her to say her most favorite line, "But you're not Mama!"

"We were just talking about Bong's family in the uplands," he answered while waiting for the smile on her daughter's face to come back.

"Do you mean your tribe, *Manong* Bong?" Her voice sounded lackluster still.

"Yes, *señorita*."

Don Jaime continued, "I will have someone accompany Bong to deliver rice grain and crops to their community. Will it be okay with you if you come with Bong, Clarissa?"

Her eyes slowly brightened.

"I know!" her father teased. He knew how she loved adventure.

"Thank you, Papa!" She kissed him on the cheek.

"But Maying and the maids cannot go with you. Your mother will look for them."

Doña Guada would definitely throw fits of protests when she found out that her mansion was drained out of servants. She would endlessly accuse them of being ingrates and unfortunate slaves with no birthright!

"Oh, that will be fine!" she exclaimed. "I have the strength of a man!"

Her father laughed.

*   *   *

The warehouse was made of long coconut lumber. It was big and was filled with sacks of rice grain, which the farmers harvested in the early quarter of the year. The grain was supposed to be sold in the barrio and to potential buyers outside, but the disaster happened. Hence, the grain was hoarded to serve as emergency supplies.

Clarissa was entirely taken aback when she saw Alejandro transferring heaps of rice grain to the cart. He carried the sacks with his back, and she marveled at how strong he was to do it. But she had hold of herself. A plain curtsy would do. She would have to learn to distance herself from him from now on. She could not, and would not, allow her mother and aunt to have a say about her conduct around men, especially with Alejandro, the man who they considered a bastard.

"*Señorita?*"

"*Manong* Bong?"

He walked toward her carrying a basket filled with corn. "Alejandro will drive the cart. It is *Don* Jaime's special instruction," said he.

Her father had contemplated of a need for her to have a companion on her way home. Thus, Alejandro was specifically appointed for the job. She saw no reason for not allowing it. She did not want to just walk miles from the mountains to the dark roads of the mansion.

"Good afternoon, s*eñorita*..." Alejandro greeted, rather lacking spirit.

She bowed without even looking into his eyes or the slightest movement of her lips. She felt terrible for acting cold around him. Alejandro noticed her subtle change of attitude, yet he dared not ask about it for he deemed it to be disrespectful.

Manong Bong sat behind the driver's seat where Alejandro and Clarissa were. He kept an eye on their loads as they journeyed the rutted, narrow road to the mountain. They were silent. The only sounds were of the rushing stream that followed the road, the sound of the wheels, and the clacking sound of the *carabao* heels. But *Manong* Bong's cough cut the awkward silence between the two.

"Will you mind if I tell you about the story of my tribe?" His eyes were at the clear sky as he recalled how his ancestors told them the story of their clan throughout the years.

"No, not all, Manong Bong!" Clarissa answered.

Oh, how she loved to hear stories!

Manong Bong started.

The Dihinari Tribe lived for centuries. Their earliest settlement in the Quezon Province dated back from the late eleventh century. They first lived on a small island in the north of Luzon and south of Zhongghou where foreign merchants from the north or even the west would come for trade. But the Dihinarians vacated the island after Mt. Harimau erupted and splashed lava and magma out from its crater. Strong underwater quakes occurred that produced large tidal waves. It was a cataclysm that occurred on a festive night when the gods gathered in the heavens to celebrate the birth of another star. Instead of celebrating the feast, the Dihinarians were masked with fear. Hence, they left the island using wooden ships they called *balangays*.

In a small harbor where trade was flourishing, they landed. There were large villages so foreign to their eyes. Majestic trading ships from all over the world docked in the harbor as strangely dressed merchants came down their ships to empty their caskets with bartered goods from spices to gold and gems to exotic fabrics. The new place was filled with people bearing different appearances yet able to communicate with one language.

Not for long, they were able to settle harmoniously with the natives of the region and build a new community. Some of the Dihinarians spread to the different parts of the country as their population grew. But *Manong* Bong's direct ancestors chose to stay in the area where their tribe first arrived.

"What happened to the island after you left, *Manong* Bong?" Clarissa asked.

"It sank into the ocean, eaten by water and earth. It was forever erased from the map of the world," he replied.

"Like Plato's missing Atlantis?" Alejandro intercepted.

Manong Bong shrugged for he had no idea who Plato and what Atlantis was. Their island was never called Atlantis for it had its own name, and no man named Plato had ever come from where they lived.

Clarissa had read accounts about Atlantis from her papa's study. She was amazed by the scope of knowledge Alejandro possessed.

"Was it punished like Atlantis?" She turned to *Manong* Bong.

"No one can stop the fur0y of the gods," he spoke in a serious tone. "If that Atlantis of yours sank in the ocean because of disobedience to the universal laws, I would say they had a similar fate with my island."

CHAPTER 14
A Secret in the Heart of the Forest

The rutted road ended at the mouth of a cave where hanging plants and veins made a perfect waterfall curtain. *Manong* Bong signaled Alejandro to continue driving.

The tunnel-like cave was not so dark for there was light emitted from the egress. Clarissa's eyes wandered. Some mires hindered the wheels and the *carabao's* movement. Mud splashed to the walls of the cart and to her skirt as well. Buzzing sounds from insects that circumnavigated the cave filled their ears with their wings fluttering in less than a second.

"Continue driving," instructed *Manong* Bong to Alejandro.

Clarissa held unto a beam of wood that connected the *carabao* to the cart to prevent herself from falling down. The road had become rougher and muddier.

"We'll be there in a few minutes." *Manong* Bong's voice reverberated and disturbed small animals that were hiding behind rocks.

A flying animal soared right before her face.

"Aahh!" Her heart skipped a beat. She leaped from her chair and searched for a safe object to hold onto.

"Clarissa?" Alejandro's eyes looked so big as they were just a few inches from her face.

Her cheeks suddenly felt warm. It was the first time she had looked straight into another person's eyes for quite a time.

139

He cleared his throat after realizing that he wrongly called her by her name, "Are you alright, *señorita*?"

Her face turned warmer and warmer as she realized that she had been looking into his eyes for quite a time now. Her arms circled around his neck, and her legs pulled up close to him as she coiled with fear. She felt him breathing heavily.

"It was just a bird, s*eñorita*," *Manong* Bong gently spoke. He watched the two with curiosity.

She hurriedly loosened her arms from him and embarrassingly moved a little farther from Alejandro.

That was terribly mortifying!

The warmth in her body would not go away.

The cart went on, but she did not dare turn Alejandro's way. *What could he be thinking after what happened?*

It was a dreadfully silent ride to their destination for the remainder of the time. She was too embarrassed to even look his way.

Arriving at their destination, Clarissa hurriedly went down the cart without waiting for Alejandro's hand.

"This is the heart of the forest!" *Manong* Bong said.

Small wooden houses stood above huge sturdy roots and beside gigantic trees with branches as high as the sky. It was all brown and green everywhere. A barren land was in the center of the small village where the natives were seen cooking their food with the use of fire woods and clay pots, domesticating their animals, and where children were playing with each other.

The women wore simple *baro't saya* and *bakya* while the men wore *camisa de chino*. Their complexion was alike, brown and darker than Alejandro's tan. They seemed like they had been under the sun for a long time. Their eyes were big, and their eyelashes were long and curled outwards.

Alejandro and *Manong* Bong started unloading the cart. Young men came to help and brought the rice grain and crops inside the first house.

Clarissa sauntered and filled her eyes with the spectacle that she had never seen before. It was like she was in a new world—a secret world that only the tall trees and animals that lived there knew about it.

People seemed to live so peacefully, not the savages the friars labeled them to be. They were lenient and smiling, and even laughing at some old jokes. They were just like the townspeople who enjoyed good company and food but secluded from the benefits received from the imperialists. She wondered what life was like in the forest, not going to church, having their own set of values and beliefs, and maintaining the strength and willpower to resist foreign forces.

What was with the Dihinarians?

Children stared at her. Probably because she looked different from them, but she gave them her sweetest smile anyhow.

Manong Bong stood at the porch of the biggest house in the village. He called for her to get inside.

"This is my sister's house. She lives alone here," said he.

Clarissa searched for Alejandro amongst the sea of Dihinarians before she entered the house.

"Where's Alejandro?" she asked as she could not stop from worrying. She lost track of him while she was busy feeding her eyes with the mystifying beauty and secrets of the Dihinarians.

"He's coming in a second," said *Manong* Bong in one breath.

The house looked spacious from the inside. There was not much inside, only a small table atop a woven mat and a few dressers. Sitting in a squatting position near the window that overlooked the backyard was an old woman whose eyes were large and dark, with her graying curly hair made into a low bun.

The woman generously offered Clarissa a constrained smile.

She could not be mistaken. She recognized *Manong* Bong's sister. She was the native who she met outside the church's gates.

She was the woman who told her foolish things like eternal suffering and not repeating the mistake of the past.

"Don't be afraid." The woman's voice sounded creepy.

"Here, *señorita*. Take a seat!" *Manong* Bong nicely placed a cushion on the floor where Clarissa could sit.

Her legs stiffened and trembled as she bent down.

"My name is Doray, Clarissa," spoke the woman without leaving Clarissa's eyes.

"How did you know my name?" her voice quavered.

"Doray is a *babaylan,* the chief priestess of the Dihinari Tribe," answered *Manong* Bong. "Some of us call her the old priestess."

"What's a *babaylan?"* The question was intended for *Manong* Bong, but it was Doray who answered.

"I am a healer, a seer, and a miracle worker. I am everything this tribe needs to survive the test of times," Doray responded straightly.

Clarissa did not quite grasp what the occupation really meant. It was new to her ears and none of which she had read from books, not even in the restricted books Ayang lent her.

"I have the gift to heal the spirit and the body," she added.

"You are like a doctor?"

Doray hesitated at first but nodded after realizing that Clarissa would not easily understand new things.

"Bong, can you let Akhil know that I will need to borrow her time for tonight's prayers? I missed the chance to talk to her today," requested Doray.

"Of course, Doray," answered *Manong* Bong, and he left the house.

Clarissa began to wonder why Doray stared at her like she was prepared to devour her, her glare threatening and dark.

"Is Ayang from your tribe, too?" Clarissa remembered that Ayang was a native. "Are there other tribes living in the mountain?"

"She is one of us. And yes, there are other tribes. Do you want a glass of water or juice perhaps? I make great wild berries extract."

"No, thank you, Doray," she answered. "You said you are a seer. How do you foresee the future?" She read from books that seers or fortune tellers used the elements of nature or runes or other magical objects to predict the future. However, she could not see unusual foretelling objects inside the room.

"The answer to that question is only known to a few."

"So I guess only you and your friends share the secret?"

Doray took a sip from her cup of green drink.

"Can you foretell the future now?" Her eyes glowed with excitement.

"Your future?"

Clarissa eagerly nodded.

"But I had already foretold it."

It was not what she wanted to hear. It was terrifying and quite impossible to happen. She could not even understand what it meant and how it was related to her. It sounded more like a joke. She wanted something serious. Something that would really happen.

"But it is not what you want to hear, right, Clarissa?"

She reads minds too? She marveled.

Doray continued, "However, there is only one thing I can tell you, and it is what you want to hear. Believe me." Doray bobbed her head, then closed her eyes. "You will be on a journey at some time in the future, not now but very soon, and you will come across two rivers. One has constant rough water flowing, going downhill and may seem the more dangerous path to take. The other is stagnant wherein you will have to row the boat and depend on where the wind will take you. Nevertheless, these two different rivers still meet at the end as they are one of the same body, only separated by time and space. The catch there is choosing either will not lead you to the end that you want but to the end that destiny chooses for you."

She fixed her eyes on Doray, wondering whether it was a riddle or a prophecy she just said. Doray undoubtedly did not fail to showcase her flare of obscurity. Having said that, Clarissa could only force a smile to let Doray think she appreciated the wonderfully made speech.

Three faint knocks sounded at the door.

"He's come to take you." Doray opened her eyes.

The door opened and revealed Alejandro.

"Is it time to go?" Clarissa asked.

"Yes, s*eñorita*," he answered. His eyes went straight to Doray. "We have to hit the roads before dusk."

"I'll come out in a minute, Alejandro," she told him.

Then, Alejandro walked back to the cart without closing the door.

"I have to go now, Doray. It has been a spectacular time spent with you. Thank you for the hospitality."

"Will you come back?"

"Sure… I will."

"Will you bring him with you again?" Doray pointed her lips towards Alejandro who was tending the *carabao*.

"Alejandro?"

Doray nodded unquestionably.

"Maybe I will," she hesitated. "I don't see any reason not to."

"And Clarissa…" Doray added before she could get pass the door. "You have a heart that loves without fear, which is a wondrous thing, but you must know that duty does not call for that kind of love."

"I'll remember that."

Clarissa did not understand why she responded to Doray, as her last words did not make sense to her at all. But one thing was sure, Doray was not an ordinary woman. What she said had a deeper meaning, and Clarissa was eager to find that out.

*   *   *

It was dusk when they returned to the *barrio*, and her father was waiting for them at the *gobernadorcillo's* office.

Once they arrived home, she immediately went to her room without uttering a goodbye to Alejandro.

Inside her room, Ayang came to light the black candles on her walls. She sat in front of her dress table to brush her hair when she found something was missing.

Her neck was bare.

Her necklace was gone.

PART 5

CHAPTER 15
Beyond the Horizon

A large galleon, escorted by an armada to protect its cargoes, set sail in the Pacific to Manila from Acapulco on the seventeenth of August. In the ship were thousands of passengers, heaps of spices, porcelain, ivory, silk cloth, and silver bullion in exchange for what the Pacific could offer.

A young Jaime del Fierro, who was then a successful university graduate from Madrid, came with an English friend to spend a few weeks of fun before the latter went back to England and performed his noble duties.

"This place is bizarre!" exclaimed Matthew Livington as he breathed the first air that stroke his face upon setting foot in the Spanish East Indies.

Four months inside a ship with only cargoes, thousands of similar faces, and vast scope of blue was quite mind-numbing. It was liberating to see different colors and appearances!

"Where do we go after?" Matthew asked as he placed his hands on his hips and examined stalls made from woods and strange thorn-like leaves and rough cloths. His eyes indulged on the uniqueness Pacific goods possessed.

The harbor where the galleon, *San Cristobal,* docked, appeared to be the melting pot of the west and the east—where one culture met another, and from there stemmed a new one.

"*Manong* Crispin should have been here by six," answered Jaime as he checked his golden watch.

"Will you not mind if I go around while we wait for the man?" asked Matthew with his confident smile.

"Okay, but don't go too far," said Jaime before he went to the waiting station.

Matthew sauntered the roads along the harbor where people of different language, color, and appearance, exchanged goods and seemed to understand business very well.

He stopped at one space where a girl was sitting on top of a patterned woven carpet with her goods around her. She was a beautiful girl. Her skin glowed as the sun's light touched it before it retired for the night. Her long black hair dropped to her shoulders and chest like rainfall. Her eyes were dreamy, and they seemed to cast a spell on him. He had never seen such beauty all his life.

She started showing him her products. There were strings of pearls and raw pearls inside a shell. To him, she was an enchanting merchant. To her, he was a foreign customer.

Matthew started with a greeting, but the young woman was totally clueless about his message. So, he took a small blue leather book out from his coat and showed it to her. The girl stared at it for a few seconds, then handed over a small pearl encased in a shell.

"No. No. No…" said he as he tried to pull the notebook back from her. But the girl was strong and seemed incessant to have it. Matthew had to let go. He intended to just write his name on it, but the girl thought that he was exchanging it for the pearl.

The girl's face flushed as she held the papers with her long fingers. Maybe, it was something she had not seen or touched before. It was, after all, the best parchment in the world!

"Matthew," he uttered, pointing his index finger to his chest.

The girl's curious eyes followed his finger as it pointed toward her.

"What's your name?" he asked gently.

He waited for her to say something. The sky was already getting dark, and the stars were ready to show.

"What's your name?" he patiently asked again.

"Hiyas..." Her head tilted to the side of her shoulder. Her face showed astonishment and wonder, and her voice was soft.

Matthew smiled.

"Hello, Hiyas!" He laid his hand in front of her.

The cordial and warm smile of the strange man invited her to give her hand to him. Once their hands touched, Matthew initiated a gentle handshake.

"Matthew?!" Jaime was calling him. He turned to the waiting station and saw a carriage approaching.

It was time to go.

"It's time for me to leave, Hiyas," he said as he held her hand. "But I will come back to see you. You will be here, right?"

Hiyas just stared at his blue eyes, marveling at how the sea and the sky were painted in the man's eyes. Before he left, he kissed the back of her hand, which confused Hiyas. Her face grew pink.

Matthew bid her farewell and then walked straight to the waiting station on a piled wooden bridge over a murky body of water. The pearl from Hiyas was safely clasped in his hands. The smile on his face did not elude the nosy Jaime though.

Matthew Livington, a nobleman from Europe, came to a foreign land to have fun, but he did not expect it would get to him. He had just fallen in love with a native.

He kept it a secret from everyone, even to his best friend, Jaime. He would go to the harbor every day and pretend that he had goods to exchange for Hiyas's pearls. Well, he really had some stuff brought like a few books, badges, quills, and even gold coins. He would sit at one spot across Hiyas and pretended that he was doing something on his notebook just for the latter not to discern that he was just plainly watching her.

He would talk to her in his language, and she to him in her dialect. It was not easy at first, but Matthew was determined to know her more and to get closer to her. With passion, he taught her his language, and in return, Hiyas would teach him hers. Not so soon, they were able to develop a mode of communication where they both understood each other, then a beautiful friendship developed.

But it was always a question to Hiyas why Matthew was always coming to her stall and giving her too many splendid objects in exchange for her pearls. For her, he did not need to come every day and stay for long hours and wait for her to finish selling. She felt it weird for a man to exert so much effort coming to the harbor to do nothing but watch her work. Moreover, she was getting tired of getting the same products over and over again. As a merchant, she would have to decline his offer if he could not come up with a fresh idea to barter.

Obviously, the head-over-heels Matthew was running out of things to exchange, and his cover-up was at the verge of being busted. In the end, Hiyas still accepted them not because they were essential and peculiar looking but because she felt that Matthew was not just a plain merchant who just wanted her pearls. He had an ulterior motive for being too uncannily generous. He was her friend and a nice one, after all.

One afternoon, Matthew gave her one thing that he had worked on for hours and perhaps perfected for days in exchange for one thing, which he knew would not be hard for Hiyas to give.

"I have something for you," he said as he laid a rolled parchment on Hiyas' carpet.

"What is that?" She marveled at the parchment that was tied with a red ribbon.

"Open it," he said.

Hiyas picked it up and slowly opened the parchment from the side.

Her eyes widened as she saw a painting of a woman in watercolors. It was a strange product to be bartered, but she did not think it was impossible to sell it to the Arabs or even to the

Chinese. She had never seen such artistry, and the colors were beautiful.

It deserves more than my pearls. She thought.

"But would my pearls be enough for this?" she asked.

"It's a gift from me," said Matthew before Hiyas could pick another pearl from her trade. "It's you in the drawing, Hiyas."

"Me?" Her eyes studied the painting once again.

"Yes, it is you. You have the same eyes, nose, lips, and hair." He had always thought that Hiyas had the most beautiful face in the world. "So you are not to sell it to anyone.

"What do I do with this then?" she asked with a flushed face.

Matthew reached for her hand and kissed it gently. The same feeling hit Hiyas that perturbed her the first time he kissed her hand.

"Can you meet me at the river tonight? I have something to tell you," he said warmly.

Hiyas nodded as she looked into his eyes.

Matthew smiled at her before he left for home.

The man's strange behavior had always bothered her but not in a bad way. She actually liked it. Matthew made her happy with his oddity, and this she always looked forward to experiencing every day. Hiyas knew it was more than attraction.

*   *   *

She waited for her *ama* to retire for the night before she left the *nipa* hut. Her father never liked his children outside the village at night for fear of wild boars and bad spirits. Her excitement could not be contained, however. She wanted to see Matthew badly, and she knew that he was waiting for her.

Her bare feet touched the soft shrubs that were growing on the bed of soil along the river bank. The ringing of her anklets and jewels was no competition to the uproar of her heart. The smell of freshly cut leaves as her feet trampled on the weeds and grasses somehow calmed her. The moon was bright, and its reflection glimmered on the flowing river.

It was a peaceful night, but her heart was clamoring like a storm. Guilt was there. She was seen leaving the village by their tribe's chief priestess, despite her full effort to be discreet. The priestess's stare bothered her. It was threatening like she was ready to expose her misdemeanor to her father.

She finally saw Matthew, standing under the shade of the biggest tree in the bank. He met her with a fervent smile. His eyes shimmered with tears. He seemed to know what she felt as he ran toward her to welcome her with a warm embrace.

He smelled the scent of *sampaguita* in her hair down to her neck. His lips landed to the side of her cheek the moment he got hold of her tiny body. She was cold and shivering, and only the warmth from his firm embrace ended her jitters.

"I thought you wouldn't come," he uttered as he pressed down his face to her hair. His anxiety alleviated. For hours, he waited for her, and for hours, he had his fingers crossed that Hiyas would come.

Tears fell down her eyes. It was liberating to let him know what she felt. She had been keeping it far too long that tonight she found a reason to meet up with him. She was full of wonder and doubt as to what Matthew's actions really meant. But tonight, the cry of their hearts unleashed the feelings that were hidden for a long time, which seemed an eternity for the both of them.

He smiled as he saw how she received his kiss. It was sweet and gentle. Her lips felt smooth and tasted like honey. His hands followed the contour of her waist then yanked her closer to him. She muttered as he pressed his lips deeper to her.

"Sorry," he whispered after he accidentally bit her lower lip.

She chuckled. She then held her hand close to his face and studied him for a while. His blue eyes were like the bright sky.

"We can't stay here," she told him.

"Why not?"

"I was seen by a villager." Her eyes roved the vicinity as she checked for the priestess's presence.

The priestess might have already told everyone in the tribe of her elopement, and they could be looking for her. Matthew would be in great danger if they found out about him. She could not bear to imagine the punishment that awaited the man she loved. He could be hung on the tree or drowned in the ocean, or even struck with an arrow in the chest. Death awaited him if they saw them together.

"They will not see us here," he calmly told her as he touched her lips with his fingers. Matthew thought it was the safest place outside the village. "We can't leave this place. I have something to show you."

"What is it?"

He pulled her nearer to the tree and laid out a carpet on the ground. He then hauled her close to him and wrapped his arms around her bare skin. They sat on the carpet with Hiyas leaning on him. The moon and the beautiful river were in front of them. He constantly smelled *sampaguita* as his face was so close to her hair.

"It will show up in a while." His voice was just like a soft blow of air that tickled her ear.

"Which part of the world did you come from?" She wondered.

Her eyes were waiting for his surprise. She had always wondered what was beyond the horizon that she always saw in the harbor. Was it a cliff or another world where strange people live?

"From a very far, far place where people look so differently, dress so differently, and talk so differently," he answered.

"Do they look like you?"

"Yes, but none of them is as beautiful and unique as you, Hiyas." His words were music that pleased her. He went on, "I got on a boat, and I traveled the vast ocean. We encountered storms, heat, and even pirates, but the wait and loneliness were paid off when we reached this paradise where everything is just simply breathtaking!"

"Will the time come when you have to leave?" Her voice turned blue.

"Yes," He did not lie. "It will, but I will always find my way back here. The world is round. In either side of the globe I travel, I will still reach you," he sweetly said after placing a gentle kiss on her cheek. "When I come back, I will bring you to my home, and I will prove to you that the world is round. That beyond the horizon there is an endless path that will lead you to my place. We will travel together. I will build you and our children a boat so that we can travel all the places in the world, which others had not yet seen."

Her face glowed as she listened to Matthew's promise. She pictured how it would be like to be on a big ship and travel the world. It would probably be an exhilarating experience, and to have children with Matthew was the best thing she heard from him. She moved closer to Matthew and shoved her face into his firm chest. She smelled the sweetness of Matthew's sweat as air brushed through her face. Then, she closed her eyes.

The silence gave her peace. Thoughts about her tribe or the scenario that might befall her when she came back to the village escaped from her mind.

"Hiyas," he called softly. "Look at the sky."

Three distinct stars in the sky shone the brightest.

"Those are stars, Matthew," she said as she marveled at its glow.

"I will make those stars bigger," he said as he reached inside his pocket.

He showed her a tiny cylindrical object that had a gold metal covering and silver carvings.

"This is a telescope," he said as he showed her the glass at both ends. "You peer through here, and you will get to see the stars clearly."

Hiyas touched the delicate carvings on the strange object in front of her. Mathew had always shown her strange things, and they never failed to amaze her.

"Here." Matthew held the telescope horizontally and placed the eyepiece on Hiyas's right eye. "Tell me if you see them."

Yes. The stars were bigger and brighter, and they flickered altogether in a rhythm.

"The next time we'll see those stars together again might be after another decade or century, Hiyas," he told her. "We are very lucky to have witnessed this rare phenomenon."

"But our children and our children's children will get to see them, won't they, Matthew?"

He smiled. "Yes, they will. But in a very long time from now."

"I have something to give you as well." She brought down the telescope and faced him. She took out a small smooth black stone from the tiny compartment in her short skirt. It was perfectly shaped into a circle. She handed it over to Matthew.

"It's a black pearl, isn't it?"

She nodded and answered, "We call it *mutya*. It is a testimony of my eternal love to you the same way it had become one to my tribe's ancestors. I want you to have it. It will protect anything or anyone who bears it. Most of all, it will take you to the place where your heart actually desires to be. It will take you back to me."

He held it with his hand and kissed Hiyas on the lips.

"I can't, Hiyas. It's yours. It's a special thing in your tribe," said he.

"Yes, I know," she answered back as she reached for his lips. "I want you to have it."

The night was still long and cold, but they had each other to warm away the chilliness. The last kiss broke down her walls. Hiyas was his tonight, and in her mind, he was hers.

157

CHAPTER 16
The Bastard

At the break of the day, Matthew quickly rolled the carpet and returned it to his bag. He kissed her for the last time before they bid each other farewell.

Last night was the most unforgettable moment in their lives. One promise had led to another, and they were both resolute to fulfill those promises at the right time.

Hiyas walked back to her little village with the sweetest smile on her face. As she reached the entrance to her village, she saw all the households gradually starting the day by opening their windows, and by creating fire to heat their houses and for cooking. Her gaze turned to her tiny house erected on the slightly elevated terrain. Her father and sisters were still asleep, and this alleviated her worry.

"Hiyas!" A commanding voice stunned her.

She turned back and saw the chief priestess, Maduri, staring at her. Next to her was the chief priestess of the neighboring Dihinari Tribe, Doray. What was a Dihinarian doing inside the Haraya village, and more so the *babaylan* or chief priestess of the enemy tribe?

Hiyas wondered. Were the two *babaylans* in talk about a possible agreement? Or did the feud between these two tribes finally come to an end?

"Where have you been, Hiyas?" Maduri asked darkly as she walked straight to the gradually turning scared Hiyas.

She faltered. "I was out early in the morning to find wild roots."

Maduri was a scary woman, and Hiyas never wanted to lie to her. *Babaylans* were highly respected people, and they would know if they were being lied to. Yet, she had no choice but to lie to protect the man she loved.

The Dihinarian priestess had her glare fixed at her, but Hiyas knew that Doray might have read her mind already.

"It's late," uttered Maduri. Her tattooed hands were on top of Hiyas's belly, gently making funny circular motions. "The seed has been planted, and all that is left for us to do is wait for nine lunar awakenings."

Hiyas stood looking so clueless and perplexed at Maduri's actions.

"By then, we will know what to do," Doray finally spoke.

"What is this all about?" Hiyas's anxiety grew. She resisted one more touch from the priestess and stepped away from her.

"It is something of significant nature for you, Hiyas," Maduri answered calmly and coldly. "Look after yourself over the next few months. We need the child to live."

"Child?" Hiyas dropped her jaw.

"Yes, you are bearing the seed of fertility," Doray replied. "And in nine lunar awakenings, a baby boy will be born."

"I will have a baby boy?" Tears started to swell around her eyes. Unexplainable happiness suddenly ripened. A baby boy fathered by the man whom she loved!

Matthew would be very happy, she thought.

Their dreams were within reach: the boat, a family, and a journey around the world. She could not keep herself from rejoicing.

"Hold your horses, Hiyas!" Maduri interrupted her glee. "The man will not take the boy as his son. He will be his bastard."

159

Hiyas froze. She felt her knees weakened and the strange numbness slowly climbed up her legs.

"You will see, Hiyas… The man has left you, and he will never come back," added Maduri in a dead sounding voice.

Tears heavily rushed down her face. Matthew would never lie to her. He promised her he would come back for her. She believed his words because she loved him. She fell down to her knees and plummeted to the ground. She felt her heart being shredded to pieces.

"By this time, your man had already boarded the galleon *San Cristobal* on its way back to Acapulco," Doray spoke.

Maduri kneeled and held her a hand. "You will not need him, Hiyas. He will not be needed in this part of the world. He has other duties in the place where he truly belongs, which is not here and not with you."

Hiyas just cried. She gave her heart to him. She surrendered herself to him, and what did he do? He chose to break her heart by making a fool out of her.

"Listen, Hiyas!" Maduri lifted Hiyas's forlorn and angry face. "Protect the child because we need him. All of us will need him."

"You will abide with our agreement, will you not, Maduri?" The tone of Doray's voice suddenly turned threatening.

Maduri turned to Doray as she held the helpless and weeping Hiyas. She told the Dihinarian *Babaylan,* "As long as you keep your word as well, Doray. I am as dumb as an oyster. Do not tell her about the boy."

"I will not, Maduri. I am not a fool to place the child in such danger," answered Doray.

"This is for the betterment of our tribes. If you want us to survive, we must sacrifice," said Maduri.

*　　　*　　　*

Nine moons passed the night skies like a whirlwind. The passing of the chieftain's beautiful daughter was made known to the entire Haraya Tribe. They mourned her demise. But none from the tribe had known of the child Hiyas bore on the ninth lunar month of the year. As Maduri advised, the chieftain secluded Hiyas from the public to keep her away from harm. Her health had grown weaker as the days passed by. She had forgotten to laugh or even smile. She had forgotten what love was about. She died even before she received the invite of her grave.

Doray trudged the green and bushy terrain of the hillside. She carried in her arms a crying baby boy barely a day old, wrapped in a neat and thick cloth. She had to deliver the baby before the Harayans caught him. The plan that was initiated nine lunar awakenings ago must be carried out. Nobody from the Haraya tribe knew about the living boy. She and Maduri lied to the chieftain by saying that the child died together with Hiyas. While everyone was busy attending Hiyas's death rites performed by Maduri, Doray had to begin the first chapter of the boy's life.

"Priya!" she called the woman who was standing under the shade of an old tree.

She was not dressed in a native's negligible wardrobe but in a simple elegant-looking *baro't saya*. Priya was dark skinned to be identified as Spanish mestiza. Her face bore the exoticness of the wild.

"I got your message from your brother Bong. What is it that you need from me?" Her curious eyes were fixed on the baby in Doray's arms.

"Bring this child with you and take care of him." Doray handed the boy over to Priya.

"Whose child is this, Doray?"

The child did not seem to have the resemblance of a native. His skin was fairer for an average Dihinarian, and his hair lighter than ebony.

"One of our women who died at childbirth," she lied. "His father is not from this land. The boy cannot stay in the mountain because he is different from the rest of us. I want you to baptize him a Christian because he's destined to be one. He has to be protected from the Dihinarians."

"Why does this child need protection from the tribe, Doray?" She wondered.

"It's his fate we cannot reverse, Priya."

Priya glanced at the boy's tiny innocent face. "What will your future be like, little boy?" She mumbled.

"Priya, he will be a vital element of time and of the world. So, please, do all you can to protect him."

"But, Doray, my husband…"

"He will not question you," assured Doray. "He will always believe whatever you say."

Priya was convinced.

"Your son was recently married, wasn't he?"

Priya nodded as she swayed her arms to stop the baby from crying.

"His wife will not bear a child in the first two years of marriage, but this boy will keep your son happy. He will treat him like his own."

"But Guada and Jaime will have their own children, won't they?" Priya sounded alarmed.

"Yes, they will, but in two years, Priya. It will be a girl."

Priya's eyes sparkled. The child in her arms had calmed down and dozed.

"Now, go, Priya!" instructed Doray. "Your husband is waiting for you."

"I will take care of this child, Doray. I promise," she said as she tickled the boy's nose. "His name will be Alejandro."

A name which Priya found in a catalog while she was browsing for a name for his son.

"And Priya, don't tell anyone about where he came from," warned Doray.

Priya, as she fulfilled her promise to the Dihinarian priestess, brought the baby Alejandro to the del Fierro Mansion and took him as her own grandchild. She swore to protect the child but little did she know that by the time she passed away, poor little Alejandro would have to suffer his fate as a bastard child.

PART 6

CHAPTER 17
The Drawing

The light flickered right in front of his eyes. He played with it using his fingers. The light was just like the sun and its light like its rays, and his fingers tried to eclipse it to see how it was like to be dark.

In his other hand was the crucifix necklace that Clarissa had dropped when the bird flew right before her, and she jumped out from her seat to him. It fell on the step of the cart's driver's seat. He missed the chance to return it to her as Clarissa dashed to the front door, obviously avoiding him.

A smile was painted on his face as he remembered how Clarissa clung to him like a scared little baby. Just like the good old days!

Alejandro closed his eyes and kept the necklace close to his chest. It was time to rest and to bury that sweet memory of Clarissa to his collection.

*　　*　　*

Losing her grandmother's necklace was the worst thing that she could have ever imagined. Clarissa looked through all the possible places where she thought she had lost it, but unfortunately, it was not there. The necklace was her only memory of the sweetest and most loving grandmother in the world.

Not even the pots and rows of beautiful blossoms cheered her up. Her mother and *Tiya* Consuelo had been preparing for the *fiesta* that would take place three days from now despite the mysterious drought that struck *Hacienda* del Fierro. The two women were clueless of the looming financial bankruptcy that was afflicting the master of the house. They continued to spend on dresses and shoes and even on other inessentials that added up to the excess.

While the women engaged themselves with tending the flowers in the garden, Clarissa stole her way out of the women's clutches and ran back to her room. She just could not bear their vanity.

She shut the door behind her and hurried to her study table. She nearly forgot about the diary.

"Ayang?" The diary slipped through her fingers as she caught a glimpse of the old woman standing near the doorstep with a *rattan* basket carried by her wrinkled hands.

Ayang's eyes dropped to the site where the diary had plummeted and opened into half. Her face twitched, something that Clarissa noted.

Clarissa hurriedly picked up the diary and hid it behind her back.

"How long have you been standing there?" Her voice quavered as she tried to recover from utter surprise. She swore she had not seen Ayang the moment she entered her room. She seemed to have blended well with the walls.

"I have been here even before you came in," Ayang answered. "I have to take your laundry." Then she swayed her body to the left and slowly moved out of the room.

As soon as Ayang was out of sight, Clarissa shut the door and positioned herself comfortably at her study table.

A charcoal sketch of a woman stunned her as she opened the diary. Her eyes could not believe what they just saw. It was a picture of her in her dress robes.

"Tell me if you are this woman. I'll wait for your response," was written at the bottom of the sketch.

She stopped right there. Her eyes curiously glanced at the picture. She had no idea how to believe such mystery nor did she know where to start questioning. It was just so bizarre.

How did the person behind these bewildering messages draw her? Was it possible that he could see her? Was it possible that he was just around, hiding and pretending to be invisible in her eyes? But she saw how the messages appear and reappear like magic. No one could have possibly penned them while they appeared right before her eyes.

What should she write back?

Yes, it is me.

Her handwriting appeared in disarray. Her fingers quivered as they held the quill and as it touched the parchment. No amount of self-control could contain her trembling. She waited for a response. Her eyes widened as she anticipated strange letters to appear. Her fingers tapped the surface of her study table joining the rhythm of the ticking clock.

Minutes passed yet the spot to where she was waiting for the reply remained clean and empty. But she was not getting bored or hopeless. She was rather excited regardless of the noise she heard from her mother and *Tiya* Consuelo down the garden.

Finally, I hear from you again!

She gulped as she saw what she was waiting for. Her fingers hurriedly reached for the quill and replied.

I wasn't gone.

Then, she browsed for her earlier entry, which was something about the mysterious whisper she heard when she was playing the piano.

She wrote.

I think I heard your voice a few days ago if it was yours.

I heard your music too if it was yours.

How is this possible?

Where are you now?

Clarissa instantly scribbled.

In my room. Why are you asking?

I need you to be specific. Tell me your location.

It sounded like an order to her, but she still answered.

By the window. At my study table.

*Is there a garden outside your window,
a gazebo, and a mausoleum near the swamp?*

Her gaze went straight away to the mentioned spots outside her room. They were there. *How did he know about them?* But one thing was missing. There was no mausoleum.

*There's a garden, a gazebo, and a swamp but a mausoleum.
I don't live near a cemetery.*

Her eyes still wandered outside looking for the mausoleum that was absolutely not there.

What time is it?

The reply appeared a bit delayed.
Why was he asking about the time?
She answered confidently, looking into the small golden pocket watch on her table.

It is thirty minutes past ten in the morning.

The sun was high up the sky together with the strange scarlet rings, which made the morning hotter than usual. The drought had finally hit the entire *barrio* as no rain was recorded for the past three days. Her room was fully ventilated by the open windows, and the candlesticks were empty but soon to be filled before twilight.

Look into the mirror!

She rose from her feet and dragged her heavy legs to her dresser table. What could he mean by what he wrote? What was in the mirror? She hugged the diary with her arms and held it close to her chest. All she saw was her reflection in the mirror, pale and curious. She slowly walked closer, observing her own reflection changed expressions as she got closer.
Nothing was happening.

I am in front of the mirror. What now?

Does she expect to see a ghost or a light? Would she bite her tongue to stop herself from screaming? Did she need to prepare herself for a possible fright?

171

What do you see?

She saw nothing but herself—a plain looking girl, holding onto her mysterious diary.

Just myself. Am I supposed to see something else?

It does not make sense! You should see me!
I am standing in front of the mirror, too!

What? Her hair on her arms rose. What did he mean by that? She looked around her room, but she saw no one and nothing odd. It was just her in front of the mirror.

I don't see you!

Her hand trembled as she wrote. It was completely ridiculous to be seeing a person in the mirror other than your reflection!

I saw you one night in my mirror.
I just don't understand why I cannot see you now
or why you cannot see me!

She laid down her diary on top of the dresser table, pulled the cushion chair, and sat down. She rested her elbows and wrote.

Enlighten me.

I really saw you! The evidence is the sketch I made of
you.

Did you not say that you look like the woman in the sketch?

Yes, I think so. But how is it possible that you have seen me before in the mirror?

She looked straight at her own reflection. Could it be that he was also sitting on the couch she was sitting on? Could he be looking at the same mirror she was looking at?

I'm not sure. I don't know.

She was fully concentrated on the diary when knocks on her door prevented her from penning her reply.

"*Señorita?*" Maying appeared.

She instantly closed the diary and hid it behind her.

"*Padre* Cito is here, and he wants to talk to you. He's at the porch having tea with your mother and aunt," said Maying.

"I will head there, Maying, in a while." She grasped the diary tightly as she felt it slipping from her palms.

Her anxiety was killing her. Maying should not have appeared like that. She thought it was Ayang or worse her mother.

Maying gently closed the door after she noticed how appalled and troubled her *señorita* looked.

Clarissa returned the diary to the drawer of her study table and headed to the porch at the back of the house. The diary could wait, but *Padre* Cito should never be kept waiting, despite her tremendous curiosity over the mystery of the diary.

Her mother's and aunt's laughter were heard even before she could set foot on the porch. Good old *Padre* Cito sat across her mother, sipping his cup of chamomile tea. Sitting beside the Spanish friar was her mother's best friend, *Doña* Stella.

"*Buenos dias, Padre!*" she greeted with a polite bow.

173

The friar's face ballooned with delight as he laid his eyes on the approaching young lady.

"Oh, Clarissa!" he called her to sit next to him.

"Good morning, ladies!" she greeted the other women around the table as she sat next to the priest.

"*Buenos dias,* Clarissa!" replied *Doña* Stella amiably.

Her mother sarcastically smiled at her as she mumbled, "Clarissa had been spending most of her time in the study, probably swimming in a pool of books!" She laughed.

Tiya Consuelo laughed, too.

"You should be spending more time studying marriage, *Hija,*" *Padre* Cito spoke. "Our church believes in the sanctity of marriage! Divorce is not an option in our religion, unlike the other denomination!" He sounded so secured with his short sermon. "Hence, you should be looking for a potential husband as early as now. Someone whom you would want to spend your entire life with!"

The women nodded altogether.

Clarissa was tongue-tied. She had never thought of marriage yet, until now. She thought it was too early to be married or to be away from her parents, and she had not yet found the man who had captured her heart.

"I have four nephews in Spain, Guada!" teased *Doña* Stella. "They are all good-looking and clever bachelors! I can always write to them about Clarissa!"

Her mother's eyes lighted.

"Oh, I do have someone in mind!" commented *Tiya* Consuelo who seemed not pleased with *Doña* Stella's proposal. "Clarissa will have to marry within the family. If things do not go well with this marriage, then perhaps we can explore with other alternatives! My husband has a nephew who has a large business in Barcelona. I think he is the best contender to be a family man, isn't he, Guada?" Consuelo's brows arched.

174

"I have yet to see these eligible bachelors!" laughed Guada. She seemed to be enjoying the topic, while Clarissa abhorred the thought of it.

Who would want to marry a man other people chose for you? She was not a top prize that was won over a game of cards and a few rounds of cockfight.

"Anyway, *Padre* Cito and I are here," cut *Doña* Stella, "to convince you to join the *sagala* or the parade to commence the festival. A lot of young women already applied but we are saving the best role for you."

"That will be lovely!" exclaimed Guada.

"Clarissa will have to wear her new dresses!" seconded *Tiya* Consuelo.

"You were chosen last year, were you not, *Hija*?" asked *Padre* Cito.

Guada answered for her, "Yes, Clarissa has always been invited to join the festival. Unfortunately, certain things always happen that prevent her from joining."

They were not misfortunes. They were carefully manufactured to avoid objectification of her sexuality, which she abhorred. It was her progressive thinking that her mother did not know about.

"But this time, we will make sure that Clarissa gets to join the *sagala*!" assured her mother with a wicked smile.

"Then, there it is! We have our Queen!" cried out *Doña* Stella.

"Isn't September a little too late for the event? Flowers are not as beautiful as they are in April or May!" commented *Tiya* Consuelo.

"Don't be too pessimistic, Concha!" reproached Guada. "This is the first time we are going to hold a pageant at the end of the festival. Perhaps next year, we can have it a little earlier. Perhaps April or May when the blooms are in bounty!"

Consuelo retreated. *Padre* Cito and Stella bobbed their heads enthusiastically.

"We will not only need young ladies, but we will need young men too! I see you have a fine looking young man in your backyard!" teased *Doña* Stella as she sneaked a peak to the backyard down below the porch.

All heads turned to the vast lot where workers built a fence to separate the yard from the woods.

"Oh, he's not allowed to join the festivity!" Guada quickly uttered in a sharp tone with her eyes narrowed in austerity.

Consuelo acerbically chortled. "He is but a helper boy! Would you want to see your daughter or niece be partnered with a bastard, and take note, not only a bastard of an unknown man but also of a native? How shameful!"

Guada added, "No, no, and definitely not! He belongs to the field with the animals!"

Doña Stella cut in, "He is very fortunate to be favored by Jaime. He is the son he never had."

Guada's face turned sour.

Padre Cito stated, "Jaime talked to me about furthering Alejandro's studies. I think he is considering sending him abroad again to get a degree. A university in Berlin, was it? In no time, the bastard boy you have here will become a proper gentleman and will rise through the ranks. He can even become a doctor or a professor! Pray, he'd be more marriageable by the time he turns thirty."

Doña Stella's round eyes enlarged, seeming to love the topic of their conversation. "Why not marry Alejandro to one of the ladies we know? It's a capital idea, isn't it?"

"What about that English lady in town? Dr. Tatterton's niece, is it?" *Padre* Cito started. "I've seen them together a couple of times in the past weeks. They'll make a great couple. Guada, why don't you talk to your husband over this?"

Clarissa felt her *Tiya* Consuelo's eyes on her, maybe waiting for her to do something stupid. But she composed herself and played with the food on her plate.

For the rest of the day, the women and the friar talked of nothing but Alejandro's bad luck and sinister future. Clarissa did not think it was a good thing to listen or to talk about someone else's misfortune especially if that someone had done you nothing but kindness, but she could not just get away from them. They were visitors and as a civil host, leaving the scene prematurely was deemed impolite.

She had always felt sorry for Alejandro being talked about by people who deemed themselves above his rank, be it in front of him or behind his back. If she only dared to butt into their talk, she could have introduced another topic like the French Revolution that ended in 1799 and made Marie Antoinette's overwhelming and unmatched grandiosity the envy of women.

Don Jaime was always humiliated because of inferior birth and deficient expectations. If there was one person who treated Alejandro differently, it was only him. He saw great talent and hard work in the young man that others did not possess. And Clarissa who was his best friend when they were young. Things just changed while growing up.

The change started when Alejandro had to leave for Mother Spain to study. Guada greatly opposed the idea, but Jaime was steadfast. He said he would pay to get the eight-year-old an education. She was six when Alejandro left. By the time he returned, she was seventeen, and he was nineteen. Things became awkward. Manners and duties became the limitations that hindered their friendship.

Alejandro changed a lot. He had become very smart and serious. He was no longer the rowdy little boy who climbed trees or played in the rivers whereas no change had ever occurred to her except for a little meekness, maybe. Nevertheless, he earned her admiration for being patient and virtuous for letting others'

177

wrongdoings against him pass. Perhaps being forgiving was a virtue that was only learned from school. Something he gained for eleven years of being away from home.

And not too soon, he would be leaving again if *Padre* Cito's words were true.

When dinner ended and when the guests had gone home, Clarissa prepared herself for sleep. Ayang had the candles set to fire, and Maying had the bed prepared.

She was raring for the two to go.

"*Señorita?*" Maying spoke after Ayang had gone out the room. "There's a package that I found outside your door this afternoon." She led Clarissa to her dresser and showed a rectangular package. "I have no idea who put it outside your door, but I made sure nobody has seen it, especially your mother."

Clarissa held the rectangular package with her hands and wondered who could have given it to her. It did not seem to be coming from the post office.

"This came along with it," said Maying as she revealed a shiny thing from her pocket.

"My necklace?" Clarissa almost jumped for joy. Her eyes smiled and started forming tears. "But who…"

Maying just shrugged her shoulders.

Clarissa hurriedly wore the necklace, afraid of losing it again. Then, she unwrapped the package.

"A painting"—Maying's mouth dropped with surprise—"of you, *señorita!*"

Indeed it was! Painting in watercolors!

But who sent it?

As she surveyed the painting, a weird idea clouded her mind.

"It's time for me to sleep, Maying," she lied.

Maying nodded and sheepishly left the room.

Clarissa dashed to her study table and took the diary from the dresser. She immediately opened it to the page where an image

178

of her was sketched. Was the man behind the mysterious messages the sender of the painting?

She immediately scribbled.

Were you the one who sent me back my necklace?

To her surprise, the response was quick.

What necklace?

Oh, God! So it was not him?

Nothing.

She felt a little sad that it was not him.

I do think there's a problem.

How did he know? she thought

I lost it a couple of days ago, and just tonight, I got it back with a painting of me.

She could not think of any other person who could have painted her.

That's impossible!
There's no way I can send you gifts or whatsoever.
It's just too impossible!

What did he mean by that?

I don't understand. Why is it impossible?

It was not like he was from outside the planet or some faraway place. Could he?

What's the date today?

Why was he asking about the date?

Fifth of September, 1812.

She could not understand what she was feeling, but it was giving her the chills. It was taking long, and waiting was causing her anxiety that intensified every second the clock ticked.

It is September 5, 2017, in my time, Clarissa.

PART 7

CHAPTER 18
One

He covered his entire face with his hands as disbelief crept its way into his consciousness.

1812. He grinned as he thought about it again. If smashing his head against the sturdy table would make him forget about what was written in beautiful longhand, he would have done it without second thoughts.

Fifth of September, 1812

Now, that was bizarre!

He was making contact with a person two centuries older than him.

He started laughing. Tears of laughter filled his face. He just could not believe everything that was in the diary.

How did you know my name?

The new message halted him.

Xander held in his hand the metallic case that contained a quill. There was a name carved in the inner side of the lid. It said, Clarissa del Fierro.

He assumed it was her, but he did not think she was from two centuries ago. Well, he had the hunch, but he did not want to believe until he heard it from her. The quill and ancientness of the diary, the handwriting as well, and the young woman in the mirror, just suggested that she was old, well not biologically old, but maybe from an older dimension.

Quill case. C.d.F.

That's funny. I have my quill case with me. As a matter of fact, it is in front of me, on top of my desk.

I know it's a little creepy and strange, but I cannot be mistaken. I have your quill case, and I am holding it right now!

Because if he hadn't, he could not have known her name.

How is this happening?

From the lines, he could identify that she was utterly shocked.

I don't know. I have no idea. Perhaps something has gone wrong with the universe or a time warp just appeared!

He humorously answered.
There was no room to be morose or be surprised anymore, he thought.

It happened. It was not like he could reverse time to stop this idiocy from happening.

You are not lying to me, are you?

He literally smirked. How could she think that he was just playing around?

I am not in the position to lie to you, for heaven's sake!
Just like you, I am in utter disbelief too!

Communicating through a diary with a woman who was possibly dead by now, in his time, in 2017, was a complete absurdity! All this time, he thought she was just in some place far from him but in the same time. But two hundred years?! Two hundred years was not a joke.

Prove to me that you're not just making this up!

Okay! For the first time in their conversation, Xander felt challenged.

It is 2017, and the current President of the USA is
Donald Trump.

He thought it was the most common fact in 2017, and everybody, even outside the U.S. would know who Trump was.

Donald Trump? Who is he?

Of course, she wouldn't know. So he wrote.

Absolutely! You don't know him
because America's President in 1812 is James Madison!

He remembered a few things from his History.

I do know who James Madison is and what happened to
America in the eighteenth century. I do read newspapers! You could be
reading newspapers, too!

Hesitation was written all over her message, so he wrote
back.

Since you do not believe my genius in American History,
might I tell you what I think is happening here?
It could be that the past and present are happening at the
same time!

Possibly the future as well, but he did not write it because
the future was always undefined and vague, and he had not seen it
yet. He could be in the present, and this present was Clarissa's
future.

The pain started to radiate from his forehead to his
temples. If only he took Physics class seriously, he would have
understood Einstein's Theory of Relativity and the concept of
space and time. He remembered something about eternalism: about
how all moments happen simultaneously. Einstein would not be
dubbed as, if not the best, one of the best scientists and
philosophers of all time if his theory was bogus.

Perhaps, he was really right! It was happening with him and
Clarissa, eighteenth century and the twenty-first century at the same
time! Nonetheless, his theory could not explain the possibility of
contact. It was like they breached the rules of a moving universe
just to talk through papers. Xander was not convinced. It was not
just Einstein's theory. He believed so. Yes, moments in time might
happen all at once but what about communicating with two
hundred years as the element that made this whole thing so
impossible?

I have no idea if I should believe this whole thing, but it seems that I do not have a choice. It is already happening. Perhaps you are already standing right in front of me now if time is not the barrier.

He halted after reading what she wrote.

Yes, she could just be anywhere in the room. Perhaps, she was sitting on the chair near the dressing table, or lying on the bed, or perhaps sitting by the window just like where he was.

My name's Xander Montejo.

He thought it was nicer to introduce himself first before continuing a flourishing conversation. The two centuries matter was slowly sinking into his logic of reality. He recognized the need to further investigate the mystery wrapping the diary and Clarissa and might as well introduce himself.

You don't need to tell me who you are though.

Still, I think it is appropriate to formally introduce myself. My name is Clarissa del Fierro, only daughter of Don Jaime del Fierro and Doña Guada del Fierro.

Hello, Clarissa!

He doubted if it was the right greeting. Well, regret always happened in the end. Oh, how he wanted to erase what he wrote and change it to something more casual.

This is really awkward, but I think I should say hello too!

How's the eighteenth century then?

187

He really sucked when it came to conversations. He just had no appeal or confidence to start an interesting exchange.

I think you should check your History books to know what happened in my time. I think they are recorded.

She seemed to be lecturing him.

Do you still think that this is a joke?
I am actually trying to be nice.
I am trying to build a relationship
so that we can solve this mystery together.

Well, it is not that easy to accept things! I am currently in a state of shock.

Alright,
so what do you want me to do for you to believe that I am real?

He found it unfair to know that she did not think he was real when he, in fact, believed that she was real.

Maybe when I see you. It is different in my time because we only believe in things that we see. I don't know what kind of world you have, but I think it is very different from mine.

He was kind of impressed by her. Her exchanges sounded clever and well-thought of.

We could be family, you know.

He wrote without thinking much about it.

Like you are my great, great, great, grandson?

Yes. Maybe. There's a possibility.

So, it means that I will be marrying someday?

Why? Don't you have any plans for marriage?
Don't ever think of becoming a nun because it will change
history,
and I wouldn't be here!

If you are really my grandson, I will reproach your parents
for not teaching you conduct!

The smile faded away from his face, and he answered.

They passed away when I was eight.

Oh! I'm sorry. I did not mean to offend you. I meant well.
Like if I were really your grandmother, I would have disciplined you
the way we do here.

It's okay, Grandma!

Does calling me Grandma mean you are not mad? Is it a
way of punishment?

The smile returned. Slowly, the awkwardness was gone.
Xander thought he was enjoying the mystery. He instantly replied
with a smile on his face.

Just relax, okay? I'm not mad, Grandma!

Good! But don't call me that. I am too young to be a grandmother!

You know what, this is actually fun! Do you feel the same?

Surprisingly, yes! I think it is fun. I barely talk to men.

So, you do not think I am terrifying. This whole thing?

Not anymore. I don't think you find me terrifying, do you?

I don't think grandmothers would hurt their grandchildren!

He wanted himself to stop laughing.

I told you not to call me grandmother!

Alright! I won't call you that anymore. Well, not tonight.

His face was starting to feel warm. He thought he missed laughing out loud or genuinely. It had been quite a time when he had one good laugh. Surprisingly, only the diary and Clarissa had made him feel so light again.

Have you told anyone about me or the diary?

No, and I don't plan to. This whole stuff is beyond their grasp, I guess. You see, I am different from them. I like to bend the norms. That's what my mother hates about me most.

That's a good thing! You sound normal to me.

Clarissa would not be normal if she would tell anyone about this mystery. This whole thing did not happen in the normal world. He was relieved to find out that he was exchanging messages with a sane individual.

There's one more thing I am really curious about you.

Alright! One question before I go to bed.

Do you play the piano?

So you heard my music just like how I heard your whisper.

There are really a lot of strange things in this world.

Maybe you'll hear me next time.

Will you play your piano tomorrow?

I play it every morning. So, yes, I will.

So, it wasn't Ayang.

Then, I will wait for it.

Good night, Xander!

Just this once, okay? Good night, Grandma!

His lips curved into another smile.

CHAPTER 19
Flare

Xander scurried to the living room.

The second he heard the music, he literally jumped out of his bed and did not bother to put his slippers on. His heart raced as he set his eyes to the unmoved piano. So, it was not just a dream. Last night was real! He thought that when he woke up, he would not hear anything and just realize that everything was just a figment of his imagination.

She was real! She woke him up with her piano just like she promised.

Excitement filled him up.

He scurried back to his room in his pajamas and pulled the diary out from his drawer. He excitedly turned on the pages until he reached last night's conversation. At the back of the page was a new message.

Good morning, Xander.

It made his day.

He cuddled the diary as he sat with his legs crossed on the settee that was just across the room.

The music was fun, fast, and colorful. It was very different from what he used to hear before. At the back of his mind, he was assuming that Clarissa was in a good mood.

He held the pen and wrote.

I am listening to you now.

Then he imagined. What if he was standing right in front of Clarissa? What if he went back to 1812 and he wore what men wore before, and Clarissa saw him? What if?

He wrote again with an unmatchable smile on his face.

This is the best morning I ever had.
You are the best alarm clock in the world!

He imagined how his joke would tick her off. He pictured how her face would blow up with fury. Despite the little time that they had talked to each other, he thought that he had known her character quite well. Clarissa, for him, seemed to be sharp but childish. Well, she easily got annoyed by his jokes. He could even hardly believe the possibility that she could be his great, great, great grandmother. He never imagined having a cry baby for a grandmother. If Clarissa could read minds, he could have probably lost his head by now.

Bravo!

He added to his message as the music came to an end.

Clarissa was not a bad candidate for a grandmother though. She played the piano very well, and he thought she could be a good teacher to her children. Coming from him, saying that Clarissa was grandmother-material just meant that he completely approved of her. Xander was a fastidious person, and he was not easily swayed by common characters. Clarissa was not a common character. She was exceptional, and by getting a compliment from Xander was as rare as finding a gem.

Thank you!

His smile got even bigger when he read her response.

Nevertheless, I think I heard some flats.

He kidded. She was perfect. His ears heard and his judgment dictated regardless of his ignorance of music.

What do you know about Bach or even Mozart?

His intention was met. Oh, how he wished he could see Clarissa's burning face.

Don't be too presumptuous, young lady!

He bit his tongue to keep himself from laughing. He might catch *Manang* Leticia and Ayang's attention.

Presumptuous? I am not presumptuous, sir!

He could feel her rising fury. He had no intention of turning Clarissa into an enemy. Thus, he gave up.

I was just joking, Grandma!

But not reading any response from her for about two minutes worried him. Did she take it seriously? Perhaps Clarissa did.

He grew anxious. He did not mean what he said.

Hey, are you still there?

I got you, Xander!

He felt his face warming. That was embarrassing! He could picture Clarissa laughing at him.

I never thought you would be a little credulous. Were you worried that I might be mad at you?

Now, I know what kind of trouble I had gone into!

I am trouble now?

I won't fall into your trap again!

You're playing my game against me!

Am I?

He smirked. He dashed towards the windowsill to breathe some fresh air as excitement was starting to congest his chest.

Are you standing next to the piano?

You are mistaken, Ms. del Fierro.
I am at the windowsill catching some fresh air.

Can you guess where I am now?

He sighed.

Probably sitting on your piano chair.

No! Try harder!

He smirked with amusement. How could she play hide-and-seek at this time of the day?

Okay. Maybe inside your room.

Can't you be a little more imaginative?

Was she trying to say that he lacked imagination? Well, that hurt!

Okay! You want me to be imaginative?
Perhaps you are standing by the window too and next to me,
playing with your hair.

He wanted to laugh at himself. He never thought he could imagine wildly.

Or we are both looking at the front yard
watching if anyone gets inside the gate!

I am happy that you exercised your imagination, but you are
wrong! I am not looking outside the window. Actually, I am thinking
that I am looking straight into your eyes.

Xander numbed. Clarissa was standing next to him! He could also be looking at her eyes. They could be looking at each other's faces!

I have not seen your face while you have seen mine. It's
unfair! I want to know what color your eyes are…

They are black.

His face felt warm. He did not want to think that he was blushing. It was weird, but knowing that Clarissa might be standing next to him made him self-conscious. There was this uncanny chaotic sensation inside his stomach, which he did not want to deny that he did not know. Of course, he knew what it was! The question there was, was it right? Was it possible? How did it happen? Did she feel the same way too?

Remember when you heard my voice?

His fingers trembled as he wrote. The disturbing heat on his face and the disorder in his stomach were slowing his pace.

Yes.

Maybe it will happen this time. Maybe we can actually talk.
I don't know if it's going to work but do you want to try?

Badly.

He added after realizing that he just exposed a part of his secret feelings for her.

You already know the color of my eyes.
I think it's my turn to hear your voice.

Okay...

Perhaps she was hesitating. The response was taking long.

197

Tell me when you're ready, Xander.

He caught his breath. He closed his eyes and thought of the excitement and nerves that were starting to kill him. But before he could write on his diary, Ayang appeared from the staircase and killed the momentum.

Xander hurriedly hid the diary away from her sight.

"You're up early," Ayang uttered darkly as she sluggishly strode towards the corners of the sala to collect the candles. "So, do you believe now that I don't play the piano?"

"If there are secrets in this house that you do not want me to know, Ayang," he replied confidently, "I will find a way to uncover them."

"It seems that you are one step ahead than what I thought."

Xander thought he saw a tiny meaningful grin on the woman's face. There was her threatening glare. His grip tightened on the diary as Ayang walked closer to the window and took the candle that was on top of the piano away.

"I think you're up to something," Ayang conveyed almost in a whisper. The holes of her nose enlarged as she approached Xander.

"I also think you are up to something, Ayang!" Xander challenged as he stepped one foot closer to the formidable Ayang.

The old woman retreated with the same mystifying grin on her face. Xander closely watched her finish her job, coming into each room to collect the candles until she left the upper floor without a word or a change of facial expression.

Ayang had just spoiled his morning. She was getting creepier and stranger as days passed by and Xander would not let her get away from his grasp the moment he discovered something more about her.

He quickly wrote before Ayang returned.

Maybe this is not the right time, Clarissa.

Why?

Our secret is not safe in this house.

He was sneaking a glance every now and then at the staircase where Ayang disappeared.

Is there something wrong? Does somebody know about our little secret?

No! Our secret is safe with me. I just don't want to risk it.

I understand.

You're not mad?

No. I am just a little upset, but I can recover.

He smiled. Clarissa was not an ordinary girl.
She was not a total cry baby, after all. He thought.
He wondered about how she looked when disappointed. Would she purse her lips? Would her cheeks puff like a balloon? Would her forehead wrinkle? How would she make a long face?

So what's in store for you today?

He read as he shifted his attention back to the diary.

Nothing really. You?

He began to wonder.

I wonder if you like to read books.

His face twitched, the side of his lips curved.

You mean you want to have a date with me in the library?

His eyes sparkled with thrill. The strange satisfaction and joy were getting clearer and clearer. He definitely liked communicating with this mysterious woman from the eighteenth century, and most probably liked her.

A date? What's a date?

I mean, you want to spend time with me?

I have been spending a lot of time with you already.

Not to count those times when they almost see and hear each other.

No. Not that kind of thing…
A date is a rendezvous with someone special to you.
If you spend your time together with a person you like or
love,
you talk and get to know more about each other, that's a
date!

Well, if you could get yourself to the eighteenth century, I
might consider your offer.

Really? You would go out on a date with me?

You don't seem to be a horrible person. So, yes I will.

200

The harmless amusement was turning into something, which he definitely acknowledged as a possibility. He did not care if it would lead there. What was so wrong about liking older women? Clarissa seemed to be a really nice person, and she was lovely! The best thing about this was they were enjoying each other's company.

*   *   *

Breakfast was simple but superb for an egg cheese omelet. Oh, how he missed fats and protein! He had gotten used to *Manang* Leticia's bland boiled foods and her exotic taste. It was good that she let go of the unusual and tried to be simpler this time around.

"*Manang*, have you heard about the del Fierros?" he asked as he swept his plate.

"No. The name does not ring a bell to me," she answered as she enjoyed watching Xander enjoy his food.

Where would he start solving the mystery if Clarissa's surname did not ring a bell?

"Do you know of anyone who might possibly know any del Fierros in the *barrio?*"

"I think Ayang might help you. She's one of the oldest locals in town," replied *Manang* Leticia while taking the plates off the table.

No, not Ayang.

"What about how life was in the eighteenth century? Do you think someone in town has any idea what it was like?" He was not giving up.

"*Manong* Tomas's family had been living here for ages. Maybe he can give you some accounts about that family," she told him.

He nodded. *Manong* Tomas sure knew a lot of things. He'd find time to pay him a visit, perhaps tomorrow or the next day after.

"What about the snowfall, *Manang?*"

"Oh!" A big bright smile was painted on her face. "The ice is melting, and people are going back to their normal routines. Everyone's helping the farms and sharing things with each other. You will really see how people care for each other! Help from the outside is coming as well. I ran into a couple of journalists in town. They're covering the incident for the news on TV. They even interviewed our parish priest."

"That's good! At least the world knows about this calamity. Everyone gets to have a fair share of the essentials!"

"Oh, but not everyone! There's a small village in the mountain that has not been reached by help yet. My husband is going there later when the supplies arrive."

A small village? He raised an eyebrow as he remembered the one village at the heart of the forest where Rina secretly went. It could not be the village *Manang* Leticia was referring to because it already received aid from Rina, most probably the first one to receive aid and warning as well.

"There is more than one village in the mountain?" His voice rose with curiosity.

"I think there are two. My husband said the villages are homes for the old tribes that have been in this place for a long time," answered *Manang* Leticia.

"Have you been to any of the villages?"

"Oh, no, not yet! They aren't very friendly people especially the village where Rina always goes." She forced a smile. "I mean, they are nice except for the one old lady whom people call their spiritual leader. She's a very strange woman!"

Could this woman be the Doring whom Rina had a conversation with?

"Why does Rina go there?"

She cleared her throat after searching her mind. "Rina goes there once a week to teach children."

"I heard Rina has a friend named Doring. Is Doring that strange woman you are referring to?"

Manang Leticia nodded. "Doring is a tribe priestess. In olden times, priestesses or *babaylan* performed sacred rites. Some people in the *barrio* go to her to be healed from their illnesses. She makes wonderful and effective herbal decoction like Ayang. If my memory serves me right, Ayang belongs to Doring's tribe."

"Does Rina always talk to this woman?"

The woman halted. She started wondering why Xander grew instantly curios over Rina and her activities, yet she did not dare to ask.

She replied calmly, trying not to overanalyze Xander's inquisitiveness, "Maybe. I don't know. Why would I know? She goes there four times a month, so I think they have a lot of time to talk."

Xander realized that *Manang* Leticia had already noticed his interest in Rina and her oddness, thus he added, "I heard that Ayang took care of Rina while growing up. Don't you think it's a little arduous for Ayang to be working for my grandpa while she takes care of a child?"

"I just know that Ayang took care of Rina after she lost her mother. She was, I think, seven years of age," replied *Manang*. "Ayang would often bring Rina here. Of course, you never met her because she started coming here a year after your visit."

Thus, Ayang had a big influence over her. She had been under her care for half her life. He had no idea why Ayang would manipulate her like telling her to stay away from him or not even trust him. Did she think she was Ayang's puppet?

CHAPTER 20
Feud

Tell me one thing about the future.

      He walked his way to the library to do what Clarissa told him to do. The library was a peaceful place, and he did not think that Manang Leticia or Ayang would find him there and his secret. He comfortably positioned himself on a rocking chair near the window sill.

What will I get in return?

I will tell you something that is not found in books.

It was fair enough, he thought.

We use cell phones when we want to talk to people who are far from us.

That sounds strange!

Does it?

There seem to be so many strange things in your time.

They do not appear strange to me though,
but there were really big changes after the eighteenth century.
In progressive cities, we use automobiles rather than carabao
carts or horse carriages for transportation.
Candles are rarely used in my time because of electricity.
There are airplanes in the sky that carry passengers
from one place to another.

It sounds fun. Is it?

Yes, it is. But sometimes I get tired of them.

Why?

He did not really know. It was strange, but Xander thought that he was slowly adapting or even had grown to like the slow-paced way of life in the barrio. Surprisingly, the anticipation that he'd miss the busy life in the city died out, slowly and unconsciously. He enjoyed the stillness and the quiet, and the free flowing time, which gave you the free will on what to do for the day—no schedules, all surprises.

Because they sometimes make you forget to be happy.

That sounds sad. I wish you are happy now.

I am. Thanks to the nice people here and to you.

Just as he put down the pen to wait for her response, his right eye caught a *carabao* cart entering the gates. There was a woman in a knee length skirt and with long dark brown curly hair tied up in a pony tail, mounting off the cart that was parked on the lot across the house's main entrance. Xander had to narrow his eyes to see what were inside the baskets. There were potatoes, carrots, and corn.

Hey, mind if I excuse myself for a while?
Just got some fish to catch.

He closed the diary without second thoughts. He found a small chamber at the bottom of a table where he thought the diary would be safe while he catches his prey. Then, he scampered downstairs to the back part of the house where the food supplies were brought.

Rina, with her undying kindness to the needy, greeted him as he set foot on the dirty kitchen. He heard her talking about being careful on the roads as the ice had just thawed out and *carabaos* are not used to walking on slippery icy roads. She also expressed her sorry for not coming with Leticia's husband to deliver the supplies.

"That's okay, dear," said *Manang* Leticia as she wiped her sullied hands with her apron. "You have been nice to them, and that's what matters!" She went out of the room carrying a tray of freshly baked bread to be included with the food supplies.

"Why can't you go, Rina?" An evil smile curved at the edge of his lips as he finally forwarded his feet to the kitchen.

Rina went ashen pale as she realized that Xander had been listening and observing her.

"You have been acting nice to everyone like you are running for sainthood!" he mocked.

He could not forget what she said about him, about being a man different from others and not worthy of her trust. Who wouldn't feel bad about it? She had not yet known him, yet she judged him so hastily! He could not stomach her unjustified dependence on Ayang's opinions.

"I am not having this conversation with you!" she uttered with surprise, wondering what got into his mind to dispute with her.

"You're just afraid, Rina!" He laughed after.

She halted. "Afraid? Afraid of what?"

"Afraid of a lot of things! Afraid of making mistakes! Oh hell, you might be afraid of spiders too!" There was laughter in his voice. "Or worse, afraid of me!" His eyebrow rose as he cornered her to the wall adjacent to the back door. "Are you afraid of me, Rina?" He grunted. His arms on her sides, the length of his body almost pressing her deep against the wall, their faces only inches away.

"Why will I be afraid of you?" she raised her voice.

She was never afraid of Xander. She just did not like him.

A stunned *Manang* Leticia surprised them both. With her stare, she signaled Rina to push Xander away.

She hurriedly said, "I'm leaving now, *Manang* Leticia. Thanks for your time." She avoided Xander's eyes.

"Alright, dear…"

Manang Leticia was still in the state of shock. Who would expect to see young people getting so close in one corner, probably doing something unspeakable? Leticia did not want to put colors on what she had seen. She believed in Rina's virtue.

She is not the same with other girls, Leticia thought!

"Good luck for the festival!" added *Manang* Leticia before Rina could go away.

"Can I go with your husband, *Manang*?" Xander inquired while his eyes were still with the leaving Rina.

"Certainly. Certainly!" replied the flustered woman as she marveled over the threatening glare Xander threw at the girl.

*   *   *

Xander sat beside Juan who had control over the tie that was connected to the *carabao*. The baskets of crops and trays of bread were secured at the back of the cart. Xander did not have a

207

hard time convincing the appalled *Manang* Leticia to let him go, and he had no intention of setting things straight with her.

Let her think what she wanted to think.

Xander believed that Leticia was a responsible and smart woman. She would probably not think maliciously. However, if being put into such a scandal would agonize the astute Rina, then he would gladly tolerate such a wild story.

"Where are we going, Juan?" he asked the man who seemed serious controlling the *carabao*.

Rina was right. The roads were slippery, and the poor beast was struggling to move its legs.

"To the west portion of the forest, sir."

Xander helped the poor Juan heave the rope to control the animal.

"What kind of people are living there?" He wondered.

"They are tribesmen, sir. Another kind, just like the tribe Rina always visits."

"How does this tribe differ from the other one?"

"I heard that there is a feud dividing the two. I am not just sure how long this feud has been going on, but I don't think they are ready to forgive each other yet," answered Juan. "I don't really have an idea what sets them apart. For me, they are the same."

"Why didn't Rina personally go there?" He was most curious about it.

"Heard that she was warned by Doring."

Doring, the tribe priestess? Why did he feel that it was not Doring who had a hold of Rina? It must be Ayang again.

"What does Doring actually do, Juan?"

The *carabao* was starting to move quicker as they got through the smooth slope of the road.

"She has a candle stall outside the church. Sometimes she would foretell customers' future," replied Juan.

They stopped at a river bank where a small waterfall could be seen from a distance.

"Here we are at last!" exclaimed Juan. He dismounted the cart and went to unload the baskets.

Small wooden houses were built on top of sturdy trees. Narrow and fragile-looking stairs encircling the tree trunks connected the houses to the soft ground filled with mosses and shrubs. This village looked entirely different than Doring's village.

"*Apo* Tawil!" called Juan with a full smile on his face, showing off a complete set of teeth.

An old man, nearly in his seventies who surprisingly walked faster for his age, approached them.

"Juan, what can I do for you?" the old man whom Juan called *Apo* Tawil spoke as his eyes smiled with marvel over Xander's presence.

"We brought food supplies for you and your tribe. We're sorry it came late."

"Oh, thank you! We are fortunate that we have stored a bounty of harvest before the snowfall," replied *Apo* Tawil. "We had to wrap ourselves with animal skin beside a bonfire."

The old man looked at Xander.

"This is *Señorito* Xander Montejo, grandson of the deceased *Don* Santiago," Juan finally introduced. "Xander, this is *Apo* Tawil, the chieftain of the Haraya Tribe."

Apo Tawil offered his hand for a handshake. "I am so honored to meet you, *señorito.*"

"No, please just call me Xander," he said as he reached for the thin wrinkled hand of the old man.

The chieftain dressed normally, in shorts and slightly yellowed top, like common people do. Xander was expecting high ranking community leaders to appear distinct from others. He thought he was going to see a tribesman wearing an ethnic costume like what he had seen from books: feathery and colorful.

"Your grandfather was a great man, although we did not have the chance to meet each other. But I heard a lot of great

209

things about him," said *Apo* Tawil as he led the two inside the village.

Juan chose to stay at the cart to tend the *carabao* and to check its condition. Apparently, the slippery icy road had weakened it a bit, and with a little grass, he prayed the beast would be re-energized before the time to go home.

"How long have your tribe been living in the forest, *Apo?*" asked Xander.

"For centuries. We have lived harmoniously until one precious possession of ours was stolen by the neighboring tribe," he told him.

"Doring's tribe?"

"The Dihinari Tribe. Yes, Doring's Tribe. You're quite knowledgeable about them. I'm surprised."

"My caretaker belongs to that tribe, and I know of some people who go there for charity." He cleared his throat then. "I learned from Juan about the feud. So did the feud stem from this theft?"

"It was a factor, but it was not the main cause according to our ancestors," answered *Apo* Tawil. "Not a single petty crime could have caused this massive scale of a dispute between two camps. It's way deeper than that."

Xander worried over the old man's bony legs as they wobbled when they walked along the pebble-covered pathway.

They were slowly disappearing in the foggy and misty thickness of the woods. Tall thin trees filled the forest, and the pathway was filled with pebbles and small wild plants. Xander had no idea where the chieftain was taking him, but he trusted the man. *Apo* Tawil did not seem to be a dangerous man. If he was mistaken about him, he was confident that he could defend himself against a frail seventy-year-old.

A feud between two tribes: the Dihinari and the Haraya! Xander could not ask for more excitement. He was looking forward to knowing more about the two. Finding out anything about the two would draw him closer to Rina and her secrets, and probably Ayang's questionable behavior, too.

"As you see, the Haraya tribe no longer keeps a priestess or a *babaylan* this time," started *Apo* Tawil. "We are in the modern times and our culture is slowly disintegrating. We are not like the Dihinarians who are almost puritans in their culture and ways. The Harayans are slowly coping with the fast-changing world."

"What do you mean by that?"

"Most of us are evangelized, unlike the Dihinarians who still have strong faith in their gods and goddesses, most especially in their Moon Goddess. Some of us work in the *barrio* or in the private farms or have even migrated to other places for greener pasture. We no longer solely depend on hunting or farming in the less arable soils. We go to places where there is work. We don't stay in one place and depend on the prophecy or promises of gods. I would say that drastic change occurred within our tribe after we lost the last tribe priestess."

"Why didn't you pick another *babaylan*?" Xander realized the importance of priestesses or Doring to her tribe. They keep the culture and tradition alive for centuries. Perhaps, not having a *babaylan* was one of the reasons the Harayan culture was dramatically dwindling.

"Because of the risks and their grueling tasks, none ever dared to try." *Apo* Tawil's voice turned sad. His narrow eyes even turned narrower as he looked up to the sky.

The sun shone brightly, and its warmth touched their skin despite the shadows the tall trees cast. No evidence of the snowfall had survived the heat. They turned into glimmering dewdrops and must have dispersed to create an afternoon or a late night rain. Weather changed. The sun and the moon came and went but the three scarlet rings, now fainter and weaker than the previous days, remained unmovable in the sky.

"Most of all, had we had a *babaylan*, most definitely will she not feel a sense of satisfaction with her job if her most important task to protect whom shall be protected would turn out futile."

Xander's head was clouded with too many thoughts that he barely grasped what *Apo* Tawil was saying.

Protect who?

"It is quite a complicated story, isn't it?" smirked the old man. "Well, the story behind the feud has a more complex plot than the priestess's job." He continued, "Long time ago, the Dihinarians accused us of stealing their precious gem: a black pearl. We called it *Mutya*. But the pearl was already with us even before the time the tribe was founded. Hence, we deemed the accusation nothing but claptrap.

"We worshipped the God of Conquest through an *anito* in the form of a sacred sword bestowed upon by the Sun God to our warrior ancestor who founded the tribe after he escaped a pandemonium in a small island that he failed to conquer.

"He built this tribe with his flesh and blood, his family dominating most of our ancestors. In this land, he brought with him the black pearl and the sacred sword. Our ancestors taught us that the black pearl will protect its owner from any form of harm and will evade painful death and will only die the natural way. It was said that the black pearl was a gift to him by the Moon Goddess, the Dihinarian deity. With both the power of the sun and moon, the Harayan Tribe was invincible. Until one day, we lost the pearl to a foreign man.

"He seduced one of our local girls, and she gave him the pearl, thinking that he will return for her. They had a child. This child was taken by a Dihinarian priestess. She was able to do it with the help of our own priestess. Because of the conspiracy, they were punished. They died to appease the wrath of the gods and the two tribes, and to close a peace treaty to cease the war. She was our last priestess: Maduri. We had not had a new one because of the missing pearl and lost child."

"Why do you need to protect a child?" He wondered. If they badly needed a child to protect, they could have chosen one among the newborns in their time.

"Because it was believed that the child was the rebirth of our warrior ancestor. The Dihinarians were so eager to take his life in payment for the death of one of their own. We needed to protect the child from the Dihinarians and from their *Muling Buhay*."

Muling Buhay?

Had he heard it before?

"Is there a problem, Xander?" *Apo* Tawil noticed the disfigurement on Xander's face.

The latter was trying to remember where and when he heard about the *Muling Buhay*.

"What's a *Muling Buhay*?" His voice quavered.

"A reincarnation of a person who is fated to correct the wrongs of the past. Our ancestors believed that the *Muling Buhays* come to life again to finish a task or to fulfill a prophecy."

Muling Buhay?

Where did he hear it before?

The chieftain went on, "This forest played a great role in the war of the tribes. We called it the War of the Sun and Moon. The Dihinarians still worship their Moon Goddess and believe in her power of healing and protection, while we, the Harayans, had long forgotten our duty to embody the Sun God's desire for unfathomable conquests. Nevertheless, I do not think that the God of Conquest stopped doing what he ought to do. His desires had always been linked to our world's history."

"You mean all the wars among nations and territories happened because of this deity?" Xander wished he could have bitten his tongue to stop himself from chortling. He knew it was bad to laugh at other people's beliefs, but the thought was just over the top. To claim that Alexander the Great's conquests around Europe and Asia, the power of the Roman Empire, and the triumph of the cunning and fearless great leaders of great empires were works of a god was a little wild.

"I know you will laugh about it," the chieftain said calmly.

He was not offended or disappointed with Xander's inconsideration. He was rather expecting such a reaction.

"I'm sorry," Xander apologized immediately, still with tears of disbelief and amusement in his eyes. "I am not just used to those kinds of stories."

"I understand."

"But I do think it is worth a space in a library or a bookstore!" he kidded. "People in the past sure had a lot of strange stories!"

"In this forest, many natives died protecting their heritage, their beliefs. You are fortunate you were not born in those times when calling the gods a joke was a sin."

The laughter died out.

The wind started to blow hard. It was slowly turning cold as the hair on his arms stood. The brightness of the sun weakened as an army of thick clouds hovered above their heads. The leaves danced in cadence as the cool breeze of air kissed the treetops. It seemed that it was going to rain or the heavens were ready for another bout of surprise.

Did the gods hear him laughing at them? Was the cold wind a sign that they were not amused by his tirades? Or was he turning a little too superstitious to believe about gods?

"Be careful," warned *Apo* Tawil. "I hear footsteps."

A soft treading sound and the ringing bells continued to intensify as it got closer and closer. Sounds of rumpling dried leaves and grasses suggested that they were marching on a forgotten meadow. Xander began to wonder about the existence of a meadow clear of the breadth of woods.

Shortly, hazy murmurs began to emerge from the copious murkiness that besieged that part of the forest.

The thick clouds moved out of the sun's view. Nevertheless, the sun was not as bright as it used to be a couple of minutes ago as it was overpowered by the shine of the scarlet rings.

Then, they heard a giggle that was suppressed for concealment.

Women's voices arose as *Apo* Tawil and Xander searched the vicinity for the arrival of unlikely guests. Silhouettes came into sight not longer than a minute of bafflement.

Rina?

Xander froze as his and Rina's eyes met after she and a stooping old woman came out from the fog.

What was she doing in the forest with that woman, who looked familiar in his eyes?

Xander studied her face carefully. The old woman wore a plain brown patterned *baro't saya* like Ayang and was carrying a wooden staff.

"Having a great afternoon walk, Doring?" spoke *Apo* Tawil.

Doring? So, she's Doring. The famous tribe priestess whom he had always heard of!

CHAPTER 21
Poisoned

"Sure, I am, Tawil!" she replied in a bleak voice without removing her gaze from Xander's befuddled face.

Yes! She was the woman whom he met outside the church grounds who "read" his future for a hundred pesos.

"Shouldn't we be going now, Doring?" Rina looked anxious. She tugged Doring's sleeves and seemed to be so eager to avoid an upcoming confrontation with him after the heated conversation in the mansion's kitchen earlier.

"Are you remembering the war that this forest holds the most valuable memories of or the outrageous allegation you pressed upon my tribe, Doring?" *Apo* Tawil stepped forward.

Apparently, the tribe leaders had the memory of the centuries-old war afresh in their consciousness. Even time could not heal the wounds. Xander felt that a mounting dispute might occur if not put off early.

"Thank you for reminding me that today was the day you attacked my tribe for the mistake of one human!" laughed Doring sardonically.

"Is it not because of that fault why everything turned worse?" *Apo* Tawil was not retreating.

"May I remind you that the robbery by your ancestor was the main root of all these?" Doring was neither in the form of drawing back.

Rina, who was standing behind Doring, seemed so apprehensive. She seemed to know the story of the feud as she was so keen to protect Doring from the rising tension.

"There was no robbery!" countered *Apo* Tawil.

"The gods had spoken!" the enraged Doring exclaimed.

"Move on, will you?" laughed *Apo*. "I am sure they have forgotten the mistakes of the past!"

"They never forget!"

"It's because you feed your minds with such baloney!"

"Weren't you the same with us when you still believed in your Sun God?"

"Stop!" Rina interfered. "This is not going to end if you continue hating each other!" Her face was so red in anger.

"Is she the *Muling Buhay* you are fostering to fulfill the prophecy?" *Apo* Tawil shifted his attention to the disconcerted Rina.

"Back off, Tawil!" warned Doring as she shoved Rina behind her.

Muling Buhay?

Rina?

Xander smirked in disbelief. He had heard Doring and an unknown voice talk about doubt resurfacing in Rina and if she could do "it." The "it" a *Muling Buhay* was warranted to do.

"A what?" Rina moved her way out of Doring's shadow. Her eyebrow rose as she patiently waited for an answer. It seemed that Rina had no idea about anything.

"You haven't told her…" said *Apo* Tawil in one breath.

Doring gulped. Her eyes rolled as if looking for an explanation.

"You shouldn't believe anything they say!" Xander spoke.

It was the best time to interrupt as he could see confusion written all over Rina's distorted face, and he hated her for playing innocent. What was she? Some fool who let other people play on her? It was obvious that Doring and her cronies were just using her to their advantage. Whatever it was. Yet, she played gullibly!

The whole reincarnation thing and the stories about ancient feud and gods were claptrap! They were just part of a primeval culture that was at the brink of total annihilation. If you gave these people a taste of city life, they would absolutely and easily forget how to make fire with woods and rocks!

"They are just making a fool out of you, Rina!" he added with a laugh.

There is no such thing as Muling Buhay. He believed.

"The young lad is right, Rina," Doring spoke calmly with her eyes narrowed sleek, glaring at Xander with utter surprise. "You shouldn't be too trustful."

"See! Take it from her!" exclaimed Xander.

"Don't tell me who I should trust, Xander!" The anger just appeared from nowhere. "I have been with Doring and her people all my life. I know that they can be trusted!"

"Yet they are feeding you with lies!" He stomped toward Rina and stood inches away from her face.

Her eyes were threatening, and he could see in them an utter disgust for him.

"They are my friends!"

"Friends who are manipulating you to mistrust others!"

Rina was not mistaken. Xander was a man full of himself, so confident that what he said was always true—a brat. She was not mistaken. From the very first day she met him, by just reading his unusual behavior made her understand that Ayang was right.

He was selfish.

He was destructive.

He could not be trusted.

Who was he to tell her what to do, whom to be friends with, and most of all whom to trust?

"Ah!" Xander growled, and his voice ricocheted in chains of expressed pain.

Hiss!!

A green colored snake with yellow markings crept slowly around his right leg with its fangs deep down to his calf muscles.

Whack!

The tip of Doring's staff landed on his calf, and the snake flew directly to the tall grass beside him. Two holes on his pants were stained with blood, and Xander felt the sting as the fangs separated from his flesh. A sudden numbness weakened his leg, prompting him to lean against the nearest tree.

"We need to stop the poison from reaching the vital organs!" *Apo* Tawil hurriedly ripped a portion of his shirt and tied it tightly around Xander's leg.

"He has to be seen by a doctor!" Worry was heard in Rina's voice. "Xander?" she called as she tugged his shoulders, making sure he would not pass out.

It's just a bite! Just a bite! He kept telling himself.

But the worst was yet to come.

The snake was a viper, one of the poisonous animals in the forest. He read from books that once bitten by it, the victim could only make one hundred steps before death comes to him.

How would he make his one hundred steps if he could not even move one of his legs?

They trudged to the road back to the village. *Apo* Tawil and Rina helping Xander walk with only one leg. Before they could even exit the forest, he felt warm little by little. His sweat started to fall down his face.

"Xander?" Her quavering voice was all he could hear.

I will be with you no matter what… I will protect you…

Was that Rina? Was that her voice?

He could not see her. His sense of sight was failing him. Only the movement of her lips and the sparkle of gold in her eyes were visible.

That sparkle that he always wanted to catch in print appeared.

But why now?

Now that he was dying.

*   *   *

Fresh.

Warm.

Pungent.

His eyes would still not open, but he was awake. He could hear two distinct voices of women, which sounded distant but clear.

"Can he be?" asked one of the women.

"I don't know, but he's alive."

"That was life-threatening. He could have died."

"But he did not." A reassuring sigh followed.

"Perhaps a miracle."

"He is protected."

"Always?" replied the woman who seemed to be more in doubt than the other.

"Maybe."

Just like how he was not killed in the car accident that killed his parents, the snake bite was his gateway to death yet he was still alive.

The depth and tone of one of the voices changed.

As he opened his eyes, he realized he was lying on a wooden bed. There was a lit kerosene lamp beside his bed and a wide window that let the wind in.

If he was not dead, then where could he be?

"I have finally found the warrior."

The familiar voice caught Xander's attention now that he was more awake.

"Are you sure it is his reincarnation?"

Xander gathered his feet together when he noticed a bandage wrapped around his leg.

220

"I am more than positive. If we fail to find today's reincarnated warrior, we could still fulfill the prophecy with reversing the past."

Ayang?

That hoarseness in her voice. He couldn't be mistaken.

He tiptoed slowly toward the doorstep, and he was not disappointed. He saw Ayang's back turned from him as she talked to the tribe priestess, Doring.

What was Ayang doing here?

Doring's glare directed him as though trying to tell him to stay hidden.

But why?

"If we succeed with this plan, it means that everything will change," Doring said, her eyes still on him.

Xander cautiously hid behind the door, but his ears remained stuck on the hole to hear the intriguing conversation.

"Yes." Ayang sounded thrilled.

"And if we fail in this—"

Ayang cut in, "Then we have no choice but to hasten our search for the present warrior."

"I thought you said that you have a hunch about this present reborn warrior."

"I do! But it will take time to prove if he is the one," replied Ayang.

"What will we do with Rina?"

"Everything in the present will be of no use when the prophecy is fulfilled. But one thing is for sure, Rina and the future *Muling Buhays* will continue to walk this earth," answered Ayang confidently.

"Without the warrior?"

"Without the warrior but with peace and harmony as what the gods promised!"

"All this is still useless if we do not have the pearl. It is the one carrying the curse," said Doring. "We have to find it. It has

221

been a very long time that the Goddess of Protection and Healing, your sister, Cahaya, has been trapped in that cursed thing."

"We will find it, Doring." Ayang slowly stood and turned her eyes to the door where Xander was hiding. She narrowed her eyes and studied the strange sensation she had with the door. "I feel like I am being watched."

"That does happen all the time in this house, Ayang," said Doring. "Many priestesses have died in that room. Perhaps you are feeling their presence."

Ayang shook her head.

Xander held his breath.

"It's time for me to go," said Ayang, and she went out the door.

"You may now come out." Doring's voice did not sound angry. "Did you hear everything?" she asked as she followed Xander walking his way to the almost bare receiving room.

"Enough for me to raise questions," he replied boldly. "Why am I here?"

Doring answered straightaway, "Apo Tawil wouldn't be able to save you from the snake bite, so I took you here in my humble abode, thinking I could help a little bit. But it seems that you did not really need any of our help."

"Sorry, I need you to speak human language here."

"Cahaya's spell is too strong. Ayang did not even feel you were here. A part of her she shared with you, so you became one with her. Did not know it would actually work."

"What?" His eyebrows raised.

"Sorry. It was not meant for your ears to hear."

Done with the tribe feuds, the stories about gods, or Doring's craziness, he did not believe a single thing about it until Ayang showed up. Her presence just sealed the urge to accommodate his endless curiosity.

Something was going to happen, and it was not going to be good. For days, he had been watching Ayang's quirky behavior, and he never felt at ease with any of it; her sudden interest with the diary, her involvement with the snowfall, and her influence over Rina. They just did not happen without a purpose.

"I want you to tell me the truth." It sounded like an order. "Tell me about what you are planning to do with Rina."

Doring's lips curved at the edge. "With all the questions in your head, you chose to ask about Rina first. I wonder why."

He wondered too. Nevertheless, he felt it was the priority at the moment. He might have grown extreme dislike towards her, but he could not deny the fact that he had always been astounded by her mystery. By mystery, it meant he wanted to know her more.

"I knew about her being the *Muling Buhay,* but I don't believe it. I feel that you are up to no good, and Rina will be in great danger," he added.

"How can you say that when you do not even believe a thing about what you heard?" Doring's calmness surprised Xander.

"This is bullshit!" His voice rose. "Making her believe those lies!"

"It is to you but not to us." A tiny smile on her face added to Xander's annoyance. She went on, "Look at you! You are still alive despite the snake bite. Strange thing, isn't it?"

Alive?

"There are mysteries in this world that cannot be explained if you keep yourself in the dark, Xander," she said slowly. Every word was enunciated carefully. "Evidence is right in front of your eyes, yet you deny them. Well, that's pathetic! I wonder what will change your mind."

He froze.

Evidence?

"Okay. Let this be. Let us wait for the day of your enlightenment," she said jokingly.

"Why do you need to protect Rina? I heard you. Even *Apo* Tawil said that *babaylans* are tasked to protect the *Muling Buhays.*"

"For her to accomplish what must be done."

223

"What is it? What must she accomplish?"

"Something that you mustn't know!"

He slammed his hand against the table, but it did not scare Doring.

"I thought you do not care about this lie!" Her stare was piercing.

"This is about Rina!" A little more disappointment from this woman and Xander would be pushed to his limit. "I do not care about the pearl, or the reincarnation of a warrior, or whoever this warrior is. I do not even understand their importance…"

It was just about Rina. He realized.

Was he actually worrying about her?

He was tongue-tied. The thoughts sank into his brain.

He was worried about her.

He was worried about what Doring and Ayang had in store for her.

"If I were you, Xander, I will stay away from Rina and Ayang," cautioned Doring as she reached for a tobacco stick from her pocket.

"Why?"

"If you love your life, protect it."

"What does my life have to do with Rina or Ayang?" His voice grew dark.

"You will know at the right time. Just be patient until the enlightenment." She smirked.

Oh, how he hated her riddles! She never helped!

Xander hurriedly stripped his leg of the bandage and was taken aback when he saw his skin free from any wound. The snake bite was gone.

"How did you do this?" His eyes almost dropped from its socket as a perfectly flawless calf welcomed his sight.

"It healed by itself," retorted Doring without even looking at it.

What?

"That is one example of the mysteries of the world that you fail to recognize," she added.

There was a knock on the door.

Juan came to take Xander home.

His leg did not even hurt.

How did it heal itself?

How did he protect himself from the snake's poison?

Doring's last words before he left her village continued to confound him.

"You should not have come here in the first place."

Why would Doring say it anyway?

*   *   *

"*Señorito?!*" *Manang* Leticia scurried downstairs with her round eyes shaped into pears as tears rushed down.

She must have heard about the accident in the forest.

"Oh, thank goodness you are okay!" A big smile spread on her face as she saw Xander walking perfectly straight. "It's a good thing that Doring knows how to cure snake bites!" she added.

When they reached the *sala,* he saw Atty. Tan standing near the window with a cup of coffee. The moonlight was strong and the three rings added to the luster of the night. The candles and the kerosene lamps were already set alight.

"Sir?" Atty. Tan brought down his cup as he saw him coming. "Do I need to call for a doctor?"

"No. I am perfectly fine," he replied with his usual angst.

"I brought you the list of potential buyers," said Atty. Tan as he laid down the papers on the table. "They are all interested in the house, sir. The bid will start at twenty-five million, but if you want, we can always increase the benchmark."

The lawyer sounded guarded with his words. He perceived Xander's wrinkled forehead, which meant the latter was not in the humor to have lengthy conversations. If he could finish talking in five minutes, he would not delay leaving for another minute.

Xander carefully scanned the names.

"This includes the farm, right?" His sharp tone pricked Atty. Tan's leniency.

"Yes, sir!" the lawyer responded hastily.

"Excuse me…"

He stopped with what he was doing.

"Will you mind if I take this cup now, sir?"

The question was not meant for him.

"No. Thank you, miss," Atty. Tan replied amiably while handing over the cup.

Rina?

She obviously dodged his stare, then quickly scampered out of the *sala*.

What was she doing in the mansion?

"Sir, as I was saying…"

But Xander could not keep his revolting interest tame always.

He hurried downstairs to the dirty kitchen and looked for her, leaving the befuddled lawyer in the *sala* shocked over his action.

"Where's Rina?" His shocked appearance surprised *Manang* Leticia who was busily mixing vegetables on a large pot.

"Rina?"

"Yes! She was here. She took Atty. Tan's cup!"

"Oh, yes! I asked her a favor since I could not leave this soup unattended," answered *Manang* Leticia. "She was here to bring some leaves and herbal decoction for your wound."

There were two bottles of dark green decoction and a bundle of dried leaves and twigs on the table where Atty. Tan's cup was placed too.

"She's gone now," added the woman.

Without any delay, he rushed out of the back door through the *zaguan* to the back gate.

There, he saw Rina walking toward the front yard with an empty basket in her arm.

How was she going home? There was no cart waiting for her. Did she think that walking by foot in the dark and dangerous road was a good idea?

"Rina!" he called. His loud voice filled the yard that had nothing except for darkness and the sounds of singing crickets. He dashed to her and took her arm with his hand in a tight grasp.

"What do you want?" she complained as she tried to loosen his grasp.

What did he want?

He didn't really know.

He just followed her because… because of nothing… because he just wanted to.

His grasp loosened after realizing his purpose was unviable.

I will be with you no matter what… I will protect you. He remembered what he heard before he passed out. The voice was Rina's. He heard it, and he could not be wrong.

"Did you say it?" he asked.

"What did I say?" Rina slowly stepped backward, getting ready to run away anytime.

"You said you will be with me no matter what happens, that you will protect me!" He grasped her arm again, and this time he had reason to do so. "Why did you say it?" Xander incessantly searched for answers in her eyes.

"I didn't!" she answered. She used all her power to slacken off his grip, but Xander was determined to not to let her go.

She did not say it. Rina began to wonder why he said it. *Was he out of his mind?*

"I do not know what you are talking about, so please let me go!" she went on.

"It wasn't you?"

"No! Please stop. You're hurting me," she pleaded. *Xander was a monster,* she thought.

"Why do you hate me?" He wrapped his arm around her waist and pulled her closer to him.

"I think you know the answer to that!" she insisted. "Ayang does not need to tell me what to think about you because I have made up my mind."

She pushed away from him, trying to counter his strength with what little she had, but Xander was as strong as a beast. She heard her heart pounding so loudly and quickly. There was anger and ambivalence.

"You are heartless! You do not even think about the poor farmers. You're going to sell everything because you're greedy. Ayang is right about you, and I do not regret..."

He silenced her with a kiss, sudden and unexpected.

He too didn't foresee that he'd do it. All he knew was that Rina was hurting his ears and that she was an enchantress. Her babbling lips seduced him.

Deep and tender.

She weakened.

He was lost too.

His grasp on her loosened as Rina's defenses were breached.

Their lips slowly parted. Their eyes fixed on each other.

Rina gasped. "You kissed me..."

"You let me kiss you," he countered.

She pushed away from him and picked up the basket from the ground.

"Wait!"

She paused. "At least, let Juan take you home," said Xander, still dazed after the kiss.

PART 8

CHAPTER 22
The Flower Festival

Guada and Concha adorned her hair with fresh flowers and pink lace. Her curls were tucked in a middle-high bun. Her neck festooned with a diamond necklace. Clarissa almost did not recognize herself in the mirror.

"You look very beautiful, dear," said her mother as she fixed her sleeves.

"She almost looks like the younger you, Guada," said *Tiya* Consuelo.

There was a knock on the door, and Maying appeared.

"*Don* Jaime is waiting in the carriage, *Doña* Guada," Maying said shyly.

"We better do our last minute touches, dear sister," mumbled Consuelo as she looked at herself in the mirror.

"Maying, help Clarissa with her train. The dress is a little heavy," said Guada before she and her sister left the room.

Clarissa laughed.

"What's funny, *señorita*?"

"Mama and *Tiya* are more self-conscious than me. They have been changing outfits since early afternoon."

"Four times?"

"No. Five times!"

Both girls ended up laughing. Clarissa pointed out how messy her *Tiya* Concha's make up had become after the grueling task of transforming her into a lady for tonight.

"Who's going to be your escort, *señorita*?" Maying picked up the long, heavy white train of Clarissa's gown.

"*Doña* Stella's son, Antonio. Oh, how I hope it rains tonight."

"It won't rain. The stars, and even the moon, are so bright tonight."

"Hush, Maying! Whose side are you on?"

"You must really detest the parade, s*eñorita*."

"I hate the idea of being displayed like a tapestry. You of all people must know that. I am not a doll to be beautified as they wish."

Maying faced her and said resolutely, "*Señorita,* it's just for one night. I'll be accompanying you, anyway."

"Oh, Maying! This must be the worst day of my life!"

"It's not as bad as yesterday."

"Please don't remind me of that letter from Barcelona."

"What was on that letter again?" Maying sounded as though she was going to burst into laughter.

The door opened and revealed *Doña* Guada in her most fabulous outfit. But behind the regality she was bearing was the uncouthness of her mouth. She started reprimanding the girls for being so slow.

*　　*　　*

The sidewalks were filled with curious spectators—women, men, and children holding candles with their bare cold hands—while the main street was cleared up to make way for the *sagala* where the makeshift wooden arches, adorned with flowers, colorful papers, and beautiful ladies, were to be paraded. It was a cold night, but it didn't seem like it was going to rain.

Guada, Concha, and Maying assisted Clarissa to her position in the first arch. Her escort was waiting for her there.

"Now, all you have to do is walk till we get to the church. Then we can go home after the mass," said Guada as she kissed her daughter on the cheek.

Clarissa's face was void of happiness, but she had the duty to not let people know.

Antonio, her partner, offered his arm.

The procession started with a marching band; a pair of trumpeters and drummers leading the flock. People were throwing flower petals to them. Light lanterns stood along the sidewalks, which made the road well-lighted. Clarissa could see elderly women smiling at her, probably appreciating her effort for dressing up, and children adored her dress and hair. Few of these people, she knew by face.

It was going to be a long walk. However, as time passed by, Clarissa thought she was wrong to say that tonight was boring and intolerable. Eyes were not just on her. People were also watching the other girls behind her, which put her at ease. She was starting to enjoy the parade.

The marching band slowed down as they arrived at the church grounds.

"Clarissa," Antonio spoke. "Did you know that your mother talked to my mother about your interest in my cousin?"

Her gaze, which was fixed on the sky above her and the dazzling three rings, shifted to Antonio.

"What?"

"*Doña* Guada. She went to our house a few weeks ago to ask my mother about my cousin, Andres, who is currently studying medicine in Europe."

"You are not joking, are you, Antonio?" She tightened her grip on his arm.

She knew Antonio and Andres. He and his band of boys always loved to kid around. They were naughty, especially around

233

girls. Andres was the biggest joke and bully in the group. She couldn't forget how he insulted and embarrassed Alejandro one time in her mother's garden party. Clarissa was just relieved he had to go to Spain to study medicine. But this relief would be short-lived as Andres sent her a telegram telling her he was on his way back to Manila to see her. Clarissa was not dumb to not know what it meant.

"Ouch, Clarissa!" He winced. "I'm not throwing shade at you. Of course, I am telling the truth."

"I'm not interested in your cousin!" she exclaimed. She had not even seen Andres for five long years.

"Well, that's how your mother made us believe. As a matter of fact, Andres is expected to arrive in a week."

Her legs numbed. Her shoulders and arms froze with cold shock.

Her mother's audacity to decide on her part was too much. What was she doing? Arranged marriage? It was the thing she feared the most. Perhaps the day would come when her mother had everything all planned and all she had to do would be to walk down the aisle and marry a man she barely knew. That was disgusting!

Well, her mother could dictate what dress she wore, what food she ate, what books she read, or what activities she did, but marriage? She just couldn't allow her to play with her heart. Not anymore. Not like this.

And with Andres? Of all people, why him? She'd rather marry a stranger than the haughty Andres Tovar!

She stopped.

"What's the matter?" asked Antonio in a murmur.

The couple behind them was starting to wonder why they stopped. She just interrupted the entire parade, and she was close to ruining it.

She felt her lungs congest; tight and full. Her heart was hammering loudly. It was like she was meeting doomsday. All she wanted was to run away and get away from what lay ahead.

She did what her heart was screaming for. Clarissa pulled her skirt up and dashed out of the procession line. She didn't care what others would think. She didn't even care about people's reaction. She just wanted to get away.

She ran and ran, not knowing where to go. She could only hear her heart pounding while she took big leaps away from the crowd. It seemed that the moon and the three rings were guiding her to which way to go, although she was clueless as to where it would be. Her legs had a mind of its own, and she was just following where her emotions would bring her.

She took off the piece of cloth or the *panuelo* that covered her chest and shoulders and loosened the corset of her dress to breathe freely. She was quite a distance away from everyone. She had no idea as to where she even was. She just recognized the road she took and a few hills that surrounded her. She didn't want to think that she was lost.

Having completely lost her mind, she still knew she was safer now than being around those people. Perhaps her family was looking for her now. Her father was friends with the *gobernadorcillo*, who could easily mobilize his guards to search for her. But she didn't want to be found. She wanted to be alone to clear her mind, to think, to release this frustration so that when she faced her mother, she wouldn't say anything hurtful to her.

Why did they have to think on her behalf? Why did they have to plan for her? She had her own brain. She had her own heart. She was very capable of making decisions and of falling in love. Did they even care to ask if there was someone she liked? What if she did? What if she liked someone but was too scared to tell them because it was not right?

When she had relaxed a bit, she continued to follow the road and walked to where it would lead her. It was dark, but the moon was big and bright and it showed her the way.

Then, she heard clanking sounds of a horse coming her way.

235

"*Señorita?*" The voice echoed.

She followed the voice until she saw a silhouette of a man riding a horse. She knew who it was.

"Did my father…"

Alejandro climbed off the horse and angrily walked toward her.

"Yes, he did. I have been ordered to take you home," he uttered coldly.

She could see veins ready to burst on his forehead and neck.

"You have no right to be angry with me!" she shouted at him.

"You ran away!"

"I ran away because I don't want to get married!"

He winced.

"You heard it right. My mother arranged everything for me: my future, my life!" Her voice cracked. "It's like I don't have control of myself." She started to cry. "They're marrying me off to Andres Tovar! Andres Tovar of all people!"

Alejandro paused.

"Now, give me the horse and don't ever follow me!" she demanded as she grabbed the reins off his clasp, but Alejandro quickly blocked her.

"I'm taking you back home," he said.

"No, you're not!"

"It's dangerous for you…"

"Why would you care? I'm tired of people bossing me around. Let me have this my way!"

Before she could say more, Alejandro grabbed her by the waist and yanked her closer to his body, and kissed her in surprise.

She was silenced.

The horse neighed, but all Clarissa could hear was the storm inside her chest. The coldness of the wind raised the hair on her skin, but it was impossible to douse the fire traveling all throughout her body.

The kiss was long, deep, and tender as if putting an end to eternal yearning or desire.

Her cheeks glowed red and felt warm, and Alejandro wasn't stopping. She too wasn't, and she couldn't understand why.

Questions swarmed her head. Why would Alejandro do such a thing? Why kiss her? Why?

Why even let him kiss her? Why was she not resisting?

After a while, loud and clear sounds of running horses interrupted their moment.

Alejandro pulled back and said, "Come!"

Clarissa knew that they were guards commissioned by the *gobernadorcillo* to look for her under her father's request. They were known to be merciless officials, especially to *indios*, and they might mistake them as such. After all, they were in the middle of the forest where *indios* roam.

Alejandro lifted her to the horse and joined her.

"Where are we going?" she asked.

"I don't know," he answered.

CHAPTER 23
By The Riverbank

The civil guards' horses were after them, and they were getting closer and closer. Clarissa clutched the reins tightly as she heard Alejandro gasp from behind. He was charging the horse to move faster. She literally felt her heart jumping out of its cavity as the civil guards started shooting at them. The fog was helping though, keeping them imperceptible to their captors.

"Ah!" Alejandro shrieked.

She turned to him.

"What's wrong?"

He winced, and his voice crackled, "Nothing."

But he didn't look okay, she thought.

She closed her eyes as their horse began to gallop quickly. Her bare shoulders trembled with the cold, her mind playing with the possibilities of being caught, yet fear was bearable. She knew why.

Then, all of a sudden, their horse stopped.

Alejandro's grip on the reins loosened, so he fell down the horse, and rolled to the side of the road where wild plants grew.

"Alejandro!" she yelled while she pulled the reins to calm the horse.

The poor man groaned with pain as he hit the bark of the tree. Before she climbed off the horse, her eyes caught a glimpse of the moon, flickering together with the three scarlet rings. The sky turned wine red, although a little lighter. Her eyes fixed on the moon as it glowed brighter and brighter. Strangely, she felt her body being pulled by it like some force wrapped around her, pulling her.

Then, a sudden gush of light appeared right before her eyes, almost blinding her. Everything went white.

"Your duty awaits you. It's time to make things right."

The strange voice from nowhere sent creeps to her nerves.

Slowly, the white light disappeared, and she saw Alejandro walking or limping, toward her with his hand pressed on the side of his trunk. He was bleeding.

"We have to find a safer place," he said, his voice cracking. He pointed to the thick forest around crammed with mist.

"Did you see the light? Did you hear a voice?" she asked him as she went down the horse.

"What light? What voice?"

"I thought I heard something." She looked up back to the moon where she thought the light and the voice came from.

Alejandro pulled the horse out of the road to the entrance of the forest where wild plants, weeds, and tall thick trees grew. She followed him, holding up the long train of her gown.

Only the peaceful sound of the flowing river, the chirping crickets, the hooting owl on top of a leafless tree where the moon shone behind, and the tearing fabric as it came in contact with the wood and grass, caught her attention. It seemed that they have lost the civil guards as the firing of guns and the clanking of horseshoes waned down. The owl's large threatening glare followed them, which scared Clarissa. She reached for Alejandro's arm.

"Where are we? Are we still near town?" she asked.

"We're slowly leaving the municipality," he answered as he tied the horse to the tree. "There's a cabin a mile from here. We can stay there for the night. Are you tired already?"

"Yes. Can we rest for a while?" She sat down on the bed of dried leaves at the foot of a huge tree. It was pretty tiring carrying the train of her gown.

Alejandro rested across her, leaned the back of his head against the tree, and closed his eyes.

She watched him peacefully fall asleep. One bullet from the officers hit him while they were running away. His trunk was continuously bleeding yet Alejandro showed no sign of pain on his face except for the exhaustion knocking him out.

She tore a piece of fabric from her skirt and came near the sleeping wounded man. He was so tired that he did not even notice her noisy footsteps. She sat on her knees, rolled the piece of her skirt around her hand, and slowly lifted Alejandro's shirt. The wound was deep, and flesh and blood were coming out.

He moved even before she could press the cloth on the wound.

Their eyes met. Alejandro caught her hand.

"You're injured," she mumbled.

"I'm fine," he said.

"No, you're not," she insisted. "Let me help you, please."

"I'm not going to die just because of this."

"You lost too much blood already. We have to take the bullet out from your body if there is one."

"I'm fine. Just take a rest before we…"

"Why won't you let me help you, Alejandro?"

"I am not in pain," he answered, taking his eyes off her.

Clarissa still forced the piece of cloth under his shirt and pressed the wound to control the bleeding.

He fell into silence as he felt the pain coming out from the wound. It began to grow as Clarissa pressed harder to stop the bleeding.

She tore another lengthy piece of cloth from her skirt and reinforced the already blood-soaked cloth.

"Where are you going?" he questioned when he saw her stand up.

"I'm going to look for some herbs."

"You can't. It's too dark."

She didn't listen. Ayang taught her to identify herbs even with the use of smell and touch. She might not be as good as Ayang, and she might not have instruments like mortar and pestle to powder the herbs or fire to heat and create decoction from it, but Clarissa always believed that natural and raw herbs were more effective and potent.

Just a few walks away from where Alejandro lay, she found what she was looking for. Small elongated or finger-like red pepper dangled on its twigs. Cayenne pepper was best for bleeding. She picked three peppers from the tree and hurried back to Alejandro.

"What's that?"

"Cayenne pepper." She split one into half and squeezed both on top of the wound.

Alejandro gritted his teeth to prevent himself from screaming. It stung painfully. The cayenne juice penetrated the bloody opening as it created a barely bearable stinging sensation. Alejandro knew that he must keep mum to stay hidden. One loud shriek from him would divulge their whereabouts and that he didn't want to happen.

He cowered every time a drop of cayenne extract fell into his wound.

"Let me see it," said she.

"There's no bullet."

"Are you sure?"

He nodded.

The last pepper was consumed, and the pain was starting to be more bearable.

"Where are you going now?" He grabbed her arm.

"I'm going to look for anti-infective leaves."

"I'll be fine now. Just stay here."

241

She did what he said. Clarissa sat beside him and waited for him to fall asleep. His forehead was sweating, probably the effect of the cayenne on his wound. She ripped most of her train using a sharp-edged rock, which she found on the soil, and used it to cover Alejandro from the cold. Then, she wiped the sweat on his forehead.

As she watched him sleep on her lap, glaring at his peaceful lips, she recalled the kiss.

It was her first kiss and a forbidden kiss at that. She knew it was wrong, and if her mother had seen it, she and Alejandro would surely be punished. Knowing Alejandro's status and her mother's hate for him, Guada and her aunt would surely do everything to put him behind bars. But if it were a different man, they would surely marry her off to him.

Why did she feel so strange, ticklish, and warm when she watched him so close like this? Her fingers traced the outline of his lips down to his chin. She had never felt this way about Alejandro before. Was it because of the kiss? Was it because she was too surprised?

Clarissa leaned her head against the tree and closed her eyes. She too was exhausted from the running and walking. It seemed that their plan of leaving the forest tonight would be delayed for tomorrow. Yet she didn't mind sleeping under the tree.

"When I die, you shall protect the tribe and shall heal those who are wounded. I may not be with them physically, but in spirit, the guidance and guardian of the Moon Goddess shall be with them." She heard a soft voice.

With her eyes closed, she saw a woman whose hair was as black as a raven and whose skin was that of a lighter shade of wood, kissing a tiny white pearl.

Clarissa opened her eyes when she realized that, in her sleep, she was dreaming about a strange-looking woman.

Alejandro was no longer there. She was all alone sleeping under the tree with her train wrapped around her.

washing it. The birds flew from tree to tree, and they joined her singing. She picked up a small stone and gently rubbed it to her skin.

Clarissa didn't notice time passing so quickly. She was obviously enjoying the serenity of the flowing river and the freshness of the morning. She owned the entire forest for now.

*   *   *

Alejandro brought back a bundle of fresh bananas and a basket of ripe mangoes. He tied his horse to the tree and sat on the flat top surface of the rock. From afar, he carefully watched Clarissa and remembered his stupidity last night. He had no clue as to why he did it. It was like he lost his rationality and just impulsively followed his heart. Though he wasn't ashamed about it, he wondered why Clarissa didn't even resist. He wouldn't want to assume, so he thought that she was just too shocked to stop him. He was aware that what he did was wrong—completely wrong—and he could be severely punished if Clarissa disclosed the incident to her parents and to the authority.

Clarissa would always be the woman he'd lifted to the pedestal. She was heaven while he was earth. He knew that he would never have her.

He turned away when she went out of the water.

"You're back," Clarissa's voice neared.

He cleared his throat.

"I got us some food," he said.

Clarissa sat across him. "So, where do we go after?" She peeled one banana and started eating. Her hair was dripping wet on her shoulders.

"You might want to…" Alejandro handed over a new set of clothes, which was a plain baro't saya.

"Where did you get these?"

"There's a village a few miles from here. They're very friendly people," he replied.

It was where he got the fruits.

"Are we going there?" she asked.

"Clearly, you have no plans of going home," he murmured. "Your parents are absolutely worried."

"Alejandro, if you really want me back home, you could have dragged me last night, but you didn't."

"It's because you said you didn't want to."

"No. I think you didn't want me to marry a man I barely know." She smirked.

He was tongue-tied.

"Is there something I should know, or you would like to say?" she asked.

"No."

"No?"

"No!" He shook his head.

She cocked her head.

"About last night…" he started, hesitating, "I'm sorry. I wasn't…"

"I got you now…" teasing him, her laughter contained to keep that serious face.

"What?"

"I know you, Alejandro. We're friends since we were little kids and I know how much you care for me," she explained as she studied the man's disgruntled face. "Everything between us just changed when you left. I hated you for that. When you came back, you became entirely different. You don't joke to me anymore. You became crazily polite. You don't even laugh boisterously like I always do when Mama's not around. You're strangely—"

"I was taught to treat ladies like that."

"Ladies?" She then crazily thought whether Alejandro had been kissing just any lady when he was in Spain. "Oh well, you must be so experienced then."

245

"What?"

"I mean you've been away for so long, and I don't believe you've never met a woman whom you like there. As Tiya Consuelo would say, the Spanish women are breathtakingly fierce and feisty."

"Oh, yes. They are! But as they say there, the wind changes every day, a woman every second," said he, stifling his laughter. "No… No… No… I didn't have much luck with women. Besides, I don't think I could love somebody else when my heart already belongs to someone." His voice turned serious this time, his gaze penetrating Clarissa's heart.

"Oh, does she know?" She found the memory of Alejandro kissing her repeating in her head.

"She might have by now," he answered softly as though trying to keep it from her, as he stood up. "Alright, señorita. Let's keep going." He thought they would need to get to the village before lunchtime.

"I always hate it when you call me señorita! Why can't you just call me by my name like the old times?" She got up from her knees after shaking fruit extracts off her hands.

"Because things change, Clarissa. So did you!"

"I didn't change," said she while following him.

"Of course, you did. You're taller, smarter, and prettier now."

Her face looked so red in his eyes.

"You're not a girl anymore." He turned on his heels and looked at her with his gaze intently boring into her pierced soul.

"Then what am I to you?"

"You're a woman."

An eerie silence filled the forest.

Face to face. Eye to eye. Clarissa felt her heart racing.

"If there's one thing that will never change, it's who we are. I am an indio, and you are a del Fierro. Does that make sense to you?"

"That did not stop you from kissing me..." Her face searched for answers from Alejandro. "You didn't kiss me just because I am a woman now. Why, Alejandro?"

His lips curved.

He said, "You already know."

"I do?"

He nodded. "Obviously. You won't be torturing me if you don't."

She stood and picked up the new clothes.

"We're going to the village," said she, hiding the amusement on her face. "I don't want to go home." She, then, went to the back side of the tree and changed her dress. "No peeking, okay?"

CHAPTER 24
Harayans

"So how did your wound heal exactly?" she asked as they trailed the path to the mountain.

The forest was so rich with trees that the sun barely touched their skin and the ground.

"I have no idea how my body does it," he answered while pulling the horse. Clarissa walked ahead of him. "One time, I cut my finger with a knife. The next day, it healed on its own. Strange really!"

"You know what? I remember when we were little kids. You were teaching me how to ride a horse, and then you fell. You broke your arm, but later that night, the doctor came and said you were okay."

"I remember that."

"How is that possible, Alejandro?"

He shrugged his shoulders. "One of the many mysteries of the bastard child, I guess." He laughed.

"Did you ever think of wanting to see your family?"

"Yes."

"Do you think they're still alive?"

"No."

"What made you say that?"

"Grandma Priya said that my mother died of childbirth and that my father left her before I was even born."

"Grandma told you that?"

He nodded.

"She also told me that I came from her tribe. That my mother was one of their women who mistakenly gave herself to the wrong man."

"The Dihinari Tribe?" She turned to him.

"You know about them?"

Her eyes brightened. "Just a little. *Manong* Bong told us about their story, remember?"

"I remember."

"So you already know that you were a Dihinarian when we went there, don't you?"

"Yes."

"Why didn't you tell me?"

"You never asked."

"Do I always have to ask for you to tell me things, Alejandro?"

"I don't want to impose, Clarissa," said he. "And it's not a big deal."

"It is! My grandmother came from that tribe, so it means I'm a Dihinarian, too. God, why didn't I ask her about that?"

Of course, she knew why. Guada!

"Clarissa, it still doesn't change a thing whether you came from what tribe because you're a rich man's daughter. You're *Doña* Guada's daughter," said he.

"I still have my grandmother's blood!" Her voice rose.

"So what? It doesn't make us…"

"Make us what?"

He sighed. He could see in her face the bursting disappointment. She was just preventing herself from exploding.

The sky dimmed. Dark clouds ruled everywhere. The drought was soon to end. The farmers would absolutely feast.

Slowly, rain poured.

"You're not thinking…" his voice cracked.

249

"I am. What's wrong about that?" Her tears mixed with the rain.

"It is wrong. This is wrong."

"I know, and you know. But still you…"

"What do you want me to do, Clarissa? I'm a poor man!"

"Do you love me or do you not?" Her voice echoed. The rain was starting to pour heavily, but it didn't match the storm of emotions inside her. "Do you want me? Do you need me?"

"Why…"

"Because I'll go with you if you want me to!"

"No." He quavered.

"It's the truth. I always liked you. But last night…"

He pulled her close to him and sealed his lips to hers.

"Are you serious?" he mumbled with disbelief, his eyes directed to hers.

She nodded, containing the surmounting rebellion in her heart.

"I let you kiss me twice already. How can I not be serious?"

He smiled contentedly but wanting more of her.

*   *   *

The rain slowly stopped. It was twilight when they reached the small village of the Haraya Tribe, holding each other's hands like how lovers did. They just needed shelter for the night before they leave town tomorrow. Their destination: somewhere people did not recognize them. Some place where they could just freely love each other, somewhere far from the del Fierros. But Clarissa still acknowledged the respect she had for her father. She loved them both: her mama and papa. But if there were one person who'd really understand her, it'd be her father.

Before they even reached the entrance of the village, they already saw a thick smoke climbing to the sky. People gathered in circles. Chants and drums sounded festive.

"Do you think it's the right time?" she asked Alejandro.

"It's getting late, Clarissa. We need a place to sleep."

The festivity stopped when the people saw Clarissa and Alejandro entering their territory.

"How can we help you?" An old woman in red and brown patterned clothes stepped forward. She had tattoos all over her body. Her neck, wrists, and even ankles were festooned with jewelry. Her eyes narrowed as she scrutinized the lovers.

"I was here this morning to ask for some food. If you'd be so kind, my wife is with child and needs a place to stay for the night." Alejandro tightened his grasp on her hand.

The old woman shifted her glance to Clarissa, whose legs were shaking, afraid to be caught at one lie, and who hid behind her man.

"You're just in time," said the old woman. "We have just ended the ceremony. I can spare a room for you two. Follow me."

The people's eyes trailed after them. One man took Alejandro's horse and kept it to the barn.

"Do not worry about them," added the old woman. "My people aren't used to seeing strangers. They barely leave the village."

They stopped in front of a small cabin. The old woman went in first and lighted the candle that was near the door.

"Come inside," said she.

The room was spacious with only one wooden table at the center.

"Is your wife hungry?"

"Are you, Clarissa?"

"No," she whispered.

"Thank you, but my wife is still full. We had fruits on our way here."

The old woman nodded.

"Here's your room." She handed over the candle.

"Thank you…"

"Maduri," she cut Clarissa. "I'm this tribe's priestess. I'm sure you have heard about *babaylans*."

"Yes, we have," answered Clarissa as she remembered Doray of the Dihinari Tribe.

"Well, if you get hungry, you can join us at our banquet."

"Thank you again, Maduri," uttered Alejandro.

Once Maduri had walked out of the cabin and joined her people, Clarissa and Alejandro set their things inside the room. There was one small bed.

"I'll sleep on the floor," said Alejandro.

"Thank you, my love." She landed a soft kiss on his lips.

"We leave for the north tomorrow."

"Can I see my father even for a few minutes? I want to ask for his forgiveness and his blessing as well."

Alejandro was silent for a while.

"Do you think it's a little dangerous?"

He nodded.

"I see." Her voice was mixed with sorrow and disappointment.

Alejandro touched her face. "Okay. We'll ask help from Maying."

A glow of hope resurfaced on her face.

*   *   *

Alejandro went out of the cabin as soon as he was sure Clarissa had fallen asleep. The laughter of the tribesmen was luring him to go out.

There, in the middle of the bonfire, was a group of men dancing and singing.

"Here is our guest!" exclaimed a red-faced balding old man as Alejandro approached the group.

The priestess, Maduri, was also there, looking at him with the utmost severity.

252

"I hear you from our window," said Alejandro.

"We are celebrating our god's descent to earth through our sacred warrior, who banished our enemies single-handedly," explained the sober man. "I, *Apo* Dula, leader of the Haraya Tribe, welcome you, our guest, and offer you this glass of wine. For the coming days, the Haraya Tribe will seal history. Our enemies will die searching for the reincarnated warrior. Their eyes will turn white, their hair gray, their knees frail but they will never succeed in breaking the curse our Sun God had put to their priestess and her reincarnations. As long as the warrior is safe, the Harayans shall continue to walk this earth!"

"Let us celebrate this victory!" screamed one man as he laid his arm on Alejandro's shoulder.

These people were filled with immense joy, though he barely grasped what they were talking about.

"Do you see those three rings in the sky?" continued *Apo* Dula. "Those are the gods who punished the enemies. With their power, they sank an island to the deepest part of the ocean. With their power, the Harayans emerged. On the day they align, and the enemy's reincarnated priestess has not reversed her mistake, we shall survive another cataclysm. No bloodshed. The rings will disappear for a long time and will only reappear when new *Muling Buhays* are born."

"*Apo* Dula, it's time for you to go to bed," spoke Maduri.

"But our guest…"

"I will take care of our guest. Besides, he must not get drunk for he has a wife waiting for him, and they are bound for a long journey tomorrow."

"Okay, then." *Apo* Dula fell on the ground and snoozed to sleep.

His men carried him to his cabin and the night eventually turned peaceful.

"He has turned like that after his daughter, Hiyas, died. *Apo* Dula never recovered," said Maduri.

"He still looks strong and able to battle."

"He does. He's a brave man, Alejandro."

"You know my name?"

"She isn't your wife," answered Maduri in a cold and dry voice.

The blaze of the fire intensified.

His forehead wrinkled with wonder.

"I read minds as I could see through time. She doesn't bear the seed of fertility yet."

Amazed with Maduri's skill, Alejandro leaned forward to hear more.

"Clarissa will bear my children?"

"It might happen."

He smiled. It was what he wanted to hear: a happy future with the woman he loved.

"I see you have a lonely childhood too."

The smile on his face waned.

"You have no family except her."

"The del Fierros have been so kind to me. They took me in like their own."

"Yet you chose to take away from them their precious gem."

He gulped. "I love Clarissa."

"Do you think it's the right thing to do?"

"No." He knew it was wrong in all aspects.

"Destiny is against you," she went on.

"I know, but I'll regret it if I don't do this. I love her very much," said he. "I'll take all the punishment just to be with her. I feel that our souls are bound together, our hearts knotted and that if one goes missing, the other one will die. It's like I had loved her the moment I've seen her or the moment I was born. It's like I already loved her even before I started breathing."

"Does she…"

"I know she does," he assured.

"Ask her again tomorrow."

"Why?"

"You have to be sure before you take the risk."

CHAPTER 25
Into the Cell

Maduri put down her quill and folded her letter into half. Her lamp flickered. Her fingers were dirtied with ink as she wrote with trembling hands.

"Take this, boy, to Doray. She's expecting that," said she to the young messenger.

The young lad flew to the west of the forest toward danger.

Maduri reached for her shawl and wrapped it around her shoulders. It was cold daybreak when the moon still reigned. She strolled out of her cabin carrying an elongated heavy object wrapped in thick scarlet cloth and organic rope. Her footsteps were measured. She didn't want to wake the entire village.

She made three quick and careful knocks against the young lovers' door.

"Are you ready?" she questioned Alejandro as she got through the opening.

"Yes, as what you told me last night," he replied.

"Did you ask her again?"

Clarissa went out of the room, carrying a knapsack with few clothes and warm blankets.

She answered the *babaylan's* question, "Alejandro did, and I gave him the same answer, Maduri."

"Well, you seem certain, young lady."

"I am." She reached for his hand and held it tightly like she didn't want to let go.

"Then you must leave before the entire village wakes up. The town will be dangerous for the two of you. The civil guards are everywhere. So it's better that you leave without anyone seeing you," said Maduri.

"I need to see my parents first."

"They can stop you. Don't you know that?"

"I know, but my father will let me go for my happiness." Clarissa sounded so confident.

"Very well." Maduri sighed. "Your maid is already awake. She can help you get into the mansion and to your father's room. You have to hurry. Your father will soon rise up to leave town and look for you in the neighboring provinces."

"You see all that happening?" Alejandro curiously inquired with awe. It seemed to him that what Maduri was saying was happening in real life.

"Yes. I have the Sight. But, of course, they change. They might not happen after all. Nothing is constant," replied Maduri as she handed over the heavy object wrapped in red to Alejandro. "Take this with you."

"What is this?"

He studied the strange thing, laid it on the table, and carefully opened the wrapping.

"A sword?" Clarissa wondered. "Why do we need a sword?"

It had delicate carvings on the silver blade, and the handle was made from light metal. Alejandro tried to decipher what the carvings or strange letters in the blade were but he couldn't.

"You will need it for protection," responded Maduri. "Take it away from this country. Take it back home."

"I do not know what you mean, Maduri." His eyes were fixed on the strange sword.

"I am simply telling you to go as far as you could. Some place where people do not know you, away from everyone here. Go to the land of the rising sun, to the island of Honshu. Stay in the temple and return that sword to the sacred box, and the danger surrounding you will go away."

"Honshu?" Clarissa, who was worried, turned to Alejandro. "We'll need a boat to get there."

"I have a friend in the north who owns a boat. He'll let us use it," said Alejandro. "Honshu sounds a safe place for us. But, Maduri, why do we need to return this thing there? Why does it have to be us?"

"Please do me this favor. That sword has long been here. It doesn't belong here. It doesn't belong to anyone from us here. Only you can take it back to Honshu. Its people are waiting for it. For centuries, they waited for it."

"Okay," uttered Alejandro.

"We'll leave now, Maduri," spoke Clarissa. "Thank you for letting us stay."

Maduri timidly smiled.

Alejandro took the sword and tied it around his waist. He brought out the knapsack and left for the barn to take the horse.

"Clarissa, please protect him with your life," Maduri said to her once they were alone. "Do not let anything or anyone harm him."

A sudden fear stroke Clarissa.

"Will something happen to Alejandro, Maduri?"

"Yes. Something bad awaits him. Hence you should protect him."

"Is it going to be my parents or the civil guards?"

Maduri pulled her a little farther from the barn so that Alejandro wouldn't hear what she had to tell Clarissa.

"He's going to be in a lot of danger because of you," said Maduri as she held both Clarissa's cold hands. She wanted her sole attention for what she was going to say was a warning that must be taken seriously. "He could die in your hands."

"I'm not going to let that happen," Clarissa hissed as she watched Alejandro prepare the horse and the saddle, and stored water in a bamboo container. She knew the danger that might befall upon him. The law was against Alejandro, yet he risked himself just to be with her. There was no turning back.

"If you want to be with him forever and have his children, you mustn't come back here. Keep him in Honshu."

"I will, Maduri."

The horse neighed and approached the two ladies. Alejandro took Clarissa's hand and heaved her up to the horse's back. Clarissa wrapped her arms around his waist.

"Hurry now! Your maid is waiting for you," said Maduri.

Alejandro and Clarissa charged away from the village back to town.

Maduri went back to her cottage, took out a ceremonial dress from her chest, and wore it. She saved this dress for the most important day of her life, and she only wore it once: during her transition ceremony. She didn't think she would wear it again. But this time, there would be no sacrilegious rituals or ceremonies for new priestesses or baptismal of newborns. She was going to wear it to hear her verdict.

A few years ago, she committed a crime against the tribe: a lie against their tribe leader, a lie that worsened the feud between two warring tribes, and a lie she made with the enemy for the fulfillment of the prophecy.

She looked at herself in the mirror. She had aged. For many years, she kept that secret, but today was the time to let her people know her sin. There was no better thing to do but to admit it to everyone after the rooster crowed three times. She had always been ready for this day.

Despite her offenses, Maduri was able to fulfill her task to protect who must be protected. For the last time, before she faced the Sun God and be punished by him eternally, she had done something good. The God of Conquest was in safe hands. It had found its guardian.

*   *   *

Clarissa carefully entered through the back door of the mansion. Alejandro was waiting for her at the forest at the back of the house. People were still sleeping. She crossed her fingers that Ayang hadn't gotten off the bed yet or she will be busted.

"Heavens!" Maying went ashen pale as she saw Clarissa in the kitchen. She loosened her grasp on her glass, and it fell to the ground and broke. "Señorita?"

"Sshh, Maying!"

"Jesus, you're alive!" Maying clearly didn't know if she were to laugh or cry.

"Oh, Maying!" She hurriedly gave her maid a warm embrace.

Clarissa was all the more amazed with Maduri's powers. Maying seemed to have just wakened up from bed and seemed clueless of what was happening.

"Where have you been?" Maying asked in a controlled voice. She kept her eyes alert. "We are so worried about you. Your father…"

"Where's Papa? Is Mama okay?"

"Oh, señorita! Doña Guada is furious. She's so depressed and she wouldn't even come out of her room. Her sister couldn't do anything but force her to eat, or she'd grow weak. And your father is angry."

"I have to talk to them."

"Where's Alejandro?" asked Maying.

"Are they after him now?"

"A farmer boy pledged to be a witness. He saw Alejandro taking you away, and he told the authorities about it." Anxiety was marked all over the poor maid's voice. "He has a price on his head."

"What?"

"The civil guards are after him, and your father paid a lump sum of money to capture your kidnapper."

Horrified, Clarissa stormed out of the kitchen to the back of the house where she assumed Alejandro was waiting. She didn't find him there. No horse, no knapsack, no anything.

"Señorita?" Maying ran behind her. "Señorita?"

Tears formed at the edge of her eyes.

"He left me…" Her voice quavered. She looked around, checked everywhere until she fell dizzy seeing only trees, green, and the wilderness.

"Who?"

"Alejandro…" She fell down to her knees. "He promised to take me away, but he left me here."

Maying embraced her and tried to calm her down. Although she didn't know the story behind her mistress's disappearance, just by looking at her in despair, she came into a conclusion that people were wrong about the abduction incident.

"Clarissa?" Her mother came running, followed by her aunt and her father.

The entire house had just awakened.

"Oh, Jesus! You are safe!" Tears of joy fell down her cheeks. She kissed her daughter.

Don Jaime took her into his arms and said, "We have been looking for you."

Tiya Consuelo cried in the background.

"How dare he do this to our family!" her aunt exclaimed angrily.

"Jaime, you must inform the gobernadorcillo about this," spoke her mother as she held her daughter in her arms. "The bastard must have not left town yet."

261

Clarissa was in too much pain to defend her captor. She just cried and cried.

Why would he leave her? Didn't he just say he loved her? Didn't they promise each other to be together forever?

Or did Alejandro lie to her?

*   *   *

The young messenger brought the letter to Doray's cabin. The priestess took it to her table and read it with a lighted candle.

> *The prophecy will no longer be fulfilled, Doray. There will be no bloodshed. The curse will stay. He will live as Cahaya promised and wanted to. Let the gods be angry again. It's time for Cahaya and the warrior to be happy. Who are we to take their happiness away? Let them be this time.*

Doray's limbs trembled. She fell unto the ground, afraid and uncertain. Maduri just deviated from their plan, and she was endangering her life because of this.

Let them be this time…

But letting them would change everything.

History would have to be rewritten.

The future would be changed.

Ayang's plan would be futile. The world would be in grave danger as the curse remained.

PART 9

CHAPTER 26
Warning

Doring hurriedly went down the mountain. Her legs scuttled through the tall wild grass. The church bell rang six times, and it was heard through the entire mountain. Birds were disturbed from their nests as Doring passed by the row of trees that was bent by a strong gust of wind. Torrential downpour was looming. A storm that none of the people in town knew about was coming, and people were supposed to stay in their houses, but Doring went down the mountain with only her *salakot* to protect her from the rain.

The sky was angry. The gods were sending warnings just like how they used to do for centuries. The reason behind this unprecedented rain was not a question to Doring.

By the time she reached the town, she met with Ayang whose clothes were soaked.

Houses were shut. Windows reinforced with timber for protection from the gushing wind.

"I was going to your village," panted Ayang. "The weather is horrifying. The day of the alignment is fast approaching yet we remain struck with calamities. After the snowfall, here's the storm."

Doring led Ayang to a corrugated steel shade near a bakery.

"I know you'll tell me to hasten looking for the reincarnated warrior. I am doing everything I can, Doring."

"That's not a problem anymore, Ayang," said Doring while catching her breath.

"What do you mean?"

"I hurried down once I received the Sight from Doray. Maduri is dead."

"Maduri? The Harayan Priestess?"

"Yes. She turned herself to their tribe jury for the crime she did in the past. She conspired with Doray. They hid the reincarnated warrior from you and told the entire clan that the child was dead."

"And?"

"They are reunited now."

"What?!" Enraged, she stomped her foot on the ground. Her eyes darkened. Her forehead creased.

"They did it to protect the boy from you. They feared that you'd take the boy only to prepare him for his end. Now, Maduri died fulfilling her duty of guarding him while Doray failed to keep Cahaya away from him."

Ayang fell back to the wall. She remembered clearly how Doray promised to be transparent with every action she made. Now, she was just too surprised that her tribe priestess conspired with the enemy to protect a person whose life was on the lease.

"Maduri let them," added Doring. "Doray appeared in my Sight to warn me about a major catastrophe. History will be changed once they leave the country. It just means that the prophecy will fail. If ever he succeeds in planting his seed to her, today's reincarnated priestess will be extinguished, and our tribe will go extinct. Doray is afraid this will happen so she gave me the Sight."

"See what secrets can do!" murmured Ayang. "Have they left?"

"Not yet. The warrior flees, but he will come back to take her."

"What else do you see, Doray?"

266

She paused as though preventing herself from showing any sign of doubt on her face.

"I don't think she will do it. It's not that she can't. She just won't do it."

"Cahaya's heart is overpowering her again. This was the thing that endangered us all, and I won't let her ruin everything the second time around." Ayang's voice was as dark as gravel.

"If she fails?"

"We have the second *Muling Buhay* to do it before she fails. You must prepare her. Two reincarnations are enough to end the curse. I don't want to wait for another century for the third one.

"You haven't found today's warrior yet, have you?"

Ayang smirked. "I would like to think that I have found him. I just wish that he is the one."

"Who do you have in mind?"

"Tiago's grandson."

Doring kept mum. She witnessed how Xander saved his life from the venomous snake, which was a capability known to only the Harayan warrior.

"But it is always safer that the first reincarnation does it. Right, Ayang?" Her voice trembled.

"In this case, it is. It is always safer to have the first *Muling Buhay* break the curse," she answered. "If Doray's priestess does it, your dear child will be spared and so does Tiago's grandson if he indeed is the warrior. If Doray's priestess succeeds, the years of misery of our people will be erased from history. It will all be changed with comfort, wealth, and glory."

"Then, we have to make sure she won't fail."

"That's why I'm going there now. I have to change her mind."

Ayang walked into the rain as Doring watched her disappear right in front of her eyes. In seconds, Ayang could travel from one time to another. She earned this mystical power while she was little, and she harnessed it to avenge the death of her dear sister. She had been using this to cross from the modern world to the colonial times and vice versa.

*   *   *

Rina piled firewood in the corner of their house. Her father, Macaryo, was resting on the rattan chair in the living room while she watched the rain pour down her window and how the moon's light was defeated by the three rings in the sky.

"How long do you think those rings would stay there?" her father asked with his eyes closed.

"I don't know," she answered.

She had been dazed and displaced from reality since this afternoon when Xander kissed her. Strange, but it seemed that nature was joining her with the confusion in her head and throbbing heart. His lips left a ghost of guilt and pleasure on her. She caught herself touching her lips and feeling again the warmth and surprise he gave her.

"I wish the storm doesn't destroy the field. After the snowfall, the farm was battered. Farmers will have a hard time reconstructing the field and the water system," said he.

"Mr. Montejo plans to sell the mansion and the farm. I don't think you need to worry, father."

"Sell it, huh?" He scratched his forehead. "I didn't think he is that kind of man."

"You are wrong this time. He doesn't care about us." Still, she recalled the beast Xander was when he just pulled her close to him.

"Maybe I should talk to him. He might listen to me."

"You will just waste your time."

"Rina, dear." Macaryo positioned himself up on the chair. "Why do you think ill of him? Has he done something to you?"

Her cheeks burned with fire.

"No!" She tried not to sound defensive, but Macaryo's facial expression just suggested that he was surprised with her response.

There were loud brisk knocks on the door.

"Who could this be?" murmured Macaryo as he rose from his chair and approached the door.

"Good evening, Macaryo!" A drenched Doring surprised them all.

"Jesus, Doring! Did you walk from your village all the way here with that little hat of yours only?" Macaryo let the old woman in.

Rina hurriedly took a dry and thick piece of blanket from her room and gave it to the freezing woman.

"Are you out of your mind, Doring? Rina, make some tea."

"Yes, father."

She hurried to the kitchen and made fire. She poured green tea leaves into the kettle and reached for cups in the cupboard.

"Why have you come here, Doring?" Macaryo asked the *babaylan*. "Did Bong come with you?"

"No. I came alone," she answered as she shivered.

"You're frail, Doring. You might get sick after this daring move," said Macaryo. He sat on the wooden chair beside Doring.

"If it's my time, then so be it. We can't defy the will of our God, can we?" A warm smile marked her face.

"Here's your tea." Rina brought in a cup of tea to the living room. "Do you need more blankets, Doring?"

"No, thank you. I am fine now," she replied after she sipped her tea. "Rina, might I have a piece of your time?"

Macaryo gathered his legs up. "I'll leave you, two ladies. If you need me, just wake me up." He walked to his room.

"Is there something you need to tell me?" Rina's curiosity rose.

Doring rarely did such precarious acts, and walking alone through the storm was shocking for a frail old woman to do.

269

"What do you think about Xander Montejo?"

"Why are you asking me that?"

"I just want to know."

"It's not something you should be wary of."

Doring grabbed her hands and fixed her glare to Rina's.

"Something is bothering your mind right now."

She was reading her, and Rina began to fear that Doring would know the state of her mind.

"Is he slowly changing your mind?"

Rina had never felt so suffocated. She felt her heart racing and her lungs expanding more than the capacity of her chest. She thought she was going to explode.

"He kissed me." Words just slipped out from her mouth when she started to feel the threat of Doring's magical ability. "And I didn't even object."

Doring took a deep breath. She looked like a ton of metal left her shoulders. She leaned back to her chair and replied, "And what now?"

"I don't know. I can't get him out of my mind," she stuttered. "I know that I should hate him for being selfish and for trying to sell the farm but…"

"You have fallen in love with him."

"I beg to differ!"

"Then what do you call that, Rina?"

She was silenced.

"Ayang had warned you about that. Her instructions are clear. Stay away from Xander Montejo."

Rina rose from her seat and anxiously paced around the living room.

"Doring, I just don't understand why Ayang has to feed me with her opinions. Yes, she is right. Xander Montejo is evidently an arrogant, selfish man, and he cares little about his tenants. You are right when you told me that I am letting her dictate my judgment, but it's only because I respect her and I look up to her. She's taken good care of me after my mother died, and she always seems right."

"What do you think now?"

"I... don't think she's always right."

A tinge of doubt raised the old woman's curiosity.

"The truth is," Rina took a deep breath, "I don't see him as a monster like Ayang does. Selling the farm is the only valid reason to hate him yet I don't think it is enough to personally loathe the man to the extent of disregarding the good in him. I was wrong to judge him right away and be swayed by others' opinions. I should have been more confident with myself in dealing with him and not let anyone tamper my judgment. Do you have any idea why Ayang does not like Xander?"

Doring cleared her throat. She had been thinking about telling Rina everything. She couldn't always keep the girl in the dark. Her duty was to keep Cahaya's reincarnation, in this case and time, Rina, safe and protected. Hence, she had every obligation to warn her and tell her all the facts. But how will she start? Ayang had successfully gotten inside Rina's head by keeping her out from the truth. Her only concern now was how to make the truth real and true to Rina.

"I shall tell you everything, Rina, tomorrow. Come to my place and bring the book you borrowed from Tomas' bookshop."

"What about the book?"

"I know you're wondering why Ayang told you to read it, but tomorrow you shall know why and how it is important."

"I have not finished reading it."

"Then tomorrow, you shall come to my house, and I'll tell you everything that you need to know."

The torrential rain subsided.

Doring quickly finished off her tea and insisted on walking back to the mountain despite Rina's offer of a warm room for the priestess.

271

Macaryo came out of his room and suggested, "I can drive you home, Doring, if you don't want to stay here. Although, I'd rather want to evade danger on the roads."

"Thank you, Macaryo, but I can't leave my village. The storm just passed but it doesn't mean it's not coming back. I must be there when another typhoon comes."

"There will be another calamity?" Macaryo took his woven hat out from the cabinet.

"Yes, and it will be stronger. I fear it's not just going to be only a typhoon."

"What is it, Doring?" Rina couldn't keep her interest unnoticeable. If Ayang was able to foresee the snowfall, then it was not impossible that Doring could. She had all the means to tell the truth. Rina feared that it would be a major catastrophic event and that she must warn the people.

"It's still vague, Rina," answered Doring as she supported herself with her staff. "Thank you for the concern, Macaryo. And yes, I'll be more grateful to you if you take me home."

CHAPTER 27
The Sight

Ashes. Fire. Chaos.

People were screaming and running while the earth shook. Children getting separated from their mothers and getting stuck between rubbles and stomped by adults. Rina couldn't do anything. She was there in the middle of the street, her legs numbed, and horror overpowered her. Her eyes fixed on the fear clearly shown on everyone's faces while a vicious army of dark clouds ravaged the place in the background, and the volcano from the neighboring municipality discharged balls of fire everywhere.

None could survive this nightmare. Fallen debris from stone houses and lamp posts injured just about anyone in the streets who tried to flee. Thick smoke made seeing almost impossible and breathing a problem.

Was this the apocalypse?

She turned back, and she saw a strong tornado coming. Anything that came close to it was just thrown around, violently flying and hitting anything. The clouds darkened as fire and cold met. The torrential gush of wind was driving her to fall. Thunderstorms suddenly appeared.

The sky brightened as it roared like a lion.

Her eyes opened. She was back to the less painful world.

Big drops of sweat fell down her forehead to her pillow. Her breathing was deep and quick. Her lungs expanded as the ghost of the horrifying nightmare slowly left her consciousness.

It was just a dream, a big bad dream.

She relaxed a bit after seeing through her window the calmness of the sky with the three rings and the moon glowing. It appeared like no hammering storm or rain once wrecked its tranquility. What a relief to see and feel peace after that dreadful nightmare!

She climbed out of her bed and sauntered to the kitchen to take a glass of water.

Her father hadn't returned yet from the mountain. It hadn't been an hour when she last checked the time before she fell asleep. He was probably on his way home now.

The coldness of the water soothed her dry throat and calmed her nerves.

Crack!

Her fingers let loose of the glass, and it broke as it hit the ground. Rina suddenly trembled. The hair on her nape stood, and her skin felt cold. The muscles in her chest and abdomen tightened. Her heart raced again.

She saw something in her mind; not her eyes, but her mind.

Her hands searched for the chair to support her weakened legs. She sat and buried her face with her hands as she recalled what appeared in her thought.

There was a body. She had no clue if it was dead or was still breathing, but it was lying on the grounds of the forest, soaked with rainwater, and sullied with mud. Thick shrubs and wild plants kept it hidden from anyone, but she saw it.

Unconsciously, she rose from her seat and went to her room to take her raincoat and umbrella out. She had no idea why her legs were moving separately from the dictate of rationality. The forest grounds were slippery and dangerous, but there she was, taking risks. It was unexplainable. It was like the forest was calling her to rescue the body, and she knew that she wouldn't be able to close her eyes if she didn't secure the body out of danger.

Alone and with only a little torch as her company, she bravely trekked the forest. Their town was shrouded with rich forests, and one must pass through dense woodland to get into their house. Strangely, her feet and legs seemed to have its own mind. They knew where to go and what was left for her to do was to alert her eyes and ears.

She paused when she saw a black horse blocking the way. It wasn't dead, but it was injured. Its leg was broken, and it couldn't move. Then, a weak shriek of pain directed her to a large sturdy tree in her left, just a few feet from the fallen horse. There were thick bushes that surrounded it, which was the exact image that appeared in her head.

The cry or groan intensified as she got closer to the tree. She pointed forward her torch, watching for any movement in the bushes.

"Help..."

Rina quickly scraped the bushes with her hands and saw a man lying on his back, his forehead bleeding and arms and legs caught by weeds and twigs.

She moved closer to catch a clearer glimpse of the unfortunate stranger and was ultimately shocked to see who it was.

"Xander?" Her heart skipped a beat.

"Help..."

Her anxiety rose. What happened to him? Why was he in the forest? What craziness had gotten into him to ride a horse on a stormy night?

"Are you okay?" She hurriedly cleared him off the wild plants.

"Rina?" A gentle grin marked his face. He seemed surprised and pleased to see her.

"You're crazy! Your back, is it okay?" She could hear her voice cracking. "Where are you hurt?"

"My head. I..."

"Can you walk?" She pulled him up after assessing that Xander could move his legs and hands.

"I don't know..."

Rina placed her arm around his waist, while Xander moved his hand around her shoulder. He tried to exert all his strength when standing up and turned a little conscious when he felt Rina bearing all his weight.

"It's a surprise that you're helping me."

"You know what? I have the choice to leave you, but I won't because I have the heart for the needy." She emphasized the last word so that he wouldn't misinterpret the aid she was giving. She too was quite surprised she was helping him. After what just happened to them in the mansion, she thought she had lost her face to see him again. But it seemed that her nature to help people overpowered her this time. She was left with no choice, but be her humanitarian self.

"I know for a fact that you hate me."

"It isn't tormenting me."

How could she leave an injured man alone in the forest? It was not like she had a heart of stone.

"I'm sorry. I have become a burden to you." It was evident on his face that he was enduring the pain in his body.

"Are you sure you can walk?" Rina already welcomed the thought of spending the entire night in the forest and just wait for help to come.

"Not more than a mile, I guess."

Slowly, she guided his steps through the slippery and muddy forest ground, gripping tightly unto him so that he wouldn't slide down the slope again and add injury to his already battered body.

"My house is half a mile away," she said. "You can stay there until you're better. I mean until you can manage to walk."

What was she thinking? She could have said that her father could drive him to his mansion with his cart and horse. She tried to hide the flush on her cheeks.

"Thank you," he responded. "Your kindness is appreciated."

Rina thought Xander shouldn't be too formal. He was kind of different tonight. Had the concussion on his head pushed the politeness and gentleness out of the beastly surface?

"Well, if you didn't come out in the storm, this wouldn't have happened," she stated matter-of-factly.

"I didn't know the rain would turn out so bad. What are we going to do with my horse?"

"My father will absolutely take the horse when he comes across it while traveling back home."

"Macaryo is as stubborn as me. He deserves your scolding, too."

"My father went out after the storm to drive a friend home while you did not."

"Well, it turned out that luck was not on my side." He managed to smile.

"You find this amusing when you nearly died!"

"I didn't. I tell you, I once evaded death, and this accident could not even measure up to what I had so many years ago."

"And you're proud of that?"

They were slowly reaching the way out of the forest.

"Is that where you live?" asked Xander.

It stood in the middle of a field. It was small and made up of cement and wood just like the houses in town. Light emanated from the inside.

"Yes. It's small, so you'll sleep in the living room. We don't have fine soft couches there but an uncomfortable wooden couch made from timber. So I'm warning you already of one long sleepless night."

Little did she knew, she was already laughing about his sour expression when she told him about the wooden couch.

"But you can have as many blankets as you want." She laughed.

"At least, you've got electricity here."

They reached the threshold and Xander propped his arm to the post to free Rina from his weight.

"Sorry about this," he whispered when Rina almost lost her balance and fell unto him.

Their gazes froze on each other, and both of them noticed the awkwardness that quickly rose between them. Rina immediately pulled back, took out a key from her pocket, and opened the door.

"Er, come in." She easily shrugged off the uneasiness, put the key back to her pocket, and assisted Xander to the couch.

Blood tainted the floor as he walked his way across the room.

"I'll get something for that." She pointed out the wound and scratches he got on his forehead.

While he waited for her, Xander surveyed the living room. It was a humble place with a few pieces of furniture. It was good that Rina had a TV and an electric fan. They brought delight to his eyes. He never thought this was how it felt to miss technology so badly. The fluorescent lamp at the ceiling made the four corners of the room so bright that it hurt his eyes.

"We're not completely primeval," spoke Rina as she went out of her room just a few walks from the living room. She had noticed awe on Xander's face and thought how the latter must have missed city life.

"I thought so, too," he responded as he eyed the first aid kit in Rina's hands. "I regret misjudging things here. It's pretty different in the mansion."

"I know." She sat beside him, opened the lid of the first-aid kit, and hesitated what to do first. She shyly uttered, "Um, I'm going to…" She wanted to look closely to see how bad the wound was on his forehead but it seemed that she was overwhelmed by intimidation.

"Is it that bad?"

"No." The wound was actually not that deep, but it was bleeding. "Do you feel dizzy or any pain on your head?" She quickly pulled out a clean gauze from the kit and dropped antiseptic solution on it.

"Not anymore now."

"Okay, tell me if it hurts. This will sting a little," she said before she gently patted the gauze against the wound.

He flinched when the gauze touched his flesh. Rina, then, placed another gauze on top of the first and gently dabbed it on his skin three times.

"Thanks," said he.

"Your legs?"

"They're okay. They will be fine tomorrow." He honestly thought he felt like he was bruised after a one-on-one taekwondo match.

"Okay."

They drifted into a long dreary silence; Rina gauging the right time to leave him and say that it was time for bed and Xander wanting to start a conversation. The silence made her recall the earlier incident. Knowing the man who owned her first kiss was just one reach away from her, threatened her defenses. She feared that she might exactly do what she did before and be swayed easily by his manliness and control. As the silence started to be a little unbearable, Rina thought of just saying a brief good night and take out a blanket and pillow for him when Xander broke the walls of silence.

"How did you find me?"

It was the question she too could not answer. She didn't really know how it happened and how it was possible, but she didn't think it was appropriate to tell him that she saw in her mind the danger he was in, and that was why she flew to the forest. For her, it was quite perplexing, too.

So she lied, "I was looking for some tree roots for my herb collection."

"Out in the rain?"

"Some roots are effective when soaked in earth and rainwater."

"So it was a coincidence?"

She nodded.

"You? What were you doing in the forest?" she asked.

"You want the truth?" His voice sounded serious, and Rina began to think that the conversation was not gearing into a good one.

"Well, I think you can keep the answer to yourself," she answered in a snap, uptight and nervous. "You look tired. I can…"

"Rina." He caught her arm before she could get up from the chair and leave him behind. "I wanted to see you. I felt the need to explain myself."

He added, still grasping her arm. Rina fell into speechlessness.

"What happened earlier today was…" He looked altered. "It was a mistake, and I apologize for it. I acted upon impulse. I should have respected you. I feel that I have violated you. Don't trouble yourself about it. It was nothing."

"Nothing?" she whispered to herself.

"It meant nothing. I was angry, tired, and disappointed. I just got saved from a snake bite. A lot was going on in my mind that time."

The situation that he wanted her to understand sank into her immediately.

"I just wish you don't hate me more because of it," he added.

"No. I clearly understand you." But why did it feel heavy inside her like there was a thorn in her chest, her throat was blocked, and her voice cracked in rebellion to be heard? "I, too, was surprised. Perhaps I was too shocked to even say no."

"So, we're okay?"

"About the kiss?" She bobbed her head stiffly. "You went all the way here to say it meant nothing?"

He nodded hesitatingly, "Er. Yes! Is not that what you wanted to hear? Can we be friends now?"

"I don't know…" Rina stood up.

"What do you mean you don't know?"

Unexplainable fury rose.

"I accept your apology, but I can't be your friend."

"Jesus, Rina! I didn't think you're…"

"Xander, the kiss I can ignore. We both admit that it was a plain mistake. But I just can't be friends with… you."

"Let me guess. Is it because I am selling the farm?"

"Yes!" Her hands on her hips, her face fuming, her reason to be mad remained questionable, at least to her.

"Rina, that was the plan even before I came here. It's not like I'd live here forever. I have a life. I do not belong here!"

"Well, maybe you should consider the lives of the poor farmers who will definitely lose their jobs!"

"They can still work in the farm under the proprietorship of whoever buys it!"

"You are so unfeeling!"

"Now you're angry with me just because I do not want to listen to you! Well, you should accept that not everything in this world agrees with you!"

"I can't believe I'm having this conversation with you. I should have known better!" she said angrily.

"I'm sorry that I turned out to be a disappointment. But you disappoint me too. I came here to make friends. I risked my life out there thinking that you, of all people, will understand!"

"Now you're blaming me!"

"All I ask from you is friendship! How can that be so hard to give?"

"How shallow are you, Xander?" she mumbled.

To think that she was very much willing to form a new opinion of him, something more pleasant, and let go of her prejudice against him, yet here he was wrecking it with his acclaimed ego. Ayang was right all along! She had always been right!

"If you only learn how to consider the little people, then I might have given you the consideration you're asking!"

The sound of Macaryo's cart entering the front yard put a halt on the growing disagreement.

"Your father's here," he said calmly now.

Rina took a deep breath and composed herself. Fury did not just subside in three seconds, so she tried her best to look unaffected. She rolled her eyes at him before she opened the door.

Macaryo came in with his raincoat drenched. Rina took it from her father and hanged it to the metal wiring by the window.

"*Señorito?*" He quickly approached Xander for a handshake after recognizing the latter's surprising presence. "What happened to you?"

"I was in a road accident."

Rina left the two and entered the room on the right side of the house.

"You own the horse?"

"Yes."

"It's badly hurt, but I took the liberty of bringing it here without knowing it's yours," answered the old man.

"Thank you, Macaryo."

"How did you get here?"

"Your daughter found me," he said with his grave glare not leaving the pissed off Rina who was now leaving the room, carrying a pillow and a blanket on her arms.

"The young man can have my room," Macaryo uttered with deliberate genuineness.

"Oh, no, thank you! But I don't want to impose," answered Xander rather spicily, looking at Rina.

"But you might find it difficult to sleep…"

"I'll be fine, Macaryo."

She gave the same excuse when Macaryo asked her what she was doing in the forest so late at night.

"So, you stay here for the night. It's too late for us to be traveling," said Macaryo to Xander.

"Don't forget to change into dry clothes, Father," said Rina. She was obviously avoiding his glares.

"Good night, *señorito!*" Macaryo smiled at him.

"I'll never forget this hospitality," he muttered as he watched her disappear from his sight as she went inside her room.

CHAPTER 28
Reincarnates

"Where is she going?" Xander asked Macaryo while he watched Rina load the cart with baskets of corns and other crops. It amazed him how she carried those big heavy baskets all by herself, and she didn't even ask help from the male farmers around her.

Macaryo replied, "She's going to the mountain to meet with Doring. I presume you already know who that woman is."

"Yes, I do."

"Doring paid us a visit last night too. She told Rina to come by at her house today."

"What are the supplies for?" He was thinking about an upcoming disaster, which Rina and her friends only knew about.

"We're taking them to town to be stored in the church. It's better to be prepared than be sorry," answered the old man.

Xander's injured horse was still incapacitated. A local veterinarian already came by earlier to check on it and said that it required rest to regain its strength.

"How did you know about the snowstorm?" Xander still wondered about how Macaryo and Rina saved town last time. What awaited everyone in town this time?

"I didn't. I just suspected that something bad was about to happen because Ayang and Rina had been talking secretly. After that, I saw Doring and Rina storing food behind my back. I knew then that something was up.

"Strange women, eh? Ayang is known for that ability; she and Doring. Last night, Doring tipped us that a super typhoon is set to arrive this week. Scary really but I'd rather believe her than die for not listening to her warning." Then Macaryo's tone hushed as though conveying a secret. "The mystical lineage of Doring and Ayang is a known secret to all. They both came from the same tribe. My wife too has a tinge of the Dihinarian blood. Her father was a native."

"Does that make Rina a Dihinarian, too?"

Macaryo nodded. "Sometimes I would think she's more of a Dihinarian than her mother. Rina sees things that normal people don't. Well, I'm telling you this so that you won't be surprised one day when she tells you what you will become ten years from now. What's strange too is she doesn't even recognize this. She thinks they're just dreams. It's good that these things have waned as she grew older. I can't imagine her being a younger version of Ayang." A tone of irony matched his concern.

Xander continued to watch Rina load the cart and began to think about the mystery that enveloped her. He soon connected the puzzle that linked Rina to Ayang and Doring. Perhaps this Dihinarian connection fortified their bond, without disregarding this extraordinary skill the three shared.

"She's leaving now," said Macaryo.

Rina drove the cart exceptionally. She seemed like she was trained to control the horse for years.

"We leave now too. I drive automated vehicles, you know."

Macaryo revealed a green Jeep CJ that was covered with white tarpaulin with a shampoo advertisement.

"Isn't she lovely? Got this for half the price." He sounded so proud. "It has always been kept here. The last time I used this was, I think, seven months ago when I took Rina to the capital for her birthday."

"This is absolutely beautiful, Macaryo!"

"Classic!"

"You should drive this more often."

"I'd love to if we only have a petrol station in town. Having vehicles is more than a want than a necessity here. We have to travel miles to the city just to fill our tanks."

"Does your tank have enough?"

"Don't worry. She's full." Laughed Macaryo. "Get in now!"

*   *   *

People marveled at the sight of Macaryo's jeep. They looked like it was their first time to see such an invention.

"It's rare for you to see cars in here. We have become a major attraction," kidded Macaryo as he drove along the busy streets of the town.

Driving through the forest was a lot easier with the jeep than a horse. Unusually, there was no hint of the storm last night except for the quagmires on the uncemented roads.

"So, tell me. How exactly does Rina execute this mystical skill?" He couldn't get his head straight after Macaryo told him about it.

Without hesitation, the old man disclosed, "Since she was a kid, she has been exhibiting a seer's skill. She would come to me and tell me about upcoming events or incidents like the death of a neighbor, a birth of a child, even problems in the field, and misfortunes of others. Sometimes she'd wake up at night and talk about nonsense like how the sun and moon try to eclipse each other. How the sky turns into the color of blood, and voices she hears. For a moment, I grew scared for her. Normal girls don't see and hear things. Then, I realized that it was probably normal for kids with Dihinarian lineage. My wife said it once happened to her when she was a kid, then it all disappeared when she turned into an adult. Fortunately, Rina subdued these things as she stopped acting strangely already. Perhaps, it's part of growing up."

Apparently, Ayang and Doring already knew about Rina's special skills, he thought. *Cause if not, they probably wouldn't spend much time with her.*

They reached the mansion and Atty. Tan was still there as the storm stopped him from leaving last night. *Manang* Leticia was distraught to see the bandage on Xander's head that she thought the latter was still in pain. For caring gestures, she hurriedly went to the kitchen to cook rice porridge.

Macaryo left once Xander was all settled. He told him that the farmers were waiting for him in the field to prepare for the typhoon and they had to harvest the remaining crops that survived the snowfall and store them as early as now. Obviously, the *barrio's fiesta* would have to be canceled because of the uncanny weather changes. Xander suddenly felt bad for the group of active women volunteers who spent most of their time preparing for the occasion.

"I'll be returning to the city, sir," spoke Atty. Tan. "Is there anything you want me to bring for you when I return next week?"

"No, Attorney," he replied as he peered over the window from his room. Macaryo and his jeep were leaving his yard. "I want you to stop the bidding for the farm and the mansion."

"Pardon, sir?"

Xander paused for a while and pondered. Last night was supposed to be a night of reconciliation. He had it already when she accepted his apology for the unforeseen kiss. But things reversed, and Rina hated him again.

Women, really!

"I'm not going to sell my grandfather's properties anymore."

"Really, sir?" The lawyer was quite shocked.

"Yup."

Atty. Tan smiled.

"But, as you said, I still have to meet the terms of his will, right?"

"Yes, sir." Apparently, Atty. Tan couldn't keep the overflowing excitement.

The first and second terms were successfully met. He had learned to appreciate and love the humble ways of the *barrio* people, and second, he sacrificed the huge amount of money he could get from the bidders just to save the farmer tenants' jobs in the field. He suddenly felt how heroic his acts were, but of course, he must not boast of them for there was one person who always chose to neglect his benevolent deeds. He wouldn't want her to think ill of him all over again. Last night was enough! However, the third term was a little difficult to fulfill. Where would he find the missing painting and the white pearl?

"Why are you smiling?"

"I'm just too surprised with you, Mr. Montejo." This just meant that he was not going after Xander's demands and picky choices. What a relief! "It's a beautiful morning we have today! What made you change your mind, by the way?"

"Let's just say that my concussion was so severe that I'm starting to make weird decisions."

"You're funny, sir!"

It was weird seeing Atty. Tan loosen himself up a bit. It was the first time the man actually appeared not stiff or afraid of him. It was quite an improvement.

"Perhaps, this will change someone's opinion of me," said Xander.

*   *   *

Xander went inside his room to sleep after Atty. Tan left, but his exhaustion faded when he suddenly remembered his grandfather's diary, which he just left on his nightstand. He checked on it last night before he went out to see Rina. It felt like forever when they last wrote each other when in fact it was just days.

288

He last wrote, trying to be as poetic as he could. "Forgive me for my absence. I promise to make you feel my presence."

Instead of the response he was expecting, he read a rather different Clarissa.

> *Oh, how I wish you are with me, Xander. I just had a terrible experience. I have been crying all day. My parents are angry with me because of what I have done. I am afraid I broke my father's heart. He won't even speak to me. My mother has become stricter, and my aunt keeps on bickering with me, reminding me of my misfortune.*

> *How can a man be so insensitive and heartless? He promised me the stars, the sun, and the moon, but none of it did he fulfill. It feels great to fall in love and to know that you are loved. But it is more painful when the person you love chooses to hurt you. I don't know why he left me like that. What's troubling me is I feel that he will never show up again.*

> *Soon my mother will take me out of the country. She expressed her utter abhorrence with me by ruling my life. She wanted me to immediately marry her friend's son whom I don't even know. I don't know what to do. I wish there was someone who can help me get out from here. My house stopped becoming a home for me. It has become my cage.*

> *Guards are everywhere, and I couldn't even leave without my mother or aunt or my maid trailing behind me. I am literally shattered now. I cannot think wisely. People around me are pushing me to hate Alejandro. Even Ayang tells me that he doesn't deserve me and that I must loathe him all my life.*

Ayang? Her name rang a bell.

There must be a mistake in Clarissa's message. The Ayang she wrote there couldn't be the Ayang he knew.

Quickly he wrote.

Where are you now, Clarissa?

To his surprise, the response appeared in no time.

Oh, God! Thanks you're here! For a moment, I thought I was going insane waiting for words to appear on my parchment. I am in my room. Why?

I don't really know how I can help you. You see, we're in different worlds and time. We will never see each other. It's impossible.

I know. But you saw me. I heard you. I don't think it's impossible. I need you to save me from this hell.

Clarissa, you don't hate this man, do you?

I want to, but I can't. I wish I could.

He started pacing around. His head hurt with questions just waiting to be transcribed by his trembling fingers and be answered.

What do you want to happen?

Let's meet. I don't know how but I know it's possible. Please, take me with you.

This was just downright craziness! Meet? How? She was in the eighteenth century while he was two hundred years away from her. How would that happen?

I have never been so shocked by you!
Do you know that nobody has invented the time
machine yet?

He thought she sounded crazy, but he felt that Clarissa was in dire trouble. A clever woman like her would never think of crazy things unless she was in danger.

Remember the instances when we almost connected? You
saw me in the mirror! You heard my music! I heard your voice!
Perhaps this time, we'll actually see each other.

Xander reached for his chair and fell back there.

Okay. We're going to try.
Where do we meet and what time of the day?

Right now. Meet me by the riverbank. There's a big old tree
there, the tallest and the biggest. You'll find me there!

Right away?

Yes! I have packed my things already since last night. I've
been wanting to leave. My maid Maying is going to help me escape the
guards.

One more question, Clarissa.

He paused, and thought for a while if it was right to ask at this situation.

Who's the Ayang you're talking about?

The house caretaker. Why?

Is she old and weird?

Yes.

Does she belong to a tribe called Dihinari?

Yes!

"How was that possible?" he asked himself. Another proof of Ayang's mystery surfaced, and Xander feared that he had not enough time to look into it.

Just how could Ayang be in Clarissa's time and his time at the same time? Or could she travel from one dimension to another? Xander left for the riverbank with those questions in his head.

CHAPTER 29
Meeting at the Old Tree

Meet her? Just how?

Nevertheless, he still went there, hoping for some miracle to make it possible.

He looked for that huge old tree by the river bank and he found it so easily. It stood alone the slope that bordered the clearest water in the forest. He went there in the middle of the day, not certain about Clarissa's plan. But he was determined to help her. She sounded so desperate. He thought she was up to something really ridiculous.

His heart froze.

His legs quivered.

A girl was standing under the tree, which he only noticed when he walked closer.

"Clarissa?"

She turned to him. To his surprise, it wasn't Clarissa but a pale and anxious-looking Rina, her hair disheveled and her feet three inches soaked with mud.

"Rina." He almost dropped his jaw. "What are you doing here?"

Rina turned back from him and continued looking at the tree as though searching for something.

"Why are you here?"

She traced the carving that was on the bark of the tree with her fingers and uttered shakily, "I don't know why I am here. But I feel as though I should be here. That I am supposed to be here to see someone I do not even know. Something's pulling me. I can't figure out what it is. What's happening to me?"

Then, the shakiness in her voice suddenly worsened like she was possessed by blinding and dazing visions and her mind hurt with all the words to describe what she was seeing.

"She was here. She came and waited, and waited, and waited. She was crying, broken-hearted, and hopeless. She had nobody. She used a rock, the sharpest she could find, and carved these words, hoping that he would come." She fell to her knees and started digging with her hands the base of the tree. Her hands soiled, her heart racing, and her mind seeing hazy pictures. A mysterious voice was guiding her on what to do. It was telling her to look for something underneath to where she was standing.

"Rina." Concerned about her, Xander tried to stop her. "Maybe you should go home now." He remembered what Macaryo said about her, her strange mystical skills, and he was scared that he was witnessing it firsthand.

"It was here. She put it here to keep it safe in case he doesn't show up." She continued digging. Then, after a while, she found a parchment yellowed with time. She breathed out as her hands held the piece of paper.

Xander followed her every action.

"She was hiding this thing when…"

"When what, Rina?"

Rina slowly opened the paper and saw a sketch of a woman barely noticeable. However, Xander recognized it. It was his sketch of Clarissa, his sketch from his grandpa's diary. She tore it and hid it under this tree.

He looked up to the carving on the tree and read in a murmur, "The window through time." Then familiar long handwriting at the far right edge corner of the paper caught his attention. It was written there.

If you find this, then it means I am real. I am no ghost or figment of your imagination. It's just sad that we didn't meet or we couldn't. But I knew you came.

Clarissa
18th September 1812

"When," continued Rina. "When a man came. She screamed when she thought he was one of them. There were armed men in blue uniform running after her, but she lost them even before she arrived here. The man didn't hurt her. She cried when she recognized him. Fear and sorrow were replaced with bliss and assurance. He came back for her."

"Who?"

Rina turned to Xander, studied his face, and replied, "You."

"Me?"

"Yes. It was you. I can't be mistaken."

Then her brown irises sparkled like gold like how they did when he first met her in the church grounds.

"There you are, Rina!" A commanding voice caught both their attention. Doring slowly emerged from the thick trees with her wooden staff supporting her walking. "I have been looking for you."

Rina fell down the ground and lost her consciousness.

Xander shrugged when Doring spoke, "She's finally found herself. Don't worry. She'll wake up soon."

Xander picked her up and carried her in his arms.

"She was saying strange things." But deep inside him, he knew she could be right.

"It's her day of enlightenment. It's when the Muling Buhays get reconnected with each other. Rina has just found her other piece. In this case, she sees what she sees, hears what she hears, and feels what she feels. They have become one."

"Hold on! I don't think I understood what you just said."

Doring hissed. "Come with me. It's time for you to know everything."

*   *   *

Doring led Xander, who was carrying the unconscious Rina, to an uninhabited cabin just a few walks from the river. He laid her to a wooden bed as Doring cleared the furniture off dust.

"Sit here," she ordered leniently.

As they were face to face, she started.

"Rina ran off when I told her who she really is. I told her she is no ordinary girl."

"What is she exactly?" He found himself holding his breath.

"She's the second reincarnation of a Dihinarian priestess who's tasked to break the curse conferred by the Moon Goddess a long, long time ago."

"Second?"

"Yes. The first one was whom Rina just reconnected earlier on. I'm afraid she's on the run with the warrior and is bound to repeat the same mistake."

Xander's hands grew cold and trembled. He was holding his sketch of Clarissa.

"What is in there?" asked Doring as she noticed the parchment.

"Nothing." He quickly hid the paper to his pocket.

Doring narrowed her glare at him as though suspiciously reading the thoughts that were plaguing his already troubled head.

Her eyes widened with shock. "You know her!" Her voice was tensed and loud. "You know the other *Muling Buhay*!" she added.

He gulped.

"But how's that possible? How did you know Clarissa?"

"Clarissa is Rina?"

"Answer me! How did you know Clarissa?"

"No, I won't! I won't say anything unless you tell me everything I need to know!"

Visible veins surfaced on Doring's forehead and neck. She was apparently just controlling the sudden rise of shock.

Xander didn't want to say anything until he knew that this secret would be safe with the *babaylan*. He just couldn't find her a trustworthy person like Ayang. He just didn't think that freely telling anyone about his grandfather's diary was a safe choice.

Not yet.

Doring pulled back and relaxed.

"Alright, I'm going to tell you Cahaya's story and your relation to this matter. So listen carefully." She breathed in and out. "You see this book?" She showed him an ancient looking book whose paper was as fragile as the papyrus. "I made Rina read this. From this, she found out the truth. Cahaya, Clarissa, and Rina are one…"

PART 10

CHAPTER 30
Eclipse

"Look here, Cahaya!" A girl of eleven years was busy mixing wax, honey nectar, oil from her collection, and pearl powder in her cauldron. She sprinkled black ashes from Mt. Harimau and her mixture turned dark. "Soon I'm going to perfect my candles!"

"What will be the purpose of your candles, Ayang?" asked a lady whose hair was as black as her eyes, and her skin color, though, not as dark as ebony, was glowing. She was beautiful, probably the most beautiful on the island. Two girl servants were washing her feet with warm water and a fresh floral fragrance.

Ayang approached her sister and picked up a comb from her accessory box, which was filled with gold and jewelry. She started combing Cahaya's hair.

"It will enshrine my spirit when I die. Father said, if I please the Moon Goddess, she might make me the Guardian of Time."

"Was it really father who told you or Sari?"

Ayang smiled shyly. "Okay, you got me! Sari knows these things because she's the chief priestess and all Dihinarians believe her. I can't be her apprentice since I lost my Sight before I turned ten, so she told me I can help you fulfill your task as the next priestess."

"She really said that?"

"Yes. She also said that the Moon Goddess favors you among all the girls in the island because you get to keep her gift of Sight. What is it like being Sari's apprentice, Cahaya?"

Cahaya looked out from the window. Their house, walled by sturdy and polished timber, was the biggest in their village. She watched the moon glow. It was the Moon Goddess watching over them. The sea was calm and from her window she saw the waves dancing as the moon glowed.

"It isn't as easy as you think," she said as she recalled how difficult it was to control the Sight.

Dreadful visions in the middle of the night always disturbed her sleep. Seeing death, calamities, and misfortunes all the time broke her heart. She always felt guilty when she knew that she could do nothing for these suffering people. She was a mere spectator of their demise.

"I can't wait to be like you, Cahaya. Next year, on my twelfth birthday, Father will veil me. I'll be a *binukot* just like you!"

Cahaya just smiled. She remembered the day when her parents veiled her. She was too young, way younger than Ayang. She was four when she was isolated from everybody. Her only companions were the four walls of her room, her maid servants or *apids*, and her family. The public never got to see how she grew up. She bet that the people already forgot how she looked.

"So I won't have to leave the house without anybody accompanying me. People won't see my face, and they'd wonder if I grew up beautifully."

There are always disadvantages in the world, Cahaya thought.

The *apids* festooned her sleek long black hair with a chain of gold coins called *pundong*. She walked behind the divider and put on her *panubok*, a white ankle-length skirt and long sleeve blouse richly embellished with gold and tiny gems at the hem. She adorned her waist with a *wakus* or a band of coins. On her ankle was an anklet with carvings of her name written in their native alphabet, *alibata*.

"Here you go, Cahaya." Ayang handed over a beautiful white veil, and Cahaya placed it over her head so that her face was covered. "You're ready for the ceremony!" said Ayang with a cheerful smile.

As customary, the Dihinarians celebrated on the eve of the harvest day to thank their Moon Goddess for a bounty of blessings. Tonight, Ayang would dance in front of a thousand Dihinarians as she would offer a jar of wine and the blood of a newly killed beast under the full moon. She had painted her arms and legs with phrases of praises for the Moon Goddess.

"Good luck to you, Ayang." She kissed her sister's cheek before she entered the litter or palanquin, which was a box-like wheel-less vehicle with a fully carpeted interior and with poles, which male servants carried.

One *apid* went out of her room and called for the porters. They were signaled to come in when Cahaya was comfortably seated and protected from curious eyes by a sheer curtain. On the count of three, the porters pulled each pole up and settled them on their shoulders.

"You'll watch for me through your window, right, Cahaya?" asked Ayang.

"I will try my best to sneak a peek at you," she answered. Of course, she knew she wasn't allowed to take her head out from the litter's window.

"I'll keep father and the elders, especially Sari, entertained so that they won't see you!"

"Thank you, Ayang!"

The porters started moving out of the room.

*   *   *

Festive music from drums, gongs, guitars, and flutes filled the open air. People were dressed with shawls around their shoulders to protect them from the cold wind from the east sea.

Mt. Harimau, a perfectly cone-shaped volcano, was the tallest landform in the island surrounded by water. Mountain ranges surrounded half of the island, mostly in the north and west. The east was left open for the sea.

The porters carried Cahaya's litter to where her father, *Apo* Umar, and the elders sat. Cahaya lifted her curtain and waved her hand to her father. *Apo* Umar waved back and smiled. None of these people here had ever seen the face behind that veil. She was much like a princess. As a matter of fact, she was. She was *Apo* Umar's, the Dihinarian tribe leader, first born child. No man would actually dare to look at her. Every male in the island would close their eyes or even look down when her litter passed by. Looking at any *binukot* would be served a punishment of death.

The drummers pounded on their drums made from clay jars and stretched animal's skin on top of the opening in brisk motion. Ayang went out in an exotic woven dress made from vegetable dyed abaca fibers. She danced around the fire, lifted her arms, and swayed her hips as she followed the rhythm of the music. The fire was lit in the middle of the open space and an elder man came there to bring out the wine and pour it over the flame. The fire blazed and the people clapped their hands as they found it as a sign that the Moon Goddess was there in spirit and that she was ready to accept each household's offerings.

One by one, children poured a bowl of rice grain to the fire. Lactating mothers burned their newborns' first clothes. Infertile women gave three duck eggs, hunters their full moon game, farmers and fishermen their today's harvest and catch, and finally, *Apo* Umar, the blood of a freshly killed beast, a *carabao* this time.

During the last full moon, they offered a goat and the Moon Goddess wasn't pleased. The harvest was sparse.

Ayang continued to dance until the last drop of blood from *Apo* Umar's shell jar dripped.

Cahaya tried to peep through the window, but one elder was so close to her litter. She was afraid to be caught peeping and being reprimanded. Fortunately, there was a small opening at the head of the litter, and there she watched her sister dance.

She froze with complete fear when her Sight suddenly warned her. For a moment, everything went silent as she tried to concentrate on getting a clear view of the vision. It was impending trouble. She closed her eyes and forced her mind to the flash of short vision.

There was a ship. A large floating vessel geared to the south pacific by the eastern wind. It was loaded with men, spices, gold, armory, and even music and laughter. It was heading to their island. She searched the men's faces to look for the captain. She knew she'd immediately recognize who the captain of the ship was. Only if his face appeared in her Sight.

From the deck, where joyous sailors celebrated with wine and meat, she continued searching through the empty and dark hallways to the cabin. She tried to see what was inside each room. There were either sleeping sailors who fell into a deep sleep after intoxication or men counting gold coins or polishing their long swords and sharp arrows.

In one room, she saw a piece of white cloth with the figure of a red sun in the middle. It was hung on the wall and below it was a sword encased in an iron holder. The sword emanated a strange aura. Something that caused her heart to race. Her mind searched closer to the room. She viewed every corner and was struck when a muscular arm, a hand, rather, with visible veins and a few hairs appeared in her Sight, touching the sword's iron holder. Not much of the face was shown, but she was sure that she saw a controlled smirk.

Danger was coming.

The foreign ship was bringing this danger.

Then, her sight dimmed. The turmoil in her chest worsened, clamoring against the walls like wanting to be freed. A tiny flare like the fire in the ritual, except that it was not too big, appeared next in her Sight. It was slowly intensifying.

There were screams and Cahaya's eyes immediately opened.

She quickly went out of her litter and saw her people panicking. The full moon was gone. It was slowly being eclipsed by a fiery ball, which was something new to everyone's eyes. The disappearance of the moon on the night of worship was a mystery, but Cahaya felt that a force equal to or even stronger than Bulan, the Moon Goddess, was deliberately showing its power to them to be feared.

"*Ayu?*" The term the local people called their princess. An elder anxiously approached her and was ready to reprimand her for leaving her litter without a veil.

"Where's Sari?" Her eyes searched the chaotic crowd in the open space.

People were running back to their shelters, scared and in tears, holding their children tightly and securing their animals inside their tiny little houses. *Apo* Umar mobilized his guards to restore peace and order, and once the people calmed, he met with his council of elders in his house.

"What are you doing without your veil?" Sari, an aged woman with long white braided hair and plain white ankle-length dress similar to Cahaya's, appeared from behind. She looked anxious too as she got the hidden message from the sky.

"Bulan is warning us," whispered Cahaya.

Sari pulled her inside the door that was behind them.

"What else did Bulan let you see?"

"A ship. A huge ship! It's coming to our direction. The wind brought it here. I should tell Father this!"

"Calm down, Cahaya. I will tell your father about what you saw. He's meeting with the elders."

"Do you feel the force too, Sari?"

"Yes, but not as clear as you." Sari was getting older, and one of its disadvantages was slowly losing her powers. "How far are they?"

"I cannot gauge, but they might arrive before dawn."

Sari nodded.

"Do you know who they are, Sari?"

"They can't be foreign traders."

"Subjugators?"

"Can be but I hope not." Sari looked up into the sky and watched the huge ball of fire eat the moon. "It does look like it is mightier than us. It will give Bulan a hard time protecting us."

"Then we shall not let our guards down," Cahaya replied determinedly.

"We shall hurry your rite of passage. You need to receive Bulan's blessing for I can't protect the tribe for long."

"But that will be on a fortnight. The subjugators will reach land in no time."

Sari rubbed her wrinkled forehead.

"We can't hasten the turning over, can we?" she asked.

Sari sighed. "It is too risky."

*   *   *

A young servant boy, thin and poorly dressed, ran from the bridge of the ship to the largest cabin, gasping for air.

"Captain!" He pushed the door open. "We sighted an island a few miles south!"

"Is it the Spice Island?" the captain asked.

The captain was as young as he appeared to be with eyes shaped like almonds and colored similar to the midnight sky, his jaw chiseled, and his nose perfectly pointed. His hair was sleek black and quite long and tied at his back with few strands falling from his forehead.

He put his sword back on top of his desk and quickly put on his armor made from iron plates and connected by leather thongs.

"I cannot say it is, Captain. But it is where the tide is taking us."

As captain of the ship, he knew his men were just waiting for his decision. "We are going there." He followed the young servant boy out of his cabin to where his men were merrily celebrating the night with wine.

He paused when he saw the odd phenomenon up in the sky.

"What's that?" he asked the servant boy, who shook his head while watching the spectacle. "It's like the moon is being eaten by a beast," he murmured.

"Sorry, Captain." One of his crew accidentally bumped him, and his attention was diverted away from it.

He, then, made known to everyone his plan to explore the newly found land. From his ship, he could see the wide and rich mountain ranges, the thick forests that occupied most of the land, and the tall and commanding volcano at the center.

"Do you think it is inhabited?" he asked his right-hand man.

"Behind those forests could be a community, Captain," answered Usui, his right-hand man.

"We shall find that out," whispered Kazuma.

He was too eager to get into the island. He felt the bounty it could offer him. The Sun God was looking at them when they found this gem, and he would be most pleased if Kazuma took it over for the Sun God's name.

"How long will we get there?"

"Not for long, sir!"

Kazuma smirked.

CHAPTER 31
The Sword Landed

The ocean was ramming their ship to the shore. It was not too long ago when daylight broke. Kazuma and his men were raring to disembark, fully clothed in their finest armors. Few of his people tossed a huge chest to the coast. Kazuma, once he set foot, kissed the white powdery sand and praised the Sun God for a successful landing.

It was a sight to behold. The sea looked blue and clear. The shore glistened like gold dust. The forest, which was a few walks from the sea, was richly populated with diverse trees, plants, and maybe undomesticated animals too.

Kazuma ordered his men to penetrate into the heart of the island when, unexpectedly, strange looking people emerged from the thick bushes. They outnumbered Kazuma's men. Though comparatively short, they were lean and had a great physique. They were dressed in vests and short trousers. Their feet were bare and their heads were tied with a piece of cloth. On their chests, shoulders, and arms were paintings of undecipherable characters. They had their own weapons, sharp rocks attached to their long and light but strong sticks, aimed at Kazuma and his people.

Kazuma, surprised and awed at the show of force from the natives, ordered his men to be gentle, to bow their heads, and drop their swords. The natives watched their every move. Kazuma cautiously walked near the wooden chest and opened it.

Gold. Lots of gold and jewelry.

"I came here to give you these," he said.

One native, taller than the rest and who seemed to be the leader of the pack, came forward. His weapon was still aimed at Kazuma while he checked the gold. He spoke to his men in his language, which sounded funny to Kazuma and the others. Three natives walked forward and carried the chest of gold together.

"We're here to make friends," added Kazuma as he thought the natives were starting to lower their defenses. "We can give you more only if you don't harm us."

One native started talking.

"What do you think did he mean?" questioned one of Kazuma's man to the other in a guarded murmur.

"As you please," answered Kazuma although he didn't understand what the native said.

"What did he say?" one of his men asked alarmingly.

"Calm down. I don't think they're going to hurt us. Just let them do what they want to do. Observe and listen," instructed Kazuma.

The natives surrounded them, two guards in each of Kazuma's man, and tied their hands with ropes. The natives started walking, and they all followed.

They were led inside the forest where rich flora and fauna met. Kazuma kept on giving eye signals to his men as though telling them not to worry. Time went by so quickly and they did not mind. They were too busy appreciating nature's beauty. They could have sauntered through several valleys already. Despite thirst and exhausted legs, they kept going.

Behind the thick trees, along the cleared pathway were tiny houses made from sturdy woods and roofed with tied dried leaves. The sound of the flowing stream decreased the tension felt by Kazuma's troop as they realized that the place they were in was more than a paradise.

As they reached the native's village, they were welcomed by curious and threatened glares from the residents. They all stopped from their chores and watched the foreigners being dragged to the middle of the open space.

The native guarding Kazuma freed his hands and pushed him forward that he fell to the ground, his face almost hitting the dry soil. But he kept his cool. It would be the wrong time to let fury overpower him. They could get killed if he showed any sign of displeasure.

A middle-aged man, well-built and with a face aged by harsh weather conditions, approached him. His serious glare only focused on him. Kazuma assumed it was the tribe leader as he looked commanding, and everyone was silenced when he went out of his shelter.

He began to speak in his language. His voice was loud like an erupting volcano, and his nose flared every time his mouth opened to speak. He could look terrifyingly blood-curdling to the normal eyes of his crew, but for Kazuma, he did not fear anything or anyone.

"Forgive me and with all due respect, but there is no way for me to be able to respond to you correctly," answered Kazuma as politely as he could. "But let me tell you that we came here to make friends. Friends. Like brothers. No war." He realized soon that he was making hand gestures just to let them understand him.

The man's face creased.

His guard whispered something in his ear and showed the chest of gold.

Kazuma could only just wish that he pleased him.

"If you'd be so kind, my men and I would be so delighted if we could have a drop of water to quench our thirst," said he.

The priestess, Sari, who had been looking from his window, went out of her house and approached *Apo* Umar. She quickly surveyed Kazuma and whispered things to *Apo* Umar's ear.

Apo Umar then nodded and told his men to give water to his "guests."

Kazuma and his men, though clueless of what was going to happen, were unchained, and they followed the royal guards into a room just a few walks from the open space. The room was almost empty with only clay jars and baskets of crops and rice grain stored in it.

Sari went inside, eyed everyone else, then her gaze finally landed upon Kazuma. The hair on his arms rose when Sari, strange and uncanny to him, walked toward him.

"I can read your mind," said she.

Kazuma pulled back. He was utterly surprised when the native woman spoke to him in his language. How did she do it?

"I learned everything about you by just merely listening and watching you. It took me that short time to know who you are, where you come from, and what your intentions are." Although she was gentle-looking and small in stature, her voice sounded sinister.

"If I am right, you are the priestess," said he.

"You are not mistaken. It is not your first time to witness such mystical prowess."

In his hometown in the north, he lived in a temple, which was protected and guarded by a shrine priestess, who was chosen by their Sun God to look after a sacred object that encased a *kami* or a mortal who had become a deity after dying.

"I have always held a high regard for your kind. I think we're going to be great friends." He smirked.

His men stared at him, fearing for his life.

"Let us see."

"I am a very pleasing negotiator, priestess," he proudly said as he rose from his feet, placed his hands on his hips, and lifted his chin a little higher.

He was taller than Sari, so she had to look up to him.

"What is there to negotiate, warrior?"

"Excellent! You easily know my occupation."

312

"I could even see your past." Sari stepped backward, moved away from him, and started walking slowly around the room as she stressed the things her sight showed her. "Won battles for your emperor. Barbaric but triumphant. Well-liked and well-loved by the people because of cunningness and bravery. Strong. Arrogant. Clever. But none of these could have happened were it not for a higher power. And most importantly, ambitious, driven by a goal." Her stare narrowed. "I just wonder how that goal would affect my people."

"Impressive. You've shown more than I expected. The priestess in my temple, however, could do the same, but I don't know if she is as good as you…"

"Sari. My name is Sari."

"Sari," he mumbled.

"Of course, you wouldn't know Akimi's abilities because you left right after she was ordained. You were too eager to show the world your vigor and power. But I can tell you. She's doing the best of her abilities to protect your people even in the absence of the *shintai*."

"It is safe with me," he replied.

"Yes. You would risk your life to keep it safe."

"What is it you exactly want from us, Sari?"

"I should be the one asking you that, warrior."

"It's destiny which brought us here."

"Don't tell me that it's destiny that shall be credited for what is bound to happen."

"What is bound to happen? I'm sorry, but I'm not following, Sari. Enlighten me, please," mocked Kazuma.

She sighed. Her face seemed to be controlling the rising rage.

"Oh, you can't see the future?" He was pleased to know of Sari's weakness. "That's shocking," he mumbled.

"You are not here to make friends, warrior. You are our enemy!"

"You are just good with assumptions, my priestess."

"Just wait and see, warrior. You will find your match. She's better than me and she's favored by our goddess," she countered confidently. "She can go deeper into your head and see what you can and will do. She was the one who saw you coming."

"An apprentice?"

"As for now. But you'll regret you came here after she's executed the rite of passage."

"Oh, I'm scared!" laughed Kazuma.

His men looked at him with terror.

Sari shrugged her shoulders and turned away from them. She told them before she left,

"Have your rest before you go back to your ship. I'm giving you time to leave."

"Won't there be a welcome party?" kidded Kazuma.

Sari frowned and left immediately.

"Captain!" His men breathed out freely.

"What the heck were you doing?" One of his men panicked.

"I was just testing the waters," he replied as he scooped water from the clay jar.

"You just annoyed a priestess! She's sacred, Captain!"

"Did you forget, men, that I happen to have the sword? We're equal," he said.

CHAPTER 32
Under the Moon

The elders met in *Apo* Umar's house for another meeting. They were in serious talk about Kazuma's arrival.

"We shouldn't be complacent, *Apo*," said one of the five elders.

"What if they came here to trick us?"

"Their gold should not blind us."

"I agree with all of you," said *Apo* Umar.

They were in a rectangular room wherein the flooring, and the walls were made from bamboo. The window was overlooking the majestic Mt. Harimau.

"We shall watch their every move."

"If possible, befriend them," suggested an elder woman.

"Sari will tell us what to do." *Apo* Umar crossed his arms around his chest.

"I don't feel these foreigners. I think they bring trouble with them!"

"Me too!"

"We must raise an army in case…"

"There will be no war!" exclaimed *Apo*. "Bulan will not allow it."

Apo Umar was just too confident about it.

*　　*　　*

Kazuma went out of the shack. His men took the opportunity to sleep. He watched the people watch him with utmost interest. They looked different. They acted different. Everything was just so different. Their clothes were colorful and they wore large pieces of gold on their body. He even began to wonder if their gift was a match to the wealth these people were hiding. They could have more than what they brought. But still, they graciously accepted it.

He approached one kid who was playing with a stick and a few pearls. He was trying to shoot the pearls into a hole in the soil. His mother was about to pick her son up, afraid of what Kazuma could do to him, but he told her gently, "I'm not going to hurt him."

The woman seemed to have understood him and allowed her child to play with him.

From her window, Cahaya watched the warrior. She found him odd. The negative energy he was channeling since he arrived was waning, and Cahaya couldn't figure out how this was happening.

He is becoming less and less threatening. She thought.

With a sheer fabric covering her face, she was tempted to take it off as she wanted to catch a clearer glimpse of him. She remembered that she must not be seen, so she pulled her window curtains down instead, thinking that it would be a good cover when she lifted her veil. The curtain was thinner and sheerer, so she could see the warrior more clearly.

He played with the little boy jubilantly as though he was his friend. Laughter followed. This she did not expect to see. Gone was the menacing aura that he emanated before he even set foot in the island. Cahaya wondered where it had gone. It disappeared dramatically each time he smiled and laughed with the little boy.

Strangely, Kazuma's senses heightened as he felt that he was being watched. Though he did not know that it was Cahaya, he looked around to search for his uncanny observer. To his dismay, he saw almost everyone, women and children, watching him curiously. Some of them were amused by his friendliness while some still in doubt. But his meticulous eye caught a glimpse of a slim figure, a silhouette to be exact, hidden behind the window curtains of a house just a few steps from where he was standing.

Cahaya thought he'd seen her and her heart began to pound loudly and erratically. She hurriedly shut her windows down as she started feeling so awful. There was something odd about this sensation. It was fluttering, warm, and perturbing.

Right after she fell down to her bed, her door opened, and Sari entered unexpectedly.

"I talked to them, to him to be exact," she spoke quickly.

"Who?"

"The man responsible for my fury. Put down your veil." She then walked passed by her to the window and pushed them out to open.

Cahaya's anxiety rose, but it was too late to stop her.

"He might see us." Her voice quavered.

"Do not be afraid of him."

Cahaya saw him still playing with the boy but not alone anymore. He was surrounded by so many kids. From time to time, Kazuma would glance at her window.

"Let him see you," said Sari.

"What? I shouldn't be seen."

"I didn't mean it that way. I want him to feel your presence. I want him to know that you exist."

"Why?"

"I told him about you. I told him that you're much powerful than me and that you are his match. Let him feel you, Cahaya."

"Sari, I'm not even a priestess yet."

317

"We will get there. As for now, he must feel threatened by you," she answered. "I'm afraid he is directly protected by a higher power."

"A deity?"

"Yes, and just like you, he is favored. What's troubling me is I could feel this deity to be more aggressive than Bulan. She is peace-loving and meek, although she's terrible when angered. But his god is ambitious and power-driven. I'm not saying that Bulan cannot match him, but we have to make her know of this scenario," Sari responded. "That man led me to believe that he's untouchable."

"What do you suggest?"

"We have to call unto her tonight," replied Sari.

"Okay."

"Cahaya, get into his head as often as possible. You need to know your enemy."

*   *   *

Kazuma instantly befriended the native farmers. For hours, he was with them in the field, observing them, and even lending a helping hand, while his troop went back to the ship. The natives were quite impressed by his friendliness despite the language barrier. They taught him how to harvest rice plants from the paddies.

Since Bulan smiled at them last night, they all believed that the harvest for the week or month would be overflowing, although they couldn't stop worrying about the unusual phenomenon in the sky. *Apo* Umar assured them that Bulan was not angry and that harvest season would be great; that the phenomenon had nothing to do with scarcity or long drought in the next few months. To their joy, the paddies looked ready to be harvested. They were drained and dry.

He took off his iron armor and walked to the fields barefooted and lightly dressed. One farmer became Kazuma's mentor in rice harvest.

He followed what the farmers did. They bent up to the waist level and cut the plants with their sharp sickles. They did it quickly and in synchronized motion. Kazuma thought he'd need more time to practice this skill and sat back to watch the farmers work.

It is different from sword fighting. He thought.

In here, he had to bend his body all the time that his hips and thigh muscles easily strained.

Once the field was cleared, the farmers gathered them in one dry space under the sun and separated the grains from the plant. After drying, some farmers took them out the drying space and took the grains inside a house to be burned and threshed.

Kazuma just watched the farmers with amazement on how they worked with zeal.

For most of the day, he was with the natives. He watched them work in groups and sometimes joined them as some of them farmed, fished, and even hunted.

He was barely missed in the ship for his men knew what he was planning.

He only returned to the ship before sunset.

*　　*　　*

With nobody accompanying her, Cahaya, in her sleeping garments, left her room and passed by each house vigilantly until she reached Sari's door. It was night and time to retire. She made sure none of her *apids* caught her leaving the house. She felt really good breathing the cool breeze of air without the veil covering her face, and she'd do anything to have this experience again.

Sari opened the door for her and let her in.

"I told you many times to keep yourself veiled. What if somebody sees you?"

"Nobody saw me, Sari, okay? If somebody did, they wouldn't think I'm Cahaya." Nobody even knew how she looked like so it was quite impossible for them to recognize her. "How do we start then?"

There was a mat in the middle of the room, and the windows were left open to let the light from the moon come in.

"Come here," said Sari as she sat on the left side of the mat. "Hold my hands then."

Cahaya sat across her and held her hands.

"Now, I want you to get inside my head. See what I am thinking."

"Is this how the passage will be?"

Sari nodded.

"Isn't it too early? I thought you said we'll just call unto her?" A tinge of worry was reflected in her voice.

"I thought this will be the fastest way to catch Bulan's attention. Now, hurry up."

Cahaya closed her eyes and concentrated. She saw wilderness instantly. Her shoulders and arms felt electrifyingly cold.

"Don't even think about letting go of my hands," warned Sari.

"It's too cold now…" she murmured.

"I know. It will worsen. Now, concentrate!"

She tightened her grasp on Sari's hands.

The cold was starting to be unbearable. She felt she was being blown by a strong wind and being surrounded by glaciers. Her body was struggling to keep the tiny amount of heat inside her. Her breathing began to shorten and her lungs compressed. Was it because of the cold?

"You're not looking into my mind, Cahaya!"

"I can't. It's too cold!"

She tried and tried to hold unto Sari.

320

"I see something," Cahaya said. "But it's not what's in your mind."

"Tell me. What do you see?"

She calmed down. "A woman. No! There are two of them."

The cold dramatically faded. She let go of her grasp and just focused on her sight.

"They look the same but different in a lot of ways... She's running... Both of them... Hiding. They look scared... No. They're not together... They can't be together. There's no way they'll be together..."

"Cahaya." Sari was worried, and she shook Cahaya's shoulders to slap her back to reality.

"They're running away from... I don't know. I can't get a clear picture of whom they were avoiding, but it could be danger... They're exhausted and only if they could just stop for a while, but they have to run because if they stay, they won't see him..."

"Him?"

Cahaya let out a big deep breath like she was under the sea for so long.

"Yes... him," she reiterated.

"Who's him? Who did you see?"

"The women. They're looking for the same man."

"Who is the man, Cahaya?"

"I don't know. I didn't see his face," Cahaya answered. "He was there. I saw him, but he never showed his face to me. Why did this happen? Why did I see them instead?"

"You've been warned."

"By Bulan? But what was that? Who are they? I don't even know them."

"Yes. Bulan warned you, but I don't know what it was for."

She fell to her back and massaged her forehead to ease the striking pain.

"Are we moving on?" asked Cahaya.

"No. That will be all for the night. I'm afraid I have exhausted you."

"Well, good night, Sari." She gathered her legs and stood up. "I'll see you tomorrow. Then, maybe we can continue our lessons."

Instead of hurrying back to her house, Cahaya went up the mountain to the hot spring. A dip in the warm water could alleviate the cold. She went there all alone. She had done this so many times without her *apids'* knowledge.

Surrounded by huge rocks and colorful flowering plants, the warm body of water was deeply seated in the heart of the mountain forest. Cahaya slid her clothes off her arms down to her waist and legs. She put her hair into a bun, and she quickly went into the water.

She closed her eyes as she relaxed and got lost in the soothing silence. The warmth slowly freed her mind from Bulan's warning.

Then, all of a sudden, the moment of peacefulness was disrupted by strange screeches on the forest floor. It sounded like a dozen feet crashing down dried leaves.

"Who's there?" Her voice was loud and tough. "Is that you, Ayang?"

The sounds paused.

"Sari?" She walked closer, step by step, holding her breath, to the nearest curve of the spring. She quickly grabbed her clothes and wrapped them around herself even though she was still in the water.

After a few seconds of careful monitoring, the footsteps started to scamper away, quickly as though being chased.

Not wasting any time, Cahaya went out of the water, put on her clothes properly, and put down her hair. She searched for the noise again, and she heard it moving farther.

She followed it until she was slowly moving out of the spring area.

CHAPTER 33
At First Sight

With bare feet, she sauntered the heavy drylands. The sound of land animals scampering around didn't scare her; snoring boars, chirping birds, and buzzing insects. She was more worried and curious about the mysterious footsteps slowly waning. It led her down the mountain and into the thick forest where the wild grows. The cold breeze seeped into her wet skin as she moved faster and faster, catching the sound of the strange steps.

"Ahh!" she squealed as she caught herself trapped between two strong arms.

"Gotcha!" A smirk from an unknown man literally stopped her heart.

It was the warrior!

"Get away from me, or I'll scream!" she warned him in her language.

"Why were you following me?" His grasp just tightened, his eyes dark with suspicion.

She then realized that no matter how she tried to speak to him, he wouldn't understand her.

"Boss!" Three men emerged from the thick wild grasses, each of them carrying game on their shoulders.

"Who is she?" one asked as he surveyed her.

"I found my own game!" laughed the warrior.

Cahaya tried to resist, but he was too brawny that all her efforts were put to drain. The warrior wasn't just cocky but annoying too—overly!

After one meaningful curve of his lips, he heaved her up to his shoulder, and his shoulder blade pressed unto her stomach.

"Put me down!" she shouted on top of her lungs.

"Shut up, or I'll throw you into the ocean!"

She continued screaming at him as she pounded her fists against his lean back, but the warrior remained steadfast. He started moving to the shoreline where his huge ship and the others were waiting.

"What do you have there, boss?" laughed one man whose face was dirty with ashes as he was obviously the one in charge of making the fire.

The men, almost a hundred in number and apparently stronger and bigger than her, gathered around the fire, barbecuing fish and a cow.

"Is she our dinner for today? Too bad we're packed right now!"

Kazuma laughed.

"No, boys! She's our special guest," said he.

He left the others who were laughing at Cahaya's misfortune. She had the option to reveal herself to intimidate them, but she chose to take everything slow.

These foreigners must not know who I am. She thought.

Kazuma brought her to the ship, into his cabin, and tossed her to his bed. Her hair was wet and in disarray, and Kazuma looked at her, shaking his head.

His glare was mockingly piercing that she felt her intestines squeezing and turning upside down.

"What's your name?" he asked cockily.

She looked straight into his eyes. In just a few seconds, she knew who he was and his language, but she kept mum.

Kazuma pulled a rope from the stocks and moved closer to her. He reached for her hands and tied them to the pole of his bed.

"I'll come back in a while," he said, and he left the room with that smirk.

Cahaya studied every corner. She felt an overpowering force compelling her to look at the wall that hanged the sword that her Sight allowed her to see. There it was, calling her. Strange, but she thought she saw it emanating light.

Bulan, I feel you, she said in her head. *I know the predicament that awaits you. You must not let this higher power overwhelm you.*

Then, her vision was suddenly whitewashed.

Her Sight showed her another astounding scene.

This time, it was in another land far, far away from her island. She saw high mountains capped with white surrounded by shimmering lakes and a vast ocean. There was a magnificently walled village, heavily guarded by what she assumed were royal guards in sturdy armors. She followed the scarlet runner that led to the palace doors. Several doors opened, from the biggest to the smaller ones until she reached the most sacred room of the palace; the Emperor's Hall.

She saw the emperor dressed in elegant gold and red robes, sitting on his throne. A man so familiar to her kneeled in front of the Emperor with his head bowed. It was the warrior in his valiant war armor, so pleased to receive the sword wrapped in gold cloth. Then the Emperor whispered something into his ears. The warrior nodded.

Before she could even see what happened next, her vision turned gray, and it shifted to another scene. She was now inside a less grand room.

A woman in a colorful dress robe approached the warrior.

"The emperor is sick and dying," said Kazuma to her as he watched the moon from his wide window.

"And I heard from your men that you are charged to travel the world."

"Yes. He's given me the Kusanagi."

"Kazuma, that's such an honor!" The woman's face brightened.

"The sword is going to be his shintai."

"Really? So, you're..."

Her vision was cut when the door opened.

Her eyes immediately turned to the warrior standing outside the door with a plate of food. Her ashen face surprised him.

"What happened to you?" he asked.

She shook her head as she kept her eyes away from the sword.

"Here! I don't starve guests." He set the plate in front of her and freed her hands.

Cahaya studied his face and tried to get inside his mind, but to her dismay, the sword seemed to be shielding him from her.

What a powerful force, she thought.

"Everything alright?"

She threw the plate away and quickly climbed out of bed. Before she could run away, Kazuma had already caught her hand, shoved her close to him, and pinned her to the closest wall.

"Where do you think you're going?" His teeth gritted with irritation.

Surprisingly, she found a hole in his mind and saw what he was thinking.

He was planning to keep her as a prisoner despite his lack of knowledge as to who she was. He was going to use her against her tribe, grasp her by the neck, and make her as the leverage.

Leverage for what?

"You don't seem ordinary," he mumbled right on top of her mouth. "You're royalty, aren't you?" He then sniffed her hair. "You are royalty." He pulled back from her.

He isn't different from me. She thought.

He too was favored by his gods; the highest power and the newly immortalized force. Two gods were protecting him.

"If only I haven't found you swimming in the spring, I would have thought the priestess have sent you here to spy on us." He smirked. "How are we going to understand each other?" He rubbed his forehead as though disappointed about communication, but Cahaya had no plan to reveal her ability just yet.

"Come!" He pulled her out of the cabin to the deck where few men were gathered in a roundtable.

She watched them closely. Everybody paused as they saw her. Kazuma pushed her to one side where empty barrels were stored.

"You stay there!" he ordered before he turned his back on her.

She looked up to the moon in the sky. It was massive, and it glimmered brightly. Bulan was watching her, and she knew she wouldn't let anything harm her. Kazuma returned and tied her hands again.

"If you want to jump, jump! You'll just drown," said he.

The sleeves of her clothes fell off her shoulders revealing her bare skin and showing off a portion of her breasts. She thought she saw the man smile.

One man whistled and teased, "Boss, someone's waiting for you back home."

A haughty façade he showed to her.

"What a spectacular night we have!" laughed another man.

"Show some respect, people!" said Kazuma. "She is a very special guest." He tilted her chin and studied her face.

"She's fair-skinned compared to the others," commented one.

"Are we going to use her?"

Cahaya moved her face away from him.

"Oh, Boss. She's feisty! She knows how to dissent!"

Cahaya realized that what they said was a compliment. There was no need to read his mind. She had known enough about Kazuma.

Kazuma stood up and went to his men. They started talking, and she listened carefully.

"Is it alright that she hears us?" asked one man.

"Don't worry. She doesn't understand a thing we say," assured Kazuma. "She's not like Sari."

He was wrong there. Cahaya just grinned surreptitiously.

"What do we do now?"

"We attack the day they least expect, on the day when their defenses are down," answered Kazuma.

"How are we going to do that?"

"Make them believe we're friends. Gain their trust."

"How do we gain their trust, Boss?"

"Right!" exclaimed one of his men. "The woman!"

"Yes. Her!" echoed Kazuma. "Now, good night, my trusted soldiers." He rose from his seat and approached Cahaya, untied her, pulled her up by her arm, and heaved her out of the deck back to his cabin.

Cahaya thought she heard Kazuma's troop laugh while they left. She could read from their minds the nastiest idea ever formed by the human brain. It was despicable!

Just after Kazuma shut the door behind him, Cahaya pulled the sword blade out from the iron case and directed it to the appalled warrior with her hands tied.

Kazuma slowly raised his hands. He eyed her cautiously.

"That sword is mine. It is sacred," he uttered carefully. "I won't hurt you. I promise. Now, put it down." His voice low, gentle, and reassuring.

There was a tiny tinge of fear, tiny but better than nothing.

Cahaya moved forward and pointed the tip of the blade to his throat.

He gulped. Fear slowly rose in him while courage heightened in her.

"Liar!" she bellowed.

CHAPTER 34
Bulan Listens

Cahaya failed to keep her identity a secret. After what those men ran in their dirty minds, she just couldn't stay meek and composed.

"You speak my language." Kazuma was shocked.

"Yes, I do. It's something only my kind can do," she assertively answered without putting down the sword.

"You're a priestess too?" His brow rose. "No! You are who Sari was talking about."

"Yes, and you should fear me!"

The tips of Kazuma's lips formed a haughty grin.

"Fear you?" A tinge of ridicule reverberated in his voice.

"Yes. Because just like the god in this sword, I possess powers stronger than you!"

"Are you saying that you'd become a god, in your case a goddess, when you die?"

She frowned as she thought Kazuma was just laughing at her.

"Mockery aside, I think that will just happen when you become a priestess, which for now is quite impossible since you are in my territory," said he.

"I have something on your throat, Kazuma," she warned. "I can end your life in two seconds!"

"Slay me with my own sword? Slay me with the god who vowed to protect me? I don't think so!"

All of a sudden, Kazuma flexed her wrist, and she let go of the sword. A resonating sound of clanking metal filled the room as the sword hit the wooden floor. Kazuma tightened his clutch on her wrist and yanked him close to her.

Cahaya gasped as she saw herself empty-handed in just three seconds.

Face to face, Cahaya stopped her breathing when his nose almost touched hers. She felt her heart racing, pounding loudly and fast, so fast that she could feel her chest exploding. His eyes were grimly fixed on hers. She had never seen an angry man like this in all her life, not even her father could look as angry as Kazuma.

"Do not try me!" Kazuma verbalized on top of her quivering mouth.

"You are shaking on your knees, warrior," she countered. "I can't blame you."

Kazuma held her hands and pulled her to the bed. She kicked him on the chest, and that triggered Kazuma to the edge of his patience. He pinned her down to the mattress with her tied hands on top of her head, close to the head of the bed, and his hips cornered hers. Anger just churned his veins. No woman had ever treated him like this. No woman had ever made him feel defeat was possible.

"Sari talked so much about you," he mumbled on top her mouth, his eyes raging with every inch of repressed anger. "Now that I have you in my hands, I will not let you get away."

"My people will find me, and they will make you pay for what you've done!" she bravely countered as she tenaciously attempted to pull back from him.

"Then they will make this whole parade easier for me." He grinned. "I just wonder how this lovely face breaks a war."

"Believe me, my people will not make it easy for you!"

"Oh, I'm scared now!"

"Laugh all you want, warrior, but victory is ours."

"I'll keep that in mind, priestess," he said while suppressing his laughter. "If war breaks tomorrow, I better get my men ready. As you said, you'll make us tremble with fear."

He picked up the sword from the floor, returned it in its iron case, and walked out of the cabin. Cahaya turned to her side. The storm had passed already yet she still felt her heart thumping in utter chaos.

She closed her eyes and uttered a silent prayer.

Bulan, you see what lies ahead. I pray for complete protection for my people. I know it will be difficult for you to go against this man's god, but I know that you will never surrender without a fight. Please let peace reign and not animosity.

*   *   *

Kazuma heaved a deep sigh as he entered the deck with a grim look.

"Why the face, Boss?" Usui asked as he noticed the look on Kazuma's face.

"We're close to taking this land," answered he. "We got the priestess."

"The priestess?" Usui raised an eyebrow.

"Without a doubt! Sari's successor."

"You mean the priestess whom we all shall fear?" He followed Kazuma to the wooden beam that made up the hull.

Kazuma looked over the silhouette of the shining moon on the steady water below his ship.

"Fortunately, she is the one, Usui."

Usui laughed, amused by the circumstances. "This is indeed great news!"

There was no better way to defeat a kingdom but by attacking from behind, slyly like a fox.

"We must not take this lightly though. She gave me a warning."

"We are going to crush them no doubt. Have you seen the weapons they carry?" assured Usui. "They can't hold a candle against us."

"Don't count your chickens before they hatch," Kazuma answered. "They might not be as fierce as the warriors from the north, but they have skills unknown to us."

"They're short, so they can be quicker. Speed will be our problem," pointed out Usui as he leaned forward to the wooden railings of the hull. "We need to know what weapons they keep in secret. Maybe the priestess can spill out some information."

"That will be a challenge, Usui. She's smart. I don't think we can easily trick her in revealing their plans. She's pledged loyalty to their deity by being a priestess herself. That just means that she is obliged to protect them from us."

"But with her in our hands, she won't be able to do that." A haughty smile formed at the edge of Usui's face. "Imagine the displeasure she will cause their deity."

"She's a priestess. I'm sure she has secret ways."

"Then, what are we going to do with her?"

"I don't know. Let's see tomorrow," he replied.

*　　*　　*

For the night, he watched her sleep soundly on his bed. She looked so peaceful and defenseless from him. He rose from his chair and pulled out his sword. His mind was dictating him.

Kill her!

Kill her?

He pointed his sword toward her throat, just a few inches from her delicate skin. One movement and it would slay her to death.

Kill her!

The voice in his head was getting louder and louder.

Kill her!

If he killed her, he would eliminate his greatest hurdle. She was just there with death smiling at her, but his hand froze every time he thought of doing it.

He finally lost grip of his sword and fell back to his chair.

What is stopping me? He asked himself.

As he buried his face in his hands, questioning the astounding doubt that was arising, he caught a glimpse of the sky turning red. The phenomenon attracted him to walk towards his window to check it out.

The once midnight blue turned bloody red, auroras filled the spaces, and the moon surprisingly increased in size right in front of his very eyes.

Just watching the spectacle, he realized that it was a message from one of the gods, not his god, but could be hers.

"Hachiman, I found our real enemy," he muttered as he glared at the burning moon.

*   *   *

The roosters in the tribe village simultaneously crowed and Sari climbed out of her bed when she recognized Cahaya's *apids* storming into her room.

"What's the matter?" she asked as she opened her window and let sunlight come in.

"*Ayu*, Cahaya is missing!" exclaimed a pale *apid*.

"What?"

"She's not in her room. She was just in there last night, sleeping!"

Sari remembered that Cahaya left everyone in her household, unknowledgeable about her coming to her house last night. It was meant to be confidential between her, Cahaya, and Bulan. But where would the Princess go? She was confident she

333

sent her home before midnight, and she knew her to be an obedient girl.

What went wrong? She wondered.

"What do you mean she's not in her room?"

"We woke up this morning not finding her in her bed, and we looked for her everywhere, in the village and in the forest."

Sari put on her shoal and slippers.

"All of the forest?"

"No. Not yet. A few of the girls are still searching for her. We're too worried that we thought we might inform the tribe king."

"No!" snapped Sari. "Don't tell anyone yet."

"But, Priestess!" The *apids* were truly worried about their princess as it was their duty to keep her safe and secluded, away from people's eyes and hands. If *Apo* Umar found out about their negligence, they would surely face the scaffold or the sword. "What about *Ayu* Ayang?"

They knew that the nosy little Ayang could easily extract the truth from them.

"Hush, women!" Sari filled her basin with water, dipped her long index finger to it, and twirled circles three times. "Give me the candle."

One *apid* handed over a candle.

Sari placed the candle on top of the basin and let the molten wax fall onto the water's surface. She heaved a deep breath as a figure formed from the molten wax.

"Cahaya is safe. She's doing us a great favor," she told them as she surveyed the uncanny wax formation on the water.

"Where is she, Priestess?"

"I can't tell you, but Bulan will not abandon her. As a matter of fact, she had already shown everyone her support to us. She already declared war last night." Sari saw in her mind the reddening of the sky that occurred last night when everyone was sleeping. She saw the warrior peering from his cabin's window, watching Bulan up above affirming her powers, and speaking to his god, Hachiman.

Sari added, "Do not tell anyone that she's missing. Tell them she's with me, preparing for the big day."

"You mean the Seclusion Week?"

"Yes. No one will question that." Sari thought it was about time for the Seclusion, the first phase of an apprentice's turn over rite, to begin.

"In just a few days, we'll hear from Adlaw."

"Adlaw?" queried one of the *apids*.

"The Sun God. The warrior calls him Hachiman," replied Sari as she put off the flame.

She recalled the story of Adlaw and Bulan from the mouths of her ancestors.

"Isn't he Bulan's greatest rival?"

"Yes, and he's come here to prove his might."

CHAPTER 35
Two Worlds, Two Gods

"Eat!" Kazuma entered the cabin with a plate of fruits.

Cahaya retreated to the corner and wrapped her arms around herself. She leaned her back against the wall and rested her head on the cabinet that stood beside her. Her clothes that were wet last night had dried already, and she thought she was going to be sick from feeling damp all night.

"If you don't eat, you'll not have the energy to call unto your Moon Goddess."

Little did Kazuma know, Cahaya was already preparing for the turnover. Since she was away from Sari and the Seclusion was impossible at the moment, fasting for days before the big day would be her preparation.

"You're killing yourself," he added.

"You don't know anything about what I am doing. You're just a loyal servant," she countered, her face marred with odium. Last night, she fell asleep waiting for his dagger to pierce into her heart, and in all honesty, she was utterly surprised to see herself breathing this morning.

"Yes, I may be clueless about your nonsense, but you can't take away the concern I have for you. I don't starve prisoners."

"Why don't you just end this for me since you're only good at that?"

"Don't pray for that," he hissed as he put down the plate in front of her. "What will I get from a dead priestess?"

She was just trying him out. It seemed to her that Kazuma had no plan of ending her life so prematurely.

"My name's Kazuma by the way." He sat a few feet across from her. He picked a berry from the plate and tossed it into his mouth. "What's your name?"

Cahaya found him so arrogant in the way he spoke. The cockiness of an established warrior who had conquered countless kingdoms slowly churned her patience.

"I know who you are," said she. "I know everything about you." Her voice sounded menacing, dark and serious, despite the confounding weakness she was feeling. It seemed that hunger was slowly overpowering her.

"I am starting to believe Sari. I must really have to fear you. You have this air that kills any mosquito that flies right in front of you."

"You're fortunate you are not a mosquito."

He smirked, showing out a complete set of white sparkly teeth and dimples.

"Sari must have taught you to be sharp."

"I was taught to never trust."

Kazuma paused. He examined her from head to foot. He knew she was hungry, but he felt that no matter how he forced her to eat something, her pride would always matter. It was the first time he noticed the exceptional beauty her face possessed.

She wasn't too pale nor was she too dark. Her cheeks complemented the color of her lips. She had long limbs as the high slit of her skirt showed them. Her bare shoulders exposed her prominent clavicle and let her long black silky hair be the major attraction of its bareness. Her figure, the curve of her hips and thighs, and the bulge of her breasts followed the cut of her dress accordingly.

She was lovely, mouthwateringly attractive.

He caught himself glaring at the rise and fall of her chest. A mortified blush spread through his cheeks as warmth dramatically rose inside his organs. He shook his head and took a deep breath to knock him off back to reality.

"Tell me about your goddess," said he as he tried to repress the mounting magnetism. "You said you know me. This has to be a fair game between you and me, so do not leave me blind on one side."

"Isn't that why I am winning this war? You don't have the resources that I do, Kazuma."

A subdued laugh came out of him.

"You'll make a great tactician in my team, you know. Too bad you're fighting on the wrong side."

"Why are you doing this, warrior?"

"Strategy. Know your enemies better and keep them close."

"I won't give you that advantage."

"It's okay. I am confident I could get that from you."

She smirked. "If I were you, I'd sail back home."

"That will come. After this."

"Don't be too confident."

"I'm sorry to say, but confidence runs through my blood. I eat, drink, and even breathe that every single second of my life." His eyes wouldn't leave her. "I would like you to know that I never lose."

"Someday, Kazuma, this confidence will eat you. Fear will be your greatest enemy."

"Shall I be afraid now?" he mocked. "Is that going to be my future? Because as early as now, priestess, I'll tell you are wrong."

"Your future? I see you having children, lots of them. They will struggle not to do what you have done. They will struggle not to commit the same terrible mistake you did. Regret will be your eternal companion. You will tell your wife someday that you want your children to be always clever but never lose heart. You will tell your wife to teach them to love because it's the way to conquer all adversity. You don't know anything about selfless love, Kazuma. All you know is create terror and animosity. Greed and pride. But time will come, and you won't be the same man as you are now."

When she said this, she couldn't believe her Sight would lie to her. She couldn't believe that an old dying Kazuma could say such powerful words. More so, she chose not to tell him what other things she saw.

My Sight might be wrong, she thought. *Kazuma is not the type of man to preach about love and peace.*

"I'll take note of that." He just grinned.

"Fear will strike you in the most unpredicted fashion. You will learn humility by then."

He smiled, amazed by her words. But he wasn't moved. He knew she was wrong.

"You change my mind, priestess. I'm not going to kill you anymore. After I seize your land and establish my power here, I'll take you to the north. You'll make a fine guardian of my temple."

"I will not worship any other god than mine."

"You will have to because you will be mine!"

She gulped.

"You will surrender to me," he added.

She had just left a desirable impression to him. Something he would want to keep forever.

He gathered his legs and rose up.

"Eat that! I don't want a sickly member in my household," he uttered coldly. He, then, pulled clothes out of a wooden chest. "And change into this. It's disturbing to see you underdressed around men." He coughed after to clear his throat of the prick of discomfort as he eyed her for the last time.

Then, the door closed into a slam.

Cahaya cared less about how she looked or what others would think about her. She must continue fasting and praying.

Bulan, she started. *Let Sari know of my condition. I will retain my strength during this entire fasting period for the turnover. I might do it alone, but please, assure me success. I need you now. Our enemy is starting to gather forces, and I need to become a priestess before they attack the village so that I could protect your people. I must stop the warrior. Be with me. Give me strength. Give me the drive to surpass the fasting.*

*   *   *

Kazuma and three of his men went to the village and brought with them a barrel of wine to present to the kingdom. Apo Umar, who was clueless about his daughter, welcomed them. The elders, still suspicious, allowed hospitality to rule them this time just to inspect the foreigners of their genuineness. As elders, they had already developed the senses to critique a person's personality through his words and actions. Though they did not possess the Sight a babaylan has, they could still say whether evil wrought a man.

While they were feasting at one long table—Kazuma, Apo Umar, the elders, and Sari—Kazuma thought he was starting to gain everyone's heart. The elders, especially the tribe king, were very pleased with the wine that Kazuma promised to bring another barrel next time.

It was indeed easier for him to converse with the natives after he forced himself to learn as much as he could of their language. His men saw a native spying on them in the coastline, and they invited him on board and talked him into teaching them their language. All of these happened without Cahaya's knowledge.

Apo Umar was very impressed with Kazuma's quick adaptability.

"Is she your daughter, my king?" He faced the very young Ayang whose hair was braided and filled with jewels. She sat next to her father.

"Yes, she is my daughter. Her name is Ayang."

Ayang timidly smiled and slightly bowed her head.

"She is very lovely."

"She is very young though," commented one elder. "And our princesses marry into this tribe."

"I have a wife," assured Kazuma as he realized that his simple compliment was misinterpreted. "I simply adore the unique beauty of your princess."

Ayang flushed.

"I have a sister who's prettier than me!" she spoke happily. "But she's not allowed to go out of her room."

"Why is that?" He turned his curious look to Apo Umar.

"Royal daughters are isolated from the public. It's tradition. Ayang will have her time," answered the king.

"I'll be a binukot next year!"

"A binukot?"

"Yes. My sister is one, and she never goes out of her room without a veil on her face. Anyone who tries to look at her, especially men, will be punished with death," answered Ayang.

Apo Umar continued to drink his wine and let intoxication bring him varied thoughts, even delusions of grandeur. He climbed up to the table and started shouting about how mighty a warrior he was in his glory days. The elders obviously could not tolerate the alcohol, and they quickly passed out. The royal guards carefully took them into their respective houses including the tribe king.

"So your sister is in her room alone now while you celebrate here?"

"That happens all the time. Although she can go out, she has to wear clothes that cover her, and she must stay inside a palanquin. Right now—"

Sari, who never touched Kazuma's wine, interfered quickly, "The princess is with me."

"Sari is—"

"I know who Sari is, Ayang," muttered Kazuma. "We've met before."

Sari left the table in the pursuit that Kazuma would follow her, and he didn't disappoint her. He left Ayang in the table and followed the priestess into the woods.

"I am impressed, Sari, on how you could keep your people calm," he started.

"What is there to be anxious about, warrior?" She turned to face him. The woods were so thick that even the tiniest light could not penetrate. "As far as I know, there's nothing to worry about."

He smirked. His tongue was raring to spill the truth about Cahaya, but prudence prevented him. He laughed at the thought about Sari pretending that everything was fine. He was very certain that the priestess knew about her apprentice's fate and that she was just creating a façade.

"In this war, I have the ace," he said.

"We both have," countered Sari with an evocative but shrewd smile. "You better be careful."

"You don't know how careful I have become now!"

"I pity you, warrior," uttered Sari as she walked in circles around him, eyeing every little action he did. "You're as ill-fated as a blind man."

He quite agreed on her about that. He was blind compared to her and his imprisoned priestess. He couldn't foresee the future or couldn't talk directly with the higher force. But he has something that they didn't; overflowing confidence and assurance.

"By the way, Sari, if you have a way to communicate with your priestess, tell her to quit being melodramatic and eat something."

"She's fasting?"

"Do you want to know what I think about it? An act of rebellion. She is starving herself to death. Maybe she doesn't want to be a priestess. Maybe she wants to die before I do it for her."

Sari paused and looked up to the sky. The trees prevented the sunlight from even touching the forest floor, so she had to find an open space to see the sun. She quickly dashed out of the woods and left Kazuma alone and shocked.

The sun was scorching and blazing, which was a terrifying message for her.

Sari stormed inside her room and shut all the openings, the door, and the windows, and quickly lit a candle above a basin of water.

The light blazed all throughout the dimmed room.

She must get this message to Cahaya to stop her with her plan.

Fasting this early? She'd die even before the day of the turnover.

Fasting? Did she think it would be a good alternative to seclusion with the incumbent priestess? Fasting was only allowed when the future priestess was two days away from the night of the turnover after Bulan had sent her the sacred object of her choosing, and when she was ready for the most difficult phase of the rite. Apparently, Cahaya was not in any of those phases. She was kept inside their enemy's den, unarmed or even clueless.

The flame doused as the candle fell to the water as she intentionally dropped it.

All Sari could wish now was for Cahaya to receive her message before she became too weak to even come home.

*   *   *

Sunset was looming. Cahaya lay on the floor, still preserving the last drop of energy her body was lodging. She felt so

343

weak, yet she refused to even take water. She could barely open her eyes. The last time she had anything was last night.

All she did was pray for strength.

The door smashed fully open. Cahaya's heart, out of absolute surprise, almost jumped out of her chest.

"Hurry!" She recognized the speaker to be Kazuma's man.

Two well-built men carried a body inside the cabin.

"What happened?" she asked as she tried to stand up.

"Boss was bitten by a snake." The man showed her the wound on Kazuma's leg. There were two tiny but deep penetrations.

CHAPTER 36
Breaking the Walls

"Is he going to die?" cried one of the men.

"Are you sure the snake is poisonous?"

"Yes. It looked me in the eye!"

While the huge and stalwart-looking men argued, Cahaya stood there, defying the weakness on both her legs and her grumbling stomach.

"What do we do now?"

Kazuma reclined his back on the bed and was sweating profusely. He began to groan and utter vague words. With that look on his face, it seemed that the bite had been there for hours and the venom was already starting to paralyze his legs.

Her Sight showed her how Kazuma was defeated by a snake. After it sank its teeth into his flesh, Kazuma fell off the slope of the hill, and his leg was stuck in between the leafless branches of trees and wild plants. It took a long while before his men found him unconscious in the woods.

"The venom is weak. I can stop it from further advancing to his vital organs," said Cahaya. She looked around and found a tie. "I need a knife."

"A knife?" one of the men queried curiously.

"Yes. If you want to save Kazuma's life, you listen to me," she declared while tying around his leg, just a few inches above the bite. "This will help stop the venom from going up his body."

They gave her a knife, and Cahaya cut a line between the tiny fang bites. She let the wound bleed for a minute and kept it open for air to get in.

"Where are you going?" Two men stopped her in the doorway.

"I'm going to look for medicines in the woods."

"Will he die?"

"He will not if you let me out to the woods. He's burning with fever, can't you see?"

"But..."

"You can come with me," she assured them.

Two men agreed to accompany her.

Barefoot, she sauntered through the woods while Bulan generously gave her light to show her the way. Cahaya could easily pick which one to uproot. They were easy to find since they grow along the trunk of old sturdy trees. She also did not forget to take its flowers.

She hurried back to the ship and asked a few men the way to the kitchen. When she reached there, she quickly made fire from wood and boiled water, crushed the herbs with a stone against the wood, and mixed it in the boiling water with a wooden ladle.

When the decoction had turned tea-green, she added the flowers and let the petals churn in seconds. The pungent smell was remedied by the flowers.

She brought the kettle to Kazuma's cabin.

His men gathered around him, hoping that he would open his eyes. She could see fear reaching the endless depth of bleakness. Everyone's thoughts were nothing but the inevitable. She read them one by one.

"Move," she instructed everyone. She poured the decoction into a cup and asked one of the men to pull Kazuma up so that he could drink the medicine.

"He's not taking it," the man supporting Kazuma's back who happened to be Usui muttered worriedly.

He was right. Kazuma was neither drinking the preparation nor opening his mouth.

Cahaya quickly took the cup and decant the medicine to her mouth. She pressed her lips against Kazuma's and let the medicine flow from her mouth to his. The men gasped with surprise.

She did another round until Kazuma was starting to respond and drink the medicine through her. She stopped when the cup was emptied.

The men's cheeks blazed with hot red after they witnessed what she had done.

"You'll thank me for doing this," said she as she wiped the side of her mouth with her fingers.

"Er…" Usui cleared his throat and shrugged his uneasiness by shaking his head. "Will he be okay after this?"

"We have to wait for a few hours to see how the medicine helped," she replied. "If he doesn't wake up, might as well start sailing back to the north by tonight." She went back to the corner to rest her legs. She had been running without much energy just to look for herbs. Now, she had become so tired that she started to feel cramps and numbing in her calves and thighs.

Slowly the room was emptied.

Usui came to bring her food and water, but she rejected them for the nth time. As Kazuma was sleeping, she could hear him groan as he battled against death. The need to find out his destiny grew, but her Sight was not showing her anything except for the dire need to drink water. Hunger drifted her to sleep in no time.

Keep yourself healthy. It's not yet time. You will need the energy.

She opened her eyes. Sari's voice was the last thing she heard before she woke up.

Kazuma was sleeping soundly. She stood up and walked toward him. His wound had stopped bleeding, so she looked for a piece of clean cloth and wrapped it around his leg. His fever had gone down too.

How did Sari know about my fasting? She asked herself as she watched Kazuma peacefully sleeping. She began to wonder why Kazuma would even speak to Sari about it. Was he that desperate to prevent her from acquiring Bulan's blessings? Was he so fearful that once she became a real priestess, he'd lose?

There was food on the wooden table just beside the bed. After thinking about what Sari conveyed to her, she picked up the food and started eating.

*   *   *

"Boss?"

Usui's face—protruding forehead, pointed nose, and hairy double chin—dazed his droopy vision.

"What's with the face?" he asked as he wondered about Usui's puffy face.

Tears that were suppressed in his eyes finally broke out. Usui cried out of complete relief.

Kazuma pulled himself up to a sitting position. When he noticed the bandage around his ankle, he quickly remembered the accident in the woods.

"Good job, Usui, for keeping me alive." He heaved a deep sigh when he realized how close he was to death. The woods could have become his deathbed if his men didn't arrive at the right time.

"Oh, you're fortunate, boss, that the priestess is a healer too."

Usui's response caught his attention. Kazuma readily searched his room.

"Where is she?"

"She's gone to the spring with Takomoto. I think she's getting water to wash your wound. The priestess executed a very radical way of curing you, boss," Usui said shyly. "Where are you going?"

Kazuma stood up.

"Takomoto is with her, boss!" shouted Usui in hopes that Kazuma would stop. To his utter disappointment, his boss exited the room, passed through several cabins and the deck, and was soon disembarking the ship through the wooden plank. Then Kazuma noticed that he left behind his slippers.

His head felt like a cracking nutshell every time he recalled the near-death experience. Something in his head was leaking. No, not blood and definitely not his sanity. However, seeing crumbs of bizarre mental pictures made him doubt about his sanity. It couldn't be the venom infiltrating his skull, could it?

He knew he reached the spring when he heard the steady and serene flow of water, the tepid warmth of the atmosphere, and the smell of sulfur. His legs froze when a naked woman stunned him.

She was in the water, her bare back facing him, and her hair drawn to her shoulder, dripping wet. Kazuma's jaw dropped. It was the second time he felt this unusual commotion in his chest, after the other night when they had a talk.

Odd.

Were his eyes fooling him?

Was the venom this potent to have affected his lungs and his stomach?

The strange warmth that was ascending from his abdomen to his cheeks worsened when he recounted the memory that hunted him while on his way here. She saved him. He remembered how she saved him. As for how Usui called it, the priestess saved him in the most radical way they knew.

The ghost of her lips left his own frozen with delight and surprise. He thought he could still taste the bitter decoction sweetened by her soft lips.

"Kazuma?" Her sweet, soft, and probing voice reverberated into his ears, and he was pulled back to reality.

His eyes went straight to her face.

"Are you well now?" Cahaya asked as she partially turned to him with her arms encircling her breasts.

He nodded stiffly.

She appeared to him as pure seduction and Kazuma battled against it by freezing his glare onto her eyes.

"Where's Takamoto?" he asked.

"I told him to wait for me at the foot of the mountain while I take a bath. Why are you here?" she said while washing her hair.

"To make sure you don't run away."

"Even coming here underdressed." She silently laughed upon seeing Kazuma run without slippers and upper clothes. "I am bathing, warrior," she stressed. "Please look away if you don't want your eyeballs scraped out of your skull."

But Kazuma was headstrong. He just remained standing under a tree.

"Tell me when to close my eyes," he instructed her coldly. From where he sat, he could still see her clearly.

"I can say that and run away from you."

"Unless you want to run away naked," he haughtily countered as he held up her clothes.

"I am now officially under your mercy," she replied almost like a whisper to herself.

Silence.

Cahaya immersed into the warm water longer than she thought she would. Kazuma's intense glare brought extreme burden on her. She should have just asked him nicely to leave.

"You could have let me die," he broke the eerie silence.

"You could have killed me that night when I was sleeping," she responded cleverly.

"So this is a favor in return for sparing your life?"

She nodded and answered, "We're equal now. After tonight, we can start killing each other. The question here is who will initiate?"

350

Kazuma thought how sharp she answered him. He pulled out dried leaves from the bushes and started weaving them.

"You stopped fasting. Why?"

"It's none of your business."

"Has Sari something to do with this?"

"Let's say she has. Why would you even bother asking?"

"Because I told her to stop you with this craziness."

"Close your eyes," she said. "I'm getting out of the water."

Kazuma tightly grasped her clothes and closed his eyes.

Cahaya, then, went out of the water, checked Kazuma if he was following instructions, and walked toward him.

"No peeping," she added when she reached him. "My clothes?"

With eyes closed, he handed them over to her.

"Even though my eyes are closed, I can still hear you."

"I'll let you know if I'm running away," she kidded.

"One more joke and I'll open my eyes," he warned.

"Prepare for the worst, warrior."

CHAPTER 37
The Seedling of the Curse

"Where are we going?" she asked angrily. Cahaya stomped her feet against the dead leaves and weeds that enveloped the muddy terrain. Rain poured heavily last night, and the skies were sending warnings for another storm.

She was tired, and her legs were slowly numbing. Kazuma had been dragging her everywhere in the forested mountain for a reason her Sight could not decode. Exhaustion and hunger could be the reason she could not get into his mind now. Was this why Sari wanted her not to continue fasting?

Kazuma walked a few distance ahead of her, heaving the rope like she was some domesticated mammal in the field. Once in a while, she'd pull the rope, waiting for Kazuma to accidentally let go of the rope.

She had planned her escape, and all she needed was for Kazuma to rest for a bit, and that would be her gateway to freedom.

"Where are you taking me?" she demanded.

"I'm just taking you out for a walk," he haughtily replied.

"This doesn't feel pleasurable at all, warrior!"

"I never intended this to be one anyway."

She could hear him silently laughing, evil seeping out with every breath he took.

"Are you punishing me after I saved your life?"

"I'm not a sadist. I'm quite generous now, Priestess."

The entire sky darkened but was quickly split into halves when lightning broke. Torrential rainfall poured down.

"It's raining!" she screamed to make sure Kazuma heard her.

Kazuma pulled the rope, and once she was close to him, he grabbed her hands and assisted her going down the muddy hill.

From there, Cahaya found a leeway. There was a shining thing hanging at Kazuma's waist.

A dagger!

She quickly pulled it away and cut the rope. Kazuma, stricken with surprise, attempted to catch her but Cahaya had already leaped a few feet away from him. Kazuma pulled an arrow from his quiver and aimed at the now distancing priestess.

In just a split of a second, Cahaya plummeted to the quagmire as she was directly hit in the waist. She wasn't badly hurt as the arrow missed her vital organs and soared to the tree behind her. Still, she groaned because of the pain.

"Trying to outwit me?" asked Kazuma.

"End this for me, warrior!" she commanded ferociously.

Kazuma pulled her up and carried her in his arms.

"We'll look for a shelter for the night," said he.

The rain wasn't getting any friendlier. Despite the injury she got, Cahaya was worried why on earth Bulan would allow such calamity to strike. Never in years did her island experience such immense rainfall and livid winds.

Kazuma stopped when he found a small hut hiding behind a fortress of trees. It looked uninhabited. He knocked the door open, and they got in in no time. It was a small abode with almost nothing in it but a few cooking utensils, blankets, and agricultural products.

"Put me down!" she ordered fiercely.

Kazuma intentionally dropped her to a bed of hay.

"You'll pay for this!" she cursed. The side of her abdomen was bleeding slightly.

Winds ravaged the windows, so Kazuma had to stick a beam horizontally on the windows to neutralize the gust. He made fire easily with a few hay and woods.

"Let me see your wound!" he uttered coldly with his hands on his hips.

"I can handle myself!" she countered. The wound, though a scratch in the standards of war injuries, was bleeding.

"Okay." He shrugged his shoulders as though he cared less. "At least tell me where to look for medicine."

"Stop pretending like you care!" She stubbornly gathered her legs up and winced when pain froze her. "I don't need your help!"

"Remember that pride is a fault," he said mockingly. "You taught me that."

"I saved you, and so I can very well do the same with myself."

The winds ravaged the skimpy walls of the hut, pounding it. The walls shook and appeared so vulnerable.

"You go out from here, and you will die," Kazuma spoke in a matter-of-factly way.

She gulped. Perhaps it wouldn't hurt if she learned to submit. Just today. Just this time.

"So, what do I have to find?" he questioned once Cahaya had turned docile.

"Heart-shaped leaves the size of your nail. Green and violet in color. The stem is short and watery. It tastes like soil. It is spongy in texture. You have to gather a handful of them."

Kazuma widened his eyes in surprise.

"Is that all?"

"I would be glad if you don't come back," she murmured.

He smirked.

Kazuma was away for a while. She lay down on the bed of hay and watched the roof and walls quiver. The gust of the wind and splashes of water pierced through the holes of the walls and roof. The roaring thunder hit her ears with utmost fright. She held her legs up and cowered like a baby as she shivered. She had never seen such storm before.

Bulan, please don't let your people suffer. They need you at this hour.

She closed her eyes and emptied her mind. It was a debacle that she could not use her Sight at this moment. It was killing her to see and know nothing. All she could do was hum with the wind.

La… La… La…

WHACK!

The door slammed open.

The wind rushed inside as Kazuma came in, dripping wet, dirty, and gasping.

"What do I do next?" He showed his hands filled with leaves.

She thought, *How on earth did this mortal survive the storm?*

She didn't expect he'd come back alive.

"Heat them first until the juice comes out. Press them with your hands to force more juice out," said she.

Kazuma did not waste time, and he did what she said. Once done, she went back to her side, looking at her.

"What?" She raised her eyebrow on him.

"Show me the wound."

"I'm doing it on my own!" She attempted to steal the leaves from his hands when Kazuma moved back, avoiding her.

"Don't be such a fool!" He knew Cahaya would not tolerate the stinging pain. His hands even felt the undesirable sting of the roughness and heat the extract created.

She was left with no choice but to turn her back at him, pull down her clothes to her waist, wrap her arms around her chest

355

so that he would not see what mustn't be seen, and lie down on her side.

Slowly, she felt the sting as Kazuma's fingers landed on her skin. She gritted her teeth as the pain traveled all over the area.

"Just hold on for a little while," he said, his voice tinged with overwhelming concern.

Later, the pain subsided as the extract caped the bloody opening of her skin, stopping the bleeding.

Cahaya could relax now.

She heard Kazuma's footfalls moving away. She did not dare look back as she realized that she just let others—in this case, a man—touch her. She knew it was absolutely wrong for a *binukot* to let herself be seen and most especially touched.

But she just let him.

Why?

Her face scorched with fires of mortification that she opted to just stay frozen in her position.

The storm was in no way stopping. As time flew by and as the evening deepened, it was getting angrier and stronger. However, Kazuma was drifting to sleepiness. When Cahaya noticed the stillness, she turned behind her.

Kazuma was asleep on the floor with only a thin blanket under him.

She sat up and pulled her clothes up to cover her bare chest. It was utterly cold that her lips were shaking.

The craziest thought passed her mind.

If I do this, I'd be freed.

If I do this, I could save the island and my people.

If I do this, I wouldn't have to worry about performing the rite prematurely.

She rose up, picked the dagger that Kazuma left recklessly on the floor, and walked vigilantly toward him. She endured the pain in her waist and made as less noise as she could.

He was sleeping noiselessly. It seemed that he was so exhausted because of the storm and being drenched by the heavy downpour. Yet, he was too lax to not tie her again.

She sat right on top of him, her dagger aiming for his life.

Wasn't he afraid that she'd run away?

Wasn't he worried about what she might do to him?

He trusts so easily, she thought.

Do it, Cahaya… What are you waiting for? Do it!

Strange voices that sounded like the howl of the strong wind murmured into her ears.

No, it was not her Sight.

It was neither Bulan. The Moon Goddess championed peace. She hated wars and killings. So it couldn't be her.

It could be desperation though, pushing her to pierce the dagger swiftly into him. The heart would be the perfect spot.

Three… two… one…

Her hands raised the dagger into the air just waiting for those voices to signal her when to strike.

Three… two… one…

The lightning and thunder bellowed together and the room filled with flashes.

Thump… thump… thump…

Her heart pounded second after second, quavered irregularly but loud and clear.

Thump… thump… thump…

She lowered the dagger and directed it to his throat. Chilliness was replaced with heat as she was about to end his life.

Suddenly, Kazuma woke up. His glare was directed to her scared ones, and he quickly grasped her hands but not to shoo them away.

"I'd gladly guide you, priestess," he uttered tauntingly.

"Sin is not a sin by doing a single act of evil," she spoke with the dagger still menacing on his throat.

"By what then?"

"By your preconceived goals and the fortitude to act on it. Only evil will become eviler."

"It doesn't make sense."

"You're not required to comprehend it, warrior," she retorted seriously.

Kazuma let his other hand loose on his grasp on her hands, but he gripped her tightly on her hips.

"Unfortunately, I understand you, priestess."

In a snap, he spun her to his side so that she was lying with her back on the floor while Kazuma was on top of her, stalwartly pressing her hips with his brawny ones and cornered her with his arms.

Cahaya, stunned and speechless, managed to keep the dagger to his throat while his eyes wouldn't leave her.

"I'm waiting," he lured her to kill him.

She advanced the dagger until his throat bled. But Kazuma wasn't even flinching. He drew his face near to hers until they could feel each other breathing, counting the times the other inhales and exhales, feeling the tempest inside their chests as they watched each other so closely, intimately close.

"What's the matter? Why are you shaking?" he questioned as he noticed Cahaya retreating after the sight of blood. "Weren't you taught by Sari to kill? How will you protect your people with just prayers? How will you win over me?"

"I'm not like you!"

He just nodded in answer.

Kazuma went for what he had always wanted and desired.

His lips pressed against hers. She, not resisting, was completely appalled that she lost grasp of the dagger and it fell to the floor.

He pulled back, caught by surprise.

Eye to eye.

Both their chests were rising up and down in turmoil.

"Tell me that wasn't a mistake," he murmured.

"I am never going to forgive you," she replied in a whisper, all flushed and warm.

Nonetheless, it didn't restrict him. Kazuma kissed her once again and this time, longer and deeper.

While nature was in a fury, passion intensified as well with every bellow of the thunder and the blows of the wind. None of the two realized the huge responsibility that would come after this.

Why did this happen? She marveled.

Why couldn't she stop him?

Just why?

CHAPTER 38
Duty Calls

Run...

Gasps...

The gravity of the burden he was carrying was breathtakingly overwhelming. He clutched her hands tightly as though not wanting to let go.

Run... Run... Run!

There was no place to go. Men in strange clothes and weapons on their hands were trailing after them. There were a lot of them. They had these long weapons that belch smoke when fired and hit the trunks of the trees. He would have to shield her to keep her safe.

Everything was dark except for the fog that was created by their captors' strange arms. He knew they were in danger. His heart was telling him to never let her go no matter what.

Ah!

Cahaya opened her eyes. Sweat plummeted from her forehead, her nape warm, and her head pounding.

It was just a dream, a horrible one though.

Death again.

The same people.

Similar fear and hope.

The storm had stopped when she woke up in his arms, her head peacefully laid on his chest.

"What's the matter?" Kazuma asked in a whisper. "Nightmare?"

"No. It was my Sight," she answered surely.

"Sari?"

She shook her head. "I don't know who they are. They all look different. I think they're from the future."

"Are they in danger?" His fingers brushed her hair.

"Yes. They're running away from death."

"Do you often get this?"

"All the time."

He sighed. "I wonder how you keep yourself unaffected."

"I already got used to this. Since I was a child, I've been bugged by my Sight. She never left me."

Silence.

Cahaya and Kazuma savored the silence. They were aware that what they did last night was inappropriate, but they did not regret it. They could not do anything against their bursting feelings. They had totally surrendered their walls for each other.

Soon, they realized how unease began to creep inside the cabin. The rain was gone, and the sun was soon to rise.

Cahaya recalled the question she had in mind last.

Why did she let this happen?

She thought she found the answer.

"Kazuma," she muttered. "This shouldn't have happened."

Her voice was swathed with remorse. It occurred to her that guilt knocked her so suddenly. She just searched his mind, and what she found out was definitely not she would choose to do.

"What you're thinking... It just can't happen." She pulled herself up to a sitting position.

Cahaya couldn't hide the devastated look on her face.

"It's just so wrong," she added.

"I won't force you," he retorted, sounding so concerned. "I know you cannot leave your people. I'm sorry for thinking about that."

It was just so wrong for him to think selfishly. She was a priestess in their tribe. There was no way she'd go with him even if he begged in front of her.

"I have a duty. We're enemies," she stated bluntly.

"I don't want to be your enemy."

"We are called to be enemies, Kazuma!" She stood up and pulled her clothes up from her waist and slid her arms to the sleeves. "You came here for that exact reason! Oh, why did I even…"

"Please, look at me." He held her shoulders and turned her to face him. Then, he realized he didn't even know her name. "Maybe we can do something…"

"We cannot defy our gods! This is outright betrayal!"

"Hush… Do you think this is a mistake? Do you regret each second we shared last night?"

She paused. She didn't want to think it was. As a matter of fact, it was so beautiful to be a mistake. Kazuma made her forget all her worries, of who she was, and what he came for.

"No," she calmly answered as she traced the corners of his mouth with her fingers.

"Then, we'll figure this out, together."

She nodded coyly.

"I'll let you go," spilled out from his mouth after a night of discretion. "I can't keep you as prisoner. Go home and take good care of your people." He landed a soft kiss on her forehead.

Letting her go was such a big sacrifice for him. He wanted her all to himself, but he realized that her people would need her at this time.

*   *   *

It was cold. The trees were dancing erratically despite the absence of a great storm. The skies were grim, pretty much a ghost

362

of last night's horror. Kazuma returned to the shore while Cahaya went home.

She realized that Kazuma only knew about her as the tribe priestess and not a *binukot* or *Apo* Umar's daughter. Both a priestess and a princess made her responsibility even heavier. Moreover, she kept her name from him, and she didn't know why.

Cahaya tiptoed into Sari's house through the back door. It was a little bit early for the tribe people's wake up call. The roosters were still half-awake.

"Sari, wake up!" She gently nudged the old woman's shoulders.

"Cahaya?" Her eyes quickly brightened at the sight of her. She sat on her bed and studied the princess' disorderly appearance. "What did they do to you?"

"Nothing," she answered. "He let me go."

"I see." Not a tinge of suspicion ever translated on her face. "I must get you proper clothes. Everyone thinks you're with me all this time."

Sari climbed out of her bed and headed toward a space in her room that stored baskets, which appeared to be where clothes were kept.

"Here, take this." She handed over a plain one. It was all that she had in her things, which she thought fitted best to Cahaya's figure.

"Cahaya!" Sari's face exploded with paleness.

"What?" She turned to her, stunned.

"What have you done?" Sari pulled up the skirt of her dress and showed her traces of blood.

Mortification astounded Cahaya. Sari looked at her with repressed disgust.

"You just broke the rules, Cahaya," Sari started in a rant. "You will be disowned by your father when he knows about this and Bulan… Bulan might stop favoring you. He's our enemy. His god is Bulan's mortal enemy! Now, you let him plant his seed in you! What has gotten into your mind?" Sari paced around her room and continued with a modulated angry voice, "*Binukots* marry within the tribe, but this doesn't apply to you. You will be a priestess, and you're supposed to remain chaste until you die. You just ruined everything!"

Her eyebrows furrowed, her forehead creased, and her cheeks red with fury.

"Why, Cahaya? Why?" Sari hopelessly fell to her knees, shaking and at the verge of crying.

"Sari," her voice quavered. "I am very sorry. I was out of my mind last night. I am still human, vulnerable and weak."

"You are not allowed to commit such mistakes! Not of this severity! Did you even think about this?"

No, she did not. It was like she was caught up by the storm, too. The sudden and inexorable emergence of ambivalent emotions, of heat and awkwardness, of passion and vacillation, of interest and curiosity but never absolute reluctance. She made it happen. She saw how things transpired but she just let it happen, and she unquestionably knew why.

"Don't tell me—"

She cut Sari as soon as she read her mind, "Yes, I do. Maybe, I do."

Sari pressed her lips into a thin line. Her paleness even worsened. She quickly grasped Cahaya's hand and pulled her out of the room, mumbling, "Bulan will never forgive you. We must remedy this as early as now."

But where was she taking her?

Cahaya knew where.

They trudged the dim, but familiar roads to the woods with heavy legs and Cahaya was being dragged by the old priestess like some child.

"You must not stop praying until you hear from Bulan," Sari said grimly. "Cry if you have to cry. Plead if needed. Stake your life to bring back her favor. This is the consequence of what you did."

A huge waterfall with the angry and strong flow of water laid untouched at the innermost part of the woods where unexplored caves, big sharp rocks, and scary-looking animals dwelled.

"You know what to do." Sari let go of her grasp and signaled her to get inside the large cave where they could hear the charging waterfall.

Cahaya went in. She heard Sari's footfalls leaving. She had never been in this part of the woods. She knew the waterfall was meant for the sinners to plead for forgiveness, especially for sacred icons like her. There had never been priestesses who had been forced to repent, so this made her the first to experience the wrath of the Moon Goddess and the monster waterfall.

With trembling legs and flailing heart, she trekked a stony lane surrounded with shallow bodies of water. It was very dark inside. She could barely see her legs. Only the sparkle of water from the tiny reflection of sunlight penetrating the few small holes of the cavern gave her the confidence to find her way to repentance.

She felt the hair on her nape rising with chills as she remembered Sari's stories about how criminals were put to trial. It was on these waters that the remnants of their sin resided for years. It was culture and tradition, imposed by the early elders and the tribe king, to judge a suspect through these waters. There was no guilty or innocent to select who deserved the punishment. Lives were never saved. These waters were a life sentence.

Criminals were drowned for punishment. The only way to know if they were guilty of the crime was to witness their bodies surface the waters. If they floated, they were innocent. If not, then they were guilty. Such an outcome was their deity's decision. They believed that Bulan decided the destiny of these sinners. Below the serene waters were dead bodies of thieves, murderers, liars, and even traitors.

She did not want to be branded a traitor, so she needed to pray for Bulan's forgiveness. She was fortunate Sari would cover for her. What was left in her was the hope that Bulan would trust her again and that her father would not know about this.

She reached the waterfall. It looked just like what she thought it would look; dark, sinister, and cold.

She went down the water as quickly as she could, and instantly felt the strong splashes that were battering her so effortlessly. It took her a long time and her complete strength to reach the pouring water. It fell down on her like rain but a hundred times stronger, hitting and crushing her bones, and hurting her skin like a rain of stones. She had to do this until Bulan appeared in her Sight and forgave her.

But will Bulan forgive her? This she doubted.

"Bulan…"

The rushing water was hurting her. She could barely get her legs and body straight.

Bulan… she cried again in her mind. "Forgive me. Forgive me…" She muttered endlessly.

Hours passed, and Cahaya lost much of her energy. When her *apids* came, they had to carry her with both hands back to Sari's house unnoticed. She did this for several days. She went to the waterfall early in the morning and came back before sunset when people were busy with dinner. And for several days, she thought she was forsaken.

On the last day of her punishment, she passed out in the waterfall and was lucky enough that she didn't drown or her greatest nightmare would have caused her sudden death. She wasn't sure if Bulan appeared in her Sight for the final time. When she woke up, it was already night, and the noise from the cheering people outside Sari's window reminded her that tomorrow would be the eve of her turnover.

They were apparently doing a ritual to secure Bulan's favor on Cahaya. Guilt enveloped her suddenly as reality struck her.

These people had no clue that she wasted everything for one man, for love, and still, they were helping her become a priestess. They were still blinded by her pureness and her faultlessness. In their eyes, Cahaya was molded to be perfect.

"Cahaya?" Sari appeared from the door. "You have to attend tonight's celebration. People have to see and feel your presence."

Bursting into tears, she told the priestess about how her Sight failed her in the waterfall. She cried about the possible failure of tomorrow's big event. Everything would just fall to ruin, and it was definitely her fault.

"I have failed, Sari. Why do we have to lie to them? I have been abandoned by Bulan," she cried.

"You abandoned Bulan, Cahaya! Not her! You abandoned us!" Sari retorted angrily.

"And I did everything to win her back! But it's over. I won't be you. I won't be able to protect everyone! You must look for a replacement."

"I just wish you realized that before getting yourself sullied by the enemy," murmured Sari. "But you still have to do this. Perhaps Bulan will change her mind if she sees you are sincere. She let you live, so there's hope. Tomorrow night, we will know if she has truly abandoned you."

What if nothing happened tomorrow night? What if Bulan wouldn't send anything for her? That would be a deliberate humiliation for her. Everyone would be watching.

"Cahaya." Sari turned to face her. "The warrior might come tonight. He's been coming here for the past few days."

CHAPTER 39
Unveiling

She stayed in the palanquin in her white dress robes, long and fully covering her limbs. Sari forced her to wear this virgin's dress to give the people impression of Cayaha being ready for tomorrow.

From the tiny hole in her palanquin, she could see Kazuma talking to the elders and her father, ignoring Sari and her meticulous and suspecting glare. He seemed unhappy. His smiles were forced and his eyes were always roaming around, hoping to catch a glimpse of her; the mysterious priestess whose name she chose not to divulge. It appeared that he had been looking for her for days.

Kazuma, too, was in a great dilemma. He had a duty to perform; to seize the land and impose his Sun God's power on its people. But he was starting to doubt himself just because of her. It was his heart which had become his greatest foe now, not the enemies he would have when his purpose was let known to everyone. His army was only waiting for his command, that strong and fearless cry for battle, but Kazuma was too apprehensive to make a move.

Not yet. Until I see her, he thought.

Seeing Kazuma's downtrodden face made her stomach cringed. It was so painful to see him look so unsure. Where did the strong and confident warrior go? All she could see was a different man.

On the other hand, *Apo* Umar, entirely clueless about the warrior's plan, had lowered his defenses. This included his elders too.

He spoke to Kazuma in an ecstatic tone, "If you want, I can adopt you in my tribe! The Dihinarians love you. You will make a good commanding guard. I might give you a good wife, someone with noble blood. We have six *binukots*, all from noble families."

"That's very generous and kind of you, *Apo*. But my heart has already been captured by an enchantress," he answered embarrassingly, hiding the shade of mortification on his cheeks.

Apo nodded, contented but not suspicious.

"Sari?" called *Apo*. "Why don't you call Cahaya and ask her to dance for us tonight? It will be her last day of being a *binukot*. Tomorrow is her unveiling. Let her dance with that veil as her official farewell to her isolated life."

Sari was tongue-tied, but she found no danger in this. Kazuma would never see Cahaya's face. She trudged to the corner where the palanquin was and lifted the curtains on the small door.

"No. I cannot do it, Sari. I won't," pleaded Cahaya.

"It's tradition for *binukots* to dance on their last night with a veil."

"But that tradition was for *binukots* who were fixed to marry for procreation."

"You are about to marry your lifetime obligation tomorrow. That is no different."

"But Kazuma…"

"He will not recognize you," assured Sari. "Just dance there and pretend that he's not around."

"He's looking for me," her voice quavered. "I can read his mind, and he wants me so much." It seemed that her tears were at the verge of bursting.

"Listen." Sari shrugged Cahaya's shoulders. "You know what is right. Your people or that man? It's your choice, Cahaya."

She quickly fixed her veil, gathered her legs together, and budged them altogether out of the palanquin door. Sari took her hand and led her to the middle of the open space where a huge bonfire was lit.

People stopped when this lady in white, fully clothed, walked like a graceful swan. Even Kazuma paused.

The drums began.

Cahaya could clearly see him watching her with utmost curiosity. With her hands on air swaying together with her hips, she followed the beat of the drums. She was put in a trance as the music got louder, but her attention was never diverted from his. She could read his mind.

"Who is she?" Kazuma asked in a murmur to Ayang who was busily stuffing food to her mouth.

"She's my sister, Cahaya," answered Ayang. "That's how *binukots* supposed to look like, covered all throughout."

"You mean you'll be like her?"

"Yes."

"She's dancing for what reason?"

"It's a farewell dance to her veil. Tomorrow, she will be accepting Bulan's blessing. I'm excited to know which item Bulan would choose for Cahaya to protect."

The words charged into his ears like uncontrolled bulls.

Cahaya stopped. Her stare fixed on his. She saw that look on his face, stunned and surprised.

He just knew who she was.

Her heart started to race. Instead of reading his thoughts, she could only hear the storm inside her.

Kazuma wasn't doing anything and this she was most curious of. She thought he'd run to her and pull her veil off her face, but he didn't. He remained calm except for the astounded face he was giving off.

Cahaya continued dancing until the music stopped. Then, she scurried out of the open space still bearing the storm in her heart. None of the people noticed her disappearance. She ran off so quickly that by the time the people saw the empty open space, they all began to think that she had returned to her palanquin.

"Wait!" a voice, not angry but not sad too, made her stop.

The forest was dark, and she was planning to go to the cave to punish herself again and to cleanse her mind from sin again.

"Cahaya?" It was music to her ears when she heard him say her name.

"Stop, Kazuma!" Her voice rose. "This is not right. We both know this is wrong."

"I'm not going to hurt your people. I won't pursue the plan," he said in just one breath.

"What?" She turned to face him.

"I just can't. I don't want to endanger you."

"And what about you? You will be punished if you neglect your duty. Adlaw isn't forgiving. He—"

She was immediately put to silence by just one kiss. A few seconds ago, he was a few meters away from her, and now, not even a gap stood between them.

"I love you, Cahaya," he whispered after that long deep kiss. "I love you that I can do anything just to have you."

"I lied to you. I don't deserve you," she replied weakly.

"You were always in my mind. I dread the day I let you go. I just want to be with you." He kissed her again, savoring the softness of her skin and the sweetness of her lips. "Come with me," he whispered right on top of her mouth, after breaking the kiss. His hands caressed the sides of her face. "Let's go somewhere. Just the two of us."

"But what will happen to your troop, to your nation? You'll put them to peril." She caressed Kazuma's freshly shaved face with her fingers. It was that roughness that she missed completely.

371

"I'll turn over the Kusanagi to one of my men I deem deserving of it. I have been thinking about this for days. I couldn't decide because you weren't with me. But now, I am more than sure of what to do. I only want you."

"I want to be with you, too. But how are we going to do it? I will be a priestess, and priestesses don't marry."

He frowned. "You don't have to be a priestess, Cahaya. Just be mine. Just be with me."

Cahaya found him too bold to go against his Sun God, which she surely knew she couldn't do with Bulan. Where did he get all this audacity to defy him?

She shook her head as questions started to fill in.

If she didn't become a priestess, who would?

What would happen to her tribe if Bulan got angry?

If she left, who would take her stead? Sari wouldn't live much longer. Her powers were waning.

But she wanted him too. She wanted to be with him so badly.

"We can be together. We can make as many children as we want," he said as he touched her flat abdomen, and as he followed her uncertain gaze. "We'll make our own destiny."

"Our own destiny?" She raised her chin up and watched the stars in his eyes.

"Yes. Just you and me."

His promise echoed into her ears like music.

"Meet me tomorrow night. Here," said Kazuma. "I'll get my men ready. We'll sail to the north before your turn-over."

"Okay." She nodded.

He kissed her again on the lips.

"Please, Cahaya," he pleaded once more.

She slowly bobbed her head. Despite the uncertainty, she still said, "Yes."

*   *   *

Cahaya was retiring for the night in her own bed when Sari stormed to her room.

"You must come with me!" she exclaimed.

Horrified, Cahaya asked, "Why?" Her heart was thumping loudly. She feared that Sari was able to get into her mind and that she was going to scold her.

"We must perform the rite tonight. The moon is calm, but it won't stay for long. I see danger."

"Tonight? Why tonight?"

"Just because!"

Then, Sari dragged her out of her room to her own house. Cahaya's *apids* were there. None of the elders knew about this. Traditionally, the elders must always be present during turnovers, but not this time.

"Kneel down!" commanded Sari.

There was a white mat on the floor. The windows were open and were showing the big bright full moon. Cahaya squinted to get a clear vision of those tiny vague rings on the sky.

"What are those?" She studied them carefully. The rings were vague and were not so bright as the moon, but they were visible.

"They are dcities. They have come together to come in between the possible war. Bulan and Adlaw."

"War?" She remembered clearly that Kazuma said he wouldn't attack.

"Kazuma is preparing his troop to attack tonight. I have been warned by Bulan just now."

"No." She trembled. "Kazuma said…"

"What did he say?"

He said he would never harm her people.

Did he just lie to her?

Did he just use her to make her trust him easily?

Was she just fooled and blinded by love?

373

"Those rings will not leave the sky when there is still looming danger," said Sari. "We must get this going.

CHAPTER 40
The Clash

Kazuma's troop marched in with swords and fire, which they used to burn the village. People screamed, their faces aghast with fear. They took everything they could from their houses and fled the village. Women and children were the first to be hidden in the forest, while the men stayed to fight.

Sari was right. She already warned *Apo* Umar about this, but the latter just doubted her. He even said Sari might only be hallucinating because of old age and her power fading as Cahaya's due day was nearing. He fell down to his knees at the balcony of his house and watched with horror as his village turned to ashes. What great remorse he felt!

One Royal Guard came and asked him to save himself and hide in the forest together with the women and children, but *Apo* Umar turned down the suggestion, pulled his sword out, and charged to the nearest foe his eyes captured. He slit his foe's throat by surprise and killed more. His tears rushed down his cheeks with anger and guilt.

No. No. No. He screamed in his head.

His line must be preserved. His tribe must flourish. He would protect his people. He would slash anyone's throat who tried to take his power away.

*　　*　　*

"NO!" Cahaya bellowed.

Her skin was dripping with sweat, and she was burning all over. The turnover had just commenced.

"Concentrate, Cahaya!" ordered Sari.

The *apids* pinned all her limbs to the floor, one in each limb.

Cahaya was in the first phase; the most critical of all phases. If she surpassed this, she could safely receive Bulan's sacrilegious object. The first phase was to experience death. The old priestess would have to summon Death to inflict sickness; a terrible and terrifying one which only the strongest could survive.

This was the reason why Cahaya needed to keep herself healthy and why the fasting was such a terrible idea. She had to experience this so that she could acquire the healing power. This would also be the ultimate test to know if Bulan accepted her as Sari's next successor, her medium to the mortals, and the guardian of the Dihinarians.

Cahaya might die if Bulan chose to neglect her. There was no way she could survive the sickness. She swayed her head from side to side as pain rose. This was a million times more painful than the last time Sari and her attempted the rite. The burning sensation gnashed her flesh. The freezing cold numbed her extremities. Her mind was confused about what she was feeling. She felt hot and cold at the same time. Her skin was punctured by thousands of sharp pins, and her neck was strangled, and she couldn't breathe.

This is death, she thought.

"NO!" Her stabbing voice smacked the wooden walls of Sari's house.

It was very dark inside with just one candle to keep themselves hidden. From the window, they could see people running, trying to save their lives. They could hear cries, pleas, and anguish, and they could smell the smoke from the fires that easily infiltrated the window.

She stopped shaking. Her Sight showed her the most despicable thing she could imagine.

"Cahaya?" asked Sari.

"My father's dead…" Her voice was trapped inside the walls of her throat, clamoring to be released.

Sari gasped. The *apids* looked down.

"He's dead…" Cahaya started crying. Her tears wouldn't stop. It wasn't just the physical pain, but also the one that was from within that was more difficult to take.

"Cahaya!" Sari gave her a resounding slap to the face, which unsurprisingly stopped her. Her palm marked on Cahaya's cheek. "This is not the time for this. Your people are waiting for you. They don't deserve this. They do not deserve to die!"

Those were the words that made her face the present and the possible future. There was no time for lament. Perhaps, after, she could do it when safety was secured.

The pain worsened.

"Sari? Sari?" Ayang appeared on the door, carrying a basket of her candle-making materials. She was breathing so hard, her face ashen pale but sullied by cinders. She had been looking for Cahaya all this while and when she saw Sari, the *apids*, and her sister, the distress on her face faded.

Ayang quickly went to Cahaya's side and helped the *apids* control her. She soon realized what was happening.

"She will die, Sari," her voice trembled. "We can't go on like this with only that small candle lighting."

"We can't risk our safety," murmured Sari. "Bulan knows we're here. She knows we're calling her."

"But why isn't she responding? How will Bulan's chosen object appear from that tiny flare of light?" Ayang pointed at the tiny candle under the windowsill. Out of desperation, she grabbed all her candle wax and set them beside the window. She tied them together with the tiny candle that was only lit. She lighted them all quickly before Sari could stop her.

"What are you doing?" asked Sari.

"I'm saving my sister!" she responded. "Big fires please gods. This won't do!" Then she sprinkled all the black ashes she just collected from Mt. Harimau this morning. The fire blazed strongly.

After a few seconds, Cahaya stopped shaking. Her moaning waned. Her breathing went back to normal.

Sari could freely breathe now. She fell to the floor and looked at the ceiling.

Bulan still favored Cahaya, she thought.

"You saved her, Ayang," murmured Sari.

"Look!" Ayang's eyes widened and fixed at the tiny object materializing from the fire. It was as big as a tomato and white as ivory, sparkling and smooth.

"A pearl?" Ayang marveled.

Sari smiled.

Bulan's chosen object.

She quickly took the pearl out from the fire. It wasn't hot. It actually felt strangely cold. Her hand wasn't even singed.

Ayang and the *apids* looked at the pearl with utmost admiration.

Cahaya was a priestess now! She passed the first phase. All she had to do now was to keep the pearl safe and unleash its powers, which she had yet to find out.

Cahaya finally woke up. Her head was spinning. She felt her nape so heavy and warm.

"Oh, Cahaya!" Ayang jumped to her arms and cried.

"Ayang." She noticed the tears of her sister. Then she remembered her father. "Father's dead."

"I know." Ayang was obviously repressing her tears. Her cheeks puffed and her lips pouted. "I saw how he was killed. You must avenge him, Cahaya! And the village is on fire! They are ruthless! I swear in Bulan's name that I will rip their throats out if I have the chance. And that Kazuma, he's such a liar! I will never forgive him!"

"Here, Cahaya." Sari handed over the pearl that now had a string so that it would look like a necklace.

"Is this…" She marveled upon the beautiful pearl on her hands.

"It's the Pearl of the Orient," said Sari. "It's yours now."

She remembered that her sacred object was a bow, which she had been keeping for years. When she dies, her bow would have to be buried with her. If a priestess's body decayed or disintegrated into ashes right after she died and the sacred object remained intact, it meant that she was chosen by the gods, who for the Dihinarians was Bulan, to become an earthly deity who would represent their most important virtue. But Sari didn't care about being a deity when she dies. She only wanted to ensure her tribe's survival.

Cahaya wore it.

"That represents protection and healing," said Sari.

"My virtues."

"Yes. And you shall do this task, Cahaya, without hesitation. Bulan still believes in you despite everything."

"Protect and heal," she murmured under her breath.

"AHH!" The *apids* screamed when the ceiling collapsed, and debris and timber started falling.

Three. Two. One.

Cahaya opened her eyes with her arms raised above her head.

"Cahaya," Ayang muttered in a stunned tone.

She turned her eyes around the room. The *apids* looked pale, and their serious glares were fixed on hers.

What just happened?

She looked up and saw the debris and timber floating. She stopped them even before they reached the ground. She saved everyone inside the room. And it happened in just a second. Reflexively and out of her control, she saved everyone's lives.

Looking at everyone's astounded reaction, Cahaya realized what her virtues were all about.

Protect and heal.

These were the virtues she needed for the continuity of her tribe. These were what she needed to stop Kazuma and his men.

"We must go to the forest. Our people are waiting for us there," spoke Sari.

Cahaya slowly brought down her arms so that the debris wouldn't hurt anyone.

"I have sent a message already to our neighboring islands to let us in. Their priestesses agreed. Boats are waiting on the shore."

"We will leave the island?" Thorn pricked Ayang's voice.

"Yes!" replied Sari.

Carefully, they left the village and marched to the forest through a secret route. Some Dihinarians died, including *Apo* Umar and two of the Elders. Cahaya couldn't stop her tears as she passed by the dead bodies. She could still hear the clashing of swords. The fire in the village began to spread everywhere. Her people were starting to run to the shore. Then, all of a sudden, the ground shook, strong and scary. Everyone went silent for a while as they absorbed the shock. Birds fled their nests and flew away in groups. She had to hold onto her *apids* to keep herself standing. Brief but strong quakes followed.

"We have to hurry!" shouted Sari who was already a few distances away from her.

In a little while, they reached the shore. People were cramming the boats. Some were still unplaced.

Cries. Screams. Fear.

Aside from the shaking land, the sea was beginning to show signs of anger. The waves hit the shore violently with short intervals turning the boats upside down. The people had to work together, women and children, to roll the boats back.

"What's happening?" cried Ayang who was holding her sister's hand tightly.

"Adlaw is furious," murmured Cahaya as she looked up the sky.

The moon was eclipsed again, just like how it looked on the day Kazuma came. The three rings flickered, gradually losing their vibrancy yet they still continued moving closely to each other, ready for the alignment.

"He doesn't want us to leave," she added.

Cahaya felt numb as she felt Adlaw's power rising, overshadowing Bulan. Not even the mediating gods could stop him.

"Cahaya!" Sari called. She was already on the boat. The *apids* were there too. "Get in the boat!"

Ayang pulled Cahaya toward the boat.

As Cahaya raised her leg to get on the boat, she heard a voice.

Her heart stopped.

"Cahaya…"

CHAPTER 41
Deep Down

She looked back to the forest.

She heard it repeatedly.

"Cahaya..."

"Cahaya!" Sari called again. "Hurry!"

But she couldn't keep her eyes off the forest. She searched everywhere for that voice. Her mind was in disarray. She forced her Sight to find him.

Sari grabbed her arm and tried to shove her into the boat when she quickly threw her hand away and loosened Sari's clasp. She scampered away. Ayang and Sari shouted for her name, but Cahaya was determined to look for him, following the familiar voice of Kazuma in her head.

Her Sight showed him, and she couldn't help but feel sorry for him. He wasn't the one who headed the attack. Kazuma was forced inside his cabin by his men. They beat him, swore at him, and even ridiculed him for betraying Adlaw. And now he was running away from them, crying her name, looking for her.

Her heart cried. He was badly hurt after the whips he received, and he was being chased. Death would come to him any time now. Cahaya ran and ran. She looked everywhere in the thick forest, neglecting the heat, the smoke that was clogging her nose, and the noise from everywhere. She just had to find him.

"Kazuma!!" she shouted. Her voice echoed.

Then, in a flash, Mt. Harimau exploded. Dark clouds of ashes emerged from the crater and quickly packed the sky. After that huge explosion, the land quivered stronger and longer than before. The trees broke and fell, clogging the pathways. The scorching scarlet magma flowed out of the volcano's mouth.

"Kazuma!" Her heart quickened.

She grasped the pearl and prayed.

Bulan, where are you? Please forgive me again for this. I know I have put you down countless times. But please, just this once, protect my Kazuma.

Mt. Harimau released fireballs.

It wasn't a good sign. Yes, Bulan was watching and listening, yet she wasn't pleased with what Cahaya was doing.

This man over her people?

How dare she ask the Moon Goddess for the enemy's protection?

Cahaya coughed as the thick smoke started to blur her eyes and suck all her oxygen out. Then just before she fell down to her knees, she heard.

"Cahaya!"

Kazuma.

It was his voice.

A smile was on her face. She started running again, searching for his voice.

"Kazuma!"

There he was! Just standing beside a huge tree with his arm against the trunk.

"Oh, Kazuma!" Tears started to burst out of her eyes.

Kazuma embraced her tightly. "I'm sorry. I couldn't stop them," muttered Kazuma, wincing.

Cahaya realized that he had an open wound on his trunk. It seemed that it was pierced by a dagger. His arms too were filled with bruises and blood. His fingers let loose of his sword, and it fell to the ground.

She caught him with her arms.

"I'm sorry. I couldn't bring you to the north. They're angry with me."

"Sshh…" She placed her index finger on his lips. "It's okay. You'll come with me." She put him down the forest floor with his back on the tree. Cahaya stroke the hair away from his eyes, and took the pearl necklace off her neck.

"Kazuma, wear this."

"What's that?"

"It will protect you. It will not let anything happen to you. Trust me. When you wear this, it means I am with you."

"No, I can't." He knew what it was.

"Kazuma, please." She forced the necklace around his neck. "I promise. You will be safe, my love. You will never get hurt. I will be with you no matter what. I will protect you," she whispered to his ears as Kazuma fell into sleep with her soothing voice. She kissed his peaceful lips and smiled.

After a few minutes, Cayaha thought she saw a figure moving toward them. The fog and the smoke made it difficult for her to see who it was.

She picked up Kazuma's sword.

"Please!" pleaded the man who looked familiar.

It was Usui.

"I'm only here to take you and Kazuma. I have a boat."

Her forehead wrinkled.

"Believe me. I mean no harm."

She saw through his mind his intentions.

"Please help me with him," she said, lowering the sword.

Usui hurriedly woke Kazuma up and told him about the plan. He assisted him with walking while Cahaya followed from behind. Mt. Harimau continuously discharged gases and fireballs. From time to time, the ground would shake.

They were passing through tall bamboo trees when Cahaya felt eyes searching for her.

"Usui, take Kazuma quickly!" she ordered.

384

"Cahaya…" Kazuma tried to speak her name, but he was losing so much energy and power as his bleeding worsened.

Without hesitation, Usui dragged Kazuma out of the forest to the shore. It was a different shore from where the Dihinarians were now. His boat and his few trusted men were waiting there.

Sari appeared with Ayang behind her. They were breathing so hard, and they looked appalled when they saw Cahaya letting the enemy escape.

"What do you think you're doing?" scolded Sari.

"Please let him go, Sari," she begged.

Ayang looked so confused. She didn't know if she were to hate her sister for defying Bulan or feel bad for her. Love was always a splendid thing to her, but it changed now as she saw her not being herself, so different, so disobedient, and so risky.

"We are all going to die here if we let him leave the island. Bulan wants him dead!" Sari pulled an arrow from her basket and positioned it horizontally against her bow. Kazuma hadn't gone too far yet. She directed her aim to the man, narrowed her eyes to find the perfect spot, and shoot!

"Cahaya!" Ayang screamed as Cahaya took the arrow. It went straight to her heart.

Kazuma paused and shouted for her name, but Usui prevented him from running back to the forest.

Cahaya dead? These words crammed his head.

For a moment, everything went silent except for a sharp piercing sound that broke his ears. He could only hear himself sobbing and shouting for her name.

As Cahaya fell to the ground with the arrow deeply punctured into her heart, the angry sea stopped, and the waves slowed down.

Adlaw was more than pleased. Bulan's guardian was dead.

Ayang ran toward her sister with tears violently splashing out of her eyes.

"Cahaya? Cahaya?" She shrugged her shoulders, trying to wake her up.

"Ayang…" Her eyes were heavy. "Sari."

Sari stood frozen a few feet away from her. Her hands trembled and let loose of the bow.

"Cahaya, please…" cried Ayang.

"Hush, sister… Look after yourself…" One drop of tear fell off her right eye. "Kazuma… Let him go… Let him live…"

"Cahaya, your eyes—"

"Adlaw's marks… He wants to show the world how he defeated Bulan through me," she answered weakly. Her irises changed its color. From dark brown, the lining turned light brown to glittering gold.

She continued, "Nobody can ever hurt him. I will protect him… I will be with him forever. And we'll find each other back…"

And life left her.

"No! No! No!" Ayang cried wildly.

Sari took Cahaya from Ayang's arms and laid her under the tree.

"What was she saying?" asked Ayang as soon as she gathered her calm. Her sister just seemed like sleeping.

"She casted a protective charm on the warrior," replied Sari.

"When?"

"A while ago. Her last words."

The words of the priestess's last breath, Sari remembered. It would never be broken unless the one who cast it took it back.

"What will happen now, Sari?"

"Bulan will never accept defeat. Revenge is next."

"Sari!" Ayang gasped.

Cahaya's body glowed. Her skin started to shed off. She was slowly turning into ashes.

"Just as I thought," mumbled Sari. "She was pre-destined to be the Deity of Protection and Healing. And she will follow Kazuma anywhere."

With the pearl.

*   *   *

Their boat sailed away. Kazuma's eyes never left the island. The silent Mt. Harimau started to spit out molten rocks and fireballs again. He witnessed how the terrain split into two after that huge explosion. The waves threatened their boat, but they kept afloat.

Without him noticing, the pearl that was hanging around his neck turned charcoal black.

"God!" Usui huffed as he watched the entire island eaten alive by the sea.

Nothing was left. It sank deep down and left no traces of civilization, not even a single soil or leaf.

Kazuma just gulped at the sight of catastrophe. All he had in mind was the picture of how Cahaya took that arrow for him.

"Kazuma, it'll take us months before we reach home," said Usui. "I think we should find an island first."

PART II

CHAPTER 42
The Enlightenment

If you find this, then it means I am real. I am no ghost or figment of your imagination. It's just sad that we didn't meet or we couldn't. But I knew you came.

Clarissa
18th September 1812

He re-read the piece of paper where Clarissa's face was sketched.

"Xander?"

He turned away from the tree and the spot where Rina discovered the letter.

Doring spoke, "I knew you'd be here."

"Thanks for this." He handed the book over to Doring as she walked toward him.

"And?" Doring's left eyebrow rose in curiosity.

He shrugged his shoulders and sighed. "I don't know how to believe all these."

"It'll take time, Xander."

Xander sat on the soil and rested his head against the trunk.

"What's the carving on the tree?"

The cross sign bothered him.

"Clarissa must have made it."

For me to find her? He asked himself.

"I never thought she and Clarissa are one. And this Cahaya and reincarnation stuff just seems so unreal. These just do not make sense, at least to me. About the curse that book was talking about, there's just not much about it. I can't make up my mind if I were to believe it."

Doring sat beside him. She answered, "Because of Cahaya's betrayal, for losing the sacred pearl, for choosing Kazuma over her people, and for letting her down, Bulan did not only punish her but all mankind. This she did to put pressure on Cahaya. Her wrath affected earth for centuries. The storms, the snowfall the village had experienced, and other weather calamities are Bulan's works and part of the curse. A curse of destruction she swore if Cahaya doesn't correct the error she made. Hence, Bulan made sure that Cahaya can fulfill the prophecy by making her immortal through reincarnation. These *Muling Buhays* will fulfill the task of breaking the curse by taking revenge on Adlaw. To make sure that this happens, Ayang travels from one time to another. She wants to make sure that one of the two will fulfill the prophecy."

He had read so much about Ayang in the book. He always thought she was strange and he wasn't wrong about that. This woman actually had powers to travel through time. From the book, he learned that Ayang fostered her hatred against Kazuma after Cahaya died, and Sari fed her with the motivation to save the world by searching for Clarissa and Rina.

He bobbed his head to shake off the confusion. "How exactly will Rina break the curse?" he asked.

"Xander, there's one more thing you must know. It's very important, I'm afraid." Doring sounded a little troubled.

She didn't want to say this, but she felt the urge to make Cahaya happy. After all, she had always believed in the power of love, and she felt really bad for Cahaya dying because of it. She didn't want Rina to experience such tragedy and to die for someone who wasn't meant for her according to the godly duties. She believed that once she told him, he might do Rina a favor.

"Do you remember how you healed yourself from the snake bite?"

He nodded.

"Do you also remember the road accident when you were a child?"

He never forgot that. It was the most painful thing in his life that he had been trying to erase in his mind.

"You're protected because you're the warrior's reincarnation. You are Kazuma's *Muling Buhay*."

His jaw dropped figuratively.

"What?"

Then Xander remembered what his grandfather, Hiroko, told him once about their great ancestor who traveled away to conquer lands under the command of the Sun God. This was the childish folly he forced himself to forget. He thought they were all tell-tales of his Japanese grandparents.

"Both of your family lines could be traced back from Kazuma. He left a wife in Japan and never went back there. Instead, he stayed here and established the Haraya Tribe, where the first reincarnated warrior came from. In your blood runs Kazuma's blood, two bloodlines from two different nations. It makes the most powerful and the truest reincarnation. You can be Kazuma himself."

He grinned. "Are you serious?"

"I have never been so sure until now, but yes, I am."

Wait! He gathered all his thoughts.

So Kazuma didn't return to Japan but stayed here. From what he read, Kazuma left a pregnant wife in the north and founded a tribe in the south where he married a local girl and produced offsprings. These children became the Harayans or *Apo* Tawil's people. His grandparents, Hiroko and Reina, had always been proud of their ancestry. Even their neighbors considered it as truth. He received ridicule from them because it was true. If he were to believe Doring saying that he shared both Kazuma's blood from the north and south, how did he become a Harayan?

Doring read his mind and gave him the answer that immobilized him.

"Your great, great, great grandfather was Alejandro Montejo. He's the warrior who eloped with Clarissa. He owned the mansion after the del Fierros left. It is from him where you got your wealth, the house, and the field. I believe your grandpa, Tiago, spent all his life studying this man. When he found out about who he is, his life as a bastard child of a Harayan Princess and a foreigner from the west, his tragic love story with the rich girl, and his relation with Kazuma, Tiago called you for a visit."

"He called me because he thought he was dying."

"No," Doring answered bluntly. "He read about the myth. He knew about how you survived the car crash. Since then, he thought you were special. So, to prove his hunch, he asked you to come here so that he would see for himself if you are indeed who you are. And he wasn't disappointed."

Unable to contain the shock, he rose from his seat and started pacing. His hands on his hips, his lips pursed to calm himself, and his ears temporarily blocked from hearing the beast inside his chest.

"I don't want to talk about this! This is bullshit!" He didn't want to remember the pain the road accident caused him and the bullying he received from everyone who thought he was unordinary. He just had enough of that!

"When Tiago learned about the curse, he sent you back to Japan where you will be safe."

"What?"

"It is Kazuma's place. It is the Sun God's territory. Bulan will not be able to hurt you there, neither will Ayang or Rina."

"Rina?"

Why would Rina hurt me? He asked himself.

"The prophecy is to kill you, Xander. Your death will break Bulan's curse."

CHAPTER 43
The Graves

"Kill me?"

"Yes. She has to kill you to please Bulan, then all these scary phenomena will stop."

"Doomsday?" He remembered the last few parts in the book about the prophecy not being fulfilled by Cahaya's reincarnation.

The three rings in the sky were the deities who cared for the people. They wanted Bulan and Adlaw to stop hating each other. The rings were actually a sign that danger was looming and that either Clarissa or Rina would fulfill the prophecy.

But who would kill whom?

Clarissa to Alejandro?

Or Rina to him?

She nodded. "She has to."

"Why are you telling me this?" He got a strange feeling about this. "You're not thinking of sacrificing my life, are you?"

"Actually, I am. I want you to let Rina kill you." It was said as sharp as a knife.

He laughed.

Why would he die? Why would he let other people take his life?

"If I don't?"

"Rina will die. It's the prophecy. Only one of you shall live. Bulan's game. We'll wait for another rebirth for centuries."

He paused.

Rina will die?

"No way! You know what? You guys are just filling my head with all these nonsense! There's no—"

"Xander, open your eyes!" Doring countered. "This is happening, and we're losing time. You have to die before the alignment of the rings."

"Doring." He suppressed a disappointed grin. "Why do you have to tell me this? If you want me killed, you should have just let Rina strike me from the back. You know clearly that I can run away after this. I can go to places where you cannot find me."

"You will not do that. You'll never allow Rina to die."

Her answer struck him to the bones. He was caught unguarded. Doring sounded so sure.

"Do you know what Kazuma's words were on his deathbed? He said to himself that if he lived again, he wouldn't let Cahaya take the arrow. He said he'd die for her if given a second chance."

"It's because he loves her." He hesitated to say it.

"Oh, yes. Kazuma loves Cahaya, unselfishly," Doring murmured, "and you are Kazuma. Your strings of fate are connected."

Xander turned his back from her and let himself drift into deep thought.

"I'll call you dumb if you don't accept it, Xander. From the moment you laid your eyes on her outside the church grounds, you know it was more than mere attraction. It's not about the color of her eyes that stunned you, but it was about the unexplainable connection you both share with each other. Strange yet so familiar, wasn't it, Xander?" Her voice intensified. "And might I remind you that it was you, your Sun God, who made Rina's eyes like those. It is for you to recognize her. It is for you to be reminded of what happened in the past. It is for you to remember that she died for you."

His legs trembled and weakened. *Why did Doring's words feel like a dagger to his heart?*

"Do something for her," ended Doring. "Return the favor."

*　　*　　*

As Xander went home, he hurried to his room and locked the door. As expected, Ayang wasn't there. He knew where she could be.

He plunged himself to his bed and wished that it would eat him alive. The confusing thoughts in his head weren't just tremendously disturbing. His head was hurting too. He felt the pain radiating from his forehead to his temporal lobe to the back of his head. Not even closing and pressing his eyes could alleviate it.

He, Kazuma's reincarnated warrior?

Huh! That was the most unbelievable and shocking news he ever heard in his life! It even paralyzed his limbs and his brain. He didn't know what to think.

And Rina killing him? Make himself a sacrificial lamb? What a stupendous blow to him!

His eyes opened, stuck to the ceiling.

It crossed his mind.

He did like her, and he felt slightly, no, weirdly different about her. After that kiss, he started to see her differently. After how she rejected his offer of friendship, he stopped seeing her as the mysterious girl who secretly went to the mountain. She had become a woman in his eyes, somebody worthy of his attention, or even…

Damn!

He felt this too with Clarissa. Now, he knew the reason why. It was the strange connection Doring was talking about.

He dumped a pillow to his face when he heard a loud noise, somewhat like wood being smacked with force. He quickly climbed out of his bed and hurried to his window just to see Rina forcing the door of the mausoleum to open.

His forehead creased.

What was she doing?

Hurriedly, he darted out of his room and rushed to the mausoleum.

"Rina!"

Rina turned to him. She was crying. Her face was all red and puffy.

"What the hell are you trying to do?"

"I can't get this door to open!" she cried as she battered the old doorknob with a piece of wood she just found along the bushes. She looked so tensed. "Please open this, Xander! Please!"

"Rina." He tried to reach for her to calm her down.

"No!" She pushed him away from her and continued hitting the door with the wood. "Don't stop me! I need to get in! Please!"

"Rina!" He finally pulled her by the arm to gain her attention. "Look at me!"

She paused.

Just by looking at her serious but worried eyes, Xander knew that she saw something.

"What do you see?" he asked calmly.

"Clarissa…" Her voice quavered. "I have to do something to save her. Open this door, please," she cried.

"What about Clarissa?" Xander suddenly got worried.

"Oh, Xander! She's in a lot of trouble. Please, help me open this door," she begged, crying.

Worried about Clarissa, Xander impulsively kicked the door. He did this four times until the lock and the hinges disengaged. The door plummeted inward, and dust briefly came out of the opening.

Rina stormed in. It was very dark, dusty, and dirty. There were so many cobwebs hanging on the ceiling, and the windows were tainted with filth.

Her eyes directly fell upon two huge marbled tombs.

Xander halted when his eyes saw the unexpected.

Clarissa?

Her picture was on top of the tomb. She was smiling and all pretty. Then, there was another tomb with a picture of an aged man. Xander quickly realized it was his ancestor, Alejandro Montejo. His name was encrypted in golden letters on his epitaph. Basing on the pictures, it appeared that Clarissa died younger.

"Am I too late now?" murmured the numbed and cold Rina. "I cannot be late."

Xander repressed the tears that were forming at the edge of his eyes. He felt tiny needles piercing his chest and a solid ball of denial clogging his throat.

"Wait!" Rina suddenly ended the eerie silence. "She isn't dead yet." Her voice changed. It sounded like that time when she and Clarissa reconnected through their Sight.

"She's still alive. She's running with him… away from them… in the forest." Rina grabbed Xander's arm for support.

"They were after him, not her. The guards were shooting their guns at him but they always missed. Oh, God! Poor Clarissa is so scared. She cannot hold her tears anymore… And Alejandro is pulling her so that she won't stop running. Then…"

"Then what, Rina?"

This time her other hand grasped his other arm. They were face to face.

"Ayang came," she said under one breath. "She stops them. She talks to Clarissa and tries to persuade her to do something… But Clarissa won't. She can't. She just can't… because she loves him. She tells Ayang she loves him… Then Ayang takes something out from her back."

Rina gasped.

"What is it, Rina?" He shrugged her.

"Sari's bow and arrow. She has them." Horror filled her face. "She aims it at him. But Clarissa… Clarissa pushes Alejandro away as she pulls out the sword from his iron case, and he rolls down the hill, and his head hits a rock. Ayang turns pale as she thinks he dies, but no! He doesn't die. He'll never die just because of that. Clarissa directs the sharp sides of the sword to her throat. She was trembling." Her grasp tightened. Her eyes widened.

"If someone has to die," Rina uttered Clarissa's own words, "it is not and will not be him. I'm sorry if I repeat Cahaya's mistake. But Alejandro doesn't deserve to die just because he loves me. I don't know why he and I have to suffer the fate of our ancestors. I don't know why we have to be contained from loving each other. This is just so unfair! You tell me, Ayang, that I deserve this fate! Why was I born to be Cahaya's replica? Why can't I just be me?!"

"Rina?"

She breathed out deeply. Her Sight shut off.

"She killed herself," Rina said.

CHAPTER 44
The Pearl of the Orient

Rina was still shaking. She sat on the lower tread of the marbled entryway of the mausoleum with her head leaned against the jamb of the door. She grew tired after those visions.

Xander came back with a glass of water.

"Here, drink this," he said as he sat next to her. "Are you feeling better now?"

She nodded as she took the water and drank it.

"I find it strange seeing you do that stuff," he stated. "Does it hurt when you see things?"

"Not anymore. I'm used to this. I have seen things since I was a child and, lately, they have been worsening. They're manageable though." She rubbed her hands together, thinking it would alleviate her shaking.

"But it's just now that you know that—"

"Yes," she answered quickly after a deep sigh. "They never told me. My father said it would just go away when I grow old like my mom's, but it didn't. So I had to keep it from everyone because I thought it is no way normal for people to have this, I don't know, stuff. It never bothered me until now."

"Clarissa, did she know all along?"

She shook her head. "She just learned from Doray, the priestess of her time. It was a blow to her much like mine."

"Did this Alejandro Montejo know that he was the warrior?" Xander couldn't stop thinking.

"No. He died not knowing a thing about it. Had he known, Alejandro might have offered himself to be killed right away than see his beloved Clarissa die," she replied looking down to the army of black ants creeping on the soil.

"If Alejandro had done it, we wouldn't be here today, Rina," said Xander. "History will be different. You and I would have never been born."

"I know, but I don't think that would have happened had Alejandro known about this. Clarissa will stop him still. Cahaya will not let him do it. That's how she loves." She cleared her throat and continued—"loved him"—as soon as she realized that Cahaya, Clarissa, and she were one.

Her words caught his attention. He wanted to ask if she'd do something like that, but of course, he just kept it to himself. He didn't want to let her have the impression of him being too presumptuous. One thing was for sure, even though she, Cahaya, and Clarissa were one, it didn't mean she automatically harbored the feelings the other two had for Kazuma and Alejandro.

No. She just didn't have those feelings, did she? He kept on telling himself.

"Alejandro left for a year. He went to some place where nobody knows him," Rina continued after her shyness waned. "The del Fierros escaped the burning."

"Burning?"

"The townspeople thought that the visiting European lady who was always seen with the del Fierro matriarch was a witch. There were accounts that people would see a woman from her window lighting candles and smoke would come out to the open. She was seen dancing erratically like she was possessed."

Xander was about to believe Rina because he knew that sorcery in Europe was an ordinary craze in there especially on the eighteenth century when Rina spoke again.

"But it wasn't true. The European lady was neither a witch nor any of the del Fierros, but the damage had been done. This property was burned down, and they had to leave the province as quickly as they could. They did not even have the chance to mourn Clarissa's death."

"Then who was the witch?"

"Ayang."

Xander felt his stomach being pinched and his insides pulled by gravity.

Ayang, again!

He shook his head with complete disbelief.

"She isn't literally a witch, is she?" He wondered about how great it was to have Rina's skills.

"No. She is not a witch, but those behaviors were perceived as seditious by the Roman Faith. You know how it was before, do you? You have to be connected with the church in any sort of way to be favored by the governing body. The church was the highest form of the government then. Ayang is a native, and she has her own religion. Religious leaders and the people would condemn natives just because they shun away from Christianity."

"Then, why execute the del Fierros when it was Ayang?" He felt rage rising.

Why would innocent people have to die because of someone else's fault? Why didn't Ayang even defend the del Fierros?

"She couldn't die," she answered. "She had to look for us. She had to find the next generation *Muling Buhays* to complete her task. She was just saving herself."

All the more, his hatred for this woman deepened.

"When Alejandro came back, the del Fierro property was given to him. His name was on the will."

"Where are the del Fierros now?"

"In Europe, living the life of freedom."

Xander thought of going to Europe to see Clarissa's family, well, her descendants now. He missed her already. He wanted to cry but he just couldn't because Rina was around.

After all, crying for Clarissa was just like crying for Rina. They were one!

He looked up at Rina. This was when he noticed that she and Clarissa looked a bit similar. He had seen a glimpse of Clarissa on his mirror, but her face never left his mind since then. He could assure that Rina almost had Clarissa's features; her nose, her full lips, her chin, cheeks, and her almond shaped eyes and its mind-boggling color.

Why did he notice it just now?

"What's wrong?" queried Rina as she grew more conscious about herself. His glance was sending fires all over her.

"Nothing. You just look so much like her." He grinned after.

"Clarissa?" Her brow rose. "How can you say that?"

"Rina, I want you to take a look at this." He pulled out the burnt leather-bound journal from the back of his pants. "I communicated with Clarissa through this."

Rina carefully opened the journal and scanned the pages. There were still memories of their sweet conversation. She traced with her long fingers Clarissa's handwriting.

"You saw her," she murmured as her vision blackened and slowly fashioned a memory, his memory. "You saw her in the mirror. Yes, she does look like me."

"You're seeing her now?"

She nodded.

"Do you know why it happened?"

She closed her eyes and searched her mind. All she saw this time was a tiny flare of light from the candles on the tapestries and the walls, swiveling each time the strong wind got through the mansion's window.

"I see black candles," she uttered.

She forced to clearly see the figure of a person slowly reaching the upper landing of the staircase. He or she was walking toward the wall to…

She gasped. Her eyes quickly opened.

"Rina?" Xander called worriedly.

Her face whitened with shock. "It's Ayang!" As Ayang's face popped out from the darkness, her heart skipped, and she lost her Sight immediately. "She's responsible for why you saw her. It's her candles. Once they're lit, they become portals. They are her gate to time travel. But it's only her who can do that and who can effectively use its magic. But they're only useful when they're lighted. It's the reason why you saw her that night."

Xander immediately remembered what the book of myths said about Ayang, the younger princess of the Dihinari Tribe; recipient of the Moon Goddess's gift of time and space. He, too, recalled the times when the old woman would switch the candles in the mansion from ordinary white to her special ones. He began to realize that it was her way to easily travel from one place to another without anyone noticing.

"Xander, what's this?" she asked as she fixed her eyes on the charcoal black stone attached in the middle of the leather cover.

He shrugged.

Rina carefully touched it, felt its texture, and studied the reflection of her face on its smooth surface.

A realization struck her.

She once more scanned the pages and looked at Xander's and Clarissa's exchanges of words.

"This is the pearl, Xander!"

"The what?"

"The pearl!" She bit her tongue upon realizing that her voice was so loud. Her eyes surveyed the surrounding, making sure nobody was listening. "It's the pearl," she hushed while tapping his shoulder.

Xander turned his probing gaze from her light brown eyes to the stone.

"Really? That's the pearl? Why is it black?"

"Because of the curse. When Cahaya died, part of her soul was trapped here to—"

"To what, Rina? To protect me?"

She shook her head. "No. You are always protected even without this, Xander. Cahaya cast a charm on you before she died. That was the promise of eternal love, her vow of keeping you alive. When this turned black, this no longer holds power to protect and heal but becomes the medium for you and her to reconnect. It happened, you and Clarissa. Remember Cahaya's promise to you? She said she'll always be with you. It's the pearl. This is Cahaya, Xander!" Her eyes lit up.

He no longer questioned Rina. Well, she was the descendant of a priestess. Realistically, she was a priestess too. She knew things that only she could understand.

So, the pearl made all this mystery possible. Aside from the overwhelming information pouring into his brain, one more thing that caught his attention was how Rina comfortably and freely used his name instead of Kazuma's while she was not even mentioning herself or even relating herself with Cahaya or Clarissa.

"Hold on a second!" He groped for words. "I thought the foreigner from the west took this stone. Why is it here? Why is it in this diary? Why did Clarissa have it and my grandpa?"

Was he asking too much from her? He began to worry that he was abusing Rina's skill. It must not be so easy handling such gift, and here he was just continuously asking questions.

"I'm sorry. You must be tired," he added quickly.

He stretched his legs as he looked up to the sky only to see the sun's glow fainting. It was nearing afternoon and rain was a high possibility. The three scarlet rings were still there, only a few inches away from each other. When would they align? When would those gods come to intervene? The last time they aligned, Cahaya died, and they probably aligned too when Clarissa died.

He looked at Rina and wondered if the rings' alignment would cause her life.

Would she even risk her life for him? Would she even do what Cahaya and Clarissa did for Kazuma and Alejandro?

"The foreigner left the stone in the guest room. Priya found it. She immediately recognized what it was, so she kept it from anyone. Because she was a Dihinarian, she knew about the curse, so she thought a way of helping Cahaya be reunited with Kazuma. She put it on the diary. Priya knew that her granddaughter had the Sight. She had been observing Clarissa since she was a child, only that the latter didn't recognize it was an unusual gift. So she gave the diary to her. And for your grandfather, he discovered it among Clarissa's things in the *zaguan*. He gave it to you because he knew that you are the warrior. And you and her happened."

She rose from the marbled tread, looked down to him, and said, "I must be going now, Xander. I'm really tired, and all these information cramming my head is way too much for me to handle."

"Sure!" He thought he had already pass through the story of the diary already. "I'll take you home." His fingers touched her elbow when she moved away from him. Rina seemed to steer clear of him.

"No. I'm fine," she said quickly, avoiding his eyes.

"Are you sure, Rina?"

"Yeah!" She turned away from him and slowly walked out of the yard.

Xander watched her leave, but she halted, turned back to him, looking weary.

She opened her mouth, rather hesitant to speak, "If you are to choose who must die between the two of us, who will you choose?"

He dropped his jaw.

Then she grinned as though embarrassed with what she just said.

"What was I saying?" She chuckled. "I must be really tired. Well, I'll go now."

Xander didn't like the look on her face. It was filled with frustration and doubt.

What could Rina be thinking?

Why did she ask that creepy question?

Would she kill him? Or would she do the opposite?

CHAPTER 45
Torn

The aroma of freshly cut leaves filled the kitchen. The kettle blew steam as the pressure built up and filled her ears with a loud whistle. Rina scurried to take it off the fire. She, then, placed the kettle on a bamboo mat and waited for it to compose. In a while, she poured the boiling water into an empty basin to cool it down. Then, she pounded the leaves with the pestle against the firewood board. It was very important that some particles of the firewood mixed with the leaves. Once all crushed and juicy, she sprinkled the leaves into the water and let the heat dissolve the particles.

Afterward, she wrapped the two pieces of wild berries and a strange-looking mushroom, which she picked from the peak of the mountain before dusk, with a piece of cheesecloth, and squeezed them until the extract came out. Then, she mixed it with the leaf decoction she just prepared.

An obnoxious pungent smell came out that made Macaryo leave his room.

"What is that smell, Rina?" He wrapped a towel around his neck.

She remembered that her father was going to town tonight to attend the farmers' meeting.

"Your medicines again?"

"Yes, father."

"I'll be back before midnight." He slipped into his boots.

"Father, will Xander be in danger?" She heard her voice cracked.

"I'll try to pacify the farmers. The news about selling the land came as a shock to them," he said before he passed through the threshold. "It's not the only matter that we're worried about. The weather station called the town mayor's office and warned us about a strong storm hitting the Pacific Ocean and it might pass through the entire archipelago and the neighboring countries. It's huge, and it could cover half of the continent."

Rina stopped what she was doing.

"We must be ready. I'd take timbers from the forest tomorrow so that we can reinforce this house's foundation," Macaryo added worriedly. "I'll go now, Rina. Be safe."

"Be safe, father." She smiled meekly at him.

Macaryo slowly closed the door behind him.

When he was out of her sight, Rina quickly decanted the decoction into the two tiny bottles on her hands. She made sure she didn't spill anything.

Knock! Knock! Knock!

Her heart nearly leaped off her chest and the liquid spilled. She covered the bottles with their lids and carefully kept them inside the drawer. She hurriedly cleared the table and got rid of the wild berries, the mushroom, and the cheesecloth.

She walked to the door, took a deep breath, and twisted the doorknob.

"Xander?"

"Hi."

She surveyed him from head to foot. He appeared to have walked from his mansion to this side of the town again, his rubber shoe inches dipped with mud, his shirt soaked with cold sweat, and his hair rowdy from the blowing wind.

"Mind if I come in?"

411

Surprised, she let him in. She carefully closed the door, looking outside first to make sure that none had seen him come in. She took a clean towel from the laundry that was piled inside a *rattan* basket.

"Dry yourself," said she.

"Thank you." His gaze did not leave her.

"If you're looking for father, you just missed him by five minutes." She tried to make her voice sound so calm despite the growing tension between her head and chest. She could only gulp at the intensity of her beating heart. The recollection of that unwarranted question a while ago added up to the mortification she was currently controlling, and it was slowly becoming a little too uncontrollable.

He pulled out an old-looking package wrapped in plastic from his back, probably to protect it from the looming storm.

"I came here to return this. It's yours."

Curious, Rina received it. She unwrapped the plastic and revealed the leather diary with the pearl.

"No." She shook her head and handed the diary back to him. "It's yours, Xander." She stepped back from him.

"Rina, this is Cahaya's. So, it's yours. You are the rightful owner, not me."

She bit her lower lip as she pondered.

"It has been with my family and me for so many years."

Rina took the diary.

"Thank you," she said. "The Dihinarians will be happy when they find out that the pearl has been found."

"They wouldn't be angry with me anymore, would they?" He repressed a smile.

"Angry about what?"

"Well, they think that Kazu... I took it from you."

"I think most of the Dihinarians nowadays knew only a little about Cahaya and Kazuma. It's only Ayang who's too dedicated and determined to put everything into place."

He nodded.

"Are you going to the Haraya Tribe to tell them about yourself?" she asked.

"Is there a need?"

"Xander, they have to know you exist. They have been waiting for you since Alejandro. They have never known him. At least, tell them that you know who you are. You might need their help someday."

Her words brought him to deep thought.

Suddenly, a sharp sensation stopped her.

"She's coming," she uttered. Rina quickly looked at Xander with worry. She grasped his arm and pulled him toward her room. "Stay here! You must not be caught!"

"Who's coming?"

"Never say a word, Xander. Don't make your presence be felt. Please!" She slammed the door in front of him.

Anxiety was too difficult to mask at this moment. Anyone would see she was hiding trouble. Her face would say so. She quickly paced around the living area to calm herself. She kept on looking at her bedroom's door. Xander's aura was too strong that a powerful woman like Ayang could immediately smell him even from the doorstep. He was discharging this energy that could warrant Ayang's attention.

Oh God! How will she keep him hidden from her? She asked herself repeatedly.

What would Cahaya do in these tight times?

Rina stormed back into the room, overlooked Xander's questioning glare, and heaved him by the neck closer to her. She reached for his lips gently and without hesitation.

Xander froze, caught by surprise.

It seemed that time slowed down.

She pulled back after four seconds.

His face went all pink.

413

"Don't say a word!" she warned him. "If you have to stop breathing, then do so." She walked out of the room, feeling all the heat raging throughout her face, down to her neck, and chest.

What did she just do?

She buried her face with her hands as soon as the door slammed behind her. What she did just sank into her mind. She kissed him! She knew she wasn't supposed to do it. It was like she wasn't herself when that happened. She didn't even remember herself thinking about it.

"It was Cahaya," she murmured to herself.

It was her who acted upon it. It was her solution to that problem; staining a piece of your flesh to anyone whom you want to neutralize his or her energy. The kiss was a piece of her, and by neutralizing his energy, she concealed it with hers. Anyone who would come to her house tonight would not think there was anyone else in the room but her. By now, Xander was stained by her; his energy hidden on her own.

"Rina!" Ayang stomped inside the house after she crashed the door open. She looked so angry, beaten, and frustrated just like the weather tonight. It was starting to rain a little and the winds starting to threaten everything.

Ayang put down her bow and arrow, which Rina recognized fairly.

She quickly glimpsed at the door where Xander was hiding. She no longer felt his energy. The kiss took effect.

"Do you want me to get you a drink?" she calmly asked while controlling her fidgeting fingers.

"No," she retorted directly. Then, Ayang approached her and took her hands in a tight clutch. "Doring has told you everything. You know the consequences. Therefore, you know what to do. Am I right?" There was nothing more serious that night but Ayang's voice.

She nodded.

"Good!" She smiled. "Tomorrow, the rings will align, and a huge storm will cause a wider scale of devastation."

She gulped at the thought of doomsday. This was what the humans dreaded.

"Tomorrow shall be the day you execute the task." Ayang sounded so resolute. "Do you understand me, Rina?"

"Yes." A faint answer.

Ayang's smile reached the ends of her ears.

"I know you will not disappoint me this time, Cahaya," said Ayang.

Rina felt strange when Ayang referred to her as Cahaya. She never really and seriously thought she'd be called that name. To be honest, Rina really never felt different after knowing the truth. She still felt the same as she never felt like a different person.

However, Rina felt bad about how she had twice thwarted Ayang, whose only purpose in life was to correct the mistake, her mistake exactly, and to save the world from the gods' curse. She was amazed by the outstanding strength and motivation she was showing.

"Ayang," she broke the looming silence. "Maybe you should go now. You need to rest."

"Yes, I do." She rubbed her forehead with her fingers. "Meet me tomorrow before sunset at the riverbank. We'll end it there."

Chills traveled from her spine to her nerves.

All she could do was nod.

Ayang picked up the bow and arrow and left the house. As soon as she disappeared through the thick fog in the forest, Rina closed the door and hurried to her room.

"She's left now!" she said in one breath.

As she turned to face him, Xander grabbed her by the arm and pulled her close to him. Their faces were only an inch away. Her eyes dropped to his lips, and a spine-chilling sensation began to confuse her thoughts.

Xander slowly moved closer, gauging every tiny reaction on her face. His hands at her back pulled her close to him.

Her chest started to congest. She could feel her breathing slowing down in contrast with her racing heartbeat.

In just a matter of a second, they kissed, neither of them pulling back, both aware why they weren't compelled to stop despite the risk.

"Just saying," he started as soon as their lips parted, "that it was my own volition to kiss you, not Kazuma's, and I presume it's the same with you."

That kiss, for her, was an extraordinary confession if it was what Xander would want her to know. All this time, she thought he had someone else in his heart when he told her that he wanted to be friends with her after the kiss in his backyard. Then, when she learned that Xander was communicating with Clarissa, she thought he was in love with her. Her heart was torn into pieces that her rival was her own self, her old self whom she did not even know existed.

What was it like that day in the mausoleum when she learned that Xander was probably in love with this woman in the diary? It was terrible.

It was terrible to see Clarissa through her Sight; looking just like her, whose smile, eyes, nose, and lips were a complete mirror of hers. Being the one that Xander wanted and not her, she wanted to cry at that time but she could only act tough.

She slowly moved back and gently pushed him away. Her cheeks were burning with fire.

"You should leave now," she told him coldly and shrugged off the awkwardness she was feeling.

"Rina, I want you to tell me what you want," he said.

"What I want?"

"I can end this," he said right away.

CHAPTER 46
The Choice

"They want you to end this. They want you gone."

"I know."

She let out a short laugh. "That means me killing you, Xander."

He nodded.

"You're also aware of how I feel about this, don't you?"

His head bobbed in agreement, then he said, "Will you let everyone you love be endangered again?"

Again, eh? He laughed inside his head. This was what destiny called him to do, and for many years he escaped death because of her. This time, he thought, was his best chance to be a man and reverse his destiny.

"Have you lost your mind?" She laughed.

What could he be thinking? She asked herself.

Did he really think she was capable of ending his life? This put an ache in her heart. The laughter was meant to hide her frustration. Even if she was not Cahaya's reincarnation, even if she were not her, and even before she had known who they were, she would never be able to lay a finger on him, more so kill him. Her feelings for him were not at all related to the centuries-old love story. This, she believed firmly. Even if she were some ordinary girl, she would still fall in love with him. Even if the curse was broken, and for some miracle, she lived again in the future, she was sure she'd fall in love with him over and over again, to the man who was Xander.

"Rina, it's not like we have a choice," he said.

"You must know that I make the choice here, Xander."

"I know. That is why I am telling you what to do."

"No! Cahaya and Clarissa made their choices by themselves. I don't need you to influence me."

"My goodness, Rina. I have been influencing you for eternity!" His voice rose. "This cycle will not stop unless I die!"

Rina pressed her eyes so that she could suppress the tears from falling.

"Xander, do you actually know what you're saying? You're giving up everything—your youth, your dreams, your chance to grow old with the people that matter. You do not have to do this. You can always run away and escape this fate."

"That's what Cahaya would want. For me to live. That's why she's cast a curse on me." His voice waned after he saw her starting to break down. "But what would you want, Rina? What do you want?"

Bafflement spread like wildfire on her face.

"Don't you want to see the world? How it will be like in fifty years' time? How your children would look like?" he told her while he held her hands with his. "I don't want you to die again and again and again. I don't want to make the same mistake they did. Enough of protecting me, please. I had that for over a thousand years. I don't want to experience the loneliness, the guilt, the frustration, and anger that they had for a very long time for not being able to do the one thing they were supposed to do. This time, it's my turn to protect you."

Tears started to form at the tips of her reddened eyes.

"That is something Kazuma or Alejandro would say, but not you."

"What?"

418

"Xander, do you know why I live? It's not because I have a prophecy to fulfill. It's not because you have to die in my hands to spare the world from disasters," she told him. "It's not because of the deities who are against us. That's what Ayang and Doring think. But I don't. I don't think the prophecy is all about that. I am a testament to Cahaya's sacrifice. I live because I have to. Cahaya died protecting you, and I live because of the same reason. I am here because of the promise she made." Her eyes moved away from him. "I will have to die over and over again because that's the essence of her death, of her love for you." She turned her back to him, hiding the tears that surged like a storm out from her eyes.

Xander approached her from the back and embraced her. He whispered to her ears "We're fools to believe that we can get away from this. What's the point of living if you're not by my side?"

"My Sight has shown me your future. I'm not going to be in it, but you will have a life, and that's what's important."

"I'm never going to be happy." His voice cracked.

"You will be. Kazuma and Alejandro had their happiness, and you will too."

He walked around her so that their eyes meet again. Rina tried to hide the sorrow on her face, but Xander had already seen the picture of surrender in it.

"I won't let you," he told her. His palms were at the sides of her face. "I know we can do something to change our fate and to make our own destiny."

"And endanger thousands of innocent lives? If Cahaya and Clarissa didn't die, there would have been more catastrophic events that could have happened. She just didn't die to protect you. She died to protect her people too."

"Listen, Rina." His eyes fixed to hers, holding in the tears that had been there for the longest time. "I think we're fortunate enough to be given three chances to live in this world and to find ourselves still in love with each other... I love you. I have been drawn to you the first moment I saw you. It was strange, but I

419

knew I was drawn to you for an unexplainable reason. Now I know why… That's three times, three chances, yet we know we can't be together."

"You don't need to do anything to prove that, Xander. I know… I want to be with you," said she. "I just want everything to be normal, to live a normal life, and to have a family. Why can't we have that? Why can't we just live as us, as you and me, as Xander and Rina, not the warrior and the priestess?"

He took her back in his arms and brushed her hair with his fingers to calm her down.

"I would want that too," he said gently as he kissed her on the head.

SLAM!

The door opened, and Doring came in, short of breath.

Rina quickly moved away from Xander as Doring's eyes widened in surprise. She wiped her tears and stuttered, "Is there a problem?"

"Yes, there is," she replied dryly.

Xander, who wasn't surprised of Doring's reaction, grasped Rina's hand and pulled her back closer to him as though telling Doring that he and she were now inseparable.

"I see what's happening now," murmured Doring. "Well, it has never been a question to me that this will happen. So, care to tell me what has been decided?" Her glare shifted to the crying Rina.

"Rina and I know what to do," Xander said as he tightened his grasp. It was his way of telling Rina that everything was going to be fine.

"Do I need to prepare my apprentice now?"

"No. There's no need for that."

Doring nodded, satisfied with Xander's answer. Rina turned to her side to look at Xander, about to contest his decision.

"So when shall we do it?" Doring cut in.

"Tomorrow," replied Xander.

Rina, out of words, wanted to say something but her voice just wouldn't come out. She squared his face with her hands and directly and intently gazed at his eyes. With this gaze, she tried to convey a message.

"Rina, I will do this," said he. "It's my turn now."

She answered him with a kiss.

*   *   *

Hammering rain hit every house's roof rather violently as water leaked inside through the tiny holes in the ceiling and the walls. The *capiz* shells cracked as the strong winds slammed the windows. The rain hadn't stopped since midnight, and it worsened as morning broke in. Loud thunders and huge fast lightning filled the gloomy sky. The angry winds battered trees, smashed terrains, cut the lines of electricity, and shattered poorly built houses. The soil softened and might cause landslides that scared the townspeople. As every minute passed, the storm grew stronger and stronger.

The three scarlet rings shone brightly—brightest today—and they aligned as one.

People were evacuated from their houses to the church as it was the strongest building in the *barrio*. Even the natives from the mountains did not escape the catastrophe. They were forced to flee the mountains and find shelter in the church and solid houses.

It was a perfect picture of an apocalypse.

The church crammed with scared and crying people and everyone praying for this to end.

Debris of wood and cement fell off the ceiling as the ground shook. The column posts and the walls even threatened to fall as the earthquake continued.

Ayang, pale and horror-stricken, searched the sea of refugees for Rina and Xander. Doring had told her about Xander's surrender, but it seemed that neither he nor Rina was in the church. Her eyes had turned gray already looking for them.

"Have you seen them?" shouted Ayang to the approaching Doring who was holding onto the long chairs of the church.

Noises from everyone around just made it so difficult for them to talk. She stepped her feet across each other to steady her gait as she held onto the chairs too. People's hands were creeping up her legs for support. As she looked at them, the fervor to regain peace, safety, and solidarity strengthened. Her fury against the warrior aggravated. If only she could find him. Whether or not she had the pearl and Rina, she'd kill him with her own hands just for this to end even for a while.

"No!" a problematic Doring answered.

"Are you sure the warrior meant what he said?"

"Yes."

"Then where are they?" Ayang's rage rose. "Do you think they…"

"No, I wouldn't want to think that they would do that," Doring answered back.

"It's possible. They almost did it twice!"

"They cannot leave the *barrio* in this condition, Ayang. Even the ports are closed. Neighboring provinces too are in a state of calamity."

"Use your Sight, Doring!" shrieked Ayang as the chair she was holding onto split in half, and she fell on her face.

Doring searched the vicinity again, looking for a man around six feet with a lean physique and short dark brown hair.

"I think I see someone who can help us," she said as she strode to the direction of a man and a woman, holding each other and praying, in one corner.

"Where are you going?" called Ayang who was now standing again.

"I see Juan and Leticia!"

Leticia saw Doring coming, and she gulped as she had always thought the priestess to be scary like Ayang.

"Where's Xander?" she asked crossly.

"He's left the mansion before we came here."

"Did he tell you where he would be?"

"No, but he said he might not return," replied Leticia whose eyes were now as red as her shawl.

"I thought he was leaving for Japan. His attorney called last night and they were talking about the farm. Heard that he isn't going to sell it anymore. Found no reason to stay here, might be," Juan spoke. He cuddled his wife who was trembling with fear.

Suddenly, the quake stopped.

Everyone was silenced in relief. Leticia kissed his husband, grateful they were alive still.

It wasn't, after all, all of the destruction. Ayang knew there was much more to come.

Doring quickly walked back to Ayang with a grim face.

"He's eloped with her, I guess."

"There's no time for guessing, Doring. Use your Sight!"

"If only I could right now, Ayang. I would have used it already," she countered, losing her patience. She wondered why it wasn't working. Could it be because of the weather or because the end was near? "I guess you couldn't use your powers too, could you?"

Ayang's silence meant yes, and she questioned Bulan for this.

Doring's eyes caught a glimpse of Macaryo, kneeling in front of the huge cross in the altar. Not the earthquake or the strong storm could stop him from praying. His arms were lifted mid-air as he closed his eyes and said his little prayer.

She hurried there and tapped his shoulder. She tried to sound nice despite the stress she was in, "Macaryo, have you seen Rina?"

"Oh, Doring!"

To her utmost surprise, Macaryo was crying.

"I don't know where she is. She left early in the morning. Said she'd go to the riverbank to meet Xander. But when Xander came in this morning to my house, I knew Rina wasn't with him. Where could she be? I told her about the storm."

Without wasting time, Doring hurried to Ayang and told her about this.

As the earthquakes stopped, the sky, too, and the winds momentarily calmed. Rain subsided. But it was a disaster everywhere. The *barrio* appeared lifeless; houses shattered, trees split into halves or threes, timbers, debris, and garbage filled the roads, and unfortunately, lives were lost.

Had it stopped?

Had it stopped because the warrior was dead?

Had it stopped because Cahaya had finally fulfilled the prophecy?

CHAPTER 47
Memory

Trucks of merchandising supplies from the capital city poured in the *barrio* as the traffic of businesses increased. One shopping mall was built a few miles from town as the market was widened to cater to the influx of immigrants from the neighboring towns.

It was the busiest day of the year. It was the feast of the patron saint Immaculate Concepcion. A parade was done early in the morning with a singing choir on a floral float where the image of the white-veiled patron saint stood for every devotee to see. The marching people stopped at the church for the mass. During lunch, people went from house to house to feast on the food the hosts had prepared. Graciousness and hospitality were what the people in town showed to their guests.

Later in the afternoon, there would a contest for a floral arrangement. Matriarchs of all household joined to show to the public their beautiful blossoms, which they flourished for months or years. Roses, sunflowers, chrysanthemum, daisies, and many more were displayed in town for the judges to see.

He focused his camera's lenses to all the beautiful flowers he saw, from one stall to another.

"Hey, mister." A plump middle-aged woman in blue-violet uniform came to approach him. "Are you judging the contest?"

"No, ma'am," he answered.

"Oh, I thought you are. Are you new in town?" she asked while admiring how tall the lad was.

I am just about half his height. She thought.

"Actually, I arrived here a few days ago. I am visiting my grandpa's house."

"Which one?"

"The Montejo Mansion."

"Grand house you have there."

"Yes, ma'am," he smiled shyly after.

"Are you enjoying so far?"

"Definitely! The food I love so much."

"What about the flowers? I'm actually a judge, and I am finding it hard to choose my winner."

"Oh, that's a grueling task"—he looked around to see how the flowers were arranged so carefully and beautifully—"with all the beauty around you. How do you judge anyway?"

"They say judging this contest is like selecting a girl with the most exquisite beauty in the room. I think men would do better in this!" Her joke was intended for him.

"Is it because we've got acquired taste?" he returned the joke.

"No. It is because you know what's pretty and what's not!" She burst into laughter.

"Then, it'll be my pleasure to help, ma'am."

The woman's smile reached the ends of her ears. She had never seen such a polite mannered boy in her entire life.

"Well, then, if you really want to help, will you please look into this side while I go over again on the other side," she told him while handing out a piece of paper to him.

"Absolutely. I'd take pictures of the flowers that catch my attention."

With his massive camera, he started capturing all the flowers he liked.

Click! Click! Click!

He stopped all of a sudden when he thought he saw something strange… and beautiful.

"Sorry," a man who accidentally bumped him said.

"No, it's alright," he replied. He quickly turned his gaze back to the stall where he saw the lady in a light yellow print dress with long jet black hair falling gracefully to her shoulders.

He caught himself speechless as he watched her attend to her flowers. Right away, he used this opportunity to take several pictures of her. It was the first time he stopped to look at a girl this long, and even find time to take her pictures.

She's definitely lovely! He thought.

He breathed in deeply for he thought he'd need the courage to approach her.

"Hi!" he greeted first with the most genuine smile he could give.

"Oh, hello!" She smiled back, though surprised by the stranger. "Are you one of the judges? Oh no, I should call on my father. He knows what to say," she jabbered, looking rather panicky.

"You will just be fine…" he told her without taking his eyes off her. "Just tell me the things you know."

Crimson spread all over her cheeks.

"Okay. Er, these are roses. We grow them in the highlands because they flourish in cold temperature. They are organic as we only depend on fertilizers produced by our farmers. They have been harvested just this morning, and I had a bit of help from friends for the arrangement."

She observed how this stranger never stopped staring at her. She was explaining about her flowers, but all he did was watch her talk.

Is there something wrong with my face? She immediately asked herself as she grew more conscious.

He found amusement in her state of bafflement. There was nothing more precious than seeing her blush.

"Are your eyes really that brown?" He even thought he saw gold in them.

"I'm sorry?"

"Your eyes, they're beautiful."

"Oh, thank you," she replied awkwardly.

"Hey, son!" The same plump woman appeared from behind him. "Oh! These roses are lovely!" She diverted her attention to the gorgeous lady in the yellow dress.

"Thank you, Mrs. Rodriguez," she answered.

The woman winked at him as though praising him for a job well done.

"I'll see you later for the program, dear!" said the woman. "You might get the top prize! You know we have an excellent judge here." She tapped his elbow with hers and smirked before she left.

"Anything else you want to ask?"

"Oh…" He flushed, looking for the right words.

The uneasiness quickly rose after Mrs. Rodriguez came. She shouldn't have made it look too obvious that he was hitting on her. Now, he could sense that she was starting to feel a little uncomfortable around him.

"I better get going," said he, his smile a bit forced and stiff.

"Bye," she answered casually.

He turned away rigidly as though he injured his spine, and he bet he looked funny walking away from her.

Damn! He could have scored right away had not for Mrs. Rodriguez's untimely and unwanted arrival. Hold on! He forgot to ask her name.

When he turned back, she was no longer there. The stall was empty except for the flowers. He searched and searched for her, but to his dismay, he failed.

*   *   *

It was still as clear as the waters in the riverbank. But today was full of peace. The horror of that day had been completely forgotten by everyone. Gone were the debris of the cataclysmic event that swept innocent lives.

Today was just one of the normal days he always had in the riverbank. He watched the water turned to gold as the sun slowly retired for the day. The hymn of the singing birds flying aboveground added up to the serenity.

Oh, how beautiful life is! He thought. *How more beautiful it would have been if she was here,* he added.

He closed his eyes and lifted his face to feel the warmth of the sun rays as it kissed his face.

"Grandpa?" a voice rocked him out from his peace.

He turned around and saw his grandson coming.

"How was town?" he asked.

"Great! So little time to explore everything! You should have gone with me."

"I'm too old for such pastime, son." He gave him a weak smile.

"Age is just a number, Grandpa! You could still beat me in a lot of stuff." He set his arm around the old man's neck and smiled. He always wondered why his old man always went to this part of the forest. He knew that the forest was uninhabited for almost seventy years, and it seemed that his grandpa was the only one who cared for this place. "I bet you'd get all the women in town talking about you."

"I was pretty popular at your age."

"No wonder you'd swooned Granny Sue so easily. Heard from Dad that you were quite the heartbreaker."

"Life had never been easy for me, son. You'll know what I mean when you get to love a person whom you can never be with for a long time."

429

Reeve instantly knew that his grandpa was missing his Granny Sue. He had always been sentimental when it came to the love of his life.

"Is that why you're always here?"

"Beautiful and bad memories, Reeve."

Xander closed his eyes and recalled the day she died again for him. In these waters, while the storm surged through the town, she drowned herself. He was there. He saw her walk into the water, pretending not to hear him. He could have stopped her if he was quicker. But the wind and the rain were strong. He couldn't go against them.

Not again.

Not again.

Not again.

Thrice she died.

And thrice he failed.

She went to these waters half-dead already. He found out that Rina drank poison before she drowned herself to make sure she died. Not even Ayang or Doring could get her back to life.

By the time her dead body rose to the surface, the apocalypse ended.

Xander faced his grandson and said, "When you find her, never let her go."

"Who, Grandpa?"

"The woman you will love. Never let her go, Reeve. Never!

"Of course, I will not, Grandpa" he replied. "I want a love like yours and Grandma."

Xander's eyes glistened.

"If she says something you do not like, never allow her to do it. Take her far away. Away from danger. Away from people who want to break you apart."

When Reeve thought his grandpa was getting a little bit out-of-hand with his melodramatic story, which he was famous for, he said to him, "I will do as you say, Grandpa."

His Alzheimers was taking a toll on him already. He was getting worse each day. And Reeve dreaded the day when his grandfather would totally not remember any of his family or these wonderful stories of true love he shared with the woman of his life.

"Never let her come here," added Xander whose head now seemed to be in some distant time.

But Reeve thought otherwise. The riverbank was a perfect place for a date, and he had in his mind to bring the beautiful lady he met in town in here if ever he found her again.

"Okay, Grandpa," he replied though. "I think it's time for your tablets. Let's head back home now."

CHAPTER 48
Fourth

"Bring him upstairs!"

Male servants brought Reeve up to the second floor after he fell down his horse. He twisted his ankle when his entire weight shifted to his leg.

"I'm going to be fine," he said, laughing. "You guys act like I'm your king. Honestly, this is nothing. I might ordain each one of you into knighthood."

"This is no laughing matter, *señorito*!" He got a reproach from his strict nanny, *Manang* Rosario. She was the one who took care of him growing up.

Reeve lost his mother giving birth to him, while his father died of lung cancer when he was fifteen. His grandpa Xander brought him up in this town, and when he grew older, he studied abroad. He was just here for a month of vacation before classes began in August.

"Okay, okay, Manang." He tried to repress his laughter for it would always upset his amiable nanny.

Manang Rosario put ice on top of the swollen ankle and then immobilized it with a splint.

"We better have this checked tomorrow by the family doctor," said *Manang*.

"*Manang*, you know I always get fine. Tomorrow morning, this ankle will be as good as new," Reeve confidently responded.

"You will never ride a horse again!"

"I'm twenty, *Manang!* I drive a car. Riding horses is an easy trick for me."

"And you fell!" Her face almost couldn't be painted. "You always hurt yourself when you ride horses."

"I only fell twice... uh, well, thrice now."

She narrowed her eyes.

"Fourth, I mean."

"Now go to bed, mister!" barked the angry *Manang* Rosario.

But Reeve hugged her first to annoy the woman.

"You are so adorable, *Manang!*" He started pinching her cheeks.

"Stop this, you naughty boy!"

Reeve quickly ran away before he received a spanking.

"Come down for dinner. We have guests from town." He heard her say before he shut the door from his room.

*   *   *

Reeve tripped and hurt his ankle again when he fell down the wooden floor just as he got in his bedroom and a second after his door closed. This behavior of his always brought him trouble. Before he could stand up, a piece of wood on the floor cracked. He thought it sounded empty and shallow when he tapped the space with his heel. Reeve bent, endured the pain on his ankle for a while and forced the wood to open.

There was a chamber!

In it was a medium-sized wooden chest with intricate carvings all over it. His curiosity and interest were stirred again. He always loved the mysteriousness of this house. He heard from her nanny's story that his grandpa used to live in here without electricity!

How primeval was that! He thought.

Lucky for him, he was born when electricity was no longer a rare necessity in this house.

This room used to be his grandfather's territory. Until one day, a miracle happened, and he gave up the room to him. He remembered clearly how he became triumphant. It was after he was rushed to the local hospital after breaking his arm from falling from a tree. When he miraculously got better after one night, his grandpa unhesitatingly moved into the master bedroom, which he never liked in the first place.

How strange was that?

He always thought his Grandpa Xander did not only live the life of a hermit but was also a little sentimental with his properties. He always fantasized about this room. He thought his grandpa would never leave it. It had a nice view outside his window. The swamp glistened every morning. The beautiful gazebo aged with time. The gothic-looking mausoleum isalmost eaten by weeds. And the old willow tree that escaped the forest boundary looked majestic.

He picked the wooden chest up and set it on his bed.

Pieces of fragile paper were safely hidden in it.

How beautiful the handwriting would have looked if the words were not a little difficult to read, he thought.

He tried to read them though, with great predicament.

Three loud consecutive knocks on his door signaled him to keep the letters back to the chest.

"Come in!"

"*Señorito,* they're here. You must come down now," *Manang* Rosario said with a smile.

After changing his clothes, he went down to the dining area. He thought of coming back to the mysterious letters later tonight. It was safely kept back in the chamber under the floor.

The table, not the main dining table though, was filled with flower arrangements, all made of roses.

"What on earth happened here?" It looked like he was in a wedding reception.

Manang Rosario replied, sounding a little sad, "It's too sad she can't join us tonight. She said her father is sick with fever and sore throat."

"Who's joining us tonight?" Reeve already knew who.

It must be the girl from the fair; the girl with the enchanting eye color. These flowers here just looked the same with the ones displayed in town. He couldn't be mistaken.

"Where is she now?" He felt his heart racing.

"She's left already," replied the stunned *Manang* who was instantly intrigued by Reeve's reaction.

He scurried out of the dining area even before *Manang* Rosario could even say the food was getting cold.

He saw her there, standing outside the mausoleum's door. Her eyes fixed on the old wooden door, probably admiring the gothic design. True, the mausoleum was a rare spot in town.

"Hi!" He hoped he didn't scare her. As a matter of fact, he was nervous she would avoid him.

"Hi," she answered back, surprised. "Sorry, I didn't know you live here."

"Does that mean anything? Like not coming back here anymore because you know that I live here?"

"No. No, that's not what I meant." She smiled, blushing with shame. "I mean, I didn't know that you live here."

"I did not have the chance to introduce myself earlier on. I'm Reeve by the way." He offered his hands.

He thought of how lovely she looked when she blushed. Those cheeks of hers turned the color of her roses. He was lucky that there were lamp posts in the backyard so that he could see how beautiful she smiled.

"Catharina." She slightly wavered.

"Nice to meet you, Catharina."

Unease slowly dissipated after the handshake, although the tumultuous beating of their hearts remained.

"Is it true that your father is sick?"

"Yes. I have to head back home immediately. I'm sorry I can't join you and the others tonight."

"Maybe next time."

"Maybe next time," she echoed shyly, removing her glance from him. "I better get going now."

"You want a ride back home?" He pointed out to his sleek black car parked just outside the main door, on the gravel walk.

"Thanks but I have someone waiting for me outside."

Then Reeve turned his gaze to the gates. A man was standing there with his hands in his pockets. He didn't seem to have a ride. Would they be walking from here to town?

"Your brother?" He thought a leech was caught in his throat.

"No." She shook her head with an amused chuckle.

"Ah, boyfriend." His facial expression changed to hidden bitterness.

"No," she cleared instantly. "Not yet, I guess."

His face lightened up. The leech in his throat went away in just a second.

"Are you sure you don't need a ride?"

She shook her head, looked at him, and smiled shyly. "It's nice to meet you, Reeve." She walked towards the gate, to the man waiting for her.

Reeve could only watch.

*   *   *

"Who was that lady?"

His grandfather suddenly appeared from behind with a cane in his hand. The old man was already limping with gout and osteoporosis yet he was so stubborn and went against his doctor's medical advice to just rest tonight.

He should be in bed now, Reeve thought.

He was too preoccupied with thoughts about her and her suitor that he didn't notice his old man.

"A friend," he murmured.

"A friend. What's her name?"

"Catharina."

"Beautiful name."

"She's beautiful too," he caught himself saying.

"Beautiful eyes, I see."

Reeve faced him. "How did you know?"

Those eyes that would pull anyone who saw them. Those eyes that made a person look without never wanting to stop doing so. Those eyes that called and screamed, "Hey, I'm here. Look at me." Those eyes that wanted to be recognized.

"Beautiful women have beautiful eyes," answered Xander.

"I see. She was looking at this mausoleum, Grandpa? Whose is this?"

"Old people. Ancestors."

Why is it that when I ask him questions about him or this house, he always gives very short answers? Reeve observed for the past twenty years.

"You see those words written on the door?" His old rough guttural voice complemented the cold wind.

Reeve read, "*A sol sojo ed leuqa euq son oma.*"

He thought he'd get a better and longer answer now.

"Is it Spanish… or maybe Latin?"

"It's an old language used by the natives a long, long time ago."

"What does it mean?"

"For the heart that sees."

"Did you decipher it yourself, Grandpa?"

"No. I've had help from good friends."

For the heart that sees.

Whatever that meant, Reeve wished it was something meaningful for his old man. It sounded important.

For the heart that sees.

Maybe it was very important, he started assuming.

"Come to my room tonight before you sleep, son. I have something to show you."

CHAPTER 49
Remains

Xander brought out the sword, the Kusanagi, from under his bed. He had been keeping this for years. He thought it was the right time to pass it on to its next guardian.

His Grandpa Tiago's room never changed. It was ironic that he stayed here now when he used to hate this room. Things changed. Opinions changed. It was for the better.

He found the sword on top of Alejandro's tomb one day when he was visiting Rina's grave in the mausoleum. He only noticed it then after he looked closely.

Alejandro died with it.

"Grandpa?" Reeve came in.

"Come in, son." He directed him to sit on his bed.

"Is that a sword?"

"Yes." Xander pulled it out of the iron case.

"Wow! That's amazing, Grandpa!" Reeve was in awe. It was his first time to see a real sword.

"It will be yours when I die."

Reeve was silenced. He always hated it when Xander talked about death. He didn't want him to die, not now, or if possible, not ever.

"I want you to bring this to Honshu. Remember when I told you that you have great grandparents living in a sacred temple?

Bring it there and put it back into the sacred glass box. The temple now is uninhabited, but the government is taking good care of it."

"Why do I have to return it there?" His eyes continued to be mesmerized by the carvings on the blade.

"Because it is its home. The sword had been away for so many centuries. It's time to appease its owner." He meant the Sun God.

"Okay, Grandpa." He agreed, thinking it was the only way to stop Xander from thinking about his death or for talking claptrap. He was probably having an episode of dementia again.

"Take it from me after I die, Reeve. Promise me that."

"Yes, Grandpa."

Xander sighed with relief. With those words, he thought he could die now.

"Good night, Grandpa," said Reeve before leaving.

When the door closed, Xander took out something from under his mattress.

The diary!

He found it under the tree by the riverbank a few days after the storm. Rina left a letter for him before she drowned herself. She wrote there where she hid the diary. She specifically instructed him to never let anyone see it. It must only be him who should know about the pearl. Together with the diary was a necklace. It was Rina's necklace. The necklace she had always worn. The necklace he thought was a crucifix. Actually, it wasn't. It was the key for the keyhole on the leather jacket.

He picked it up and fit it there.

The black pearl detached, just like that.

Xander brought the pearl and the sword to the windowsill where a waist-high table was waiting. He carefully placed them on top as he watched the moon brightened.

The Moon Goddess was watching him, them, he thought, only waiting for the next warrior.

Cahaya and Kazuma were together now, he thought. And so were Clarissa and Alejandro. Rina was waiting for him, and he could feel it. Right now, he could hear her voice calling his name. He could hear her saying she missed him, that she wanted him by her side, that it was time to be together, and that seventy years was an awfully long wait.

He took out a piece of paper from the table's drawer. It was his sketch of Clarissa where she wrote her message. He studied and came into another conclusion how Clarissa and Rina looked alike. He just marveled how she would look when old. How he wished he knew.

Then, a thought crossed his mind.

How did the curse begin?

Cahaya and Kazuma falling in love, both defying their deities. The Sun God was angered when the Kusanagi was never returned to its home, and for the betrayal his trusted warrior did against him. The Moon Goddess felt betrayed too that she cursed Cahaya with a big duty of ending the misery of her people by taking out the life of her love.

Love or duty?

Both chose to love.

Was it a good choice?

What would have happened if Cahaya didn't choose love? Earth would have been safe now: no calamities, no war, no anger, and no strife. It would have been a perfect place.

It was all because they loved. Who would think that the most wonderful thing on earth could cause so much pain and misery to everyone involved? How could love do this to him and Rina when it should have binded them together?

Had they been selfish? Cahaya and Kazuma? Was it selfish that they chose to love and disregard the wellbeing of the majority? Was love selfish?

Xander thought otherwise.

Perhaps, it was.

"Perhaps, it was," he muttered.

But if given a chance to reverse things now, would he change his choice?

Love or duty?

He would choose love still. He would even live a million lives and die a million deaths just to be with her again, just to see her. Perhaps, someday, the gods would grow tired and stop this. They might lower down their pride and let people destined to be together, be together. This he prayed for constantly.

But what if the gods never stopped?

It would be a forever cycle.

The next warrior and Cahaya would have the same fate.

Xander's lips curved at the edge as he looked at the black pearl.

What if... he said in his mind. Just for a little experiment. He had already seen the worst. How much worse could it get?

The pearl was where Cahaya was trapped after Bulan cursed her. The pearl was the curse. Cahaya was the curse. He, too, was the curse. If all these were gone, would the curse be broken?

He looked up to the sky to see the moon again when he caught a glimpse of the familiar scarlet rings reappearing. It was the first day of its appearance after seventy long years.

It just meant one thing. History would repeat itself.

Xander pulled out the sword from its iron case and lifted it high up the air. It was heavy now as he was already frail and old. He could feel his chest pounding. He knew it was a risky idea and the consequences unknown.

But he would try still.

He would try for the next *Muling Buhays,* who deserved nothing but the happiness that he and Rina never had.

The black pearl lay peacefully on the table, shinning and enticing him to pursue what was on his mind.

In one blow, it broke into half. The sword's blade hit the table and split it like how it did with the pearl.

Xander thought time slowed down when the pearl divided into many tiny pieces and shards flew into the air.

STOP. Time stopped.

His heart stopped beating too, so to speak.

The trees outside swayed as the wind blew strongly that put chills all over him. His hair on his skin rose. The clouds in the sky moved and started overlapping each other, even the moon. The clock on the wall stopped working.

Xander looked outside. His eyes widened, and he saw the three scarlet rings fade.

"Did I make it?" he murmured.

Epilogue

"I'm sorry for your loss, Mr. Montejo," said a man in a plain white shirt while offering his hand in condolence.

"Thank you, sir," Reeve politely replied with a nod. "He wants his body to be laid in this mausoleum."

Reeve saw the other tombs, but he didn't pay much attention to them. As his grandpa said, they were his ancestors.

"It's tragic that he died in his sleep."

Reeve nodded. He remembered how he saw his grandpa's cold body yesterday morning. He thought he was just sleeping. He even had the sword in his hands.

Reeve wiped the tears from his eyes.

Xander's marbled tomb didn't look different at all from the two except for the fresh flowers and the candles.

The man gave a light tap on his shoulder before leaving. The guests too were slowly emptying the backyard. There would be a little gathering with food, drink, and prayer tonight, and these people would come.

"Reeve?" a sweet, soothing voice rocked him out of numbness.

"Catharina."

She gave him a friendly hug. "I'm sorry for what happened."

"Things happen," he answered.

"Will you be okay?"

He nodded. "I have to. Grandpa doesn't want me to be helpless, so I'll be okay."

"I know this is untimely, but I would want you to meet a person who had been your grandpa's friend. She's outside waiting for you."

"Okay."

Catharina led him out of the mausoleum.

"Reeve, this is Ayang," introduced Catharina to a woman who seemed younger than his grandpa. Her back curved and her face bore a large mole with a whisker.

"Hello, Reeve," greeted Ayang in her coarse voice, her glare not leaving Reeve.

"Hello, Ayang!" He offered a handshake, which Ayang accepted right away.

"Ayang is a friend of mine. She sells candles outside the church," said Catharina. "I've known her since I was a child."

"How did you become friends with Grandpa, Ayang?"

"I used to live in this house as a caretaker even before Mr. Montejo came here. I would like to apply for a job, Reeve."

"A job?" He scratched his head. He didn't think it was the right time to think of other stuff right now because of his grandfather's death. And he clearly had no idea what job to give her. "I'll refer you to *Manang* Rosario. She's my nanny, and she takes care of everything here. Maybe she can give you work. But I'd love to see you around, Ayang, especially now that I know that you used to work here."

"Thank you, Reeve." There came out another creepy smile from her. "I'll go now. I left my stall unattended. Again, I'm sorry for your loss."

"Thank you, Ayang." He shook her hands again.

Catharina and Reeve watched Ayang march out of the backyard to the gates, body bent forward and steps so slow and little.

"She's very sweet," said Catharina. "Thank you for giving her a chance. She lives all by herself now; no family, no friends."

"Yeah, I think she's sweet."

"So, what happens to you after this?" She turned to face him.

"I'll leave for Japan. I have things to settle there. My grandpa's last wish."

"Oh!" Her face looked stunned. "Will you come back?"

Reeve thought he saw her cheeks flush.

"Maybe," he said in a whisper as his fingers reached to touch her face. "Yes... I think I've found a reason to come back."

Reeve noticed the change in Catharina's eyes. He thought the brown color darkened, the gold lining slowly fading.

"Maybe I could invite you for a hot chocolate on your return," she said, her subtle smile hiding the butterflies in her stomach and the sparkle in her eyes.

The End

BOOK YOU MIGHT ENJOY

SHOULDN'T HAVE ASKED
Mara Lynne

You were money in my eyes, Damien. Nothing more. How can that be amusing to you?

Angel Mohr sold for a staggering price!

Not that she has any experience in that department...

Princeton University straight-A student, Angel Mohr has her back against the wall. In between her dad's sky-high hospital bills, her pricey university fees, and the creditors hot on her feet, she's like a cornered animal frantically clawing for an escape. And you know what they say about desperate people.

With nothing else to do, she's forced to strike a deal with the high and mighty college playboy, Damien Etheridge. With his looks, body, and sexual appetite like that of a Greek god, filthy rich kid Damien would be the perfect client.

Funny how a single question can change your entire life.

When Damien uses his power to control her life, her future, and her family... Angel is left regretting that one thing she shouldn't have asked.

Will she ever get herself to do the deed? Can a stuck-up playboy open his heart to love? Will their moments of sexual tension turn into something deeper?

Up for a billionaire new adult romance to turn your insides into mush with a little steamy twist? Here's a college love story you shouldn't miss.

BOOK YOU MIGHT ENJOY

SHOULDN'T HAVE DEALT
Mara Lynne

"I don't sell myself to anyone anymore, Mr. Stone. I don't pretend to love someone I don't and will never love."

Angel Mohr's college life has ended, and so is her short-lived romance with the university playboy. Now a little less starry-eyed and a lot more frustrated, she tries to make her way into the publishing world. She's the family breadwinner, after all.

All goes relatively well until the company she's working for, McGarry Publishing, goes under... via suspicious circumstances.

With Damien Etheridge out of the picture, Hunter Stone plays his cards and plays it superbly. The cold-hearted business magnate is hell-bent on having Angel for a pretend wife and will stop at nothing to woo her—even if he has to resort to the most unconventional of ways. And god knows what the callous billionaire has up his sleeves.

What was a one-time girlfriend for hire deal ends up to be a great deal of mess, and it's not looking so well for poor Angel.

The contract has been drafted, and he wants her in. Jobless and desperate, Angel Mohr is put in the spotlight once more.

Will she sign along the line? Will this little game of pretension turn into something more beautiful? And what about those random visions she has of Damien? Is she just imagining things?

ACKNOWLEDGEMENTS

I'd like to acknowledge all of the lovely team at BLVNP Inc. Without their belief and hard word, this book would have never had that amazing paper smell.

My father-in-law, David Cole, for reading my work and showing support even though it's a "chick book". I'm only sucking up maybe a little. Your support means more than you know.

Last but not least, I'd like to acknowledge the downtrodden. To those born with less, to those who've lost it all, and to those who think they can't. My hope is that this story will help to inspire at least one person to spare some change to the old man on your corner. If it does, I've succeeded.

AUTHOR'S NOTE

Thank you so much for reading *Amor Eterno*! I can't express how grateful I am for reading something that was once just a thought inside my head.

Please feel free to send me an email. Just know that my publisher filters these emails. Good news is always welcome.
mara_lynne@awesomeauthors.org

Sign up for my blog for updates and freebies!
maralynne.awesomeauthors.org

One last thing: I'd love to hear your thoughts on the book. Please leave a review on Amazon or Goodreads because I just love reading your comments and getting to know you!

Can't wait to hear from you!

Mara Lynne

ABOUT THE AUTHOR

Other than reading and writing stories, Mara Lynne loves to daydream. Sometimes she would have a hard time falling asleep because of the many stories going on around her head. Unusual characters and twisted plots keep her company each night and would only leave her once she had breathed life to them. She discovered the passion for writing when she was eleven years old--the time when she met the well-loved red-haired Anne Shirley. She fell in love with the kindred spirit Anne because she sees herself in her. There was a time when she even thought she was Anne of Green Gables! Seriously! It was like a mild case of identification, a defense mechanism for wanting to be somebody you adore or worship but whom you can never be. After Anne Shirley, she fell in love with all of Jane Austen heroines, with Anne Elliot as her most loved. She just loved everyone whose name is Anne!! When she is not writing, Mara Lynne works as a full-time registered nurse in England. She hailed from a city in the southern part of the Philippines.